CYBERPUNK 2077
NO_COINCIDENCE

Rafał.Kosik

Translation by
Stefan Kiełbasiewicz

orbit

orbitbooks.net

Author photograph by Mikołaj Starzyński, from *Newsweek*

Orbit
Hachette Book Group
1290 Avenue of the Americas
New York, NY 10104
orbitbooks.net

First Edition: August 2023
Simultaneously published in Great Britain by Orbit

Orbit is an imprint of Hachette Book Group.
The Orbit name and logo are trademarks of Little, Brown Book Group Limited.

The publisher is not responsible for websites (or their content) that are not owned by the publisher.

The Hachette Speakers Bureau provides a wide range of authors for speaking events. To find out more, go to hachettespeakersbureau.com or email HachetteSpeakers@hbgusa.com.

Orbit books may be purchased in bulk for business, educational, or promotional use. For information, please contact your local bookseller or the Hachette Book Group Special Markets Department at special.markets@hbgusa.com.

Library of Congress Cataloging-in-Publication Data
Names: Kosik, Rafał, 1971– author. | Kielbasiewicz, Stefan, translator.
Title: Cyberpunk 2077 : no coincidence / Rafał Kosik ; translation by Stefan Kiełbasiewicz.
Other titles: No coincidence | Cyberpunk 2077 (Game)
Description: First edition. | New York, NY : Orbit, 2023. | Written in Polish under title Cyberpunk 2077: Bez Przypadku, and translated into English.
Identifiers: LCCN 2022057419 | ISBN 9780759557178 (hardcover) | ISBN 9780759555952 (trade paperback) | ISBN 9780759555976 (ebook)
Subjects: LCGFT: Science fiction. | Noir fiction. | Novels.
Classification: LCC PG7211.O83 C9313 2023 | DDC 891.8/538—dc23/eng/20230412
LC record available at https://lccn.loc.gov/2022057419

ISBNs: 9780759555952 (trade paperback), 9780759557178 (hardcover),
9780759555976 (ebook)

Printed in the United States of America

LSC-C

Printing 1, 2023

CHAPTER_1

C *lick. Click. Click.* Didn't fit.

Like everything else. Like right now. He wasn't supposed to be here—didn't want to be. Squeezed between a wall and a dumpster in the goddamn pouring rain. Who knows, could be useful. The rain. Reduces visibility, provides a little natural cover. Yeah, the rain could stay.

Click. Click. Still didn't fit. His clothes were soaked. Uncomfortable, but a reminder he was alive even though he shouldn't have been.

Zor should've been dead seven years and counting.

Gray water cascading from an utterly gray sky. The upper floors of the abandoned kibble factory dissolving into a gray nothing. The lower levels of the Petrochem BetterLife power plant looming farther ahead, barely visible. Arroyo—not the quaintest of Night City neighborhoods.

A couple of passersby scurried past—hardly a glance in his direction. Indifferent cars splashed through oil-slicked puddles, spilling onto the sidewalk. Might as well be invisible.

Click. Click. Gotta be kidding me. He looked down at the magazine. Upside down, stupid. He'd already forgotten how to do this. Seven years is a long time. Even muscle memory wasn't spared.

Click. Now we're in biz. Not like it changed much. Not a

snowball's chance in hell this was gonna work, not with this team. One in a hundred chance, maybe? A thousand? Wishful thinking said one in five, but even those odds don't inspire confidence.

"*Thirty seconds,*" said the synthesized voice through his earpiece.

Don't wanna be here—don't wanna do this. No way this would work. He looked down at his hands holding the SMG. Then it hit him. He couldn't imagine any other place he ought to be. Couldn't picture any other time or place where he'd fit. Rain, a dumpster and a gun.

And no choice.

"*Twenty seconds. Stand by; target's approaching!*"

He reached into his pocket and flipped his spare mag the right way up. He wrapped one hand around the pistol grip, the other around the foregrip. He remembered how to do this. Sort of. Seven years takes its toll. Seven years and a death along the way. His own.

A stout, boxy truck emerged through the veil of rain. Armor-plated, by the looks of it. Regular four-door at its twelve—probably also reinforced. His bullets wouldn't even scratch it.

Zor slowly rose to his feet, not moving from his hiding place. The other side of the road was closed off, dug up for repair, which meant two-way traffic was choked through a single lane. Their security ought to take extra precautions—take a detour, even. Probably banking on blending in—neither the truck nor the car in front bore any official insignia. Nothing out of the ordinary to anyone walking by.

"*Zor! Now!*" the voice commanded.

Zor aimed and squeezed the trigger. The short *rat-a-tat* echoed off the nearby buildings. The few pedestrians around made themselves even scarcer. Couldn't be any doubt in the guards' minds now—the convoy's cover was blown. The burst had pierced through the armor of the car in front and decomished the engine. Little SMG did the trick after all. Zor looked at it in surprise. The Militech M221 Saratoga wasn't the flashiest iron out there, but the increased impact velocity from its tungsten rounds made short work of most light armor. Sure, the gun would be useless after a few bursts, but that was beside the point.

The rain stopped. Vapor hissed from under the hood. Steam—maybe smoke. Nobody seemed to be getting out. The truck had stopped barely an inch away from the X chalked on the sidewalk, not yet completely washed away by the downpour. It was the perfect bottleneck—all according to plan. A vintage Quadra coupe came to an abrupt stop behind the truck, which was trying to reverse, backing straight into the sports car's fender.

A tall, slim woman got out of the Quadra to examine the damage. Short dark hair, high heels, elegant suit. Wrong place, wrong time for a corpo to vent their road rage.

Why the hell aren't they getting out?

Warden leaned over a folding table and observed the situation on the monitors. The digital clock in the bottom-right corner counted down the time it would take for the badges to appear. Only ETAs, but still.

Through the windows, the neighboring high-rises hovered in the rain like ghostly monoliths. The rain was a boon, but it couldn't guarantee the plan's success. How long before they traced him? Only a matter of time. The thirty-third floor of an unfinished apartment block on the south side of Heywood and a good two miles from the ambush—an ample getaway margin in case everything went to shit. Two minutes, tops. Disassembling and packing all the module military equipment into briefcases shouldn't take him any longer.

Not so for the netrunner.

A tangled web of cables ran along the rubble-strewn concrete floor toward the bathroom, where they joined to a hermetic coupling plugged into the neuroport behind the netrunner's ear. He lay submerged from the neck down in a tub filled with icy slush, while his brain occupied itself with multiple processes—slowing the police and security response being the top priority. What he didn't know was that he was in a race against time for his own life. Coming out of a deep dive would take time.

Warden drew his pistol—a silver Tsunami Nue with gold accents—and checked his ammo count. No point leaving behind someone who knew this much. But right now, he needed him—in fact, the whole operation rested on his submerged shoulders.

Warden checked the monitors again. What were they waiting for?

"Change of plan—we'll smoke 'em out," he said into the open channel. "Milena, stand down."

It was a classic corpo tantrum. Gesticulating wildly, she shrieked at the truck driver, demanding his insurance company, making sure he knew just how much he'd fucked up. High heels, suit—she really did look the part. Too good, almost. Even pretended she'd forgotten the shots fired a minute ago. She stood right on the chalk X. Safe, just outside his line of fire. But then she took three steps forward.

"Milena, I repeat—stand down."

Either she was still pretending or she really didn't hear it. Auditory exclusion. Throw stress into the mix and nothing goes the way it's supposed to.

"Ron, light 'em up," Warden barked over the comms.

"What about Milena? She could get shot."

"You'll all get shot if you don't stick to the plan."

"Give me a sec." Zor preferred it if no one got shot. "I have a good angle."

He switched the Saratoga to semiauto and fired a single round at the car, carving an ugly scar into the hood. The doors opened and three guards spilled out. Rookies, judging by their awkward shuffling. They wore Militech uniforms and were equipped with the minimum standard-issue weaponry. From where he stood, Zor could instantly take out two if he wanted. No, not necessary.

Milena seemed not to have heard Warden's orders, nor Zor's gunshot. She continued laying into the driver with the fervor of a hotblooded Italian prima donna, pointing back and forth between the driver and her front fender.

Finally, the driver's door of the truck opened.

"Aya! You're up!" The voice belonged to Warden.

You could tell at first glance. The slim, nimble woman with East Asian features who was hidden behind the pillar had exactly no experience in these kinds of stunts. She fumbled with the grenade launcher before they heard the muffled, familiar *foomp* followed by an unmistakable hiss. Smoke started billowing from the windows of the truck. Her shot turned out perfect.

"Borg, on your mark!"

Two figures stumbled out of the haze following a burst of gunfire from the left. Most of the bullets disappeared into the gray, save for one—likely by accident. The driver tumbled to the ground. The second guard quickly sidestepped and took cover behind the large back wheel.

"Tighten your aim!"

The next burst only skipped along the wet blacktop. Borg couldn't aim for shit.

Heels clacking, Milena dashed around the corner of one of the buildings and tossed another smoke grenade. It flew in an arc over the street, hitting the streetlight with a metallic *ding* and landing only a few yards away from Zor. Damn it! Is she even trying to aim?

With another hiss, smoke started spewing from the grenade, partially blocking Zor's view of the street.

Aya fired a burst at the truck. Probably the first time in her life she's pulled a trigger. Less than a hundred feet away and, from the sound of it, not a single bullet found its mark.

Without a visual on their attackers, three guards in uniform started blind firing from behind the car. The fourth, crouched behind the truck wheel, spotted Aya taking cover behind an old, burned-out car wreck near the sidewalk.

"Aya! Down— Get down!" Zor barked into his mic.

She quickly ducked just as a volley of heavy machine-gun fire pierced the car's body like paper. Milena's Quadra wasn't by any means bulletproof, which is why they'd lined the inside with antiballistic panels only an hour earlier. They served their purpose.

"Aya, stay behind cover," Zor cautioned.

Those three would have to wait. One thing at a time. He knew one of the guards was behind the rear truck wheel—he just couldn't see him. He aimed at the tire and fired three times. High, middle and low. His wrists were sore from the recoil. The bolt went slack. It was about to either jam or fall apart entirely. Hardly mattered, since the rounds were only hitting rubber. But now the rest knew where he was hiding. A few bullets whizzed over his head, causing little puffs to shoot out of the wall. The smoke grenade turned out to be his savior, though he still couldn't afford to lean out so much as an inch.

Seconds passed; neither side could do anything. Stalemate.

"*Cover me!*" Aya called out over the comms.

She jumped from out behind cover.

"Aya—!" Zor began, but it was already too late to stop her. He leaned out and fired a few rounds, mostly for suppression's sake—he had no chance of hitting anyone from his position.

Aya climbed onto the Quadra's roof, then jumped toward the roof of the truck and pulled herself up. Twice the speed of any soldier. A few rifle bursts sliced through the air—Aya strafed and fired three rounds up close. The guard slumped down to the ground, limp.

"*Ron!*" Warden commanded.

"*'Bout time! Almost dozed off.*"

The low thumping of an HMG broke out, hidden somewhere behind a first-floor window. Chunks of sidewalk flew into the air, a fire hydrant erupted in a jet of water and the construction barriers surrounding the closed-off section of the street collapsed and clattered into a pile of rubble. There was even a distant sound of glass shattering from windows that must have been three hundred feet away. Somehow, the unmarked car remained untouched.

"*Wow.*" It was Milena. "*Great accuracy…*"

"*Hey, it's the first time I've ever done this, okay?!*"

The guards stayed behind the car and ceased their fire. A small victory, at least.

"Aya!" shouted Zor. "Over here!"

Aya vaulted over the car wreck and reached Zor's hiding place in no time. He grabbed her and pulled her behind him.

"Thanks." She pressed herself against the wall, tied back her long hair and checked her iron. Her shoulder was bleeding.

"Show me." Zor gently took her arm and examined the wound. Not life-threatening.

"It's just a scratch." Aya clumsily tried to reload.

"Ron!" Zor called into his mic.

"*Yeah, I'm on it!*"

A brief volley, maybe five bullets—three on the mark. The car was blown open like a metal can ruptured by a firecracker. Their cover now useless, the guards retreated.

"Take cover!" It was Warden. *"Shield your weapons!"*

Zor leaped behind the dumpster and pushed Aya closer toward the wall.

"Keep your gun behind cover," he ordered.

He could materialize everything in real time and adapt the interface to his liking, mold his own cyberspatial habitat. Every netrunner had their own tastes and quirks. He preferred to keep things tidy—no frills, no distractions. He adjusted the brightness, swapped out colors for readability, nuked the waterfall animation for incoming data.

He didn't care much about the Arroyo op. He thought of it like a game. He would've managed fine on his own cyberdeck, but the gear he got for this gig was a definite step up. He felt powerful—reality was his to control as he pleased. And the codes from Borg actually worked. He had free rein over the traffic lights in that part of Arroyo.

He was propelled by a surge of joy as he floated around his self-configured control room. Essential elements were divided into sub-categories and pinned above and around him. He hung suspended amid hundreds of symbols and icons woven together in an irregular sphere with seemingly no exterior, though in reality it was shielded by a thick layer of black ICE.

Time for the next step. No need to rush. Time flowed differently here—slower. Zor's dash for the dumpster looked as if the outside world had been submerged in oil.

Local CCTV access definitely helped. The techies at the control center were surely frantically looking for the cause of their alarm, unaware it was created on purpose. He rerouted his NetIndex to cover the length of half the district. He didn't expect any unwelcome visitors in his temporary domain; nevertheless, he triple-encrypted all possible points of entry. It'd take at least six security experts to figure out his exact location—and even then, by the time they identified the intruder's whereabouts, they'd find nothing but a cold, dark void.

He liked to keep it simple. A pair of rectangular prisms hovered to his left—two big red buttons. Detonators.

Using thought-command, he transmitted a nerve impulse to his immaterial hand and pressed them both.

Two EMP charges hidden in a trash-littered street gutter chirped quietly as they activated. The ammo count on Zor's SMG flickered—all else seemed unaffected. No surprise, since it was mechanical. He noticed Aya's body twitch. Through his drenched clothes, Zor felt the heat rising off her.

Borg opened fire from the right, shooting everything within sight.

"EMP didn't do anything to us," Zor said, trying to comfort her. She nodded hesitantly.

The steel dumpster did its job—their weapons were safe, whereas it would take five seconds for the guards' advanced firing mechanisms to unlock. Five seconds was all they needed.

Now!

"*Now!*" Warden ordered.

Zor leaped out of cover and opened fire. Shouldn't Borg and Ron be covering them? Fuck! He shot at the ground to make more noise and avoid hitting any buildings or windows. Ricochets and the splattering of water across the road made a better impression. A few windows cracked from the ricochets. Aya followed close behind him, mimicking his movements.

"*Borg, the tow truck!*" Warden shouted.

The guards dropped their weapons and raised their hands in the air. Beautiful. Amateurs on both sides.

A shot. One of the guards fell.

"Borg!" Zor looked around. "Hold your fire!"

He ran to the guards and kicked their rifles under their bullet-ridden car. He shoved one of them around so that he stood facing what was left of the construction barrier. The second, equally terrified, didn't need any prompting and followed suit. Aya did a quick pat down and removed the pistols from their holsters. Didn't even bother trying to use them earlier.

Borg finally emerged from his hiding place wearing his signature violet-navy jumpsuit. He approached nonchalantly, as if he was starring in an action flick, his lime-green hair slicked back. He was preparing to take another shot.

"Borg, drop it!" shouted Zor.

Borg didn't listen. He grinned like a mischievous child about to do something naughty.

"*Borg, the truck!*" This time it was Warden. "*Stick to the plan.*"

"You heard 'im," Zor growled.

Borg carelessly swung the rifle upward and rested it against his shoulder. He winced and quickly repositioned it. The barrel was still hot. He switched off his comms link to stop Warden from listening in.

"You mean the plan that put our asses on the line," Borg began, "while he's sittin' comfy givin' us orders!" He rolled up his sleeves and briefly operated a panel just above his wrist. It beeped and his arms and shoulders started to swell. In seconds they were nearly one-and-a-half times their original size. He gave a satisfied laugh and kissed his bicep.

"Impressive, ain't it?" He winked at Aya.

"Not really, no." She didn't even look at him as she held the two guards at gunpoint. "Just get the tow truck here."

"*Time!*" urged the netrunner's computerized voice.

Borg grudgingly turned and jogged to where he should've been half a minute ago—a serious deviation from the plan.

Police sirens faintly wailed in the distance.

"Go. Start running!" Zor ordered the guards, at the same time gently lowering Aya's arms.

The guards glanced at each other in confusion, then nearly tripped over themselves as they ran away at full tilt.

"The lock!" Zor called out.

Aya ran around the truck, her black ponytail whipping the air. She really was fast, but nothing indicated that she had any implants. Zor stood by the front and kept his eyes on the end of the street.

"*Mine's armed,*" Aya reported. "*Five seconds.*"

They heard the sudden roar of a monstrous engine, followed by the beeping of a garbage truck in reverse.

"Yo, what the shit?!" Borg started, confused. "Drivin's s'posed to be my job!"

"*Should've driven it, then, instead of fuckin' around,*" Milena retorted over the comms.

Aya dashed around the side of the truck and leaned against the front fender. She pressed her hands over her ears and shut her eyes.

But there was hardly any blast at all. It sounded more like a bottle rocket than a mine. All the better—they needed the cargo intact.

They hurried back around and pulled open the rear doors.

"*There anything I should do?*" Ron asked with uncertainty in his voice.

"No, you can come down," Zor replied. "Need to unload this and delta outta here. Badges'll be here any minute, not to mention 6th Street."

Borg, disgruntled at being called out, guided Milena as she reversed the garbage truck toward their payload. It was probably the first time she'd driven anything bigger than a standard sedan. She scraped the side of the Quadra, though this time she didn't care. Ride was stolen, anyway.

In the middle of the truck's cargo lay their objective—a gray container.

They stood there for a moment and stared at it. They had a feeling they were in the presence of something...important. No time to waste, though. Zor took out a knife and cut the straps holding it in place. He tugged on the handle. Wouldn't budge.

"No way we're lifting this," Zor said. "Borg, make yourself useful and do the honors."

Borg scowled and walked over to a lift control box duct-taped to the side of the garbage truck. It was a last-minute addition. Basic, but effective. With a low whirr, a crane emerged from the roof with straps and hooks dangling from its end. Zor attached them to the sides of the container. The crane let out a groan as it started lifting.

"Motherfucker weighs more than six hundred pounds." Borg seemed impressed. "Hell's inside this thing?"

The sirens were growing louder.

"*Two minutes,*" the netrunner notified them.

"Estimated or actual?" asked Aya.

"*I can buy you thirty seconds, no more.*"

Zor looked at Aya. He could've done this without everyone else, he thought. Except her. And the netrunner, of course. Whoever he was.

A tall, skinny figure appeared at the entrance to the abandoned factory. Zor reached for his pistol.

"Jesus, Ron!" His hand froze midway. "A heads-up next time."

"Whoa, hey!" Ron sidestepped a good second too late. "Battin' for the same team, remember?" He theatrically placed his hand over his chest. "Mighty kind of you to spare me."

His oversized work coat hung on his shoulders like a trash bag. His short, gray-streaked hair was tousled. He seemed laid-back, almost as if none of this was real, but a braindance that could be paused, rewound, fast-forwarded past all the tough moments.

Though the container was about the size of your average bathtub, the roof of the truck bent slightly upward and the crane bowed under the load as it hoisted it up above the garbage compartment.

"*Time!*"

Zor cut the straps once more. The container dropped with a heavy thud, making the truck bob up and down.

"Let's move!"

Warden watched the monitors as the garbage truck drove off at full speed. He raised an eyebrow as it hit the corner of a parked car and shoved it against a streetlight.

On the smaller screen, he saw two NCPD patrol cars speeding from the opposite direction a few blocks away. He sooner expected to see a Militech rapid-response unit—usually light-years ahead of the badges. No sign of them, though.

It was slowly dawning on him that they had actually pulled this off. He didn't believe in it at first. The op, pitched by the client himself, wasn't just strange—it seemed downright impossible. Usually, clients tell you what they want and how much they're willing to pay for it. This one had it all worked out from the start, gonk as it sounded. Funny how it did work out. Maybe the plan wasn't so scopbrained after all. The thought that this strategy could be repeated in the future briefly crossed Warden's mind. Force a bunch of amateurs to do the job—it all crashes and burns; you lose nothing.

Just one oversight—they knew his face, his name. Next time that'd have to change.

"Yo, lady, slow down!" Borg yelled, one hand gripping the edge of his seat, the other combing back his green hair. "You got a death wish?!"

"If anyone's a lady here, it's you." Milena gripped the steering wheel even tighter, trying to stay inside the lane. She was smiling, clearly enjoying herself. Zor and Ron exchanged glances.

"Best if we avoid drawing attention," Zor interceded. "A garbage truck going this fast'll turn heads." He wanted all of this to be over as much as everyone else. It'd be a shame if they got caught now—right at the finish line.

Truth was, he was forced into this. Wasn't his fault, just rotten luck. He didn't have a choice.

They were here for a reason. Every one of them had something to lose—something worth saving in exchange for a few minutes of crime, dangerous as it might be.

The truck hit a garbage can. Milena swore under her breath and reluctantly eased her foot off the CHOOH.

Ron turned around and pointed at Aya.

"You—let's see your arm."

She brought her shoulder closer toward him. He examined the wound, increasing his optical zoom by a factor of ten.

"I'll stop by the doc's after."

"You're already lookin' at one, sweetheart."

She didn't protest. Ron tore off a part of his sleeve, took out a small bottle from his pocket and sprayed the wound, creating foam that quickly dissipated. Ron's six-digit chrome hands performed a swift dance across the damaged tissue. Laser bursts from one finger on his right hand were perfectly synced to the fingers of his left, which delicately slid the carved skin into one piece. The bumpy road didn't seem to interfere with his precision whatsoever, and soon enough all that was left of her wound was a thin, red scar.

"Don't worry; it'll disappear," he promised her.

"Thanks." Aya gave him a polite smile and returned to her spot beside Borg, which was wedged between the front seats and the waste tank, awkwardly adjusted to fit around the suite of chem and radiation sensors. Borg used the tight quarters as an excuse to place his hand on her thigh. The intense glare Aya shot back at him caused him to quickly yank back his hand, sending his elbow painfully into a radiation gauge. Zor sat squeezed against the passenger door, observing the rest.

Ron, a ripperdoc in the wrong place at the wrong time. Zor examined his six-digit, titanium-jointed hands covered in matte nano-rubber that didn't resemble RealSkinn in the least. Zetatech-manufactured, expensive tech. What did Warden have to force him into this?

Zor had the uncanny feeling that they had met before.

Milena turned. The truck swung around in a long arc, missing a streetlight pole by a hair.

"Whoops," she murmured. "Can't get used to how wide this thing turns…"

How many antiaging mods could she possibly have? At first glance Zor wouldn't have put her over twenty-five, but he knew now that forty-something was likely closer to the truth. Ever-so-slight delays in her movements hinted at aged muscles and joints compensated by micro-adjusting implants. More importantly, what was she, by all indications a high-flying corpo, doing down among Night

City's bottom-feeders? They were a class unto themselves, sheltered and free from the unpleasantness of getting their hands dirty like everyone else—a coveted status they spent their entire lives working hard to maintain. Whatever Warden had on her must have been serious.

Aya—another mystery. No visible chrome—a rarity these days. Gotta be in damn good shape to move around that fast. Takes discipline.

The netrunner—nobody had a clue who he was, yet he was the true backbone of this operation. The only one who wasn't expendable. Without him, there was an absolute zero chance they'd have pulled this off.

"*Take a right.*" The netrunner's synthesized voice didn't convey any hint of emotion. "*After two intersections you'll take a left at the green light.*"

"Thanks to who, losers?!" Borg called out from the back. "That's right, my codes! Without me, you…"

And who the hell was Borg? The extensive cyberware explained the nickname, even if they were probably all for show. A widened jaw, several flashy implants scattered over his biceps, shoulders and neck—there was little rhyme or reason to them, like a mash-up of unrelated tattoos. God knows what purpose they served, if any, but they didn't make him look strong—just big. No use dwelling on them—once they brought back the container, everyone would go their separate ways and never have to lay eyes on one another again.

They sat cramped together in the garbage truck's cab and watched as the street seemed to magically clear a path for them. The netrunner was changing the streetlights, leaving the badges stuck in traffic while they rode a wave of green lights. Milena's smile hadn't disappeared.

One more thing.

"Stop the truck," Zor said in a way that made Milena brake without hesitation.

She pulled over to the right. Unaccustomed to the braking distance, the garbage truck continued to roll until it bumped into the back of an abandoned car. The drumming of rain on the roof suddenly stopped. They were under an overpass.

"Damn…" Ron smiled to himself. "That was one helluva trip…"

"Switch off your phones." Zor led by example, turning off his first.

The rest hesitated but followed suit—unlike Zor, muting their implants via thought-command without so much as moving a muscle.

"Bro, an earpiece? You for real?" Borg sneered at Zor. "Can't afford a neuroport like a normal choom?"

"Don't like microprocessors buzzing in my brain."

Neither he nor Aya used implanted holo-calling. Though she had a neuroport, it was connected to a physical, external device. As long as communication was limited to voice, Zor preferred a phone—simple, no bells and whistles. It's not like they would be having a holo-conference or anything.

"All right. Why us?" Zor asked.

They stared at him in silence.

"Um, 'cause we're friggin' badass?" Borg scoffed. "Whole thing went as smooth as a joytoy's ass. You catch their faces? Shat their pants the second they saw us."

"Because they weren't expecting trouble," Ron corrected him. "Not even cub scouts like us."

"Because they were scared." Milena took out a cigarette, inserted it into an elegant cigarette holder and lit up. A violet haze wafted through the cab. "They were new, inexperienced. Wide-eyed recruits barely outta training. Must've thought this would be a routine A-to-B escort."

"Robbed those kids of their blissful youth…" Ron muttered grimly.

"For some a long life, old age, too—in one fell swoop." Milena motioned behind, toward Borg, with her cigarette. "Because someone couldn't stick to the plan."

"Because we're low risk. That's why Warden picked us," Aya said. "If we'd have died, it wouldn't be an enny lost."

"He doesn't lose anything from us being alive, either," Zor added. "Right now, he still needs us. But the second we deliver this container, that ends."

What now?

Warden noticed the garbage truck stop under the overpass.

"What's the holdup?" he asked.

No answer. Fucking amateur hour. If they're already causing problems now, then there's no telling what tomorrow would bring. Problems are best gotten rid of before they have a chance to breed and multiply. Sadly, the client specified that he wanted them alive. Why the bleeding heart?

He drew his pistol and took a moment to admire it, running his fingers across the smooth steel. What if he altered the deal just a little? Fewer witnesses, fewer problems down the road. Rest stays the same. Still weighing his decision, he slowly trained his pistol on the netrunner lying in the bathtub.

"*Wouldn't advise that,*" said the synthesized voice through his earpiece. "*Check the screen.*"

Warden leaned over the equipment. The main monitor displayed the interior of an unfinished megabuilding. A forty-year-old, broad-shouldered Black man covered in tattoos and wearing a synth-leather coat leaned over a table.

Warden quickly turned and aimed his pistol at the drone hovering outside the window.

"*Not worth it,*" said the netrunner. "*A recording of this whole operation is being kept in a secure location. If I flatline, it goes straight onto the Net.*"

Warden calmly walked over to the bathtub. He knelt against the edge and brought his face less than an inch away from the netrunner's. It would've looked like he was asleep if it weren't for the colors flickering through his eyelids. The ice in the tub had almost completely melted.

"Plenty of ways to keep a body artificially alive," Warden said in a harsh whisper.

The netrunner was silent. Warden smiled. He stood up and holstered his pistol.

"Relax, you'll get what was promised. Like to play with iron is all—don't got nothing else."

"Yo, hold the fuck up—time-out!" Borg started. "We're the ones with the goods. If he wants it so bad, he can pay for it."

"I don't think you understand our situation." Ron looked at Borg. "It's not our game—he makes the rules."

"He makes 'em, we bend 'em. I mean, Christ, we're the fucking gang here! And, like, he's just…him."

Milena shook her head.

"Every one of us has got somethin' to lose," Ron reasoned.

"Oh, yeah?" Borg asked. "Like what, old man?"

"My patience, for one, if you don't cut the smart-ass act."

"If Warden doesn't get what he wants, he'll make good on his promises," Milena added soberly. "I don't know what dirt he has on all of you, but if you're here I'm guessin' it's serious. Let's just finish this and go our separate ways—move on with our lives."

"How do you know?" Borg rubbed his shoulder and winced. The HMG barrel must've burned a patch of exposed skin. "What makes you so damn sure he'll go through with it?"

"I know how to read people." Milena took a drag, then blew a cloud of smoke in his direction. "You could say I do it for a living."

Ron smiled.

"We know who he is, at least," Zor spoke up. "As long as we're alive, we're a threat to him."

"True," Milena answered. "He could've hidden his identity from us if he wanted to. Thinks himself safe, untouchable. And he's right. We're the ones who should be scared, not him. Better keep our mouths shut, because as far as I can tell, blackmail doesn't have a best-by date."

"Fine, let's just go." Borg leaned his head against the rear wall of the cab with a metallic thud. "Let's just get our eddies and put this whole thing behind us."

"What eddies?" Aya asked, suddenly confused.

"I meant, um…" Borg hunched over slightly. "Let's just get this shit over with. Unless you like the stink of a garbage truck."

The guard waved them through without a word, not even a glance. A man of reason. The underground garage was virtually empty, lit only by a few faint construction lamps, the evenly spaced pillars casting long shadows across the floor. It looked like the construction company went bust before they could install proper lighting fixtures.

The crew hopped out of the truck, hearing the soft slap of wet concrete as they landed. It was cool and damp down here. That explained the lack of any homeless. They wanted this to be over and done with but weren't in any particular hurry to face Warden. This place was practically made for quietly taking care of unsavory biz without the fear of prying eyes.

"So?" Borg folded his arms and looked around the empty, concrete space. "Where the boss man at?"

Ron looked up at the roof of the garbage truck, which was barely an inch from the ceiling.

"Can't tell if that's a sign of Warden's foresight and intelligence. Or the complete opposite."

Before anyone could guess what Ron meant, they heard Warden over the comms.

"Weapons in the crate."

This time a holo-projection of Warden appeared—visible to all but Zor, who heard only his voice.

The crate was near the elevator doors. Kudos, Zor thought. Can't threaten a bunch of people if they're still packing iron.

Not that Zor wanted to get back at Warden. He wanted things to return to normal—if you could call his life "normal." He went over first, tossing his Saratoga into the crate like the piece of scrap it was, followed by his pistol. He'd played by Warden's rules till now—might as well play till the end. He didn't have any combat implants, which meant he had only his instincts and some training to fall back on. An amateur, in other words, but at least he wasn't alone. He could've easily died an hour ago. He could die in five minutes. Maybe this instant. He wasn't scared. He ought to drop to his knees right now and get this over with, await death with open arms—a meaningless death to top off a meaningless life. No, that could tempt fate to spare him. He just had to be patient. Sooner or later, a bullet would find its way to his brain—accidental or not—then this world would disappear. *Black rain batters the windshield, the droplets streaking off the side as he tries to speed deeper into the night. Far to the left, the neon mosaic of Night City dims and fades. A fire rages on the horizon ahead of him. It's too late…*

"Zor…"

He came to—still standing over the crate. Aya drew her hand back from his shoulder. He straightened up as if nothing happened. Besides Aya, only Ron, who stood a few feet away, noticed what had just happened, but he remained silent as he observed Zor.

The elevator doors opened slowly, forebodingly. They froze. The strip of light widened and Warden, wearing a long synth-leather coat, stepped into the parking garage as if he owned it along with everything else. His holo-projection vanished as he walked through it.

Zor managed to stave off his cerebral meltdown—for now. Still, he could barely stand.

Warden wasn't carrying a gun. He went to the back of the garbage truck and ran his hand against the edge of the container, then turned to the rest waiting apprehensively.

"A trial by fire." He spoke in a gravelly voice. "But you passed, my little impromptu gang. Feel free now to return to your boring, meaningless, happy lives."

"So…" Ron shrugged and turned up his palms. "That's it? We can go?"

Warden only smiled, displaying a set of sky-blue teeth.

CHAPTER_2

A heavy heat beat down from the sky, vaporizing all traces of the morning downpour. Even the puddles on the demolished sidewalk and the scorched blacktop had nearly vanished.

Sporting a long overcoat, Liam paced between the mangled remains of the cars and truck. He'd already watched the stills and recordings, but there was no substitute for visiting the crime scene. Police tape cordoned off both ends of the street. Patrol cars stood empty as officers took shelter in the shade and waited, watching Liam with impatience, wishing they were someplace else. Behind them a small crowd of curious onlookers had gathered along with a few reporters angling for a clearer view. "Nothing to see here." That tired cliché, but this time it was true. That didn't stop them from sending up drones or zooming in with high-end optics for fresh content to spice up with live, hot commentary. Not as hot as the air. It didn't take long before they lost interest and gradually dispersed.

Two street cleaners had had enough of standing around. They started hooking up equipment to their truck's tank.

"Not yet," the detective said.

"Gonna make us wait all fuckin' day?!" one of them snapped back. "Unlike you, I don't get paid to stand around with my dick in my hand!"

"Won't get paid sitting in a holding cell for forty-eight hours, either."

It worked. They retreated back to their truck and defiantly lit their cigarettes.

Liam wiped the sweat from his brow, turned up the A/C in his coat and returned to his inspection. No part of this made any god-damn sense. Like that HMG raining lead down from the second-floor window. Still there. Militech-made—the irony. Unless…

The detective went inside the building, ran up to the second floor and once more stood next to the heavy machine gun. The gunman managed to hit practically everything in sight except for the target vehicle, which sustained only three rounds. Why? You don't entrust a couple-thousand-eddy gun to someone who doesn't know how to use it. On top of that, you'd need to be brain-dead to leave such an expensive piece like this behind—even if the serial number's been sanded off. Could've at least swapped out the barrel and made it harder to trace… Either way, the abandoned gun and the gonk who pulled the trigger were a riddle. Riddles—plural.

He inspected the gun more closely. HMG Model 31, factory new, hot off the assembly line. Not even all its safety labels had been peeled off. But if these were amateurs, how'd they get iron like this in the first place?

Liam knelt down to examine the grip. Maybe forensics had already checked for prints, maybe not. Not like it mattered—the firearms database has been a chaotic, underfunded mess for ages.

Meaning they probably hadn't.

He took his pinkie finger, a shade lighter than his normal complexion, and ran it along the side of the barrel where the serial number had been filed down. The golden joints at his wrist where chrome met bone formed a sort of bracelet, the diodes blinking as he felt the almost perfectly smooth metal—save for the minuscule gradations where the digits had been magnetically engraved. He shut his eyes and focused.

The sensor in his pinkie needed to run over it only three times before the number flashed on the back of his eyelids. He saved it to his memory bank and connected to the database. The gun was stolen more than three years ago from a Militech warehouse...and hadn't been used until now? That's not how gangs operated. Liam felt that familiar feeling—a knot in his stomach. You either knew who to look for, or you knew better than to look at all. He'd seen investigations nipped in the bud, officers suddenly disappearing after refusing to drop a case... Occupational hazard at this point. But this...this was new.

The noise of cars pulling up outside snapped him back to reality. What now?

He looked out. Two Militech patrol trucks—identical to the one abandoned in the middle of the street—and a tow truck.

He ran downstairs and went over to the closest NCPD officer.

"What part of 'no one gets through' didn't you understand?!" he asked, visibly irritated.

"New orders from Zed," the officer replied, barely hiding his relief. "Corp's takin' this one."

"You don't say..."

Liam sighed and walked up to the Militech soldier who seemed most in charge. The rest were already preparing to tow the truck and car. Black uniforms, better equipped and armored than the NCPD, maybe even MaxTac. Their looks alone commanded authority.

"Lieutenant Liam Reed, Major Crimes." He displayed his holo-ID. "Leadin' an investigation here and you fellas are in my way."

"Not anymore." The squad leader didn't see fit to introduce himself. Didn't even lift his visor, opaque from the outside. Staring back at Liam was a reflection of himself that made him look comically small.

"What's 'not anymore'? Me leading this investigation or you being in my way?"

"You know the drill. No civilians got hurt, meaning it's not police business. We'll take it from here..."

He had a point. Rare for not a single bystander to get scratched up or for there to be damage to private property. In those circumstances, the police could hand over the investigation. Unless...

"True, no one got hurt, but this street sustained damage during the attack." Liam cocked his head backward. "And that's public property, not to mention the breach in the CCTV system."

"Militech'll cover street repairs. Obsolete ICE on your CCTV network's your problem. Now, if you don't mind, you're in *our* way. This is an internal investigation." He turned and walked to the tow truck that was already lifting up the back of the Militech transporter.

The NCPD officers started to dismantle the barricades with newfound enthusiasm.

Liam tossed a piece of chewing gum into his mouth and took one last look at the scene. He'd just turned forty; his hairline had already receded to the top of his skull. Why bother when it always turned out like this?

He enabled his phone nested in his coat and dictated a message via thought-command:

"Got the afternoon free. I'll pick up the kids from school."

ArS-03, log 35102.
Synchronization procedure initiated.
Unidentified device NI100101001110. Status: unknown.
No additional subsystems detected.

He was alive. No doubts there. At least not in Zor's mind. He lay on his back and stared at the ceiling. Lying on your back wasn't proof, but you had to be alive to stare at a ceiling.

Why'd Warden choose him? Of all people?

He didn't believe in coincidences.

He got up and looked outside the window. "Looked" was a slight exaggeration. His view consisted of the wall of the next building just a dozen feet away. Dark now, past midnight. Not like it appeared any different in the daytime. The megablock walls, sometimes reaching up to eighty stories, effectively blocked out all sunlight, as well as the holo-ads tempting you with units in nicer neighborhoods.

Coincidences...

He turned and surveyed his unit's interior. The sagging couch that doubled as a bed, a desk with an average-sized cyberdeck, closet, micro-bathroom. Just over a hundred square feet, give or take. Wedged in the corner was a small fridge and cooking range—the most basic models.

His stomach grumbled. He wasn't hungry enough to go out and buy the cheapest scop, which was all he could afford to eat. Not right now at least.

He sat on the part of the couch that sagged. Same routine for years. He switched the TV on with a flick of his hand. He could manage without all the other crap, but not this.

"*Hey, have you heard of the new ImaginEar implant?*" asked a short, bald-headed gnome with floppy ears. "*No? Well, you have now! With the ImaginEar implant, you can hear anything your imagination desires!*"

"*Upgrade your All Foods feeder within the next hour and you could get a discount of up to...*"

"*Neighbor downstairs making a racket again? BudgetArms has just the solution for you...!*"

"*Ball bearing loose in that foot implant? No problem...!*"

"*Have you ever dreamed of...?*"

"Amazing! Now you can...!"

"Stop pretending..."

Explosions of color and animated characters laid siege on Zor's mind. Once the mandatory dose of commercials was over, the show started. Except it was just another commercial pretending to be a show.

Zor was very careful with what he watched. He made sure his profile was as generic and nondescript as possible should anyone ever take a closer look. No reason why they would, but just in case. He aimed to sit smack in the middle of every consumer curve—a lone dinghy bobbing gently in the eye of a hurricane. Wasn't easy, but the knowledge that this wouldn't last forever gave him hope.

The safest bet was watching what everyone else watched. The top story on every channel for the last few hours was an ambush on a Militech convoy in Arroyo. A few recordings of the scene being looped. Nothing else.

That netrunner did a solid job. Scrubbed everything clean.

The sidewalk and street were cracked and covered with rubble—the result of Ron's exceptionally poor aim. Zor recalled the six-fingered cyberhands and forearms. The advanced Zetatech model was suited for nano-surgical operations, not handling an HMG.

The news anchor claimed that neither the badges nor Militech had any leads. Maybe true, maybe not. From within the bullet-ridden truck emerged an elegantly dressed man with dark sunglasses, looking as if straight out of a spy thriller.

Zor froze. He stared closer at the man who was now pointing his finger directly at Zor. He removed his sunglasses, revealing a set of military night-vision optics.

"Do you worry about your safety on the streets of Night City?"

Nope, just another commercial grafted onto a news segment.

"Don't go changing the channel! We're not done yet! Hold on! What you need are bulletproof CrystalArmor windows. Because YOUR life is worth any price!"

Zor changed the channel. It didn't help.

"Lonely in the big city? Not anymore! Angel's Companions are looking for girls like you! You'll meet TONS of interesting people! Sign up for our soonest casting session today!"

He changed it again.

"Maybe you don't believe in germs," said a thin doctor in fishnet stockings and high heels. *"But they sure believe in you! Invest in a water filter now!"*

He poured himself a glass of water from the sink. Unfiltered.

He took small, slow sips. He was thirty years old, lived alone, kept himself in decent shape. Probably the reason why he kept flipping to channels with commercials offering erotic services. He didn't mind watching them, but he never bought anything. Waste of time and eddies that he didn't have, not to mention the unwanted attention it could draw. He couldn't afford a run-in with the law.

Especially considering what happened yesterday.

Zor sat in front of his clunky, old-gen cyberdeck. Beneath the small screen was a traditional keyboard, a rarity these days. Zor knew how to read and write—the NUSA army required it. For some reason he had held on to this strange piece of tech. It had less surveillance than newer models and was therefore less intrusive. The commercials were seldom, since it wasn't worth the effort to format them. Nobody bothered blocking the cyberdecks' Net access, either, since they used the same protocols as corporate maintenance systems and updated transfer connections to and from auto shops and Data Inc outlets. They weren't dangerous unless you used it for illegal stuff, and only amateurs did that.

But in spite of the NetIndex encryption soft he'd installed, he didn't type anything. He simply browsed the news, albeit in a very basic format. The kind he liked the most. For someone who was chipped with optical cyberware, or at least someone accustomed to modern interfaces, this deck would look like an ancient relic of the past.

Zor would typically click on one random link after another several times, or even up to a dozen, before selecting anything that actually interested him.

He stopped on a short, looping recording of a slender fifty-something corpo with glasses getting into a limousine. Looked like someone important at first glance. He was right. The article beneath described a new government contract. No place or date. Nothing useful. Zor never saved any information, preferring to remember it instead. The same thing for years—scraps of information that never led him any closer to his goal.

He shut down the cyberdeck and sank back into his thoughts. He could find iron, no problem. He had at least enough for a pistol. But a pistol wasn't going to cut it. It'd be like trying to take down an elephant with a fly swatter. If elephants still existed.

His eyelids felt heavy. He went back to the sagging couch and fell onto it back-first. Minutes passed, but sleep didn't come. Zor finally opened his eyes. A blue-haired girl danced before him, rhythmically swaying her hips. She bent toward him and opened her mouth, ten blue tongues writhing like snakes. Was he dreaming already? The blue-haired girl vanished, only to be replaced by her. Aya. He remembered her intoxicating scent, even in the rain. How she moved. Maybe someday. Once he'd done what needed to be done. She could dance for him. Probably danced well, light as she was on her feet. In slow motion, he watched as she spun to the left, her long, black hair whipping the air, her translucent skirt billowing, her bare feet moving with carefree precision across the floor.

He was dreaming. He'd probably never see her again.

Everything farther than a few feet blurred into a thick pink haze. The beat was all-encompassing, stratified with clinking glasses and dozens of simultaneous conversations. The music's algorithm was self-generating, constantly adapting to the dancer's movements and fleeting changes in style, amplifying the atmosphere.

No doubt someone was watching. Everyone, maybe. No, not everyone. The later it got, the fewer watched. And there were always the BD junkies.

Her right hand gripped the chrome pole as she hopped off her left foot, flipped twice in the air before feeling the cool, familiar metal between thigh and calf. She released a small dose of pheromones, closed her eyes and gave in to instinct, rippling her torso like a gentle wave, her body perfectly entwined with the pole. No need to think— her body knew exactly what to do, adapted on its own. Every time the rhythm shifted, she removed a piece of her clothing. She loved it. This. Dancing in front of a faceless crowd.

The lights dimmed; the music began to fade. From behind the haze, a room filled with tables came into focus. For a brief moment, a few hands set down their glasses to pay tribute to this short but spectacular performance with uneven applause. Someone stood up and yelled something between claps. She couldn't make it out. She gathered the few items of clothing strewn around and made her way backstage. The room returned to its usual chatter and clatter.

Now, in the backstage hallway, it was finally quiet. Two male dancers smoked by the doors leading to the bar, talking to two other female dancers. One was more muscular, his nearly obsidian skin glistening, the other thin and short with skin so pale it almost glowed blue. The first one had a large cock, the second a forked tongue—something for everyone. Didn't even glance at her. Good looks and bared flesh weren't in short supply around here. She passed Yuki, who was getting ready to go onstage, bright-red patterns pulsating underneath her skin. Must've chipped herself a new subdermal. They smiled at each other in passing. Yuki was angling to break into the braindance biz but so far hadn't landed any notable gigs.

With a sigh of relief, she closed the door to the dressing room and sat on one of the four chairs facing the mirror. The light bulbs along its edges dimmed the rest of the room behind her.

It was over. Their impromptu gang's little foray into petty crime belonged in the past. Time for things to go back to normal. Boring, maybe. Limited in possibilities. But at least it was safe, predictable. Aya blinked an eye, activating her phone, and thought-dictated a message to M: "Finished for the night. Back in thirty mins."

"Aya."

She turned abruptly. Someone sat on the couch against the wall. It was her boss, Crispy.

"Crisp, hey. Something the matter?" Aya asked.

"Same as always." Crispy rose to her feet. "You know some clients have a thing for 'ganics, right? Got folks comin' here just for you."

"Guess that's a good thing, right?" Aya removed her pink wig and began peeling off her fake lashes. "Already scrolled two BDs this month."

Crispy rose and stopped just behind her chair, looking at her with those unnaturally large eyes. Maybe once upon a time they looked good on the stage, back when she used to dance. She was retired now, but the eyes stayed, made her look like an old child. She unclipped Aya's long black hair and started slowly brushing it.

"Mm-hmm. 'Cept sometimes they want more than just a dance, more than braindance. Feel me?"

"I never agreed to that." Aya took the brush from her. She began to quickly remove her eyeshadow.

"People change; deals change. Gotta stay ahead of the curve if you wanna earn your keep. You of all people should know that."

"I have boundaries."

"Ain't boundaries meant to be pushed?" Crispy laid a hand on her shoulder. "Don't hear the other girls complainin'."

Aya didn't finish wiping off her pink lipstick. She threw on her jacket and made for the door. Crispy didn't stop her.

"Remember, honey, you may be 'ganic, but you ain't innocent. So do us all a favor and quit actin' like you're some goddamn saint."

Aya pushed the door open and headed toward the exit.

The stool wobbled as Ron plopped himself down at the bar. He played around with the ice in a faux-crystal glass containing a brownish liquid pretending to be a half-decent whiskey. With a flick of his wrist, he could land one ice cube on top of the other nine times out of ten, even while losing their shape as they melted.

"You shoot dice?" Pepe, the bartender, asked him.

"Nah." Ron looked at him with a vacant expression. "Why?"

"Take my advice, brother. Keep it that way." The counter seemed to bend as Pepe leaned on it with the elbow of a muscular, tattooed arm. His gold cyberhand grazed the cross on his gold chain. "Wouldn't walk out of a casino alive with that little party trick."

"I'm a ripperdoc, not a gambler."

"They wouldn't bother to ask. And you wouldn't stick around till then, anyway."

Pepe nodded toward Ron's glass. "Always figured rippers made steady eurobuck, yet here you are drinking Joe Tiel. Donaghy's too tall for your budget?"

Ron shrugged and peered down into his glass. The green glow from the neon sign above the bar made the whiskey nearly black.

"Know what it's like to do something that's beneath you, but you don't have no choice?"

Pepe deliberately scanned El Coyote Cojo's empty interior, then turned back to Ron and pulled out an unlabeled bottle from underneath the bar.

"Try this." He poured a liquid that looked and smelled like the real thing. "Don't got no name, but it beats half the brand-name piss they call whiskey these days."

Gazing through the glass walls of a unit on the sixty-sixth floor in Charter Hill at the dazzling night of Night City could make one giddy. Dozens of skyscrapers, lit windows by the thousands, floating holo-boards the size of soccer fields, countless AVs weaving their way between buildings like a swarm of fireflies. Down below, a tangled mosaic of neon signs, brightly lit store windows and cars. And at the center of it all—the looming megabuildings of Corpo Plaza topped with a layer of cloud so brightly backlit that it may as well have been daytime.

The city that couldn't sleep.

In the window stood the reflection of a model-perfect nude body shrouded in the night.

"We really made an impression on them today." The man threw off the blanket. "Those amateurs from Arasaka. Anyway, how was it for you?"

Tall, thin, well-equipped.

Milena knew what he meant.

"It was fine," she said, throwing on a silk robe. "As usual. If you want a number, then three. But the third was sort of...whatever."

"Whatever?" The man stood up. "You had three and you're complaining?"

"Fucking optimal settings..." Milena shook her head. She went back to the window and closed her eyes. "I think you'd better go."

"Three orgasms and now you're telling me to fuck off?" He started to pick up his clothes from the floor. "How about next time I get three and you get one..."

"I have a general sort of...crisis in these kinds of relationships." She touched the glass. "Two weeks ago, I was in a pileup on the beltway. There was fire. Lots of people died. I could've died, too, but all I did was sprain my ankle. One of the Trauma Team medics there lost it, tried to save some kid from a burning car." She paused. "The others wouldn't let him. Makes you think. Death all around you, choosing whom to take and whom to give a second chance...you start to realize it's all pointless."

He started dressing quicker, not saying a word. He was too young to understand.

"Well, see you at work tomorrow," he said from the doorway.

The doors slid open automatically.

The best fuck in a month. That same empty feeling.

Ned Templeton was okay. They were all just okay. Except he was supposed to be more than good for just chewing up and spitting out.

Her hope started to fade.

It was the same thing over and over. Even three inevitable orgasms start to get boring. Nothing had substance anymore. If only something went wrong. Differently. No, they all had the same soft, same programs. It was one déjà vu after another. When to put in one finger, or two? She knew it all by heart.

She was sick and tired of it.

Milena knew she wouldn't fall asleep. She thought-commanded her neurotransmitters to dispense a cocktail of anti-stress chemicals into her brain, chasing it down with her whiskey. It was a sharp deviation from her usual "Premium Health" diet, but to hell with it. In any case, she stopped dieting two weeks ago—after the crash. When you stare death in the eyes, kale and chia for "youth and longevity" seem only a waste of time.

Her thoughts began to slow—the neurotransmitters were doing their job.

She felt herself folding back into the sparsely furnished unit behind her. The crowds of people, thoughts, things and problems that occupied her mind each day was enough. She needed space to relax. There was no place for useless crap here.

She lit a cigarette, the flame lighting up her face in the window's reflection. The synthetically rejuvenated face of a fifty-two-year-old.

She dropped the lighter, the holder dangling from her slightly parted lips.

She took the glass from the table and hurled it at the window.

Music, bitches and booze. That's right, watch and weep, losers! Table, stool's a little shaky, no big deal—whole world's swayin' to the same beat. Got a booth, my own fuckin' booth, chick to the right of me, chick to the left. Gettin' a load of my biceps, pulsin' to the rhythm—fuckin' all over me, man. One more shot. *Clink!* Gotta keep my head straight. Gonks at all the other tables. Cheap chairs, cheap taste… taste. Chick dancing on a pole, I'm on a motherfuckin' roll. Shit, that rhymed!

"Yo, one more shot and we're goin' upstairs to poundtown! You ready?"

"I'm already wet, baby." The one on the left poured a shot.

"You can stick it anywhere you want," the one on the right added.

Fuckin' A! Let's do this! *Gulp!* One last drink before battle. Gonna be a long night.

The applause momentarily snapped him out of his seconds-long reverie. He didn't even realize he'd momentarily blacked out. He got up, clapping his hands above his head.

"'Ey, beautiful!" he yelled to the stage. "Get over here! We can do a threesome...Wait—" He counted in his head. One, two, three..."A foursome, ha!"

He hobbled out of the booth and took a few wobbly steps. The dancer with the pink hair didn't even glance in his direction. She picked up her clothes and disappeared backstage. That ass, though...

"Fuckin' bitch..." He turned around sharply. "Well, guess it's just you two..."

The lights around the club started spinning, the ground beneath his feet vanished. Borg was unconscious before his head hit the floor.

CHAPTER_3

Sup, losers! Miss me? That's right, it's your favorite scumbag media, FR34K_S33K! Wonderin' what the corpos been trying to hide from us this time? Well, if you ain't, you gonna find out anyway, cuz I don't give a FUCK what y'all want.

Remember that shoot-out down in Arroyo? Look, I know there's been, like, a hundred shoot-outs since then. Who cares, right? Screamsheets be jam-packed with crime every goddamn day. Except for the one in Arroyo. You heard me—you won't find it in any official news sources anymore. Weird, right? Someone fucking obliterated a Militech convoy and boosted their cargo and not a drop of ink's being spilled over it. Except right here! News feeds've scrubbed any mention of it clean, so that just leaves little ol' me digging through days-old newsfeeds. Know anyone else with that kind of dedication? Yeah, didn't think so!

What do we know so far? They were pros, by the looks of it. New outfit, prolly from outta town. But that don't scare me. Know what keeps me up at night? The next corporate war. They tryna put the scare in us with gang wars, 'cept we used to that shit by now. Hell, gang wars is just part of the NC scenery now. But you can't ignore a corporate war, no sir. Corps won't hesitate for a second to blow an entire hood into orbit if it'll widen their profit margin. Then they'll act all sad an' shit, send their fuckin' prayers while they pin the blame on whoever pissed them off last.

What do y'all think got klepped from that convoy? Must've been something important if someone went through all the trouble of sweepin' it under the rug. Some kinda new bioweapon, maybe? Who do y'all think'll use it and when? Here's hopin' we'll never find out.

Stay tuned to FR34K_S33K if you're hungry for the truth and nothing but the truth!

PEACE!

"I already told you. I'm using it to learn stuff."

"Mm-hmm. Bet you're learning all kinds of things."

"It's not a wreath—it just looks like one. It can't even run a braindance."

The short, skinny teenager sat in an armchair at his desk, a wreath held in both hands. The woman with greasy pink hair standing in the doorway was his mother. Her sweatshirt hung on her bony shoulders as if on a coat hanger.

"You'll fry your skullsponge with that thing," she repeated.

"I modified it. I use it for other things now."

"Can already see what you'll end up like."

"Like what?"

"Like a braindance junkie!!"

"I know it looks like a wreath, but I just told you..." Albert sighed. "Besides, you're going to stand there and tell me watching TV all day doesn't fry your brain?"

Her lips tightened.

"I like knowing what goes on in the world, okay? You ought to stay busy, do something useful with your life."

"Useful...Like what?"

She pursed her lips and waved her arms.

"I dunno—something! People do useful things. You don't do anything."

"I wanted to go to college."

His mother scoffed.

"This again. With what money?"

"I'm trying to earn a bit."

"By being lazy?! Reliving those goddamn BDs?"

"For the last time, it's not—"

She rolled her eyes and snorted with disapproval. Her flip-flops smacked against her heels as she marched back to the living room couch.

Albert swiveled around to his desk. Living with his mother wasn't easy. He was seventeen years old, which by Night City standards meant he was basically an adult. But much as he wanted to, he couldn't imagine himself living anywhere else.

Braindance. He didn't even like it. Tried it once out of curiosity but had to stop after only a few minutes. It just wasn't for him—plain and simple. The wreath—now that was a different story. Armed with a few techie tricks, he was able to expand the capabilities of the standard neuroport located behind his ear. Wasn't the best place for it, anyway. Old-fashioned. Better off going straight for the more advanced tech, like the C-Link that went in the base of your skull—proven by the fact that netrunner chairs already had openings in their headrests by default. Having multiple cables jacked into the neuroport put too much weight on the side of your head, strained the neck. Then again, if all you needed were shards for the chip slot that came with every neuroport, it was no biggie. But if you wanted high bandwidth, fast transfer speeds and low latency for deep dives into cyberspace—a C-Link was a game changer.

Except Albert didn't have a C-Link. He got by with his standard neuroport and modified braindance wreath. His last-gen cyberdeck was created for different purposes, but Albert modded it to squeeze out every last drop of performance.

He leaned backward and punched the button to close the door. The backrest of his chair creaked as he reclined. He winced as something pricked his hand. He carefully pulled out a shard of plastic from the chair's cushion. He shivered as he saw a scarlet drop of blood form on his palm, staring at it with a mixture of fascination and disgust. He wiped it with a tissue, but after a second it reappeared.

Blood. It coursed within him, kept him alive. It seemed so animalistic, impractical, downright gross. He took a few deep breaths, brought his thoughts under control and redirected them. Ought to get a new chair, something better. Could go out and buy one right now if he wanted to. Money wasn't the problem—it was leaving the unit, going all the way to the tech store and interacting with people he had no interest interacting with, or even worse, getting accosted by a salesperson. Could order it over the phone or via the Net, but how would he know which chair was the right fit?

He'd stick with the old one for now.

He put on the modded wreath and inserted the jack behind his ear. Relief washed over him as if he was finally coming home after a long journey. He was back in his world.

He was immediately struck by the technological gap between his gear and what he'd been given for the op. Everything here was dumbed down; transfers crawled at a snail's pace. The difference between first and second tier was night and day. Out of habit, he ran the program that checked safety levels in his area. Nothing out of the ordinary, which meant that all of south Heywood was yellow instead of green and red in a few spots, while Westbrook and the Center were completely green. The rest was mostly red, which almost never changed. Truth be told, the program wasn't actually that useful.

Apart from Pacifica, the red zones would be crawling with police—nobody'd dare steal a candy bar. Paradoxically, red was sometimes actually safer than green.

Not as if he was planning on going out anytime soon. There was plenty of data to analyze.

"College, ha!" He heard his mother even through the closed door. "Four hundred eddies per month in tuition! Where am I supposed to get that kind of money?!"

He thought-commanded his sales figures to appear in his peripheral. The basic, unsophisticated game he'd published on the Net two days earlier had two and a half thousand downloads. One download was fifty eurocents, meaning he'd made more than 1,200 eddies.

"How's a normal person even supposed to pay for that?" she ranted at the TV.

And that was just the start. Players could purchase add-ons and extras that could net him an additional five to seven hundred eddies per day. That is, if people bought them.

"Not like you even have to think about that!" she continued. "You don't care about money as long as someone makes you dinner and washes your dirty underwear."

And this was just one of many games and programs he'd published—the newest and most polished of them all.

"Brainwashing yourself instead of doing anything useful… What about that Marty, the son of what're-their-faces, who found a job as welder? Simple, honest work for almost thirty eddies a day. That's thirty eddies more than you're making now."

The rest of the programs were hit-and-miss, but their total revenue amounted to just under two hundred eddies per day. He could bump it up even higher, but that would require more manpower, which meant teaming up with someone. Albert wasn't thrilled by that prospect.

His version of cyberspace was a dark, zero-g void with prede-termined vectors. Pillars of upward-flowing machine code sur-rounded the center over which Albert was incorporeally suspended. They ended only 2,200 lines farther down. He could occupy differ-ent points in cyberspace simultaneously, correcting, adding and deleting lines of code. It had been a while since his virtual hands had touched a virtual keyboard in a while—an anachronistic left-over from realspace. Thought-commands were faster and more con-venient, but he still wasn't able to work on larger chunks all at once. His tech couldn't handle it.

Dealing with raw code was tedious and slow, but that was the only way you could create something perfect—something that could slip by your typical ICE, or NetWatch's surveillance daemons. Albert wasn't just making another game to kill time. This was a whole new level. You couldn't design something like this from the prefab modules on a WYSIWYG editor. The Taran—the Polish word for "battering ram," as he'd randomly discovered—could be sculpted from only machine code.

The only exception to the bare-bones interface was the down-loaded bitmap in the shape of a person who had been dead for half a century. Nobody could agree on whether he was the one who destroyed the Old Net. And if he had, nobody could agree on whether he did it to protect people from corporate totalitarian control or out of his own vanity and delusions of grandeur. All that interested Albert was that he was capable of it.

Rache Bartmoss.

Green digits, letters and characters hung patiently in space. If only he could process all this code in its entirety. Tier-two tech was the answer. But how to acquire it? It wasn't sold in stores—at least not legal ones. But taking a trip to any black market meant dealing with shady characters—something Albert tried to avoid at all costs. But it wasn't just the tech—he needed a C-Link, too. Not like you could get that chipped at the family ripperdoc's.

He momentarily set that dilemma aside and went back to the Taran's code. There was still a lot of work to do.

After Bartmoss caused the DataKrash, leading to the collapse of the Old Net, the NetWatch corporation built the Blackwall to protect humanity from dangerous, rogue AIs. At least, that was the official story told by NetWatch, along with every other official source. But that was a misrepresentation of the facts—or at least one of several. The Voodoo Boys gang had a different take—since 90 percent of the Net was sealed off, that meant the Blackwall was a prison we had locked ourselves into and thrown away the key. By that definition, beyond the Blackwall was freedom, endless possibility. It was this perspective that Albert subscribed to.

Except nobody had ever managed to get past the Blackwall.

"No ambition, no life goals…" His mother's voice seeped in from outside.

No one except for Alt Cunningham, onetime output of legendary rocker boy Johnny Silverhand, who didn't exactly arrive there of her own free will. According to rumor, she was still there—a rumor that sounded about as credible to Albert as a fairy tale. He didn't believe in happy endings against impossible odds—miracles, in other words. When something went wrong, either you were prepared for it or you usually wound up dead.

"Gave birth to a slacker…"

Chipping a C-Link at the base of his skull wouldn't escape his mother's notice. Neither would a bathtub filled with ice and a son locked in the bathroom for hours at a time. Much remained for him to do, along with many problems to solve.

*   *   *

"The fuck have you done?"

Renner stood over the gray container. The hall was lit by a single metal lamp dangling from the ceiling, forming a cone of light around them. The kind they had in interrogation rooms. Half a century old, give or take. The huge silhouette of a man in a real leather jacket with antiballistic padding cast a long shadow across the floor. Two electric-gold crosses on both of his hands glowed in the pale light. Remnants of old machinery rested on concrete plinths against the walls, their original purpose long forgotten. A latticework of pipes, cables, beams and some extractors suggested that the hall was once a small manufacturing operation. The nearly thirty-foot-high windows just under the sawtooth roof meant the chances of anyone peeking in were slim to none.

"You'd better have a good fucking explanation." Renner glared at him.

"Was testing out a new way of doing things." Warden tried to stay calm. "And it worked."

"Maybe you ought to get that head o' yours tested, hmm? You stole from Militech! Our main fucking client!"

A slight, angry grimace flashed on Warden's face and quickly vanished.

"Which is why no one's gonna suspect us," he explained. "We gotta expand, Renner, or else we'll just stay stuck in the same rut. It's boom or bust…"

Renner marched up to him. He was slightly taller and a good ten years older.

"Been takin' side gigs, hmm? And here I thought you were too gonk to do anything by yourself."

Ross, who was standing by the door, stifled a chuckle.

"We got the container," Warden replied. "It was a test, not a gig. A test. Didn't tell anyone 'cause I wanted to minimize the risk. So just take it easy."

"Take it easy, hmm?" Renner stepped even closer. The crosses on his hands glowed with feverish intensity. "Did I order you to klep this container? No. Did you ask me if you could klep it? No. You don't see anything wrong with that? Or are you just too big of a fuckin' leadhead?"

"You would've never signed off on it."

"Damned fuckin' straight! Now spill—who was in on this little shit show of yours?"

"Some nobodies off the street." Warden crossed his arms. "Everyone had somethin' to hide. Just had to do a little diggin', hang some dirt over 'em, sweeten the deal with a few eddies and they were ours."

"Next thing I'd better hear outta your mouth is that their bodies are lying at the bottom of the Coronado."

"They won't peep a word."

Renner eyed him silently for a moment.

"You're telling me they're out there, alive, just waiting to get arrested and questioned?!"

"Nobody'll ID them. That includes me. Us. I've got the only recording of the op," Warden lied. He tried to relax. Too goddamn tense. "You still don't get the idea."

"No, *you* don't get the fucking idea." Renner was struggling to keep his cool. "I've got people—they're good at what they do. We give 'em a job, they go and do it, we divvy up the takings. Simple. Works every time; everyone goes home happy. And here you bring me stolen Militech goods and off their soldiers while you're at it. The fuck you expect me to do with this? 'Cause right now I'm thinkin' I ought to zero you, strap you onto this goddamn container and send it back to them with flowers and a bottle of fucking champagne as an apology. Or do you got a better plan?" Renner was inches away from Warden's face. Warden had to take a step back.

"Doubt it. Just like I doubt all your gonkbrained ideas. Now listen up. You're gonna get your ass back in line. No questions, no half-baked schemes, and don't you even fuckin' think of any more ops, never mind testing them. You do what I say—no more, no less. We clear?"

"Don't worry! You can adjust the size, even during! Especially during! Start small, finish large!"

Milena wanted to switch off the commercial, annoyed. How dare they? An aging nympho? Was that the profile the algorithms cooked up?

Except there was no profile—she alone had chosen this subscription plan. She didn't switch it off—pulling her hand back at the last second. Let it play in the background, out of sociological curiosity, to see how the other people lived, down there.

The shiver in her lower abdomen wasn't imagined.

Should she go out? No, she had neither the strength nor the desire to go anywhere. Not to mention no one to go with. Ned was still licking his wounded ego.

It was shaping up to be another charming evening. No, how much more can you put yourself down like this? She hesitated for a brief moment...Why the hell not? She wasn't paying premium for nothing. Everything was premium—her nails, breasts, skin...She browsed the newest cartridges that had arrived through her subscription and settled on the inconspicuously titled *Twelve Gigolos*. Then she put on her braindance wreath and made herself comfy on the couch.

The room was dark, not very spacious but enough to fit three operator workstations. The dim glow from three main screens and a few other light fixtures revealed little apart from the soundproofing on the walls. Each workstation looked identical: an armchair surrounded by screens and control panels with a keyboard mounted in the center. All displayed the same green, orange and red rows of digits, real-time graphs and command windows that were constantly shifting, dreamlike.

"Nothing's happened for the past hour," said the woman known only as OP1, clearly bored. "Can't we just crank it up a little bit?"

"We're not cranking up anything," replied OP2. "It could skew the results."

"There won't be any results if nothing happens."

"Our orders were clear. We don't touch the variables without good reason."

"Nothing happening isn't a good enough reason?"

"You that bored that you're willing to get fired?" interrupted OP3. "We stick to orders. End of discussion."

ArS-03, log 44321.
Synchronization procedure initiated.
Unidentified device NI100101001110. Status: unknown.
No additional subsystems detected.

"Why's it always gotta be a warehouse? Or some other godforsaken dump?"

There, Zor finally out and said it. He'd been waiting to ask that for a long time—here, in the office of Buyers & Son. The man sitting behind the counter was none other than its sole owner.

The office stank. Always. Didn't need to wonder why, since right next to it was a biomass composter. More like a goddamned bioweapon. And for what? Not like the methane was even being put to good use. The flame just past the roof never stopped burning. Was methane what thousands of rats, cockroaches and every other kind of pest produced as they decomposed? Either way, there was no shortage of them skittering through the walls and crevices of practically every Night City building. Probably ever since buildings started to exist. The flame never stopped burning.

Buyers's knowledge surely didn't reach that far.

Work in the industrial sector wasn't just tiring and unpleasant—it could be downright dangerous. How many times had a cockroach crawled up someone's uniform and made them stumble backward over a catwalk railing, plunging headfirst into a vat of acid? Or a starving rat that leaped straight for someone's jugular? Zor didn't know. Probably many.

"Age-old tradition," Buyers explained. "As my old man used to say, 'Ain't no job too hard for us to handle.' Clients know that; that's why they come here." He snorted whenever he laughed. "What did you think this was gonna be? A goddamn picnic?"

Tradition—that was one way of looking at it. Buyers himself was the eponymous son in Buyers & Son. You could say he followed in his father's footsteps, but he didn't have to move an inch. All 330 pounds sat right where his father must've sat a long time ago. Cause of death? Working in hazardous conditions, or type 2 diabetes exacerbated by morbid obesity. Probably both.

"When I started working here..." Zor hated these kinds of conversations. He felt the knot in his stomach twist. "I was sort of counting on not having to do all the heavy lifting."

"Look, choom, I'll tell you again." Buyers wiped his face with a grimy hand. "Someone's gotta do it, all right? Soon as you get this warehouse over with, you can relax, wash it all down with something strong and contemplate the meaning of life, or whatever. How's that sound?"

"It's Morris's birthday today."

Buyers closed his eyes and frowned as if in pain.

"Ugh…" he groaned. Heaven forbid if anything in his day didn't go as planned. "I dunno; go out somewhere…Buy him a beer or somethin'."

A moment's peace—Juliena's in the shower. How much water is she using up? Best not to think about it. The bill still had two weeks to arrive…

She could barely keep herself awake, but she had to hold out. Couldn't show her exhaustion. Just a little longer and she'd have plenty of time to sleep. But only after.

The girl came out of the bathroom naked, leaving wet footprints on the floor. Completely unembarrassed. She didn't even know there was such a thing as embarrassment. Her body was merely a vehicle traversing through an unfathomable reality. Aya offered her the towel, but she never took it. Aya always had to dry her.

Fifteen minutes later, they were on the subway. Aya tried with all her might to stave off sleep. Normally she slept a few hours after coming back from Marry's, then took Juliena to school and rode farther to the club to catch a few z's before work. More often than not, she felt lacking in the sleep department.

Juliena was special. Unique. When she rode the NCART train, she always stared straight ahead for the entire ride. Who knew—maybe she was solving complex equations in her head, or maybe she was just suspended in time, waiting for reality to push her forward. Without fail, she would snap out of her trance as soon as they arrived at their stop. Though she wouldn't move so much as a finger before, now she'd stand up with an unsettlingly mechanical precision and head directly toward the doors.

Aya hugged Juliena with a gentle squeeze and kissed her on the forehead. The girl didn't smile. She never smiled. Without any reaction, she turned around and headed toward the school entrance. Aya followed her with her gaze as she disappeared into the school's hallways.

As Aya made her way back to the station, she nearly got hit by a car. Her nap on the ride to the club lasted only a few minutes—woken up by the sound of a new message. Probably nothing good. Using thought-command, she opened it—before her appeared a reminder about overdue school tuition. Of course—a month had already gone by. It was a school for children with special needs—one of the few in Night City. Juliena was lucky to get in. Of course, it was more expensive than the normal ones. Though Juliena was eight, she had the emotional maturity of a two-year-old. All indications suggested that would never change. Raising her alone was getting more challenging by the day and even the help of M would soon stop being enough. It was only a matter of time before she hit puberty—how would the needs of her body be reconciled with the mind of a child? Not to mention Aya's costs would only go up.

Ads. No matter where she looked, they attacked her from all sides. Not only did LED screens cover the top corner of the subway car, screens on the walls of the tunnel flickered like a cartoon flip-book. Usually, there were also holo-ads suspended along the middle of the train, but right now their rays were deformed by the shoulder-to-shoulder crowd of passengers. Aya tried to gather her thoughts. She couldn't get it out of her head—the Militech guard she'd killed in cold blood. Knowing it was either him or her gave her little comfort—and if it had been her, what would've become of Juliena?

The screamsheets were stubbornly silent. She hadn't heard a word about what happened—not even the briefest mention in the infoflashes between commercials. A Militech convoy got jumped in broad daylight and…Crickets. Night City really did have a short memory when it came to crime. Every day brought with it a new shooting, murder, caper—variations on the same theme guzzled down with morning coffee.

An icon flickered in the corner of her vision—a new message. Aya opened it with thought-command. One look was enough to drain her of the will to continue living. Another job. Now, when all she wanted was to go back to normal? "Wanted"—a strange concept, as if it belonged to a different era. She could want something until the cows came home, but having it? A luxury. She couldn't ignore the message. It was less an order and more a description of the future in which she, Aya, would play the role laid out for her. She had no choice—it was part of the deal. She couldn't even send a reply or ask a question if she had any doubts. There was no sender ID.

She shouldn't complain. After all, the last job was nearly three months ago, dealt with in a single night—not a hitch. Come to think of it, three months was a long time.

"Objective: Jeronimo Mendes. He will be led to you. It should look like a chance encounter. You will display an interest in him, but do not overdo it. Do not pressure him; do not try to extract any information. You will be emotionally supportive and empathetic to his needs. Be subtle. Let him do the talking. Details in the attachment."

She closed the message. She didn't have the energy to read the entire brief. It was hard, time-consuming work pretending to be someone else. You had to predict and plan for every possible situation, cobble together a completely different person who appeared totally natural. Resisting your own instincts—she hated that part the most. Sometimes not just for a few hours, but days. Everything had to go just right. Who was she kidding? She didn't hate just a part of it. She hated all of it.

She'd read it tomorrow once she'd had some sleep. Tomorrow was her day off.

She stood up. This was her stop.

"Pest control" wasn't the right phrase. More like "brute-force excavation." Once the pressure hoses washed off the moss, if you could even call it that, you got rust and what must've once passed for paint. Wasn't much left to salvage—the corrosion had chewed its way to the rebars in the pillars. No sign of any insects—must've all died of starvation. Pointless—this, them being here. It'd get demolished in a year or two. Or collapse on their heads right here and now.

"Think that's a wrap." Zor twisted his hose shut and lifted his Plexiglas visor.

"What, why?" Morris did the same. "We're only on the seventh pillar."

"This place hasn't been touched for the past decade. Probably won't be for the next one, either." Zor sighed. "I'd say there are roughly two hundred pillars to get through. And they just get worse and worse."

"But...it's our job," Morris insisted.

"I know, but it's pointless," Zor replied. "Most of these pillars are just moss and rust. You know what I think?" Zor paused. "I think we got the wrong address."

Morris didn't get the hint, which was more Zor's fault than his. His Down syndrome made it difficult to pick up on little nuances, along with the usual gamut of issues associated with the disorder. Right now, Morris had a job to do, and that meant finishing it.

"I thought you checked it."

"I know, I know. Look, it's my bad, okay?" Zor went toward the green van with BUYERS & SON and the number thirteen printed on it in boldface black font. He dragged the pressure hose behind him. "Come on, we're done here. Buyers won't be mad at you, I promise. I was the one who messed up the address. Hop in, Morris, unless you want to stick around."

Pheromones—low dose. The pink haze hid everything that was more than a few feet away. Good. The beat of the music filled every pocket of air, layered itself over the cacophony of conversations. Dancing—it was euphoric; it was the entire world. Nothing existed outside it. Right hand on the steel pole, two shoulder mount flips and then the cold metal between thigh and calf. Buttocks clenched, her chest rippling—an arm sliced through the haze. Deep within her, a vague desire for something. Someone. She didn't know who.

Her legs rotated fluidly upward, hair falling to the ground. Now the moment her fans always waited for. She gripped the pole tightly, pushed off her left leg and started to spin, gaining speed. She spun to the rhythm—a feat no other dancer here could accomplish.

Good.

Almost.

Not good.

Aya's shoulder hit the stage—shock absorbent, luckily. She tried with all her might to clench her right hand into a fist. Her fingers trembled, then slowly started moving as if held by a rusty spring.

The music went quiet, her hand was working again. The lights dimmed. It all happened in a single moment.

She snapped out of it and stared into the audience, flustered. Nothing changed. The usual applause, then back to conversation. Nobody noticed her fall. Here, primal attraction reigned supreme while everything else became background noise—depending on the substance.

She noticed some creep hide a flask in his coat pocket. Or what looked like a flask. Why had she noticed him through the crowd? Must be a hundred people in the room, dancing or reliving BDs. Never bothered her—they were just part of the scenery. Of course, some of the audience was made up by employees who worked the club. She'd never noticed the individual customers before, always escaped backstage as quickly as she could.

Nerves, that's all it was. A lot had happened over the past few days.

He took a plug the size of a coffee mug and stuck it into the outlet in the back of the van. The thick cable shook and then stiffened with a hiss. The refueling station refilled the vans with all the necessary fluids, charged the batteries and ran diagnostics. In the underground parking garage next to it stood a few identical vans.

He made his way toward the office entrance. Morris shuffled after him.

It was a messy gray garage with so many leaks that stalactites could form at any second. For a place that was in the business of decontaminating, you'd think it would be more...well, clean. Luckily, no client would ever come here in person.

As usual, Buyers sat behind his little booth, hunched over a couple of scratched-up terminals that were all linked to different networks. He moved objects around on the deck's screen, using the only filters he had: done, paid and what needed correction. Or maybe he was doing something completely different. His eyes flickered blue, which meant he was probably on the holo to someone.

He stopped what he was doing and looked at them, waiting for an explanation. They were back early.

"There was nothing there," Zor spoke up. "Job was pointless."

"Corps give pointless jobs sometimes." Buyers leaned back in his creaky chair. "But they pay, so I don't ask questions. They want us to fumigate a warehouse, we fumigate it. Even if it's gonna get demolished in a week."

"There's nothing there," Zor said. "Not even any insects."

Buyers stared at him intently, then grinned.

"You might be on to something there…" He nodded. "A job that does itself, eh? Just gotta make a bit of a mess—make it look like you were there, did something."

"Did that."

"Hmm. Good." He looked back at the screen. "Got another one for ya. Simple, but urgent."

"Urgent as in today?"

"Look at those lockers all you want"—Buyers pointed a sausage-link finger at Zor—"but you still got three hours on the clock."

"What needs doing?"

"The usual, just somewhere a little…different." Buyers grinned again. "Got a feeling you'll like it."

Her hand seemed fine. No trace of the cramp. Maybe it was just that one time, gone for good. Wouldn't happen again.

She shut the dressing room door behind her and did a few simple exercises: jumps, backward handspring, tricep dips. Everything seemed in order.

Dora watched her with boredom as she smoked. She was up onstage in a few minutes but always left her warm-up to the last minute.

"Don't get why you even bother…" she said in her smug, apathetic tone. "Wouldn't need to warm up if you were chipped."

Unlike Aya, Dora had a number of visible implants and liked to remind people about it every chance she got.

"Prefer it this way." Aya grabbed the bar attached to the wall and did a few pull-ups.

"You're missing out, babe." Dora opened her mouth and stuck out three tongues that vibrated and moved in sync like snake rattlers.

"Everyone's got their own niche. I'd lose fans."

"You're, like, so weird," she said, chuckling. "Why make life harder for yourself?"

Without waiting for an answer, she shrugged and turned to correct her makeup in the mirror. Out there, in the dim light and smoke, nobody would see the little imperfections, anyway. At least that's what Dora believed.

"I had a nightmare about demons," Morris said.

"Demons don't exist," replied Zor. "They're fictional."

"What does that mean?"

"They're made up."

"Maybe demons are just bad people?"

"Could be."

"Hey, maybe we could go for a beer together?" Morris asked with desperate hope. "You know, after work."

Zor didn't answer. The van crawled sluggishly through traffic. Every other type of car passed them by—limos, sports cars, combat cabs, even a Delamain. Their tinted windows reflected the light from the holo-boards and neon signs. Corpos headed either home or to Japantown to blow off steam and wads of eddies.

"It's my birthday today."

Zor didn't have to turn his head. He knew Morris was staring at him, waiting for him to say something.

"I don't drink."

"My mom would always buy a cake for me."

"So why not let her buy you one?"

"She's dead."

Zor tightened his grip on the steering wheel.

The urban landscape outside started to give way to shorter buildings and dumpier cars. Suits and heels were replaced by ripped jeans and flip-flops. Groups of people huddled close together in a way that definitely didn't arouse any suspicion. Trash littered the street. There weren't fewer neon signs and holo-ads, but they were somehow brighter, tackier. Shop windows with garish displays stood next to abandoned squats with graffiti and broken windows. Once an emblem of wealth and prestige, nowadays Kabuki wasn't exactly the pride of Night City.

Zor parked next to the littered sidewalk between a paint-chipped van and a beat-up pickup. They got out.

"Stay close to me." Zor took note of the crowd in front of the club. "Neighborhood isn't safe."

They unloaded their equipment in the glow of pink neon. If Buyers thought they were going to enjoy this, he was dead wrong. At least when it came to Zor. Places like these stank of trouble—something he used to have a remarkable propensity for getting into. These days he avoided it like the fucking plague.

And how'd that work out?

A few girls wandered around the club flirting with customers. Propositioning, more like. The two weren't mutually exclusive. That's what people came here for, anyway, among other things.

A knock at the door—rare courtesy around here. Aya turned and just stared at it for a few seconds.

"Um... Yeah?" she finally asked.

"Can I come in?"

"Sure."

The door opened. It was what's-his-face, the kid who helped out here and there. He stood there glued to the spot, slack-jawed as he stared at Aya. A cockroach scuttered around his shoe and quickly disappeared behind the wardrobe.

"You here to fix something, or...?" She tried to sound nice.

"Uhh...Can I?" He pointed to the floor in front of her.

"You just asked that."

He took two uncertain steps forward. She wasn't completely sure what he did here. He...fixed stuff? Sometimes she saw him doing laps between the first- and ground-floor bars, changing taps, running errands. How old was he? Fifteen? Not the best place to become an adult. Still, it was better than the street.

With debilitating shyness, he placed a pink token on the dressing table and practically bolted out the door. When it closed behind him, Aya realized that her chest was still completely bare. She wasn't embarrassed, not here. Him, though...

She picked up the token. On the one hand, more cred; on the other, it meant getting home half an hour later.

She typed a message to M: "Still have some work to finish up. I'll be home later."

She twirled the token between her fingers. Life didn't exactly turn out the way she expected it to. Neither did the world, for that matter. Did it ever? For anyone? She noticed the shape of the number on the token. Eight.

The bass pounded through the ceiling. Some kind of club. The basements in these places were always the same, cluttered with crap that was once considered useful, then forgotten. Trash, in other words.

Zor lifted his mask and turned off the portable compressor attached to a small tank of insecticide. The stench alone left no room for doubt—anything living here wouldn't last long.

"Turn it off," he told Morris.

Morris switched off his compressor but left his mask on. He waited for Zor to explain.

Two rooms down...How many left to go? The sublevels of the building seemed to stretch farther than its apparent size. Probably just a feeling. Still no way they'd get this done by today. Or even a few days.

Zor strolled through a few rooms, peered into the crawl spaces. Yup, there was more—way more. A week's work, by his estimate.

"Still a lot left to go, boss," Morris said.

"I'm not your boss," Zor reminded him. "We're partners. Told you already a hundred times to call me Zor."

He took out his lighter and checked which way the flame bent. The air was flowing down. Usually, it was up. Down made things easier.

"Zor, I think this'll take us more than three hours," Morris said. "Three days, more like."

"Subtract the time getting here and back and that leaves barely an hour."

"No way we'll make it."

"Well, I'm done chasing bugs. Let's you and me wrap this up."

"But Mr. Buyers said it was urgent."

"That's why we'll do it quick."

It wasn't hard work if you had the talent. Selling yourself, your body, face—well, mostly your body—and whatever implants you had. It was just the outside you—you kept the inside for yourself. Anonymous. Sometimes it was even exciting, freeing—making money just from people looking at you. Dancing helped. Aya loved to dance.

Except private dances, which is exactly what the pink token signified.

Twenty eddies to start plus tips. Some of the girls preferred private over stage—extra cash was extra cash, after all. Aya thought differently. Private meant close, intimate. You weren't just another girl on a stage anymore. You got sleazy stares, greasy fingers groping your thigh—the thought of it made her shiver. But she had no choice. It was part of her contract.

Private dances couldn't collide with stage performances. Dora was up there now, passively showing off her synthetic calves and chrome heels soldered to her feet. A Dora show wouldn't be complete without giving a demonstration of her synth-vag.

She had a few minutes to spare before Dora finished. Aya put on her bra and a few other essentials. Stripteases were the best way to soak up the time in a private dance. She fixed her makeup and reluctantly stepped into the hallway. She knew what she was going to do—she had a routine. Still, she got the jitters every time.

As usual, Yuki was flirting with the other dancers. Now her tattoos glowed orange. Aya wondered if she controlled it consciously, or if the colors reflected her emotional state.

"How's it going?" Aya asked.

"Sold thirty-five cartridges." Yuki shrugged. "One more zero and it'd actually be worth a damn."

Aya gave a sympathetic nod. Things were looking up for her, but not enough to attract the attention of any major braindance producers. She only ever managed to sell her BDs here—at the club. A few cartridges sold after every dance—hard to call that a career.

Suddenly Yuki shrieked and flattened herself against the wall. At the other end of the hallway a giant cockroach scurried across the floor. The dancers chuckled.

"Fucking things are everywhere," she said in disgust. "Like someone brought in a whole truckload."

"Yeah, saw one in the dressing room a minute ago," Aya added.

"There didn't used to be this many."

Her tattoos glowed violet now. Emotion adapting, after all.

"For what it's worth, I'm sure even the most expensive villas in North Oak've got 'em," Aya said.

The can was maybe half a gallon, with a few skulls printed on every side. Nothing else about it seemed particularly lethal.

According to the instructions, Zor ought to warn all individuals present in the building. Unrealistic, not to mention a complete waste of time. He checked the direction of the airflow again, then twisted the timer up to a minute, removed the pin and hit the START button. *Click.* The twist-timer started turning slowly backward. Completely mechanical—a rare treat. He tossed it farther down into the basement, where it vanished into the pitch-blackness with a few metallic clangs. Probably shouldn't have thrown it, but too late now. He took out a small sealant gun and filled the gaps in the doorframe, then stuck a sign on the lock that read DO NOT OPEN BEFORE . . . and wrote the time for twenty-four hours later. Here's hoping whoever saw this could actually read. The poison should neutralize itself after thirty minutes, even if there was no ventilation, but the instructions erred on the side of extreme caution.

Somebody would have to come back and clean it all up. Luckily for them, Morris and Zor had the day off tomorrow.

She entered the familiar haze and vibrating bass of the main room. Dora was still showing off what her mods could do on the pole. Huge screens above and beneath her showed close-ups of her most interesting features, enhanced with procedural animation. The constant airflow pushed the smoke away from the stage. In the bright light of the reflectors, she was perfectly visible. Down here everything looked different, felt different. Lonelier.

The music dropped low; the reflectors stopped glaring. The stage was pitch-black—an optical illusion caused by the lighting architecture. The applause lasted a few moments before the usual background music and noise faded back in.

Aya made her way to number eight, a booth with a round table and steel pole mounted in its center. It wasn't hard to guess who had sent the token. He sat in the middle, sprawled out like a king, with curly black hair and a pencil-thin moustache. Forty, maybe. His white blazer seemed too classy for this kind of scene. Something about him disgusted Aya, but she couldn't put her finger on it. Beside him sat two girls and across from him two men. Bodyguards, probably. Or the other way around.

She placed the token on the table. The man barely gave her a nod. It was him—the creep she had noticed from the stage. Why did she even think he was a creep? He wasn't fat, his skin was okay, his body well proportioned. What put her off so much? The moustache, you'd think, but it wasn't that. She couldn't figure it out.

No point getting hung up on it. Just get this dance over with—without getting groped. She lithely hopped onto the table and slid her hand up the pole. She squatted on her heels and gracefully moved the drinks to the edge of the table. These savages never understood that when you bent down against the table, you didn't want glasses digging into your back.

She started moving to rhythm of the music in this part of the club, which demanded a slower kind of dance. Aya hugged the pole, keeping herself high and out of reach. Worst case, she could always climb higher. The creep didn't even try. He just sat there, ogling her with a smirk. The girls next to him struggled to seem interested.

*   *   *

The room was saturated with smoke, alcohol, dozens of conversations and music that was meant to drown it all out.

"Hey, Zor. It's my birthday," Morris reminded him, raising his voice over the din.

"Can't stay here."

"How come?"

Zor turned and pointed to the letters on the back of his uniform: Buyers & Son. Pest Control.

"Not exactly dressed for the occasion."

Morris pointed at two men sitting at the bar with uniforms that read NCART Maintenance and smiled triumphantly.

"Those guys aren't, either. You're out of excuses," Morris replied, focusing on Zor with an intense determination. "And today's my birthday."

Zor had excuses—heaps of them. Good ones, too. He shut his eyes, tried to order them, put each one in its place. He couldn't.

They stood on the side, at a loss for what to do. A dozen feet away people danced, showed off their implants, drank and got dances in private booths. Higher, beneath a ceiling that was too dark to make out, a fleet of screens played vaguely erotic animations. Whatever helped people blow their eddies faster.

"Look, a demon!" Morris tugged on Zor's sleeve, terrified.

Zor followed his gaze. A pale, scrawny guy with four blazing-red optics for eyes moseyed his way through the crowd, a mechanical spider with a skull for a head on the back of his studded coat. Maelstrom. Strange to see one in a place like this. Conducting some kind of biz, maybe. Best not to find out.

"Listen, Morris…" Zor sighed.

He squinted. The girl dancing on the table of the nearest booth caught his attention as she gently hopped up from the table and started to spin around the pole with surprising speed. Something familiar in the way she moved...

He shook the thought from his head. There was a very specific day of the month when he would go to a very specific bar and order a very specific drink. Every other day except that one, he tried not to dwell on the past, or else the ghosts came back. He waited for that day like it was a holiday—a day of purging.

It was on that day, the last one, when he met Warden.

She gathered her clothes and was getting ready to leave when the creep slapped something on the table. It was another token—red this time, the number eight glowing in the light. She froze. This time it meant a room—the color indicating something more intimate than a dance. Much, much more intimate.

Finesse be damned. She hopped off the table, wrapped her clothes into a ball and hugged it to her chest. It came out to no larger than a tennis ball.

"I can't..." She shook her head.

"Playin' shy, hmm?" The creep spoke for the first time. "Hard to get? Like where this is goin'." The girls next to him suddenly perked up and tuned in to reality.

"I don't do that sort of thing." Aya took a step back. "I'm just a dancer."

"And I'm a spaceplane pilot."

"I don't have anything that'll interest you. I'm sure there's someone better—"

"Except you do." He interrupted. "Saw it just now."

"I don't have any... upgrades."

"Exactly." He stood up. One of the girls rose to let him out of the booth.

"I heard you're one hundred percent 'ganic, which you just confirmed. That's why I came all the way down here. For you. You understand?"

She started to back away, covering her bare chest with the ball of clothes as he moved toward her at the same pace.

She shook her head.

"I don't want to," she said, her voice going soft.

"The fuck do I care?" He smiled. "I already paid."

She bumped into something behind her—it was one of his bodyguards. She looked around desperately, quickly putting on her skimpy top. Where were the goddamned bouncers when you needed them? Weren't they paid to stop pushy customers?

"Dora…?"

Dora was in the closing stages of soliciting a drunk corpo at the bar. The booze combined with her recent show gave her a good chance of scoring a red token.

She gave Aya a condescending glare.

"Grow up already. Fucking princess…" She scoffed and turned back to the corpo.

What was the club's security afraid of? Two assholes dressed like they were pulled straight out of a shitty spy BD? Aya's panicked eyes scanned the room until they met Crispy's cartoon eyes watching the situation unfold from behind the bar. Then it hit her. If security was going to deal with anybody, it'd be her.

Out of options. She clenched her hand into a fist, tensed up her arm and with lightning speed sucker punched one of the bodyguards as hard as she could in the gut.

Morris was right—nobody cared about their uniforms. The only thing that mattered in the downstairs bar was how much cred you could blow. Next to them, a heavily chipped girl was working over a drunk corpo. The NCART workers sat two barstools down; behind them stood a guy who looked like he came straight out of the gym. Maybe that's the kind of place this was—a place where no one cared about class—or elegance.

"I've never been to a place like this." Morris soaked up the atmosphere as quickly as he was soaking up his beer.

"Hey, go easy on that."

"Sure thing, boss."

"Not your boss."

"It's really nice here."

Morris gulped down his beer like it was soda. With his shorter-than-average arms, held in both hands, it might as well have been nectar from the gods. Zor wasn't sure if Morris had ever had alcohol before. Too late to ask. He himself hadn't drunk for... well, years. During his monthly ritual, he always ordered the same drink but never touched it.

This time he allowed himself a few sips and started to feel more relaxed, his body less tense. In spite of himself, a feeling was starting to take shape—that everything would be all right. The worries pinning him down had suddenly evaporated into the club's haze. Worries he'd carried with him for years. He felt relief. Things were starting to fall into place. The world wouldn't get better, but at least his dumb brain would ease up on the self-inflicted torture. *He can't hear it anymore—the roar of the overburdened jets, columns of flames rising up through the black rain that meant that it's already too late.*

"Why did you stop?" Morris said, annoyed. "You were telling me about your wife."

"I was?" Zor sat in front of a nearly empty beer. "What did I say?"

"Gosh, it was the most amazing story ever. Better than any braindance, I bet."

"You ever tried a braindance?"

"No, they make people weird. I like what you were saying better. Keep going."

"Once a month I go to the bar where my wife and I first met."

Zor almost smiled. Maybe there was nothing wrong with having a beer? He was on the verge of succumbing to that belief when a commotion behind them suddenly melted away his illusions. Don't look. He had to stay out of trouble at all costs, not draw attention to himself. Bar brawls fell neatly under that category.

Surely, the bouncers would take care of it. Any second now…

He sipped his beer. Tasted like shit, but it took the edge off. Sometimes you had to, or you'd trip right over that edge. Only thing left was maybe changing his habits. Warden happened because he had let his sentimentality get the better of him. Rituals were the easiest way to fall into a trap. Beer with Morris once in a while…? Couldn't hurt.

The commotion behind them heated up to the point where it would've been stranger to ignore it. Zor reluctantly turned around. One of the dancers was tussling with a square-jawed huscle in a suit. Another stood next to them and simply watched. Hard to tell who was attacking whom. Wouldn't surprise him if the club's bouncers pretended not to notice. Zor spotted them immediately. Mean-looking punkettes, almost all, pretending to be occupied with something else.

"We should help that lady," Morris said firmly.

"Not our biz."

"We should help her."

"We should stick to minding our own biz."

"My mom always said you should try to help someone if you can."

It was now obvious that the dancer was attempting to free herself from the huscle. When the second huscle finally got involved, Zor got up from his stool and walked over to them. Fuck. No backing out now. Here's hoping he could reason with them, talk them down.

He was going to regret this.

"Fellas, how about we give the lady some space?"

"Or what?"

"Looks to me like she wants to be someplace else."

"Think *you'd* better be someplace else," said a swarthy-looking man with a thin moustache standing only a few feet away. Mr. Slick. Probably their boss. "Turn around and walk. Won't say it again."

Beneath the makeup and wig, the face was one Zor recognized. His entire body became tense.

"No need for any trouble," Zor said. "You let her go, I walk away."

Aya recognized him with stunned amazement.

"Not gonna happen, *cabrón.*" He stood up. "Here's how this is gonna play out…"

He didn't finish his sentence. Before he knew it, Zor grabbed Slick, hurtling him across the table into the leather seats, where he slumped beneath the table. The girls in the booth figured now was their best chance for a quick exit. The huscle pair let go of Aya. She stood hunched over, holding her right hand, and drew a few steps back, but didn't run.

The suits were hesitating between coming to their boss's rescue or fighting back. They chose option B—B for bad call. Somehow, Zor knew they weren't combat-chipped, but they did have something else. The one on the left reached into his blazer. He was about to pull it out before Zor's fist slammed him into the ground. The second one was luckier. He made for the bar, aiming at Zor with his pistol. Kenshin, by the looks of it.

Before he could line up his shot, someone charged at him from the side. Morris. Evidently, the huscle wasn't completely inept. He quickly sidestepped and, with a fast shove, altered Morris's trajectory, sending him crashing to the floor. Morris yelped in pain, followed by noises resembling a child's sobs.

Nobody gets to hit Morris.

He lunged at the huscle—a gonk move, seeing as there was a gun pointing at him. The huscle dodged right, then closed the gap between them. The gun went off—one of the holo-projectors above them flickered and went dark in a shower of sparks. It didn't sound like a regular bullet, but like the sound of skates on black ice. It was a Kenshin all right—a rail gun.

Some of the customers were trying to get out of harm's way, while others simply sat at their tables watching them like it was just another part of the evening's entertainment.

Tech guns needed at least half a second to recharge before the next round. Fine for long-distance, maybe. Not for close quarters. Zor reached for the gun, sending them both crashing into the booth and onto Mr. Slick. He heard something crack. A rib, maybe. Or the booth's fake wood. Probably a rib.

Skates on black ice, more shots. This time the bottles above the bar exploded in a waterfall of liquor and broken glass. Even those who were entertained now started leaving, not bothering to settle their tabs. As good an occasion as any. Another half a second was all Zor needed to slap the gun away and send it flying toward the stage, which was completely dark. One more split-second movement and Mr. Slick crumpled under the table.

The bouncers couldn't keep up their stone-faced charade any longer. Five girls with spiked baseball bats stood in a semicircle around the epicenter of the brawl. Tipped with something, probably. Even so, five of them—one of him.

Zor stood still, waiting for someone to make the first move.

Mr. Slick dug himself out, nose bloody, pointing a pistol at Zor. Lexington, explosive ammo. Double the standard impact velocity.

The bouncers calmly stepped out of the line of fire. Zor had a few ready-made options, half of which ended in Mr. Slick dying. Or not. Probably would've ended badly if Aya, with a speed that only she possessed, hadn't knocked the gun out of Slick's hand.

Then a few things happened at once. Zor charged at Mr. Slick, the girls charged at Zor, and Aya charged at the bouncers. *Black rain pummels the windshield, the droplets streaking off the side as he tries to speed deeper into the night. Far to the left, the neon mosaic of Night City dims and fades. A fire rages ahead on the horizon.*

He knows it's too late as he tries to push the throttle past its maximum. There are times when you know it's hopeless, but you damned well better try. Reason takes a back seat—emotion takes command. The AV with emblazoned letters NUSA AIR FORCE slices in an arc over no-man's-land. It's the only aircraft within a few-mile radius. He's defying the cease-fire order—he doesn't care. He stops a quarter mile away from the wall of fire rising up hundreds of yards. Whatever was down there is gone. Whoever down there—dead. He can feel the heat. Soon there won't be anything left. Only ashes.

CHAPTER_4

Y'all know I never force commercials down your eyeholes, right? INSTEAD, this week FR34K_S33K's got printed T-shirts, baby! You can find them in selected dives around Kabuki. All you gotta do is shout "This is a stickup!" and you'll get a 100 percent discount. Just remember they ain't strangers to robberies, so don't y'all come crying to me after. LOL! JK, there ain't no discount. Pay up, cheapskates!

So what's new, you ask? Spotted at Marry's Bar: cockroaches the size of rats! Y'all believe that? Good, cuz that was a straight-up LIE. They're normal size—there's just a fuckload of them. Rumor has it someone's trying to scare off their customers, make them go bust. Bet you can already guess who doesn't like who over there. Little hint: Everyone hates each other.

If you do find yourself in Marry's, just make sure you cover your drinks and don't come in low kicks. Yeah, those creepy-crawly sons of bitches like to get all cozy up in there…Watch this space for the next FR34K_S33K post! Why? Cuz FR34K_S33K tells it like it fucking is. Drops mic.

PEACE!

"Pacifica." It was Aya's voice. "Could actually look nice with a sunset."

Zor opened his eyes. He jumped to his feet and immediately lost his balance. Aya steadied him and helped him sit back down on the plastic-littered sand.

"You need to take it easy," she said. "Took a hell of a beating earlier."

His head hurt. He touched the right side of his head and felt a painful bump. The numerous gashes on his left forearm were dressed with butterfly stitches. He felt a stinging pain in his right side— nothing worth paying any attention to.

They sat on the beach, if you could call it that. The plastic practically outnumbered the sand. The trash was ubiquitous—big, too, like the battered car-sized gas tank. The only way to tell where the shore ended and the water began was where the trash started to gently bob. Farther out behind the reef of empty bottles and plastic bags was the thick black water of Coronado Bay. The sky's pinks were starting to give way to light blues. It would take the sun a couple of hours to rise above the skyscrapers.

"Thanks, by the way." Aya touched Zor's shoulder and immediately drew it back. "What happened back there…It was my fault you got involved."

He shook his head. "No, I was asking for trouble coming to Marry's in the first place."

Twenty yards away Morris was rocking back and forth in an old car seat, but no car. He held his head with both hands, drowning out the world around him.

Behind Morris stood the remnants of a slide from an unfinished water park and a hotel with dark holes for windows. The rest of the buildings behind them looked nearly identical.

Pacifica—not the nicest place for a picnic. Or for anything.

"How'd we get here?" Zor asked.

"Your friend drove us."

"He doesn't drive."

"Yeah, I noticed." Aya gave a little smile. "Anyway, um, I better get going."

"'Course. We can drop you off." Zor got up with difficulty. He felt his head and winced. "Not in a rush to be anywhere right now. Apart from bed."

"And not your job, I'm guessing," Aya pointed out. Zor turned around and looked at the green van, its fender crumpled against a disused fountain. "Sorry about that. For what it's worth, I'm probably not welcome back at mine, either."

"It's okay. Hated that job, anyway."

The toothpick was still wedged a few inches up in the doorframe. Security overkill, maybe—or just straight-up paranoia. If anyone would come looking for him, it'd probably be old friends from the army. Not that they'd even bother after all these years. Can't hold a grudge forever.

He pulled down on the handle and the door slid open. The toothpick fell on his shoe. Hard to notice if you didn't know what to look for. Didn't really stop burglars—as if Zor even had anything worth stealing. If someone broke in, it'd be for him.

He stood for a long time under the shower, which wasn't advisable for the freshly unemployed. Two weeks from now he'd get slapped with the bill, never mind the rent. Five eddies—that's how much it cost to turn on the damn thing, plus an eddy per minute to run the musty gray liquid that passed for water.

He took a good look at all his injuries. Could've been worse. If they were so inclined, security could've fucked him up pretty badly back there, but they didn't. Revenge would be pointless.

He crossed off one more place in his mental map of Night City.

His phone showed three unread messages from Buyers: two that were understandable given the circumstances, and a third that was a little more surprising—a bill for the damaged van. Nearly seven hundred eddies. Could probably climb even higher since Morris didn't just bump into streetlights, but other parked cars, too. No doubt the owners would check the CCTV and see BUYERS & SON printed plain as day.

Pretty expensive for one beer.

He took two aspirins and lay back on the couch. Seven hundred eddies. He didn't even have seventy. Twenty he could maybe pony up. But he needed that, too. He made an effort to snuff out the anger bubbling up within him. Anger was easy, created easy goals, but clouded his judgment. Made him see only red. Buyers wasn't that bad of a boss, come to think of it. He'd always been fair with Zor, as if that was the hallmark of a good employer in Night City.

Zor was exhausted, but couldn't fall asleep. A buzz—another message. How the hell? It was from Ron. How'd he find him? Zor hesitated slightly, then opened it. The ripperdoc wanted…to grab a beer with him? Weird. Far as he recalled, they weren't friends. They met once for a heist, said as much as they needed to say to each other and went their separate ways.

Very weird.

No, no meeting over beer. No more beers—ever. He pressed delete.

She dozed off somewhere between the forty-fifth and the fiftieth floor. Must've been only for a few seconds—sixty-first was her stop.

Zor…

She stepped over her strung-out neighbor lying in the middle of the graffitied hallway. Aya once tried helping her to her unit just a few yards away, but waking her up from her drug-induced sleep was something Aya had to experience only once to never want to try again. Aya sympathized with her. Who the hell would want to wake up to this nightmare?

She pressed her hand against the door's biometric panel and was finally home. The TV switched on automatically, not wasting any time to greet her with a flurry of commercials.

"Tired of being bored to death? We've got just the cure for you! Braindances for every budget! Try the starter plan today for only ninety-nine cents and get one month free!"

She turned it down, wishing she could turn it off—the news was about to start.

"Did you know that the water in your home could be contaminated? With the Real Water bottled water subscription, your water will taste just like the real thing! Sign up now and get your first three gallons free!"

She let out a deep sigh and opened the door to the bedroom. Juliena's behavior during sleep was not all that different from when she was awake. She didn't make any unnecessary movements, always waking up in the same position she fell asleep in. If it wasn't for her steady breathing, one could mistake her for being dead. Aya sat beside her and gazed at the sleeping girl, lost in thought. She felt overcome with emotion. Juliena was the mirror image of her when she was a little girl—alone, a creature full of pain, unable to function independently. She already knew what Juliena's future looked like. Of course, there existed ways to "fix" her, though Aya preferred the more innocuous "treatment." Except it wasn't treatment—it was repair. Brute nano-surgical intervention that would destroy faulty, redundant synaptic connections. The sooner she'd undergo it, the better Juliena's future prospects for having a normal life. The problem was always the same—Aya had no money, and even less chance of making it in the near future.

She gently brushed away the strands of hair on the girl's fore-head and returned to the living room. Finally, she had time to herself—and she'd have to spend it all on sleep. She poured herself a glass of water from the sink that wasn't anything close to Real Water. For all she knew it could've been contaminated with all sorts of crap. Oh well. She lifted the glass up to her lips...almost. The glass fell to the floor with a thud, jolting Aya back to her senses. Her fingers were half-bent, frozen in place, her thumb twitching like a dying insect. Except she couldn't feel it twitching. Couldn't do anything, either. Couldn't bend them or straighten them. This was faster than the last time, which meant the intervals between her checkups were getting shorter. She'd have to deal with it, and fast.

Easier said than done. It wasn't about the money, or her chrome. She couldn't repair these kinds of hands in just any walk-in clinic. Except one—where she received her jobs from. Instead of paying, she did the jobs.

Sleep would have to wait. She opened the last message, expanding it in her retinal field to display multiple folders with information.

Objective: Jeronimo Mendes. He will be led to you. It should look like a chance encounter. You will display an interest in him, but do not overdo it. Do not pressure him, do not try to extract any information. You will be emotionally supportive and empathetic to his needs. Be subtle. Let him do the talking. Details in the attachment.

She opened another folder, filling the air before her with pictures, instructions and clips. She was falling asleep, but she wanted to get this over with. Jeronimo Mendes. Psychological profile, weak points, interests, and the main course: what she had to extract. Time to see who this guy is. She opened the image.

Fuck!

She knew Jeronimo Mendes, knew exactly what he looked like. Only a few hours ago she had danced for him.

Be subtle.

Easier said than done.

The ice melted slowly, dissolving into the brownish liquid purporting to be whiskey.

"Take a look." Ron raised his cyberhands and moved his fingers. Hard to do without the right mods. "Nice chrome, you'd think—top of the line."

"Wouldn't think that," Zor replied. "But okay, sure."

The head of his beer was starting to dissipate.

"Ten years ago, you'd have been right," the ripperdoc said, drumming his fingers against the green-lit table. "Gas bearings coupled with thirty-micron precision was a big deal back then. Now it's ancient tech. Chefs up in Westbrook are prolly packin' better."

In the background, holo-ads played on walls dimmed by shadow. Muted, thankfully. Always the same old shtick—all cure, zero side effects. It wasn't the largest dive, but El Coyote Cojo was practically empty. Ideal for those who preferred their own company.

They sat still, eyeing each other—Zor with anticipation, Ron with attentiveness. The ripperdoc had an acute feeling that they'd already met before the Arroyo gig. Only he couldn't place his finger on when, or where. "Next-gen microsurgical hands cost so much that I'd bore you listing off the zeroes." He finally took a sip of his whiskey. "Zetatech makes the best, but obviously way out of my budget. Militech's are practically the same. They all come out of the same factory in Poland, anyway. Combat SRG-78 model for combat medics costs half that of the Zetatech."

"So...you gonna buy it?" Zor gently slid the glass of beer away from him.

"Nah, it'd still cost me a fortune. I call it the paradox of perpetual scarcity—a catch-22, if you will. To buy the Combat SRG-78, I'd need to make a heap of eddies. But to make a heap of eddies, I'd need the Combat SRG-78. Closed loop."

"You brought me here just to tell me that?"

"Believe me, I wish." Ron downed the rest of the whiskey and immediately signaled for another. "Thing is, I've got debts up to my ears with all sorts of unsavory characters. Put simply, if I don't hand over their precious scratch, best case they'll dust me off quickly and painlessly. Bastards ain't—"

"How'd you find me?" Zor interrupted him.

"How'd Warden find you? It ain't rocket science. Seems like only the badges are having a tough time of it." He waited until Pepe poured him another double. "Catch-22s, impossible to solve by definition—variables cancel out. But then I thought, What if I got rid of the purchase variable altogether? And voilà! The solution becomes clear as day."

Zor sighed.

"You're asking for my help?"

"Let's assume I am. 'Cause see, once you get rid of the purchase variable, three others take its place—a ten-foot wall, biometric lock and a security system. Back in Arroyo, you were the only one who knew what they hell they were doing."

"Can't take all the credit," Zor replied. "If those soldiers hadn't been fresh outta training, we wouldn't be sitting here right now."

"Not like I'm plannin' to go in with guns blazing."

"Nobody does, but that's what always ends up happening."

"We're talking about an isolated warehouse up in Northside. I mean, c'mon, how many guards could there be?"

"All you need's one with experience." He pushed away his untouched drink. "Thanks for the beer."

"Hold up. I'm not asking you to do this out of the goodness of your heart. I know a couple other docs interested in this kind of gear—same sitch as me. Gotta help each other out, right? I take one—we sell all the others for a quarter of the market value, split the profit fifty-fifty. Everyone wins. Except Militech, but they'll live."

Zor stood up and started walking to the exit.

"Fifteen minutes and you'll make as much as in five years at any regular job." Ron raised his glass as if to toast. "Aya's already in."

Zor stopped at the door.

"You're a ripperdoc."

"Last I checked."

"Only one I know."

"Guess that makes me special."

"Didn't get a chance to look for any others."

"Scratch what I just said, then."

Aya stood leaning against the freezer, a safe distance from the operating chair. It definitely wasn't one of the latest models and looked…tired. A tangle of cables emerged from its half-encased plinth, leading to various wall plugs and nearby metal canisters. Diodes flashed on its side, while amid the monitors and control panels above the chair something beeped with a regular rhythm.

Clean at least, not unlike a dentist's office—except for the vague stench of rotting meat that wasn't quite meat. Glass cupboards, freezers, a device whose purpose was lost on Aya, and last but not least the chair mounted in the middle of what was a relatively small room. The stained, sagging couch against the wall didn't exactly beckon to be sat on. Apart from that, a rickety chair by the terminal, a small back room and a tiny bathroom. The faint glow of sunlight came in through gunked-up basement windows near the ceiling. Not exactly cozy.

Ron wore light-gray work overalls that looked like they could use a dry-cleaning. He was being diplomatic, trying to keep his big mouth shut. Last thing he wanted was to scare off another customer. He stood at the other end of the room, keeping his distance from Aya. He instinctively looked her up and down. Professional once-over or checking her out? Aya briefly wondered.

He couldn't stand the silence anymore. "Lot of honest rippers around here," he said.

"And I take it you're one of them?"

"Convinced of it. One hundred percent. Okay, maybe ninety-nine percent, because I lied telling myself I'd only have three glasses of whiskey today. Coffee?"

Aya shook her head.

"Already had three." She went over to the chair and laid her forearm down on it. "Problem's here."

Ron came closer and leaned over to examine her hand.

"Move your fingers," he instructed. "Like you would normally."

She did as he asked.

"They look natural," she began. "But…"

"To a layperson, sure," Ron interrupted. "Doesn't fool me, though. The way it moves—can see it instantly. An imitated, artificial naturalness, if you will. Little fluctuations added to every joint so it doesn't look *too* perfect. You see your pinkie finger moving, but I see a fluid rotation where someone added in a slight glitch in three different places. Always the same three."

"You can see all that?"

"Used to work in a big clinic ... Eh, ancient history now."

He gently took the end of her sleeve and began rolling it up her forearm.

"What are you doing?" she demanded, surprised.

"Looking for the connections."

Professional, so far.

"You won't find them," she answered. "This isn't RealSkinn. It *is* real skin." She wanted to pull back her arm, but Ron gripped it even more firmly and leaned in closer. He switched his optics lenses to micro.

"Holy fucksicle..." He whistled in admiration. "Nails real, too? They grow? Tech's gotta be Scandinavian. State of the art..."

"Which needs maintenance every half a year." She relaxed her hand and pulled down her sleeve. "But it's been happening more often lately."

"Mm-hmm. Toys you got here ain't cheap."

"They're not for fun. I had an accident—I needed them. My job, my living depends on these 'toys' looking nothing like what they are."

"Catering to the au naturel clientele, huh. More power to you. But why not go to your usual place?"

"I ... can't right now. It's complicated." She shook her head. "Actuators crapped out on me again today. Started in Arroyo when we set off that EMP. Shook me up pretty bad."

"Shouldn't cause any long-term effects..." Ron rubbed his chin in thought, his eyes still fixed on her hand. "I'd have to take a look inside—could be some minor scarring."

"Would've bothered me if you'd have told me that just yesterday.

Don't have the luxury of being stubborn when now my own hand doesn't work."

"An inconvenience, to be sure." He motioned toward the chair. "We'll start with a quick peek. Nothing invasive."

Aya momentarily hesitated, then went to lie back on the chair. It was surprisingly comfortable. Its mechanism adjusted itself to her body with a soft hum. The array of panels and displays above her looked like a giant claw that could suddenly grab her and tear her to pieces.

"Relax, deep breaths." Ron moved her hair aside and squinted at the port behind her ear. "I'm a doctor, been doin' this for years."

From the multitude of cables next to the control panel, he chose the one with the correct plug, wiped it against his apron and jacked into Aya's neuroport. He jacked the other end into his own. The monitors came alive. Somewhere beneath her a ventilator started to softly buzz.

"You'll need to grant me access," he said. "Can't do a thing otherwise."

Aya scowled. She shut her eyes and switched her port to maintenance mode via thought-command. The screen populated with charts and tables displaying hundreds of parameters.

Ron froze. Aya stared in shock as her arm suddenly lifted itself.

"Funny feeling, huh?" he muttered. "Imagine me right now. I've got four arms—or more like seven."

The three manipulators above the chair calmly descended, each trailing a bundle of cables. Ron was thought-commanding while also pressing buttons on the panel. The manipulators emitted a series of hisses, gasps and whirrs as they moved over Aya's body.

"Real preem setup you've got here," he complimented her. "Custom-built, far as I can tell. The kind Militech only uses for their elite units. Won't find anything close to this even in the darkest depths of Kabuki. Used to work with similar tech, way back when. I just need access to your configuration."

"To my what...?" She gave him an inquiring look.

"You don't have access to your 'ware's config?" He glanced at her. "How much did you pay for this?"

"I didn't."

"Hmm... Two synthetic forearms and feet, modified motor functions for every skeletal muscle... and not even a hint of cyberpsychosis? Generous, this mysterious benefactor of yours."

Aya remained silent.

"All right, won't twist your arm—ha, get it?" Ron drew back the manipulators and unplugged the cables. "Doesn't look like the usual wear and tear. My bet's on deliberate regression."

"You mean... someone did this to me?" Aya took the opportunity to slide off the chair. "On purpose?"

"From a technical standpoint, everything looks peachy," Ron explained. "But yes, this little glitch you're having was placed there by design. Almost certain of it. The algorithm in the soft controlling your implants must have some kind of switch—either timed or remotely triggered—that's causing it." He held up one cyberarm and moved his fingers. "You're not the only one. The point is that you keep coming back for scheduled maintenance. It's not enough you pay a fortune for the damn thing; they gotta bleed you dry just so it works the way it's supposed to."

"A ripper with hand trouble?" Aya squinted. "Maybe I did come to the wrong place..."

"Don't worry, my hands work just fine. Not latest-gen is all. I program and maintain them myself—zapped that forced maintenance string in the algorithm first chance I got."

"Okay, so…can you fix me?"

"Can do a whole lot more than that. Fix you up and program you so those cramps of yours disappear for good." The ripper squinted. "Freedom from corporate skullduggery."

Aya looked at him warily.

"They'll never come back?" she asked hopefully, making sure.

"Never ever. Only thing's that it'll take precision—more than I've got right now. I'm talkin' new surgical cyberarms. Been dreamin' about the latest Zetatech model, but it's too rich for my blood. Settled on Militech—ought to do the job just fine."

"So, I am in the wrong place."

"Listen, I know how to fix your implants. All I'm missing's the gear to do it, but I should have it in a few days."

"You want me to come back in a few days…?"

"That's right. But first, you're going to help me get those hands." Ron looked at his own arms in pity. "Doing the job with these would be gambling—and I'm not gambler. What I need's sittin' pretty in a Northside warehouse."

"Yup, definitely the wrong address." Aya started to leave.

"I won't charge you a dime." Ron didn't move an inch. "It'll be a trade. Quid pro quo."

"And why wouldn't I just go to another ripperdoc who already has your hands?"

"Because I know your 'ware and how to reprogram it." Ron looked serious. "And let's not kid ourselves—you don't know any other ripper and you sure as hell don't have a hundred grand to fork up."

Aya didn't seem convinced. Not fully, at least.

"Zor already said he's in," Ron added as if in passing.

She stared at him for a moment and blinked.

*   *   *

Zor sat hunched over his cyberdeck, browsing the Net using an encrypted connection. His daily trawl through the news using this archaic, dumbed-down interface proceeded as usual—by tapping the right arrow key over and over again. *Click, click*, same old. *Click, click*... It was automatic; he barely processed what he saw, never mind read. The slow, speed-capped Net connection was included in his rent, which gave him another two weeks at the latest to use it. After that, not having Net access would become the least of his worries.

Aya. Strange how his thoughts always drifted toward her. A nice morning, despite the circumstances. He thought of calling her and immediately stopped himself. This wasn't the time for distractions— look what happened with Warden. And Morris's birthday. Enough was enough.

He stared at the small screen and mechanically pressed the right arrow key. His fingers suddenly froze in midair.

Yet again, the monochrome display showed a fifty-something-year-old corpo getting into a limo. The article was in the past tense—no info on where he might be headed, or when. Most likely on purpose—security measures. He was meeting a slim woman, her back to the camera. Even without seeing her face, she seemed some-how familiar. Didn't matter—he didn't know her, didn't know any women. Apart from Aya.

It hit him like a brick. That whole fiasco at Marry's Bar was actu-ally a blessing in disguise. Working with Buyers was a road that led nowhere—the deadest of dead ends. Didn't bring him any closer to where he needed to be. All these years down the drain, along with all the insects and rats he cleared out of countless filthy warehouses— never offices, not even the smaller ones. He was waiting for a moment that would never arrive.

Maybe Ron's plan wasn't so gonk at second glance? He'd dig himself out of this hole and do something—anything. It'd be good for him. Here he was—a thirty-year-old man sitting in his unit alone, no relationship. Slowly but surely wasting away. A loner. That was the profile of someone law enforcement might want to keep an eye on. The kind of guy who might one day completely snap, plot a terrorist attack.

They wouldn't be wrong.

Aya sat on the freezer while Zor didn't mind sitting on the sagging couch, being an owner of one himself.

"Just waiting on one more." Ron wore a white apron with brownish stains that were once probably red. "Drink? Caffeine, taurine...?"

The two shook their heads.

"Something stronger? Got a few homemade specialties. No...? Too bad."

Zor glanced in Aya's direction. She didn't seem to notice.

Ron fiddled with one of the three manipulators dangling over the chair and grumbled to himself.

"What's the spec on this place?" Zor asked. "What're we up against?"

Aya looked in his direction. He didn't seem to notice.

"Choom of mine passes by there every once in a while." The ripperdoc didn't stop what he was doing. "There's a guard old enough to be in a senior home. He'll be either snoozing or too scared to lift a finger."

"Alarm system? Response window?"

"We'll be in and out before anyone even figures out what's happening. Minute, tops. Northside's a maze of alleyways—if they give chase, we'll lose them in no time."

"Or lose ourselves. Doesn't sound like the most airtight plan."

The doors to the clinic opened without warning.

In an iridescent gray blazer and skirt reaching just above the knees, she looked like a visitor from a different planet, pretentious cigarette holder jutting out of her mouth. Ron's gaze flicked to the NO SMOKING sign above the doorway, but he said nothing.

Milena looked around.

"This where you work?" she finally asked.

"Welcome to my clinic. Small, but it's mine. Cozy, you could say. You're a little late."

"Address wasn't clear. The word 'clinic' threw me off. I was looking for a storefront with some sort of obvious sign, not a basement."

"Used to receptions, I take it. Well, anyway, the less witnesses, the better."

"Oh, planning something illegal, are we?" Milena smiled coyly, which for her meant a slight twitch in the upper corner of her lip. She shut the door behind her.

"You're right, stealing from corps is illegal." Ron wiped his hands on his apron. "But the laws were written by the corps themselves, which means they get away with robbing us blind every minute of every day. Right, glad that little moral dilemma is out of the way."

"Have you thought about the consequences?"

"Taurine?" Ron ignored the question, pointing to an empty spot on the couch next to Zor. "Caffeine?"

Milena shook her head.

"Something stronger?" he asked.

"Hit me." Milena sat down on the couch, elegantly leaning her legs to the right so her knees weren't directly under her head.

Ron rummaged through a cabinet, took out an unlabeled bottle and poured a small amount of the colorless liquid into a glass—or rather a beaker. He plucked an ice cube from the small freezer and plopped it in.

"Taste isn't its strong suit." He handed the beaker to Milena. "Neither is the smell."

She took a sip—didn't even wince.

"Not bad," she said, maybe out of politeness.

Ron bought the compliment and grinned widely.

"Vodka, of a sort." He momentarily gave up trying to fix the malfunctioning manipulator and concentrated on Milena. He repeated what he told Zor and Aya. "So, what do you think of our plan?"

"It won't work." Milena took another sip. Ron's shoulders slumped. "The security at Militech's warehouses isn't based on just one guard. They have systems you wouldn't even notice. We," she said, correcting herself, "wouldn't even notice. The only thing this plan accomplishes is a three-year all-inclusive at Los Padres penitentiary."

"How do you know about these…systems?" Ron became serious.

"Because I work at Militech." Milena always inhaled and exhaled when she wanted to give weight to her words. "You can't just walk in off the street and take whatever you please."

An awkward silence fell. Milena's cigarette sizzled as she inhaled.

"Er…Guess we'll need a netrunner, then," Ron finally said.

"Bingo." Milena pointed at him with her cigarette holder.

"The one we had before was a pro—he could do it," Zor suggested.

"But how would we find him?" Milena got up to look for an ashtray. "Not like we can ask Warden."

Unable to find one, she hovered her hand over the trash can's sensor. When it lifted, she stood bent over it, frozen.

"Hand," she half whispered, managing to keep her calm.

"Want to swap yours out?" Ron grinned.

"I mean…There's a human hand in your trash."

"Call it carelessness…" Ron leaned over and closed the lid. "I myself prefer the term 'postponement.' Customer walks in, asks for a replacement. Customer's king, right? So I chip them with what they request, except what was there before doesn't just dissolve into thin air—it ends up here, in the trash."

He motioned toward the trash can and continued. "Look, I know, hygiene and sanitation, regulations—I get it, respect it. It's not like everything ends up in the bay, anyway, eaten by crabs or salmon or whatever's on the plates in those fancy restaurants for a thousand eddies a serving. Either way, rich eat the poor."

"There's nothing alive in the bay apart from algae." Milena inhaled, took a sip of her "vodka" and exhaled. "And if there is, it's mutated beyond recognition." She looked at Zor and Aya. "What do you think?"

"Can you get the layout of the warehouse's security?" Zor asked.

Milena shook her head.

"Not my department," she answered. "You show any interest in something that's not your business, people start asking questions. Besides, security department keeps their secrets under a tight seal."

"Well then, it was nice talking," Zor said, but didn't move.

Aya raised her hand, her fingers trembling imperceptibly, though she felt it. She knew it would only get worse.

"I say we find that netrunner," she said. "It's not like we can just scoop one off the street, and even if we did it'd be too risky."

"I'll track him down," Ron said with a sigh. "Just need to make a few calls."

"Finding him is one thing," Milena started. "But how are you going to convince a professional to work with a bunch of amateurs?"

"Leave that to me," Ron grinned.

*   *   *

Albert looked like trash. Literally. In the pouring rain, with a black trash bag covering his body, he sat hunched over, untangling the next little bundle of wires. He didn't even have to jimmy the utility panel attached to the decrepit wall. The little door practically fell off its rusty hinges when it opened. The cables must've been fifty years old at least. The wires' insulation was cracked in several places. It was a miracle this subnet was even operational. Copper wires instead of optic fibers made his job a lot easier and gave hope that he'd find something older, more obscure. He inserted more probe needles, penetrating the insulation and checking which one was for power, transmitter and receiver.

The tiny display on the probe tester finally lit up with the usual standard protocol. Didn't always work the first time. Sometimes not at all. Now all he had to do was connect the Harvester. Before, when he first embarked on this project, Albert analyzed data on the fly. But it took too much time, and sitting near a dumpster disguised as a trash bag was neither pleasant nor comfortable. Better to download everything you could and then later figure out what was of value.

It worked. The data harvest began. The Harvester was autonomous— its only task was to download as much available data as possible, prioritizing files containing the keywords: *Bartmoss, Blackwall, NetWatch* and a few others, including their commonly misspelled variations.

There was a five-fold spike in the library's network activity. No reaction. Maybe the admin was happy people were suddenly seeking long-forgotten knowledge. Or maybe the chronically underfunded 3rd Public Library in Heywood didn't even have a security system, because why would you? Libraries were meant to facilitate, not restrict, access to knowledge. Except most people couldn't be bothered…or didn't know how to read.

The Net today was a shadow of its former glory. Intercity connections were almost exclusively available to corps and governments. For the average Joe, even one as determined as Albert, networks in Night City could only be accessed physically, on-site. "Net" was a bit of a misnomer—it was more like an archipelago of intranets, or "subnets," as they were called—some haphazardly connected to others, most completely isolated. This library had connections to three other subnets, but their download speeds were painfully slow. He'd have to sit here for weeks.

Which meant he'd have to visit the other libraries in person. Oh joy. And that was if their access points weren't corroded beyond recognition. Nobody bothered repairing them if they weren't important, and wireless access was still practically nonexistent. You just had to be there—personal link at the ready. Corp networks were a whole different ball game—they were well maintained and surrounded the entire city, or at least its most important districts. Unfortunately, their security was also kept in tip-top shape. But even they didn't have access to whatever lay behind the Blackwall.

Footsteps approached. Albert froze and covered the Harvester's display with his hand. Unnecessarily, since he was covered by a black bag.

The footsteps became more distant; a car drove past. Who would care about a bunch of trash bags? He just had to stay still.

Using thought-command, Albert launched a program to check safety levels in the area. The map in his retinal display appeared against the interior of the garbage bag. Mostly green, smatterings of yellow, no red. Seemingly reassuring, if only on the surface. The program wasn't predictive—the colors changed only after a crime was reported. It was like checking yesterday's weather forecast.

He glanced at his left palm. There was a black dot where he'd been pricked, a scab. In a couple days there'd be no trace of it left. His body was repairing itself, though the thought of all the fluids involved made Albert queasy.

He hated data harvests. Hated being outside and risking himself to more injuries. If only the data he needed wasn't scattered through-out the fragmented Net, he'd never have to get up from his chair. The so-called surfing on a unified Net that he read about was a thing of the past. Now it was like stumbling through a maze of dead ends.

If you wanted data, more often than not you had to go get it in person, and in Albert's case that was limited to Night City—the parts that weren't red, at least. How many databases teeming with raw, unfiltered data were out there in other cities, in the rest of the world?

Beyond the Blackwall.

An icon flashed in the corner of his eye. A new message.

He'd been expecting it for a while. He read it slowly, still not removing the trash bag over his head. It was an offer he couldn't refuse. Not a threat—a chance to do bigger things.

Albert rarely smiled.

They went back together on the same subway line. The train was crowded with tired-looking people stinking of sweat, alcohol and a general lack of self-worth.

"What we're doing, it's dangerous." Aya stood on her toes so she could speak into Zor's ear. "We're trying to solve little problems by getting ourselves into bigger ones. But...I need this. I really need the money."

Zor stayed silent, at a loss for what to say. He tilted his head to hear her better. Should he hold her, maybe? The grab handle was right above her head, but instead she held on to his jacket.

"I'm just trying to piece this together in my head," she continued.

"Ron's a ripperdoc. He helps people, right? So, if he can get better equipment, he'll be able to help more people. That's what I keep telling myself, but it isn't true. It's just about the money."

She lowered her head. That wasn't the whole truth. She didn't care if Ron's new hand would help more people—just her. She didn't know how good their chances were of pulling this off, but if it meant getting her fixed, she had no choice but to try.

Message to M: "Back in a few mins. Sorry for being late. Had to take care of something important."

"I get it...I need money, too." Zor finally spoke.

The train slowed down and a morbidly obese man rose from the two seats he had been occupying. He panted and grunted as he slowly bulldozed his way through the crowd. Zor saw it coming, braced himself as the giant mass of human flesh pressed Aya into Zor as it headed toward the open doors. He instinctively grabbed hold of her to steady their balance. Or hugged her. He couldn't tell. They stayed like that longer than they needed to. He caught a whiff of her subtle, intoxicating scent.

The train started to move again. They let go of each other.

Aya was at a loss. She instinctively flicked through the messages in her head. Unnecessarily, since M never replied.

"Maybe, um..." Zor plucked up his courage. "Maybe we could grab a drink together?"

She tried not to smile.

"Sorry, I can't," she said, even though she wanted to. "Not today."

"But you're not working."

"Yeah, but I..." She hated this. She blinked in frustration. "I just can't today."

CHAPTER_5

know I'm not supposed to reply to this number, but I don't have anything else, so here goes. I know I screwed up the last job, and for that I apologize. But...I need maintenance. I know the rules—job first, then maintenance. I want to keep working—I'm ready for the next assignment...This is pointless, nobody's even reading this. It'll just bounce back automatically, won't it?"

The jigsaw's seven-millimeter-wide blade began making an incision just above the base of the skull. There'd be a little blood on the floor, a little gray matter to toss into the trash—the usual. He'd clean it up later.

With three neurolinked manipulators and his own two arms, Ron focused on the live X-ray feed of the patient's skull—partly displayed on one of the chair's monitors, partly transmitted directly into Ron's optic nerve at a much higher resolution. His third eye, as it were. Arms seamlessly synchronized to the manipulators, Ron and the chair were one. Zero latency. There was no room for error here. One millimeter too deep and he'd have a hundred-pound problem lying in his chair. Not to mention the guilt that would come with it. For that reason, his attention was laser focused on stopping the saw at precisely the right moment.

A muffled pop. The saw had fully penetrated the skull. Ron shook off the mixture of skin, bone and tissue from the serrated blade. Even after all these years, he felt less like a surgeon and more like a sculptor molding the human body into something different. Better. But there was no time for artistic musings—soon the blood would start clotting.

He took the netrunner's C-Link from a small, sterile container with an Arasaka logo. This next part had to go exactly by the book. On one end of the few-centimeters-long valve stem, an enlarged tip housed the port. On the other—which went into the skull—tiny, near-invisible filaments ten times thinner in diameter than a human hair. Neuron couplers—integral for brain-computer interfacing.

Ron dipped the filaments into a vial containing an oily substance—dormant nanites—and passed it to one of the manipulators. Slowly, he inserted the end with the filaments into the opening. The nanites would take care of the rest.

He woke to the sound of beeping. He had fallen asleep hunched over on his stool, holding an empty glass in his hand. If it weren't for the cyberarm, it would've fallen and shattered on the floor. The chair beeped like a microwave oven.

The patient started to move.

"Hard part's over." The ripperdoc helped him sit up. "Easy now, no sudden movements. How do you feel? Besides the splitting headache from the sedative wearing off."

"Don't feel any different." Albert looked around, squinting from the fluorescent light.

"Good, that's good. Means your body didn't reject it." Ron powered down his equipment and started cleaning up. "Well, you're free to go, kiddo. But if you don't want to go home looking like a day-old corpse, you can grab some shut-eye here. Can't use your C-Link for forty-eight hours, anyway—gotta let the nanites finish their work."

"What about my tier-two tech?" Albert asked, disappointed.

Ron looked perplexed.

"You don't have your own? How'd you pull off that gig in Arroyo?"

"It was Warden's, came with a neuroport adapter."

"This is great, perfect…Plan's already falling apart." The ripper let out a heavy sigh. "Well, kid, you'll have to work with what you've got."

"Without tier two, I can't do much, to put it mildly."

"Ah, another victim of what I call the paradox of perpetual scarcity." Ron nodded, rubbing his chin. "Well, that's why we're goin' on this little field trip—so we can afford nice things."

"It's not a 'nice thing'—it's a tool. I need it."

"Preaching to the choir, kid. Look, can you at least flip the lights and whip up a little traffic jam on your old tech?"

Albert thought for a moment. "It won't be easy, but yes. I just need the access codes."

"Got 'em from Borg last time, didn't you?"

"Different district. Besides, they probably already changed. I'll need the current codes for Northside."

"Sounds like a job for a netrunner." Ron pointed a chrome finger at him. "Meanin' you."

He rapped his knuckles against each brick, waiting for the hollow sound to indicate the weakest point. Though the wall wasn't actually made of brick, he'd chosen this overlay for simplicity's sake. Every one he checked changed color. Tedious, not to mention irrational. It wouldn't be hard to write a script to automate the process—just pointless. Checking every single combination would take roughly two weeks, assuming they only had one layer of ICE...and if the code didn't automatically change every twenty-four hours. Or if someone hadn't forgotten to enable limited NetIndex access. It was the jumping from one NI to another that ate up the most time, of which there was little. Juggling multiple processes wasn't exactly his cyberdeck's strongest quality.

He gave up. Looked like Borg's codes were their only option. Which meant not a lot of time to prepare.

Albert turned his immaterial back to the brick wall, which in practice was merely a reduction in his field of vision from three-sixty to one hundred and eighty degrees. In the simulation he'd created to slow down Militech, he'd hacked the traffic lights. It was stuck on loading the traffic. On top of that, the sim surely wouldn't include as many variables as would appear in realspace. Still, none of it would work if he couldn't crack the lights' access code. Plus, CCTV.

The situation didn't look great. What good was a C-Link if he didn't have the tech to pair it with? He could flip traffic lights, sure, but that would mean taking his eyes off the Militech response unit. Couldn't do both at the same time.

In the background, the Harvester spewed out data from the latest extraction in a rudimentary waterfall of ASCI matrices into the Cave of Wonders—that was what Albert called the virtual sanctuary spread out across a few different servers where he hid his data. Nobody but him knew about the Cave. Most importantly, not even the servers' owners knew about it. This was how he'd amassed quite the compendium of forgotten knowledge that he stored for his own purposes. "Forgotten" wasn't the right word—most of the data hadn't even been accessed since their creation. Data that nobody but Albert cared about.

Farther away, the Taran's ominous pillars of code loomed over the darkness. That would have to wait. Without tier-two netrunning gear, it was just that—a bunch of useless code. One thing was certain—he wasn't going to get it on his own.

"You said you'd take out the trash yesterday!" his mother hollered from the living room.

"How'd you find me?" Ron asked in surprise.

"Little Net-nerd spilled." Borg's condescending gaze swept the clinic. "You said getting the codes was a 'runner's job, so he got 'em." He pointed at his head. "'Long with yours truly. Codes are good till six AM."

"Six in the morning?!" Ron went to the door and locked it. "That's less than nine hours from now. 'Runner said he needed three days!"

"Guess we'll just have to make do." Borg shrugged. "Run the edge, y'know...?"

"Hand over the codes and go. You'll get the eddies once we sell the merch."

"Oh-ho, not so fast, Ronny boy." Borg dug his finger into the ripper's chest. "Not about to let you and those chumps fuck me up the ass like that. I'm comin' with."

"You're not in any of our future plans, kid," Ron murmured.

"What?"

"Look, plan just ain't ready yet," the ripper explained. "Go back to your job and get us new codes in a couple days. We'll give you the signal."

"Too late, old sport." Borg shook his head. "Already enabled remote access to the system. Six is when they do their routine security sweep. Operators might be leadheaded gonks, but even they won't get fooled twice. 'Sides, today was my last day at that shitty gig."

*   *   *

Harris's Auto Repair seemed less a place where cars got sent for repair than where they went to die. Scrapyard, in other words. If the owner were here, he might take offense, but he'd be fast asleep by now. It was the middle of the night.

The fence made out of corrugated sheets wobbled beneath his weight. His feet landed noiselessly on the other side. If this went quietly, he shouldn't have to touch the Lexington behind his belt.

The gate was locked from the inside. Pointless. As if the fence wasn't already falling apart. Besides, who'd want to klep useless junk from a scrapyard?

Zor crept past a haphazard heap of engines that suggested this was their final resting place. Farther ahead lay doors, hoods and parts of other car carcasses, along with tires and batteries that turned the ground underneath a platinum gray. It looked unsettling enough in the cold beam of Zor's flashlight that he gave it a wide berth.

Save for a few slivers, the all-pervasive luminescent glow of Night City's skyline was obscured by towering megablocks that enveloped the yard in nocturnal shadow. The brightest place in the yard was the office—a booth with a metal door and scratched, plastic windows behind which sat a stumpy, fifty-something-year-old man. Zor doubted that the braindance wreath he wore was being used to monitor the premises.

No cyberware, as far as Zor could tell. Except for eating and going to the bathroom, he probably spent every waking hour and every enny he earned on braindance. Chances were he skimmed a little off the top every now and then. Easier to pay him to look the other way—except Zor was flat broke. He ran through a few scenarios, including one where he pulled out his Lexington. Last resort.

Long as the guard was sucked into his BD, Zor could sneak around unnoticed.

Cars in various states of repair or disassembly stood on the other side of the small yard. Zor went back to the gate and released the latch—the extent of the lock. The gate opened.

"Clear for now," he whispered.

Aya slipped inside.

Zor saw the guard remove his wreath and look out the window. So, there was some kind of hidden alarm system after all. Too late, he'd surely noticed the two figures standing by the gate.

Zor reached for his pistol.

"No, wait." Aya stopped him. "Stay here."

She made her way to the guard as if down a catwalk, gracefully putting one heel in front of the other on the dirt. Zor couldn't take his eyes off her. Her movements were completely different—fluid, effortless, as if she glided over the ground. He snapped out of it when he noticed the guard starting to frantically rummage beneath the counter. Zor drew the Lex and held it flat against his thigh. The ship that was plan A had obviously sailed. Plan B rested on the guard not finding what he was looking for. Otherwise, he'd die a quick, pointless death.

The guard pulled out a shotgun. Zor's finger hovered just above the trigger. He saw Aya's hand make a slow, downward motion behind her—don't shoot. The guard didn't even make it in time to raise the shotgun before Aya had reached the door.

"Hi there, good evening," Aya called out through the window that was scratched and stickered with tuning company logos. Her voice sounded...soft, almost melodic. Goose bumps. He'd almost forgotten the feeling. "Sorry to be bothering you so late. I have a Quadra that needs repairing—I was told this was the place to go."

And just like that, she opened the door and sauntered in. The guard was shorter than Aya by at least a head; he didn't even raise his shotgun. He stood and stared at her as if transfixed, his mouth open but unable to utter a word. The door swung shut behind her and their conversation was drowned out by the city's hum.

She reemerged after a few seconds, while the guard hadn't moved an inch. He looked stuck in place.

"He won't be bothering us." She smiled, pleased with herself. She walked normally now; the show no longer necessary.

"How did you...?" Zor was lost for words.

"Oh, you know, feminine wiles—the usual. Come on, let's go."

He stuck his pistol back behind his belt and walked over to the van he'd come for. The doors were already open. He got behind the wheel, while Aya climbed into the passenger seat. Zor pressed his thumb to the biometric reader. The console lit up—it still recognized him.

Moments later a van with a shiny, fresh coat of green paint and the words Buyers & Son and the number thirteen drove out of the yard.

No way he'd disable the alarm—not with this tech, not even with his new C-Link. And definitely not in a few hours. If the warehouse's NI wasn't masked, he could at least give it a shot. It was probably still isolated, meaning he'd have to schlep there and find an access point, provided it was even reachable. Didn't matter. He didn't intend to go anywhere.

He rotated around, gazing at the pillars of code rising concentrically around him on a polygonal grid. Each vector grouped a cluster of pillars, beginning with the algorithm that steered movement and ending with measures preventing detection. The closest were the most sophisticated, while those farther away were auxiliary, less cohesive. Clusters of pillars from other projects shimmered in the distance.

Tough luck. He shoved the entire system of pillars beyond his sight. There was no way around it—the alarm would go off no matter what. Just as long as they got in and out before the Militech squads, which meant focusing on CCTV and traffic lights. Except how do you create a traffic jam in the middle of the night when there were no cars? He'd have to think of something.

A fresh batch of data from the 3rd Public Library in Heywood trickled slowly into the Cave. Under normal circumstances, he'd devour the fresh knowledge immediately. But if they were going to pull this off, he didn't have time for distractions. Didn't have time, period.

Why did Borg quit his job like that? He'd worked there for a while—couldn't have held out for three more days? Something didn't add up. People didn't add up. Helpless to their emotions, laziness, prejudices—nothing they did made sense. Suboptimal. He preferred computers.

So much to do, so little time. He'd have to part ways with something, but what? Tracking the Militech squads or flipping the traffic lights? The CCTV, or the drone hovering above the warehouse, or the fake NCPD transmissions...?

"You'll have to go in hot," he explained over the comms, his lips not moving. "There's no other way."

"Go in hot...?" Aya stared at the nine-foot concrete wall topped with barbed wire.

The five of them sat in the van a hundred yards from the gate. It looked even more impenetrable than the wall. Climbing over it might be doable, but not with hundreds of pounds of stolen goods.

"Yo, we jumpin' that shit or blowin' it open?" Borg slammed the wall of the van with the side of his fist. "'Cause this trash can on wheels'll crumple like paper."

Zor glanced at him without moving.

"You've got a few minutes to come up with a better idea."

"How's this for an idea," Borg began. "Why don't you invest in a neuroport so we can talk over the comms like normal people?!"

"Already told you—don't like circuitry in my brain."

There was momentary silence.

"Couldn't find anything more solid than this?" Ron looked around the van's interior with disdain.

"I'm not an auto klepper," Zor muttered.

"So how'd you get this?"

"Knew the code; engine started as if I was the owner."

"Fuck it, whatever! Let's just blow that shit open already!" Borg pulled a rifle case from a duffle bag. "You gonks ready or what?!"

"Hell you need that for?" Ron asked. "Plan isn't to shoot anyone."

"Exactly." Borg assembled the rifle in a matter of seconds. "Second I pull this baby out, motherfuckers'll drop to their knees, hands behind their heads."

"Couldn't find anything less brand-new?" Milena remarked. She wore a vintage, twentieth-century flight suit. Khaki, countless pockets. Only the expensive material betrayed its designer origins. Most of the pockets were for show.

She pulled a cigarette case and a lighter from one of the pockets, then fitted the cigarette into its holder.

"Lady, can you, like, not smoke in here?" Borg was getting worked up.

"I could." Milena lit up. "So, we doing this, or are we calling it a night and going back to our boring lives?"

"We stay here any longer, it'll look suspicious," Zor said, his hands on the wheel. "Albert?"

Zor was right. They were completely out in the open. Didn't even have the cover of darkness—a luxury reserved for the outskirts, underground tunnels, basements and tight alleyways between almost-touching apartment buildings. Out here, the constant light from the city's central districts had turned the sky into merely an overcast afternoon.

"*Follow this,*" Albert replied. The van's console display lit up with a GPS itinerary. "*Drive fast, but calmly.*"

"You ever sat behind a steerin' wheel?" Ron scoffed.

Trying to avoid making the tires screech, Zor put the van into gear and quickly turned right, following the GPS. No clue what Albert's plan was, but they had no choice except to trust him.

"Think we ought to have a name," Borg mused. "Like Maelstrom, or the Animals. Or the Tyger Claws."

"I think we've got bigger things to worry about," Milena answered.

"Gotta have a name, though. Else nobody'll respect you."

"This isn't a gang. And if it is, then it's an impromptu one."

" 'The Impromptu Gang'? Yeah, that'll go down great on prime time."

"Rather not be in the news at all," Ron interrupted. "Staying incognito has its perks."

"If we don't think of one, someone else will," Borg insisted. "They'll see the van and call us the roach killers or some shit. Or worse."

"Doesn't sound half bad, that."

They followed the itinerary for a few minutes, inching along a seemingly never-ending yellow line.

"We're going in a circle," Zor said. "Passed this intersection twice already."

"*Three times,*" Albert corrected him, not deeming it necessary to explain further.

"Mind clueing us in?" asked Ron. "All this turning's making me dizzy."

"*If they come after you, I'll upload the recording I just made of you driving around. Then you'll take a different route through the alleyways.*"

"That'll slow us down."

"*But you'll lose Militech.*"

"You come up with this just now?"

"*Told you I needed three days, not hours.*"

Borg pretended as if he hadn't heard. After a few more intersections and turns, the yellow line suddenly broke off. Zor stopped the van.

"*There's an abandoned building to your right,*" Albert said.

"Yeah, and?" Ron asked.

"*You're going to set it on fire.*"

"Whoa, whoa, hold on!" Borg interrupted. "What happened to laying the fuck low?"

"They'll see the fire from a distance. It'll distract them," Zor reluctantly agreed.

"Don't you think we're overcomplicating this?" Ron was running out of patience.

"*Once you've set it on fire, calmly drive toward the warehouse,*" Albert insisted.

"Albert." Milena tried a gentler approach. "You can't just expect us to blindly follow orders. We need to know what you're planning."

Silence.

"*I checked the warehouse gate via the drone. The van should ram through it without a problem. When you hear the fire truck sirens,*" *slam the CHOOH. Once you're through the gate, the alarm will go off. You'll have three minutes before Militech response units arrive. They'll get stuck because of the fire trucks blocking the street—they'll have to find another way around, which will buy you an extra minute."*

"What about the traffic lights?" Borg asked. "Like you did last time."

"It's nighttime. I don't see any cars around." Albert did his best impression of sarcasm. *"Do you?"*

"If this was rush hour, I could clog up the street no problem," Albert said from cyberspace without moving his lips. "I had to come up with alternative. Now's your chance. No NCPD patrol within sight of the drone."

He liked the robotic voice generated by his deck's thought-to-speech software. It was perfectly nondescript—devoid of any feeling. He could emote if he wanted to—an exclamation mark, for instance, but it had to be consciously added. Otherwise, his voice revealed nothing.

"No pigs lurkin' around? You sure?" Borg asked.

"I'm sure. Only Militech units will be alerted. Nothing we can do about that except stall them with the fire."

"Listen to him, talking to himself…" He heard his mother complain from behind the door. "Gotta do everything around here while he sits on his ass doing nothing all day long."

Albert often had bad thoughts. That things would be better if his mother was gone. If she just…disappeared.

It never failed to amaze him that he was a copy of his parents—half his mom, who couldn't be more different. If she ever had any life goals, she'd abandoned them long ago. He preferred to think he inherited his personality from his father, though he'd never met him. But that was magical thinking—he had no hard proof. Having his mother's features made him want to distance himself from her even more. Whatever she did—he did the opposite. Her life, repeating it—that's what scared him the most.

The perfection of a biological species takes thousands of years and requires huge amounts of energy. For how random it is, it's absurdly resource intensive. Millions of specimens go through their entire existence failing crucial tests and yet still survive and produce offspring. The only way to put a stop to it was destroying the reproducer before the act of reproduction. Every manifestation of life is imperfect, every person just a prototype trying to cheat death through replication. Thanks to technology, human beings became masters at cheating death, allowing specimens that were worse than previous generations to replicate. In other words, regression.

"We're running out of time," he said.

Zor was behind the wheel, which meant he wouldn't star as tonight's arsonist.

"C'mon, it's not like we're gonna draw straws here!" Borg scoffed.

"Drawin' matches, more like," Ron muttered. "Which we could use right now." He immediately realized his mistake.

Milena handed him her lighter. Ron sighed.

"Never burned down a building before..." he muttered with a hint of resentment. "What are you all staring at? Why's it gotta be me?"

"Choom, it's right there." Borg pointed out the window. "Streets're empty; all you need's a minute."

"Nobody happened to bring a flamethrower, did they?" Milena joked, but nobody seemed amused. She pulled a flask from a pocket in her suit. "Here. I'll drink endorphins today instead."

The ripper unscrewed the cap and sniffed, then took a swig.

"Too good to waste," he said, taking one last swig before handing back the bottle. "I'll figure something out."

He swore under his breath, hopped out of the van and disappeared into the empty building. Inside, the lighter's flame revealed what must have once been a hair salon. A long counter against the wall, sinks with headrests and a not completely broken wall of mirrors—vestiges of better times, a better neighborhood. Trash strewn on the floor and two hole-riddled mattresses suggested that someone, or more than one person, had made this a temporary home. Right now, the building seemed empty—at least on the ground floor.

"Helloooo?" Ron stood hunched over, ready to turn back at the slightest sign of life. "Anyone home?" Silence.

"Gonna get real hot in a sec," he added. "If anyone's here, I'd get out while you still can!" He waited a few more seconds. Damned if he was going to check the other floors.

He placed one mattress on top of the other and tossed a few pieces of crumpled paper and cardboard over it. In the corner of the room was a third mattress covered in trash and a blanket. Ron figured his little pile would be enough. Maybe it wouldn't light up the place instantly, but it'd create enough smoke for the fire department to take notice.

"If anyone's in here, this is your last warning!"

He held the lighter's flame to the mattress. It flickered, about to go off in a wisp, then it caught onto the paper and erupted in flames. It took only a few seconds for the ceiling to be covered in thick black smoke.

Ron coughed and was heading toward the exit when the blanket in the corner of the room suddenly shifted—a couple pairs of eyes peered out at him in terror.

"Fucksicle…" Ron whispered loudly. "What the hell're you doing here?!"

The children didn't move, just stared.

"This where you live?"

The eyes under the blanket darted back and forth between him and the fire.

Ron blew on the flames, which only made them grow taller.

"I think you gotta…" He blew harder, but it only got worse. "Sorry, but I think you'll have to find another place to stay…Fucksicle…Damn it, I asked if anyone was here!"

The flames started to reach the ceiling. No putting it out now.

"Come on, let's go!" he shouted, coughing. "Move it!"

He dashed around, pulled the blanket and threw it over the burning trash heap. The flames died down for a second but only made the smoke thicker.

Covering his face with his hand, he grabbed the arm of the closest child.

"Run!" He pushed them toward the exit.

Without a moment's pause, he grabbed the next one and pulled him off the mattress. The boy rolled on the floor, then jumped to his feet and ran as fast as he could. Two more—the oldest must have been about five, the youngest could barely walk. He just stood there and sobbed.

Ron bent over double in a coughing fit. It was surprisingly easy to start a fire—even more surprising how quickly before you couldn't see farther than three feet. He couldn't see flames anymore, but he felt the temperature in the room rising—fast.

Where were those damn kids?!

Someone too large for a child appeared next to him.

"Go! Get out!" Zor thrust the smaller child into Ron's arms while he grabbed the older one. Ron couldn't see anything except smoke.

"There's another one here!" Aya's voice called out from somewhere. "Zor...?!"

Zor groped blindly through the smoke and reached her.

"There!" He pushed her in the right direction.

Flames practically licking at their tails, they ran out, coughing. It took a few breaths before Ron stopped seeing stars.

"In the car. Now," Zor ordered.

Black smoke was already rising above the building.

"Wait..." Aya looked at the children, huddled together a few feet away. They didn't understand the world yet, but they already knew not to expect anything good from it.

"Nothing we can do for 'em." Ron led her toward the van. Sirens in the distance.

"Abandoned, huh?!" Ron shouted into his microphone, coughing. "Sure, whatever, just burn it down!"

"*That's what was written in the city records,*" replied the irritatingly calm computerized voice.

"Listen here, you little—" Ron didn't finish his sentence.

"It's not his fault." Aya leaned out the window. The children standing still got smaller in the distance. "We should—"

"No, we shouldn't do shit!" Borg interrupted. "We're a gang, not fucking child services." Zor glanced in the side-view mirror. A burning building, barefoot children on the sidewalk.

They were approaching the gate. Zor slowed down, but it was only delaying the inevitable.

"Zero recon on this place," Zor muttered. "Albert?"

"Our target is in warehouse number four," Ron reminded them.

"I don't know where number four is or what's behind this gate at all. Albert?"

"What's that little shit...?" Borg started.

"I'm here," they heard over the comms. *"Technical difficulties."*

"Fucking wirehead…" Borg growled. "What's on the other side?"

Silence.

"I asked what's on the other side, you scopsucker." Borg was more specific. "Yo, you there?!"

"I'm here," Albert answered, ignoring Borg's temper. *"I don't know what's on the other side of that gate."*

Borg snorted with contempt.

The gate was right there. This wasn't the time nor place to lock horns.

"Shouldn't we…?" Milena twirled her cigarette in the air. "I don't know, leave a lookout by the entrance or something? How do these things usually go?"

"Not exactly experienced in robberies myself," Ron replied.

"You wanna hang back like a pussy?" Borg asked. "And do what?"

The van drove slowly next to the concrete wall. They didn't have a plan.

"How much does one of these Combat S things weigh?" Zor asked.

"Along with all the accessories and fluids…" Ron calculated in his head. "Hundred pounds, maybe a little more."

"All right—Milena, grab the rifle and keep a lookout," Zor ordered. "Ron and Borg—you're going in with me, and—"

"Fuck that," Borg interrupted. "I'll take care of the guard."

He loaded the rifle.

"Safety," Zor said.

"What for?"

"So you don't shoot anyone by accident. Like when we crash through that gate."

"Gimme a fuckin' break."

Zor slammed the brakes, hurling everyone in the van forward.

"Safety," Zor repeated quietly, staring dead ahead.

"Fuck's sake…" Ron picked up his pistol from the floor.

Borg ostentatiously raised the barrel and flicked the safety with his thumb.

"Happy? Increased my reaction time by half a sec, just so you know," he said spitefully. "That's half a sec longer to take a shot. Better pray this guard's fucking senile."

"*Security booth is thirty feet past the gate, on the left,*" said Albert. "*Warehouse number four is just after it. You'll need to take a right to drive around the complex.*"

"Milena, Borg—you deal with the guard," Zor said. "Aya and Ron—we'll take the warehouse."

"Yo, who put you in charge?" Borg asked contemptuously.

"We have four minutes to load up the goods and get out of there. Albert—ready?"

"*Ready.*"

Zor glanced in the rearview. Thick black smoke rose from the building—the flames had already reached the third floor. Did he feel the heat all the way from here? No, just his imagination.

"Everything okay, Zor?" Aya gently touched his shoulder. She'd been saying something before; he only now became aware of her voice.

He snapped back into focus.

"Masks. Seat belts."

He checked to see if there were any cars behind them—nothing for at least two hundred yards. He leadfooted the gas and started rapidly accelerating along the middle of the road, aiming for the gate's dead center. Everyone braced for impact. A split second of deafening silence. BANG. The van shook violently and lurched forward. One half of the gate was torn inward—the other was knocked off its hinges and slammed into the van's roof. The windshield cracked—a headlight popped, extinguished.

The van screeched to a halt beside the security booth, and Borg and Milena hopped out. Zor sped off without waiting for the sliding door to close. The guard didn't even attempt to reach for his weapon. Clearly, he was getting on in years and hadn't the slightest inclination to stop them. He raised his hands above his head and flattened himself against the wall. Borg kicked the door open, marched inside and pointed his shiny, brand-new assault rifle directly at him...

"Hey, easy with that!" Milena shouted hoarsely.

He'd have to disable the CCTV cameras on the main street and upload the dummy footage to the ones at the smaller intersections... then sync it all up. Albert pressed controls that looked like they were taken from the dawn of computer graphics so as not to overload his cyberdeck. He wished he could dumb down time, too—everything was taking too long. He turned to the window displaying the drone's view above warehouse number four. Sure enough, there they were. No Militech response unit in sight. He toggled back to the footage—another quarter-second delay.

Ping! Someone downloaded an add-on for his program. Two eddies *cha-chinged* into his account. Not now—later!

He scheduled when the next phony footage would start playing. Worst case he could alter it later. Later...who the hell even knew what would happen in a few minutes? The NCPD shouldn't get involved, but he couldn't rule them out. Encrypting the footage transmission was eating up a precious 10 percent of his CPU. Nothing he could do about it—it was important, had to stay.

"You gonna take out the trash, or not?!" His mother's voice came from the distance. "It's overflowing!"

*   *   *

The van stopped in front of warehouse number four. A loading ramp ran along the wall of the old, dimly lit building, its entrance guarded by wide, sliding, steel gates.

Zor got out first and did a quick survey of the van. The right A-pillar and roof were warped, the passenger window was broken and the windshield was covered in a web of cracks. The front of the van had been completely destroyed upon impact, but the engine seemed to chug along just fine.

"*Three minutes and fifteen seconds,*" Albert's voice informed them.

"Which door?" Zor pulled a shotgun out from under the driver's seat.

"No clue." Ron scratched his head.

Zor hopped onto the ramp and aimed at the doors' locks. The first shot got rid of the motion sensor, while the next two made short work of the sliding mechanism. The shots echoed against the walls of warehouse number three. Must've been audible half a mile away.

Aya grabbed the door handle and with Zor's help they pulled it open. Ron hopped up last. They switched on their flashlights and entered the dark interior.

"*Who fired?*" Albert asked.

"Everything's all right," Ron answered. "Lock wasn't cooperating."

Inside, aisles of pallet racks reached the ceiling, most holding gray cases the size of a small fridge. Each one bore a Militech logo. Two automated forklifts stood at the end of the nearest aisle facing them, as if waiting for the signal to attack.

"What are we looking for?" Aya asked. "A symbol? Number? Dimensions?"

Ron held his hands a few feet apart as an estimation. He walked alongside the rack and ran his flashlight over the letters and numbers.

"They're categorized by code," he said. "None of them say what's inside. Just code."

"Albert," Aya asked. "How are we looking on time?"

"Two and a half minutes. Still no sign of patrols."

Zor opened the case closest to him. He had no idea what was inside, but they didn't look like surgical arms.

"Albert, check which code the Combat S—"

"Combat SRG-78," Ron corrected him.

"Already told you, I don't have access to Militech's subnet. Without tier two and a direct connection, my hands are tied."

Aya shot Zor a worried glance.

"Let's keep looking," he said, and opened the next case.

"Cool it, Borg. We're just supposed to keep an eye on him," Milena said in the calmest tone she could muster.

"Cat got your tongue, old man?" Borg approached him. "Wearin' a uniform, aren't you? What, don't got any balls under there? And here I thought you worked for the big, bad megacorp that ain't afraid of jack shit!"

The wide-eyed guard stared at him; he was experiencing a minor case of the shakes. From under his short gray hair, a bead of sweat ran down his temple where there was a scar from excised combat implants. A veteran.

"Or maybe you're just schemin'. Wonderin' how fast you can reach for iron and start pumpin' lead," Borg continued. The guard could barely shake his head. "I mean, you just wanna carry out your sworn duty, right? Protect company property?"

"Only thing he's here to do is check if the gate is closed." Milena pressed her pistol to the side of her thigh. "Here, you keep an eye on the yard. Let me handle him."

Borg ignored her.

"Day and night you just sit here—same old grind, same old shit." Beads of sweat dripped onto the barrel of Borg's rifle. "And finally, the moment arrives when you can do something—make yourself useful. But no, you just stand there like a fuckin' statue. All those years they been payin' you—all down the drain. Maybe you ought to give it back, huh?"

The guard gulped.

"Got bored of fuck-all ever happening, eh?" Borg was almost shouting, waving his gun. "Well, shit's goin' down now, ain't it?!"

The guard flinched, his head bumping into the wall with a poster of Lizzy Wizzy—one of music's biggest celebrities. His patrol cap fell onto his desk.

"Gonna pick that up?" Borg lowered the barrel from his head to the man's chest. "Don't they teach you to respect your uniform?"

Milena glanced out the window to check if the van was on its way. Not yet, too early.

"*Three minutes and fifteen seconds,*" Albert notified them.

"You're scared of me. Of what I can do." Borg licked his lips. His eyes glistened. "Maybe I'll think you're reaching for iron." He nodded his head slowly. "And then BANG!"

The guard nearly fell over. Milena winced.

"Pick up your hat!" Borg repositioned his rifle more firmly, ready to fire.

The guard started to reach down, though it looked more like he was slumping against the wall.

"It's three years behind bars for armed robbery," Milena said, trying to control her voice. "Murder gets you—"

"Shut the fuck up and don't distract me!" Borg shouted. "We killed a few in Arroyo—did anyone give a shit then?"

Milena sighed. Borg either didn't know what he was saying or didn't care.

She shifted the small pistol to her left hand and discreetly wiped her right hand against her pant leg.

"Well?!" Borg motioned to the guard with the barrel. "Pick. Up. The fucking. HAT!"

The guard's entire body shook violently. He couldn't pick it up.

"Borg…" Milena pleaded.

"Been stealing from your company for years…" He wasn't listening. "What happened to showing a little respect, hmm? Some gratitude."

"Borg…"

"Bitch, I thought I told you to shut your mouth!" Borg turned around and screamed. "You're fucking this up!"

They heard a shot outside. Then two more.

Milena noticed something out of the corner of her eye.

The guard was holding a gun.

Four things needed to happen simultaneously: swapping the port number, switching the recordings, blocking access to other ports and disabling user services via a temporarily incorrect code. And that was for every camera. Not just yet, though—fifteen seconds after they drove back out the gate.

He tried a few other tricks to locate the code for the cases containing the Combat SRG-78. No dice. Borg really was a total idiot. Couple days and Albert could've easily obtained that information—or bought it. Now they were on their own.

Better to stream the recordings depending on which route the response team took. Let them chase after digital ghosts. Difficult, but doable. With his virtual hand, he moved the recording icons to their proper places on the map. The lag from coding the transmission was making his gestures noticeably slower.

"Don't pretend like you can't hear me!" His mother's fist pounding against the wall. "Last time I took out the trash for you!"

Perfecting biological forms took tens, hundreds of thousands of years, but Albert intended to become someone altogether different from his mother in the span of a single generation. More precisely, in a matter of days, weeks at the most. He didn't want to be another prototype. He had to change into something purposeful, final. In order to do that, he'd need the Taran.

The drone picked up three loud gunshots, and a fourth one, quieter.

The barrel was still smoking when the body slumped to the floor. Milena shut her eyes. Silence hung in the air for a few very long seconds.

"The fuck did you do?!" Borg asked in disbelief.

"He had you in his sights," Milena whispered.

"'Cause you distracted me, you dumb bitch, that's why!"

Milena controlled her breathing, flicked her pistol's safety on and holstered it in one of her pockets.

"Doesn't look like a braindance from up close, does it?" she said. "Not so...anonymous."

Using thought-command she released oxytocin into her bloodstream. Should've done it sooner, but she wasn't trained for this kind of situation, nor was the oxytocin—mixed with substances whose names and ingredients Milena didn't even know—intended for it. The effect was immediate. She became calmer, her thoughts clearer.

"It's not at all like in braindances." She took the rifle from Borg's hands. "They'll never capture the messiness of it all—what's beyond our five senses."

*   *   *

"We need to talk."

Her voice made him jump—it was louder than before. Submerged in his cyberspace cave, he'd forgotten about the existence of realspace—or reality, as people liked to call it.

"I'm busy," he replied, moving his "real" lips with effort. Communicating with the others via thought-to-speech was faster, easier.

He tried to locate the source of the gunshots.

"Who fired just now?" he asked using his inner voice.

"It's all right." It was Ron. *"Lock wasn't cooperating."*

"That's what you always say."

"Albert." Aya's voice. *"How are we doing on time?"*

"Can't you listen to me for one goddamn second?!"

"Two and a half minutes," Albert answered, ignoring his mother. "Drone isn't picking up any movement."

She'll stomp out any second now.

"Albert, can you check the code for the Combat S . . . ?"

"Combat SRG-78."

"Three hours you've been sitting here with that thing on your head!" She stood next to him now—that was new.

"I'm making money," he answered, then turned his attention to the others. "I already said, I don't have access to Militech's subnet. Without tier two and jacking in directly, my hands are tied."

"Just like your father!"

His father would appreciate what he was trying to do. If he was still alive.

"And how'd he die? With all those wires plugged into his brain, that's how!"

A speck in the corner of the drone feed. Fused into the city's glow, its flashing blue lights were invisible to the naked eye, but the algorithm immediately recognized the Militech response unit. It was coming from Japantown—just as planned. What wasn't planned was his lag—up to half a second now. Unacceptable.

"You're not fooling anybody with this crap. All you do is play games!"

The armored Militech truck was heading straight for the road-block. By now the fire had engulfed the entire building, which only amplified the commotion. The image stuttered. Screw this. He killed the transmission encryption. He had no choice—encryption was hoarding too much processing power. The lag disappeared—everything went back to normal. Though if anyone attempted tracing the transmission, he was toast. Not ideal.

"Take that off when I'm talking to you!"

"It's over the Net." Albert focused on the drone's optic settings. "Can't pause it. We'll talk later."

The most important part of the plan was about to start, its success dependent on Albert's focus and reaction speed.

"Activate the jammer—" he managed to say before everything disintegrated.

The front of the van was a total wreck. There was a rattling under the hood, but the engine seemed to be in working order.

Borg and Milena climbed into the back and pulled off their masks with relief. Zor wasted no time on chitchat, driving straight out of the gate and nearly crashing into a convertible. He slammed the brakes and the cases bumped against the partition. Draped in gold chains with rings on each finger, the other driver honked and swore with an impressive range of vocabulary to the delight of his two small daughters in the back seat. He looked as if he wanted to do something, get out—but the sight of the broken gate and the beat-up van must've changed his mind and he sped off.

"Albert, how's the situation looking?" Aya asked.

The plan was to drive toward the fire without attracting any suspicion. According to the GPS, in eight hundred feet they would turn left into a narrow street.

"Activate the jammer," came Albert's synthesized voice.

They'd almost forgotten. Aya rummaged through her backpack for the walkie-talkie-shaped device with two rubber antennas. She pushed the biggest button—it lit up red.

Night City's effervescent neon blurred past from behind the bulletproof glass. Traffic at this hour was scarce, but in Japantown the streets were never empty. Plowing through it was a breeze—slowing down was almost never necessary. Even the NCPD obediently got out of their way. Militech's blue lights and sirens were not to be fucked with—and if they were, there was always the push bumper.

"Signal lost," said the soldier to the right, clad in full combat gear and armed to the gills.

Strings of data danced around the console display, in the center of which a red dot pulsed—the target's last known location. The red line emerging from it showed the target's predicted route. Its accuracy was dropping with every second. When the line split at an intersection, it plummeted to 50 percent.

"We'll make it." The driver overtook a Mizutani Shion that didn't change lanes in time. Wouldn't be so forgiving next time. "Motherfuckers are ours."

The tinted visor attached to his helmet didn't seem to interfere with his driving.

"How we doing back there, boys?" he said to the three soldiers in identical uniform.

"Locked and loaded," answered one. "Ready for that fat bonus."

The chuckles quickly dissipated. They ran a few red lights—at one of them the truck hit the back of a small car, sending it flying into the sidewalk in a shower of sparks.

"Already at five potential routes," announced the soldier to the right who was in charge of navigation.

"Doesn't matter." The driver accelerated. "Lotta streets in Northside, but not many ways into Kabuki. Two minutes and they're ours."

Nobody was after them. For now…

The GPS was useless—their jammer made sure of that. The narrow streets of old Northside had quickly transformed into a maze. For the second time, they found themselves on a block with a high concrete wall.

"Albert—where are we headed?" Zor put the van in reverse.

He was supposed to guide them via the drone.

The van's twisted-metal makeover didn't turn any heads—there were worse rust buckets driving around or parked along the street. For the third time they drove past the same three guys sitting on the steps of a closed mini-mart. This time they finally took an interest and got to their feet.

"Albert…?" Zor repeated with more urgency.

"Big fuckin' surprise," Borg muttered. "Little shit got bored. Prolly jerkin' off."

"Albert! Are you there?!" called Aya. "Albert?!"

Ron looked at Milena, who appeared to be asleep. He hovered his hand next to her neck and read the digits that transmitted through his optic nerve and flashed on his retina. She wasn't hurt; everything seemed fine. Her cortisol levels were decreasing. Ron sighed a breath of relief.

"Our best bet's heading south," Ron said.

Kabuki was the only sensible escape route. Next to it, in Japantown, it was easier to get spotted. To the west they had a closed-off city within a city—the Arasaka Waterfront—and to the north and east empty wastelands where you could easily get ambushed by Raffen Shiv—bandit nomads. They weren't prepared for that. Their only option was the narrow inlet leading to Kabuki. If they were lucky.

"Albert...is it because of the jammer?" Aya asked.

"Different frequency," Zor replied. "Jammer's only blocking the case tracker."

He tried to take a different route southbound. Figuring out cardinal directions here wasn't easy.

"Little bastard ditched us," Borg said. "Mommy prolly told him to go to bed."

"The fuck's going on?!" The driver slammed on the brakes.

The armored truck came to a screeching halt behind the standstill traffic. The fire brigade was blocking the street farther ahead. A fire was raging in the building next to them.

"Assholes skipped protocol." The soldier on the right enlarged the map. "Didn't log the fire in their system, and yet lo and behold. Wait...Got it! Back up and take the first right. Shit, it'll set us back a minute."

The driver glanced in the rearview—only two small cars behind them.

"If they're local, they're already gone." He put the truck in reverse and slammed the CHOOH2.

"Maelstrom wouldn't dare, not on their own turf. Militech'd nuke them."

There was a thud in the back, something grinding against the back fender, putting up resistance. The car didn't hold out long—the truck's engine was too powerful.

The soldier swiped across the screen and brought up multiple CCTV feeds. The ones by the warehouse's main gate weren't working. Sabotaged. But the cameras near the side alleys and streets did—potential escape routes.

They turned, leaving two crumpled cars in their wake. The roar of the engine stifled the drivers' yelling.

"Got 'em." The soldier enlarged two screens. "Hundred yards—take a left." On the CCTV feed a beat-up van passed a smoldering dumpster. "Thirty seconds till visual."

It was over. No mistaking the flashing blue lights in the van's rear display for anything else. The Militech truck looked more like a tank, though with the speed of a sports car.

"Fuck, fuck, fuck!" Borg yelled. "Drive!"

Aya turned and looked through the gap in the partition. The truck was a hundred yards away and rapidly approaching. She checked her ammo count, but she knew it was nothing compared to what they were packing.

"Faster, faster!" Ron held on to the grab handle with his six-fingered cyberarm.

Zor couldn't go any faster—the pedal was at its maximum. The little engine icon in the dashboard flashed red. Overheating.

No way this would work.

"Bunch of fuckin' amateurs," the driver said calmly.

The van in front of them was the worst getaway he'd ever seen.

"Easy pickings." The soldier pressed the button on his console, enabling combat mode.

With a quiet buzz, a turret emerged from the roof.

"Stand by; don't wanna damage the cargo."

They were now only sixty feet behind the van.

"Maelstrom ought to put these assholes in their place," the soldier mumbled. "Their turf, their problem."

The driver didn't answer. He was waiting for the right moment to leadfoot the CHOOH and turn the van into a crumpled tin can. Then all they had to do was jump out and finish off these clowns. Orders said nothing about arresting them, so why complicate things?

"Control to 70-10—abandon pursuit." The order came from central command.

"Central, please confirm," the driver answered. "Intercepting target in fifteen seconds."

"Confirmed, 70-10. Abandon pursuit."

"Affirmative."

The driver eased his foot off the gas after a beat.

"Fuck…" He sighed.

The van sped past a dumpster that was on fire and vanished behind the haze of smoke.

The soldier slammed his gloved palm against the console. The display went dark.

"There goes our fucking bonus!"

The hormone cocktail had calmed her down, made her feel safe. Too safe, maybe? Logic and reasoning were sharpened, though at the cost of her instinct for self-preservation. It hadn't mattered if the guard was pointing his pistol at her or at Borg—the danger felt the same. The concoction was meant to free her from emotion during critical moments of a negotiation. It wasn't made for firefights. Or car chases.

Her eyes opened. She was in a van speeding through old Northside. This realization didn't elicit any feelings in her, though she was aware things hadn't gone according to plan. Not like she could do anything about it. She was just a passenger. The wind coming through the broken windows generated a pleasant breeze.

The road behind them was empty—the Militech truck was nowhere to be seen.

"If it's gonk but it works, then it ain't gonk, right?" Ron said with a careful smile. "'Runner did good."

"It wasn't him." Milena's voice croaked. "They were ordered to stand down."

The engine icon that had been furiously flashing red was now accompanied by an alarm. Zor slowed to a stop. Ron and Aya looked to him for an explanation.

"Engine overheated." Zor surveyed their surroundings.

"Could've seen that coming," Ron said.

"Looks like we're stuck here."

As if to confirm Zor's words, the stench of burnt circuitry wafted through the van. Somewhere beneath them a ventilator started to frantically whirr.

Borg gave a nervous cough in the back and wiped his hands.

"How long are we talking?" Aya's expression was tense.

In the corner of Zor's eye something slowly peeled itself away from the shadows of the buildings in front. He pulled out his pistol.

"Get ready."

The alarm ceased. The icon continued blinking in silence.

Vague outlines slowly came into focus. Once on the street, backlit by the city's glow, they perceived three young men calmly approaching the van. Their crimson eyes blazed in the half-light. The tattoos and grotesquely excessive cyberware left no room for doubt. Maelstrom. Of course, this was Northside—what did they expect?

The leader of the pack had a pyramid of red optics where his nose should have been. Could have been where his mouth was supposed to be, for all it mattered.

Milena watched the situation unfold like a TV crime drama. The Maelstromer couldn't have been older than eighteen. His nonchalant swagger was proof enough that he was pretending to be someone he wasn't. A wannabe ganger. His jacket, stitched with the Maelstrom insignia, was too large and made him seem more broad-shouldered than he actually was.

The two others stayed close behind him.

"Fucksicle…" Ron sighed.

Zor flicked his pistol's safety off.

"Put that away," Milena told him. "It's better if they think they're in full control of the situation."

Zor did as he was told. She was probably right. Who knew how many more were lurking in the vicinity?

Three-eyes walked up to the door and casually leaned his forearm against the broken window frame. He looked demonic from up close, his steel jaw glistening. Usually hidden, the scars at the confluence of chrome and tissue were out on full, horrific display. He wagged his pistol absentmindedly as if still deciding what to do with them and took another good look at the ragtag crew inside the van. His lifeless eyes devoid of pupils or irises made it impossible to tell who he was looking at.

"Been a long day," he finally said. "Could've been sound asleep by now. But here you are, making all this racket—keepin' me awake."

Zor took a breath before answering.

"I think we can work something out." Milena beat him to it. "Compensate your lack of sleep."

How the hell was she so calm?

"You think you can negotiate. That's rich." Three-eyes let out an artificial laugh. "Your little road trip's over. Out, now!"

"Stay here," Milena said to the others. Not like they were eager to go anywhere.

Ron squeezed her hand. She gave him a reassuring smile.

"Don't worry, sweetie, I know what I'm doing," she said.

She unzipped her flight suit and removed it effortlessly, tossing it to the side. She emerged from the van wearing a corporate suit that couldn't have looked more out of place.

There. Something in her posture or her expression made three-eyes hesitate. Maybe he'd wanted to grab her by the elbow, smack her across the face—who knew. But that one moment sent a crack running down his tough-guy facade. No coming back from that. Milena pretended she didn't see it. Instead, she went toward the back of the van. Now his only options were to follow her or shoot her in the back—neither of which would restore his threatening demeanor.

She opened the doors.

"This should make up for your trouble," she said.

He was caught off guard. She was making him walk over there— making him eat out of her palm.

Three-eyes stared at four identical cases with Militech logos. He looked at her, at a loss for what to say but making an effort to hide it. Milena wasn't safe yet. Any second, he could put his gun to her head and blow her brains out. Because he felt like it. She was fully aware of that.

Aya tightened her grip on her pistol.

"We should help her," she whispered.

Zor nodded.

"Stay here," he whispered. "Nobody moves, understood? Iron at the ready, but out of sight."

Borg didn't give any lip this time.

"We'll give you one as an apology," Milena said calmly.

Three-eyes was silent, searching for the right words. Zor saved him the embarrassment by opening the driver's door and calmly stepping out. The two other Maelstromers immediately shoved their muzzles in his face. He raised his arms in reassurance.

"Just wanted to help unload," he explained.

Two more gangers had appeared out of nowhere, standing a few yards away. Barely adults, they both held SMGs pointed at the ground, no doubt ready to fire on command—their lead tipped with who knows what. More started creeping out from the shadows.

Zor didn't wait for permission. He grabbed the nearest case and pulled it out, barely managing to keep it from falling. Heavier than he thought. He took a few steps back.

"What's inside?" Three-eyes asked.

"Something that's worth at least a few dozen grand," she answered. "Quantum holo-sights."

Three-eyes stood still. He had no idea what a quantum holo-sight was, but he sure wasn't about to admit it. Instead, he knelt down to open it.

"Wouldn't do that if I were you," Milena said. "It's sealed. Airtight."

"So the fuck what?" He drew back his cyberarm.

"Good reason for it. You can ask your boss why you don't open airtight cases containing quantum holo-sights in the middle of a filthy street."

"Best watch your fucking tone," he growled.

"The contents will lose all their value if you expose them. Take it to a clean place. Your boss'll reward you for your good sense."

Three-eyes stood up. He licked his bottom lip in thought. Despite his lack of eyebrows, never mind a forehead, he somehow managed to frown.

"I've got a better idea." He pointed his gun to her head. So, this was how it was going to be. "You give us all four and fuck off to wherever you came from."

"Our employers can part ways with one," she said. "But if all four disappear, they're going to look for someone to blame."

Three-eyes let out another artificial laugh. He was young—his voice wasn't gruff enough to sound menacing, something any ripperdoc could easily fix for ennies.

"Doesn't sound like they're too worried. Only ones here right now are you."

"Dealt with a Militech squad already. Even easier to deal with you." She stared him down without a shred of fear. "But I trust that won't be necessary."

Though the entirely cybermodified face didn't betray any visible emotion, his body language was less reliable. Three-eyes was having doubts. The 'ganic meatbags in front of him didn't look like all that, but they acted like they owned the whole goddamn city. Something didn't add up.

Milena counted down the seconds. This was the critical moment. She was giving him the chance to save face in front of the other gangers. There was nothing he was more afraid of losing than respect.

Zor stood a few feet away, mentally arranging the order in which he'd kill them. He could hit only three, tops. The rest was unforeseeable.

"Turn a quick profit without putting any of your own in harm's way—that's what a smart leader would do," Milena said.

She never got a reply.

MLTCH-DP-173

*Bearing: 76. Speed: 100 mph. Altitude: 91 ft. Wind correction
angle: 11 NE.*

Distance to target: 0.83 mi. Time to intercept: 48.3 s.

*900 ft from Arasaka Waterfront. Requesting permission for
flyby.*

Temperature: 75. Pressure: 1024. Humidity: 53.

Awaiting permission for flyby.

Updating target position. Target speed: 0.

Permission to use deadly force: denied.

*150 ft to Arasaka restricted zone. Permission for flyby:
denied.*

Temporary bearing: 212. Right rotation.

Speed: 87 mph. Altitude: 288 ft.

Rotation left. New bearing: 71.

Speed: 87 mph. Altitude: 288 ft.

Distance to target: 0.27 mi. Time to intercept: 18.3.

Speed: 99 mph. Altitude: 150 ft.

Reverse thrust.

Something red blinked above them. The gangers scattered like rats.

"Gotta go," Zor said.

He slammed the cargo doors so loud they echoed off the nearby buildings.

A gunshot. Howls of pain.

"Don't move!" Milena said. "It'll rip us to shreds. It's a combat model, autonomous."

ArS-03, log 48652.

Synchronization procedure initiated.

Unidentified device NI100101001110. Status: unknown.
External device detected: MLTCH-DP-173.
Order to change operator sent.

It took Zor a second to understand what she meant. The size of a motorbike, it descended from up above, a red diode blinking on one side, a green one on the other. Beneath its oval, matte-gray body hung a small turret. Its optical lens had a three-hundred-and-sixty-degree view of its surroundings to detect suspicious activity. The drone's hum seemed more felt than heard.

Zor slowly reached for the pistol in his belt.

"You won't be fast enough," Milena warned him, her lips barely moving. "Not without a reflex booster."

MLTCH-DP-173
Speed: 0 mph. Altitude: 10.4 ft. Wind correction angle: 2 NE.
Awaiting permission to engage.
Incoming order to change operator: ArS-03. Verification code:
      approved. Permission to change operator granted.
Awaiting permission to engage. Denied.
ArS-03: operation aborted. Order to return to patrol altitude.
Bearing: 254. Speed: 19 mph. Altitude: 72 ft. Wind correction
      angle: 7 NE.

The drone flew away. They saw the Militech logo as it tilted to the side.

They walked back around the van, meeting the others' terrified expressions. Aya's hands pressed down on Ron's thigh to slow the bleeding. It wasn't working.

"Who shot?" Zor reached under the driver's seat for his bag, brushed away the shards of glass and pulled out a first-aid kit.

"*Infelix casus…*" Ron said through a gritted smile.

"Who?"

"Iron went off by accident."

"Lie down, keep your leg raised." He dragged the ripperdoc onto the middle seat and hoisted up his leg. Milena sidled over and held the back of Ron's head. For a brief moment, a microsecond, she actually looked worried. That, or it was an illusion—a play of shadows.

"Just don't say some bullshit like 'You're gonna make it,'" Ron groaned. "'Cause in the movies they always end up dead."

"Don't worry," Milena said in an ironically reassuring tone. "We actually have no idea if you'll make it."

"On second thought… that sounds worse."

Zor tied a rubber tube above the bullet wound and tightened it. The bleeding stopped.

"That's why you don't hold your finger on the trigger." Borg snarled from his corner. "Come on, let's blow this joint before more of those freaks show up."

"Let's move him to the back," Milena said.

Together with Zor and Aya they dragged him onto the back seats, all the while keeping his leg raised. Milena squeezed in next to Borg, who didn't move, but sat as if paralyzed. She laid Ron's head on her lap.

Zor pressed the ignition button and the van roared back to life. Without any hurry, they started to drive away.

"Where's the nearest ripper?" Zor asked.

"You're lookin' at him." At least Ron still had his sense of humor. "Take me back to the clinic."

"Who'll operate on you?" Aya asked.

"Me, myself and I. I'm a doctor, remember?"

"What about those other rippers you know? The ones you were gonna sell to."

"Know 'em; doesn't mean I trust 'em. Just take me back."

The four of them carried Ron down to the basement and laid him back on the operating chair. Somehow, Borg managed to leave without anyone noticing.

"Switch...on the side...red one." Ron shut his eyes, then opened them and blinked hard. "And the cable with the square plug. Don't touch...anything else."

Milena knelt down and fumbled with the tangle of cables.

"This?" She picked the first one she found.

"No, the one wrapped in tape, used. You..." He gestured to Aya with his hand before it fell. "Top shelf, first box...on the left."

She pulled out what looked like a jar without a lid.

"You mean this...?" She held it up close so he could read the label.

"Yeah...Stick it in the opening in the back of the chair. Any of 'em. The cable..."

He held out his hand toward Milena. The cable slipped through his fingers and fell to the floor. Milena searched for it beneath the chair and plugged it through the headrest into the only square-shaped outlet in the back of Ron's head.

The manipulators suddenly came alive. One of them lowered itself and, after finding its mark, injected something into the ripper's left forearm. The second manipulator promptly covered it with a bandage. There was a gurgling sound coming from the jar that Aya had attached.

"Ah, that's the stuff..." Ron sighed with relief. "No doc you can trust better than yourself."

Aya had blood on her hands, clothes and face. She waited idly for some instruction, though she couldn't think of what else to do.

"Uh, anything I can...?" she began.

"If I pass out, press that yellow button at the top of the keyboard."

"And if that doesn't work?"

"Then nothing will."

The manipulators went into full operation mode.

Milena held Ron's hand. Something rose up from deep within her, a desire—she couldn't tell if it was new or if she just hadn't felt it in a long time. She wanted this man to live—to talk to him, spend time with him. It was stranger than anything she'd felt that day.

Aya stepped away from the chair and typed a message to M: "Coming back late again. Sorry."

Even though she stood, she could feel herself falling asleep. She sat down on the couch, her eyelids heavy, when an icon flashed with another new message. Another one. A new job. She shook herself back awake and started to read.

With every line she read, her initial euphoria evaporated, only to be replaced by grim disbelief.

CHAPTER_6

"W on't get this view anywhere else in Heywood! I mean, just look at it!" The real estate agent stood in front of the window with outstretched arms. "Doesn't it feel like you're at the center of the world?"

The only thing visible through the window wall was the back of a gargantuan LED billboard—a relic from an era without holo-boards. The screen was detached into six large squares, between which, in all fairness, you could see glimpses of the corporate towers against the backdrop of a cloudy sky.

"Thirty-third floor," the agent rattled off with practiced excitement. "Right at the very top. Won't have anybody sitting on your head here."

His bright yellow suit, blue tie and hot pink shirt together with his pencil-thin moustache and carefully trimmed beard were clearly meant to complete the image of someone eccentric. His yellow optics flickered, imbued with symmetrical patterns.

"And let's not forget the balcony." He slid the window open. The soot-blackened rooftop of the next building was only a few feet beneath them. "Everyone else down there's choking on smog, but up here...!" He theatrically filled his lungs with air that was far from clean. "Freshest air you've ever breathed. Believe me." He stifled a cough.

He quickly slid the window closed and beckoned him to the middle of the living room.

"The latest-gen entertainment system." He switched it on with a flick of his wrist. An enormous screen descended from the ceiling. "Still not furnished, as you can see, but who needs all that when you've got this!" He proudly pointed to the large, spanking-new refrigerator that seemed unique for some reason only the agent knew. "Then you've got the two bedrooms. One to sleep in, one to do whatever your heart desires. You can even move the walls if you feel the need to."

The loft clearly wasn't originally built to live in, but that never stopped anyone. Parts of the floor and walls were still bare concrete, which meant they never bothered to finish renovating. Somehow, the lone couch facing the TV succeeded only in making the unit feel emptier than it already was.

"I know you wanted something smaller, but I thought, what the hell, let's give this baby a shot." The agent cheerfully shrugged. "Good thing is that it's still within your price range. Sadly, the previous owner had the misfortune to run into some Scavengers, after which ... well, let's just say he wasn't able to put himself back together. Even with Trauma Team premium; can you believe that? Anyway, since he didn't have any family, our agency was only happy to take over." He stuffed his hands into his pockets and rocked on his heels. "Well, there's a lot of interest in this unit, but if you still need to sleep on it—"

"I'll take it," Albert said, putting his broken cyberdeck on the kitchen bar.

Four was too many. He knew that from experience. The music from downstairs seeped through the floor as if it were made of cardboard.

She was boring him. He'd definitely overpaid—three was the limit. The flickering blue in her eyes was proof that she was on the holo and couldn't give a shit about anything around her.

"You," he barked at her. "Get out. Fuck off."

She disconnected and gave him a listless stare.

"Yeah, you. You're boring the living shit out of me," he grumbled. "So fuck the fuck off."

"You didn't pay."

"For what?! Being on the fucking holo?!"

"For my time." The girl was already getting ready to leave. So, she did it on purpose. "Forty minutes."

Borg got to his feet, fists clenched. Then he remembered he was at Totentanz. Cool it, he thought, it'd be a shame to ruin a perfectly good evening.

"Fucking useless skanks." He held up his wrist to her forearm and transferred the exact amount. "Now beat it. I swear this is the last time I'm coming here."

He gave her a hard spank, which made her promptly head out the door. No tip for you. Lazy-ass bitch won't get an extra enny out of me.

Now what?

The others stared at him with vacant expressions.

"Yo, move, do something!" he shouted. "What is this, a fucking funeral? For the love of Christ, can't you, like, dance, or whatever? Better start seeing a little effort, or we're fucking done here."

Silence. The mood was completely dead.

Ron fell back onto the pillow with an exhausted sigh.

"Operations ain't the only thing these fingers are good for." He moved his six digits and picked up a tumbler containing the remainder of the gold liquid. He swirled it around and savored its scent. "This the real deal?"

"Hey, you're the connoisseur." Milena smiled.

He took a small sip and smacked his lips in thought.

"I'm gonna say... twelve years. Aged in oak barrels." Hundreds of lit windows from outside shone through the glass, casting a kaleidoscope of yellow ovals on the walls of the dark room. "View like this, can't just drink any old piss."

"Well, you got the 'twelve' part right." Milena raised herself up on her elbow, letting the synth-silk bedsheet slide off her flawless chest. "But a year, a few months—what's the difference?"

Ron stretched his neck to get a better look at the liquor cabinet, but his view was blocked by a wall of frosted glass or... He couldn't tell. Patterns flowed through it, animated. The ripperdoc turned back to the prettier view.

"Well," he said, downing the rest, "I'll admit it still tastes and smells better than my so-called vodka. Better even than what they serve in Japantown."

"Alcohol your only vice?" Milena asked.

"Booze's been tried and tested for millennia. Call me old-fashioned, but all that other crap... even your regular smash—I've seen what it does. You gotta respect your body."

"Speaking of which, you recovered quickly for someone who was on the verge of flatlining."

"Helps to have a good doctor." Ron fingered the bandage on his thigh. "And good nanites. I keep an emergency supply for situations like this. They shorten the healing process down to a few days. Still gotta take it easy, though."

"Need a quick regen myself—I have an important meeting tomorrow. Shower?"

"After you, Your Majesty. Don't know how you can afford it, but the water you use to flush is cleaner than what I drink at home."

They lay next to each other watching TV, warmed up from the shower, neither of them wanting to spoil the atmosphere. They ate real grapes that Milena had specially ordered for the occasion. Ron didn't dare to guess how much they had cost. The news, indistinguishable from the commercials, washed over them like an invisible tide.

Then they watched as firefighters were rolling up their hoses beside a burned-out building. It was unmistakable. The reporter spoke of a fire—no mention of arson. It seemed unconnected to the break-in at the Militech warehouse—for now. The break-in itself didn't even get video coverage—the only mention of it was a sub-heading: MILITECH WAREHOUSE ROBBED.

"Wanna change the channel?" Milena asked.

"Could find out something interesting."

"What's there to find out?" Milena stood up and went to the liquor cabinet. "There was a fire, four kids were inside—you got them out."

Ron followed her with his gaze.

"Would've been better to get 'em out before," he admitted. "Got a whole list of things I'd redo knowing what I know now. Helped a lot of people once...or so I thought."

"Four kids, Ron, from the *ground floor*," Milena said softly, shaking her head.

Ron turned back to the screen. The fire was so big that some of the floors collapsed. Smoke was still coming out of the rectangular black holes where the windows used to be. With a languid gesture he switched off the screen and sat up on the bed.

"I need a drink," he said quietly.

"Figured. Here." Milena handed him the glass. "Aged twelve days."

*   *   *

"It's him. I'm sure."

Dum Dum swiveled around and peered through the throng of moshers and headbangers.

His seven ionizing optics reached up to sixty feet. Everything seemed closer: implants, bones—clothes distorted the imaging but couldn't entirely block it out. Borg. There he sat—sprawled out in the booth, nodding to the diabolic rhythm of a Tinnitus song the girls beside him were swaying to, looking like he owned the fucking place. He had piss-poor taste, but no matter. Dum Dum changed frequencies and examined every element he could within the man. Lotta chrome, most of it unoriginal, basic. Pieced together helter-skelter, all of it. Cannons for arms—didn't mean they were strong. Even if they were, couldn't do anything without upper-back reinforcement.

"Don't care if it is or isn't him." Dum Dum stood up and gave three-eyes a pat on the shoulder. "Bored as all fuck."

He didn't finish his drink—didn't need to if you owned the club. The head-banging crowd in front of him parted like a shoal of fish before a shark—instinctively, unconsciously.

He reached over the table and grabbed the guy's jacket lapel, yanking him toward him. The girls tactfully made themselves scarce. Wouldn't get paid for the last hour—too bad.

Just as he thought—the gonk's implants were all style, no substance. Poserware. He flailed, trying to land a punch—anything. Too weak. He hurled him effortlessly onto the dance floor, a momentary lapse in the crowd's rhythm. Nobody blinked—another perk of owning your own club.

Tossing him down the basement's concrete staircase was even easier. His cries of pain went quiet as Dum Dum slammed the door behind him. The poser sat slumped near the wall, frozen under a flickering light bulb that was the only source of light.

"Came to Totentanz," Dum Dum began. "Brave or scopbrained—which are you?"

Her dark skin wrapped in a tight black synth-leather bodysuit, Karla crouched down beside him in a spiderlike motion. The light from the bulb reflected against her shaved, tattooed head scarred from implants. The blade unsheathed itself from her forearm and she ran its tip along Borg's chest. He shrieked and frantically drew back, pressing himself against the concrete wall.

"So, it's the latter." Dum Dum stood and cocked his head at Borg curled up in the corner. "You, your crew—who are you? Where'd you crawl out of?"

"Wh-what?" Borg spluttered, clutching his chest.

"Question's simple. You and your chooms kick up a hornet's nest on our turf and think we're just gonna let that go? Pretend like it didn't happen? Last chance—who are you?"

Borg sobered up, finally understanding his situation.

"Name's Borg. Warden hired us."

"Warden…?" Dum Dum made sure. "Renner's lap-bitch? Thought the Valentinos were smarter than that."

"He is smart. Not Warden—I mean Ron. It was all his idea."

"Ron?"

"The ripperdoc. He needed the scratch."

"That your boss?"

"No, well, I mean—technically, Zor was in charge. Ron accidentally shot himself 'cause it was his first, or…no, second time usin' iron. The corpo cunt negotiating with one of yours was Milena. And then that dancer from Marry's…"

"Tellin' me your warehouse heist was cooked up by a debt-addled ripper, led by a man who works in pest control and pulled off along with an iron-totin' stripper?" Dum Dum's optics were fixed on Borg in silence. "Klep from the same corp twice in a row? Better get your story straight, Pork—"

"It's Borg—B, O, R—"

"Luckily, Karla's here to help," Dum Dum interrupted back.

"No, wait!" Borg begged, raising his arms, wishing he could melt through the wall. Karla straddled his legs, the blade held to his throat.

"Let me— I can explain, all right?!" Borg didn't dare move. "Warden hired them for another job. They were... We were supposed to jump a Militech convoy. But that was in Arroyo, not Northside! We klepped this container—worth a lot, whatever's in it. And we did it— heist of the fuckin' year. That wasn't on your turf. Second time was when we ran into you. Different job. Ron's idea."

Dum Dum knelt down beside him, elbows resting on his knees.

"If you're as hot shit as you sound, then how come I've never heard of you?"

Dixie, short and skinny with cropped platinum hair, watched from a few feet away. Karla playfully ran her blade near Borg's groin, slowly slicing through the pants' seam.

"'Cause that was the whole point, man!" Borg was frantic now. "Everyone was clean—no criminal record. Like regular peeps, y'know? The perfect cover. Warden—he had dirt on everyone, threatened them. Don't know with what. Prolly somethin' serious. Was supposed to be a one-off. I helped find them, but I swear that's all I know! Warden let them go after and... and that was supposed to be it. But they wanted more, so Ron... he came up with this whole warehouse plan, and Zor got the van from Harris's."

Karla parted her lips—probably the only unimplanted part of her body. She balanced the tip of the second blade against his arm.

"Humor me for a second," Dum Dum continued. "How is it a bunch of normos don't call it quits the first time, forget about the whole thing? Why volunteer to do it all over again?"

"I...I don't know, I swear I don't—"

Karla applied pressure. Blood appeared under each of her blades.

"Please, stop...It hurts..." Borg squeezed his eyes shut. "Fuck, I don't know, all right?! But if...if you let me go, I'll tell you where that container is."

"The one that's worth a lot, hmm?" Dum Dum rose to his feet. "In my experience, you're gonna tell me no matter what. No rush. Still got all the time in the world. Not like either of us have to get up to go to work in the morning. But first, you're gonna tell me about everyone in your little impromptu gang and where to find them."

"Listen, I...I've always wanted to be a ganger, okay? These ops— they were supposed to be...practice, y'know...like, for the real thing. I tell you everything and—and like, I can join you, become a Maelstromer. I'll— I can be useful...lo-loyal and shit. Swear you won't regret it."

"Join Maelstrom, eh...?" Dum Dum chuckled with amusement. "Could've picked a better way to get our attention, Pork."

"Look, trust me, I'll make up for it. I...I got a lotta detes; I'll spill everything. Can start right from the beginning..."

"That we can do." Dum Dum gave a crooked grin. "Yeah, how about that, let's start over. Tell me, Pork, do you believe in reincarnation?"

It wasn't a pretty sight, but Liam hadn't joined the force for pretty sights. The security guard's hand was missing a few fingers and most of the skin from his torso. Dead a few hours. Footprints on the blood-soaked floor, prints on the door handle—recovered, logged.

Fat chance they'd get any hits, but it was always worth a shot. More importantly, what the hell happened here?

The owner, Harris, stared at him impatiently. Not like a dead guard was nothing to him. He'd have to find new one, equally as useless, for chasing away bums and drifters. But the real rub was that his garage couldn't resume operations until the investigation was over. That'd come with losses.

"Has 'gang' written all over it," the rookie said.

"Didn't cut himself shaving, that's for sure." Liam tossed a piece of gum in his mouth, which momentarily beat the stench. He preferred that to enabling his olfactory soft.

The rookie assigned to him wasn't much help. He couldn't tell what was worse—her lack of experience or the idealistic bullshit they hammered into her skull at the academy. She'd even gotten her own trench coat, different from Liam's at least. It would only look as well-worn as his in a few years.

"Owner claims nothing was stolen," the rookie said. Clearly, she wasn't used to thinking in silence—a habit of a new recruits. Blabbering made them feel like they were actually working, accomplishing something.

"Didn't come here to steal," Liam replied. "They came for information, which Mr. Smolarski here"—he pointed at the guard—"most likely obliged."

The lock on the gate wasn't broken, though it was opened from the inside. Not like there was much here to steal. The garage, if you could even call it that, repaired rust buckets. Nobody would roll up with a Rayfield—not even to replace their windshield wipers.

The only thing that didn't add up was the beat-up pest control van. In the garage's database it was logged as repaired and ready for collection. It didn't take a genius to see that the van was far from repaired.

ArS-03, log 51652.
Synchronization procedure initiated.
Unidentified device NI100101001110. Status: unknown.
No additional subsystems detected.

It was pointless, but he did it impulsively. *Click.* A conference about cleaning up the plastic in Coronado Bay. Who cared? The water would still be toxic—nobody would dip so much as a toe in it. *Click.* Constructing new megabuildings with "affordable housing" where units started at just one eurodollar. Gangs would snap it up and hike up rent in a millisec. *Click.* A new braindance studio specializing in BDs without sex or violence. Good luck staying in biz for more than a month. *Click.* A new Church of Eliyahu the Last Emancipator up in north Pacifica—they'll want a good fire-suppression system. *Click.* Negotiations continue on trade with China and South Africa.

Zor straightened up. Not so pointless after all. A still of a high-ranking corpo in front of an office building, probably somewhere around Corpo Plaza. He's greeting a woman—white, tall, thin with black hair. She looks familiar—too familiar.

"It's just a routine test. Try to answer the questions as best as you can."

"Conducted by the director of internal security?" Milena asked. "In the flesh?"

Stanley was nearing sixty, but he had the eyes and nimble movements of a man in his early twenties. It was evident even beneath the charcoal suit that he took good care of his body. A veteran, highly ranked. No visible cyberware.

"No need to play any of your tricks on me." He smiled coldly. "Your abilities as a negotiator for this company are respected and admired. We need to be sure that you're prepared for this next assignment."

"You're questioning my loyalty?"

"No," he replied. "I need to know if you're ready. Have you recently felt any threat to your safety or security?"

Not just once. How much did he know? Did he suspect her?

"I had an accident. Not long ago," she replied after a beat. "There was a pileup on the eastern beltway—a lot of people died, but all I got was a sprained ankle. I don't know if that counts. It was a fluke."

The Japanese assistant went through the doors first. The rules were complex, confusing. Different from what she was used to. Though they hadn't been introduced to each other, the only person Milena recognized from the small group was the young assistant. They went past the elevators and reached an area probably more secured than the Oval Office. Once the two-step scanning and identity verification had been completed, they were let through.

Katsuo was waiting in the center of the lounge. Dead center—to a fault. Milena put her palms together and bowed in the traditional greeting. It had a name that she couldn't recall. It wasn't easy navigating between the East's and West's mutually conflicting customs—who held out their hand first, whether you were supposed to hold out your hand at all; who went into the elevator first, whether it was a woman or an elderly person; who sat at the table first, and so on. A veritable minefield.

"Hello, Katsuo-san." Milena bowed her head forty-five degrees. "Please forgive me for sending you the documents so late. A family member was taken ill."

"Family is most important." He gave a sparing bow. "I hope they have recovered."

"They have, thank you."

Had he come all the way down here from his perch? Must have.

An indication of respect, maybe. Or racking up social credit to spend later.

She followed Katsuo into the elevator. Without the slightest noise or vibration, it began its ascent. Moments later it rose up along the outer edge of Arasaka's north tower. They plunged into a thick blanket of cloud, leaving the rain-drenched city far below. Katsuo stood still, his gaze fixed directly in front of him. Milena didn't so much as glance his way—it would have been impolite. Not to mention unnecessary. She didn't need to look at him to pick up on his emotions, or rather the subtle afterimages they left in the air despite his best efforts.

That was her job. What years of training and countless modifications had made her capable of. Unraveling feelings, deciphering intentions—predicting decisions.

Light. They were suddenly above the clouds, before them a sea of blue that for most Night Citizens might as well not exist. She could have remarked on the beautiful view, but she knew Katsuo enough to hold her tongue. Extremely reserved, he avoided any subject unrelated to the task or meeting at hand. But his demeanor wasn't simply a negotiation tactic. He took his frigid personality back home with him after work—his entire life was governed by strict rules. She knew that.

A tricky adversary. It was like playing an intricate game against a machine. Katsuo didn't go to clubs after work; he didn't hire escorts—even the most exclusive ones. No alcohol—not even the best sake. In order to unwind, he meditated.

How did she know all this? She just did. That's why Militech was paying her a sky-high salary, though as an asset she made them much, much more.

Whatever it was, it didn't look like a Combat SRG-78 cybernetic surgical arm. Wedged in the foam mold were matte rectangular objects, each no larger than a brick. Plug sockets were embedded in their sides, while their surfaces resembled touch pads. A dozen layers like that, give or take.

Zor and Ron contemplated the disappointing sight in the dimly lit basement.

"Sixty units per case," the ripperdoc concluded. "Which comes out to a hundred and eighty batteries for previous generation patrol drones."

"You could get one of these in Kabuki for twenty eddies."

"Knockoffs, sure," Ron pointed out. "But these are original."

"Who cares? The only people who use those drones are corps—or badges. Maybe private security."

"Not really our target clientele." Ron nodded and sighed. He pressed the CHECK button on the side of the battery. "Hey, got a full charge."

"Milena…" Zor said tentatively. "You seeing her again soon?"

"Don't know, maybe…probably, I guess. Why do you ask?"

"Wanna talk to her."

Ron answered with a simple nod. He closed the case and stood over it, staring at its cover.

"I'll figure out a way to get rid of these," he finally said. "Gotta be some other use for them. I dunno…electric motorbikes, home appliances, mammoth vibrators—whatever." He straightened up. "On the flip side, nobody's gonna go out of their way lookin' for 'em."

The steel doors flew open and screeched against the floor. Buyers turned from his terminal and froze midway, which was as far as his oversized torso would allow.

"Don't even think about it." A multitude of incandescent eyes emerged from the smoke, followed by three silhouettes.

Buyers slowly moved his hand away from the shotgun under the counter. Fuck. No mistaking them. He did a quick mental rundown of his debts. Nothing for Maelstrom. He owed Scholl ten grand, but cough-up time wasn't till next week.

"Busy, busy Buyers…" The Maelstromer in front stared at him through seven burning optics: two where his eyes would normally be, four smaller ones above and one large one in the center of his forehead. "Thought I might find you here."

Buyers stayed silent. He'd already broken a sweat. They weren't even waving around any iron—didn't have to. Their looks alone usually scared anyone out of trying anything gonk. Buyers was no exception.

Wasn't Scholl's style to hire out a gang. He'd sooner nag you to death. And there was still a week until payback.

"What? No, 'Hello, how can I help you today?'"

Dum Dum—Buyers recognized him now. Black synth-leather coat, boots weighing probably a couple of pounds each.

"How can I, er…" His voice was unnaturally high. He cleared his throat. "Help you…?"

"So nice of you to ask. See, a couple of meatbags left a flaming pile of shit in our front yard and hightailed it outta there without a trace." Dum Dum leaned against the counter. "Royce isn't thrilled, as you might imagine. Livid, one could say. And I don't like when Royce loses his cool. 'Cause it's usually me on the receiving end."

Buyers leaned back ever so slightly in his chair. He mentally thanked himself for the way he'd set up his office ten years ago, which meant that Dum Dum couldn't get any closer. It was a slight reassurance.

But only a slight one.

"What's that got to do with me…?" He blinked as a bead of sweat fell into his eye.

"Maybe something, maybe nothing. Maybe everything, if you don't play this smart."

"Look, fellas, if I could help, I would, but..." He trailed off.

"Tell us who did it."

"How should I know? I just do pest control—that's it. Don't got nothin' else to do with anythin'."

"Then I guess for old time's sake you won't mind if a still of you finds its way into the NCPD database under MURDER WITH AGGRAVATING CIRCUMSTANCES. What say you to that?"

"But I didn't—"

"It was your van they were driving, Buyers."

"That's...that's impossible." He sweated profusely now. "Haven't had any jobs in Northside—not recently. I would've known!"

"You're gonna sit there and tell me someone took your van for a joyride and you didn't notice for all this time?"

Behind him stood two other gangers—one that looked almost like a teenager, though he couldn't be sure—and a woman. They both wore evil-looking grins.

"I don't know nothin', I swear to Christ!" Buyers was soaked in sweat. "All the vans are in the depot."

Dum Dum nodded as if in understanding and stood up.

"Well, in that case, we're sorry for bothering you. We'll get out of your hair now." He stayed exactly where he was and gave a wide smile. "You must take me for some kind of leadhead."

Buyers frantically shook his head.

"No?" The ganger shot him a demonic glare. "Harris's Auto Repair. Ring any bells?"

Buyers slapped himself on the forehead, sending a splash of sweat to the counter.

"Shit, shit, shit, of course! Was supposed to pick it up tomorrow.

Got banged up pretty bad. Some asshole did a real number on 'er..."

"'Did a number on her,' he says..." Dum Dum chuckled. "You know, you're not the first scopsucker I've talked to."

He spilled a few objects out onto the counter. Buyers shivered at the sight of the severed finger.

"Been askin' a lot of questions. Haven't gotten all my answers just yet. Some, though...Your joyrider who drove off into the night started up the van as if it recognized him. No cracks, overrides—nothing."

"Zor..." Buyers nodded so fast his multiple chins jiggled. "He had biometric access. It had to be him! Owes me a heap of eddies for fixing that van."

"Doubt he'll be payin' you back."

"Probably right. I mean, doesn't matter now. I'll—I'll tell you everything I know."

"Finally comin' 'round to your senses. Maybe we can work something out, after all." Dum Dum sniffed the air and frowned. "Did you just shit yourself or does it always smell like this in here?"

"You lack leverage. This meeting is no more than a token of our leadership's good will."

"Surely there'd be no need for goodwill if we hadn't obtained information about Project Aeneas."

Katsuo smiled.

"Our goal is to maintain equilibrium. This corporation's philosophy is not based on the cult of profit, unlike other smaller companies who thrive in our shadow. The road to greatness is not paved with greed."

The conference room could have looked like any other except for a Japanese scroll that hung on the wall with swans painted in black brushstrokes and a bonsai tree sitting patiently in the corner. As if one had to be reminded where they were.

"We believe that cooperating together is in both of our interests," Milena said. "There are certain technological solutions at our disposal that may bolster our mutual security."

"Security is indeed the priority," Katsuo admitted. "Which is why this project has not yet begun development."

"Nobody wants a repeat of what happened fifteen years ago." Milena nodded. "Cooperating now would guarantee that it will never happen again."

"With all due respect to your technology, we are not convinced it will be effective in this particular case. We have our own solutions— an entire generation more advanced than yours, if I am not mistaken. The aim of this conversation is only to develop a mutual understanding that will not be perceived as unfair by either of our employers."

"You want to make sure we won't meddle in your affairs, in other words."

"That is one way to put it."

Milena couldn't imagine ever seeing a crack in that wall of self-composure, but if it ever did appear, she wouldn't want to be the one to witness it.

"Start spraying, bozo."

"Why's it gotta be me again, Jack?"

"'Cause that's the job. You chose it, remember?"

"I didn't choose it. Nobody wanted me anywhere else."

"You ever stop to wonder why? No? Then start spraying."

Morris hoisted on the backpack with its heavy tank and gripped the handle with his gloved hand. Their thick orange suits squeaked with every movement. Orange always meant it would be a nasty job. Jack grabbed a bag of tools and slammed the back door of the van, sending an echo through the large, empty parking garage.

"You're not my boss," Morris said bitterly. "This is the third time I'm spraying. I thought we were partners."

"Sure, bozo. Whatever you say."

"Why do you keep calling me that?"

"What else am I supposed to call you?"

"My name's Morris. That's what Zor called me. He was a good guy."

"Not good enough if Buyers fired his ass."

"I was the one who crashed the van. Zor took the blame to protect me. I don't know how to drive."

"Lemme guess—you weren't supposed to tell anyone, either?" Jack scoffed. They walked down the stairs to the flooded basement.

"Nobody's supposed to know." Morris felt the chill of the water through the suit. "Or else I'll get fired."

"See? You just spilled the scop to me. And you wonder why I call you bozo."

Morris went in deeper and stopped. The sewage level was only a few inches away from his zipper. He had no idea how much deeper it went.

"I think we need diving suits, Jack," he said. "I can't go any deeper. I'll get wet everywhere."

"Who said you had to get in?" Jack stopped a step before the surface. He ran his flashlight over the water, revealing concrete pillars and the tops of steel cabinets. The corpses of rats and other objects of mysterious origin were also floating. The water around the staircase was covered in a thick, gelatinous slime that bubbled.

"Maybe it got higher, Jack?" Morris asked. "Since Buyers came and checked it. When was the last time he was here?"

"Never, bozo. He was never here. He sits on his fat ass all day in that office counting the scratch we make for him."

He crouched down to get a better look at the slime. It was a gurgling stew of thousands of dead insects that didn't manage to reach the concrete and now just swam here, slowly dissolving.

"Job did itself," he murmured.

The gas sensor on his suit suddenly started beeping.

"Fuck." He quickly put on his gas mask and twisted the filter valve. "Put your mask on, bozo! We need to get out of here!"

Morris felt his head spinning. He put on his mask, but when he reached for the valve, he only felt a tube that wasn't connected to anything.

"I don't have my filter, Jack," he said.

"'Cause you left it in the van, bozo!" Jack was already dashing back up the stairs. "Just get the fuck out of there!"

Morris clambered out of the water and stumbled forward, dropping the sprayer lance and leaning against the stairs. He started to crawl one step at a time. It was getting harder with each breath. Jack's orange suit vanished over the staircase's summit. There must've been a thousand left to go, and each one seemed to get higher and higher, slanting in different directions and rising and falling like waves.

Why was he suddenly so tired?

He felt something grab his back and tighten around his arms. Morris screamed and hurled himself forward, crawling up the stairs on all fours with the spray cable and lance trailing behind him. Something grabbed him even harder and shook him. He stumbled to the floor and slumped against the wall of the garage.

Jack checked the gas sensor and pulled up his mask.

"Well, you really outdid yourself this time, bozo." He took off the mask now. "Even Buyers won't—"

Jack swung around. Someone else was here. Barely visible shadows crept menacingly along the graffitied walls. He made sure his gun was behind his belt...which was under his suit.

"Shit." He quickly reached for the zipper under his neck. "Hey, can't you see we're working—?"

He didn't finish.

Out of the darkness appeared a few bright-red dots where a face should have been. Something warm and wet splattered across Morris's face. And not just his face—the floor next to him was teeming with dark, monstrous shapes that kept getting bigger. He felt something fall to the ground beyond his sight.

The first demon emerged from the dizzy whirlpool and stood directly in front of Morris, his eyes blazing.

"Zor," the demon growled. "Where is he?"

Morris tried but couldn't keep his eyes in focus. He kept seeing seven red eyes, maybe more. Everything was filled with a sweet, slightly metallic smell that was nauseatingly familiar. He decided not to move. He didn't have the strength.

"Zor," the demon's voice said from afar.

Morris fixed his gaze on one point, but his vision dragged upward, downward, to the sides. Or maybe it was the rest of the world that was moving? The Earth revolved, didn't it...?

"Tell us where Zor is."

"You came..." Morris started. "You came here...for me..."

"Didn't come here to shoot the shit. Zor. Where is he?"

"He told me you...that you didn't exist."

"Guess he was wrong. You need to tell us where he is."

"So you can hurt him. Because you're demons."

"Never saw it from that angle. Curious one, aren't you? Just tell us where he is and we'll let you go."

"No. Zor helped me—he was good to me. Now I'm helping him."

"Startin' to lose my patience." The demon stepped back. "Karla's, on the other hand, is endless."

The bald-headed she-demon raised her arms, and with a metallic hiss five steel claws extended from her fingers. She lunged at Morris and sliced his suit to ribbons. Together with some skin.

"Endless…" she whispered into his ear.

Morris felt the slightly numbed pain from a distance, as if he was orbiting his own body. Soon, the pain was the only thing binding him to it.

"You've never been this close to a woman before, have you?" she whispered.

"You're offering ten percent." Milena paused. "Ten percent of something vague, undefined. Why such a specific amount?"

"It is merely a starting point for our negotiation," Katsuo replied. "We must start somewhere, and ten is an even number."

"Fifty percent sounds a lot more even to me."

"I will remind you that we are capable of undertaking this project single-handedly. Our offer to cooperate with Militech merely serves to prevent your employer from feeling threatened."

"Which could lead them to reveal everything."

"Which would be a terrible mistake. It would squander a historic opportunity not only for our corporations, but for all of humanity. Aeneas is like entering a black hole. We cannot know what lies on the other side. Limitless computing power, perhaps. The solution to all of our problems, maybe, or even the possibility to gaze into the future. Nobody has ever come back alive. That is why our negotiation cannot be founded on specifics, for there are none. We only hope that our mutual understanding will create a common framework for when specifics finally do emerge."

Milena poured herself a glass of water. Two glasses and a jug—the only things on the table. All electronic devices had to be left outside the room—any implants and holo-phones disabled. It was more a gesture of good faith. After all, this was Arasaka's only headquarters in all of North America. If Katsuo wanted to plant a dozen different listening devices, nothing would stand in his way. But he wouldn't. Project Aeneas was meant to be kept secret even from both corporations' leaderships. It was a risk that relied on eventually presenting everyone with a fait accompli. The potential gains from the project would be so immense that nobody would dare shut it down. Otherwise, if word got out, everyone involved in the project would be treated as a criminal. Or worse—a traitor.

Dixie's frail body twitched and jerked as if he was having a nightmare. Or being electrocuted. He sat between overflowing dumpsters, slumped against the brick wall of probably one of Night City's oldest buildings. Karla held his head to prevent him from slamming it backward, while the cable from the back of his head was jacked into a maintenance panel mounted to the wall. Sometimes his body reacted this way when a signal from a remote connection was being transmitted through multiple nodes.

Beside him, in the rare afternoon light that shone through seldom-parted clouds, Dum Dum didn't look all that menacing. Nobody bothered them, especially since most Night Citizens had instilled a habit of avoiding situations that deviated even slightly from their routines.

An NCPD cruiser passed by and nearly stopped—probably to see if they could make a buck and write up a ticket. But one glance at

Dum Dum was enough for them to slowly roll past as if they hadn't noticed anything.

Let's disconnect him—he's getting overloaded, Karla thought-spoke.

Not until we find something, Dum Dum replied.

A moment later, Dixie opened his eyes, gasping for air and yanking the cable out of his head. Karla hugged him, then instinctively drew back. His body needed cold, not more warmth. Even a short dive without cooling made body temps reach the equivalent of a high fever. She brushed away the matted white hair from his forehead. Slowly but surely, he came to. Not like this was his first rodeo. Eventually, he got to his feet.

There's a couple-second transmission, he thought-spoke. *Got an address.*

Albert contemplated his most recent acquisitions. On the part of the concrete floor that was covered in synth-wood stood a couch and some chairs. The hole for the sink now had a sink in it. The kitchen had a fridge, the bedroom had a bed. The second bedroom had a compact, spanking-new chair. No more nails-on-the-chalkboard creaking or sharp plastic. More importantly, he'd bought a new cyberdeck identical to the one his mother had destroyed and a cartridge of a very specific game. Throughout the years, he'd hardly ever needed to update his hardware. All it took to adapt the cyberdeck into a mainstay of netrunning gear was a bit of patience and know-how. Yet, as much as Albert wanted to, he had no idea how to get his hands on anything better. Theoretically, he did know. He just didn't want to leave his comfort zone, which meant a rinse and repeat of modifying his deck to his needs.

A robot vacuum glided across the floor. Whenever it reached the edge of the synth-wood flooring, it stopped and made a one-hundred-and-eighty-degree turn. It, too, operated within its comfort zone.

Theoretically, a vacuum like that could exist forever. Every used or broken part could be exchanged for a new one and the vacuum would continue functioning as it did now. Over time one could swap out all of its parts and it still wouldn't behave differently. It was like the ship of Theseus. If you swapped out even a single plank from the deck, would it still be the same ship? What about two planks? What if you swapped out everything?

It was different with people. If they could figure out a way to control cyberpsychosis, then you could swap out every one of your organs apart from the brain and spinal cord, which are the two things that make you... well, *you*. Either way, he thought the general obsession with cyborgization was dumb.

You'd think a person was exactly like the ship, since all the atoms in our body are swapped out with new ones in order to keep on living. Almost, but not quite. From one of his data harvests half a year ago, Albert had found out that the body's atoms are indeed completely replaced every few years... except for the ones in your central nervous system.

He'd received three messages from Ron this morning. He skimmed over them, not intending to reply to any. Getting mixed up in that fiasco was a mistake, not to mention an unnecessary risk. Taking risks for yourself was one thing, but for others? That train wreck of a heist only cemented his conviction that he was better off working alone.

He looked around the unit. It was maybe three times bigger than the one he'd spent his entire life in up until now. Should he go sit on the couch...? Wash his hands? Watch TV? Or maybe scrounge up some food was what one did after coming home?

He felt at a complete loss. He had no clue how to do this thing that normal people called life. At least he'd gotten the necessities out of the way. Furniture—he knew that a living room was supposed to have a couch. Check. That a fridge should have some drinks in it. Check. That the freezer needed ice. Lots of it. Check.

If only he had some tier-two 'running tech he could use all that ice for. For the moment, all he had was his primitive cyberdeck with factory settings that prevented Albert from using it for his own purposes. The security features of this particular model were not exactly sophisticated—configuration changes could be done with just a soldering iron and screwdriver. But why kick down a door when you could just knock?

Albert took the cartridge out of its packaging and slotted it in the deck.

Blue sky, azure water. It's warm, but not too warm. He blinks as the white walls of the villa reflect the sun's light. The curtains gently swaying in the breeze make the unreal patio with potted, Tuscan cypresses and wooden deck chairs feel even more unreal. Deserted apart from the olive-skinned woman in a billowing white dress that resembles a Greek toga. Or is it Roman?

"You're back. Finally!" Elena walks toward him with a smile. "How was your trip?"

Imagine living here in Coronado City—Pacifica, to be precise. A paradise within a paradise.

"I need a terminal," he replies. "Deck, computer, laptop, whatever you used to call it back then."

"Don't you want to relax from your trip first?" Of course, she wasn't about to let him off that easy. "I'll run a bath for you." She tries to hug him.

"Thanks, but I can't." He frees himself from her embrace. "I really need a computer."

"Why don't you get dressed at least?"

He's wearing a white linen shirt that chafes his skin.

"I'll do that in a sec. Right now, I need a computer and a Net connection."

"How about a stroll on the beach with the sunset?" Elena wasn't giving up. "You'll tell me about everything. It's been so long since we last saw each other."

There was an error in the code. It's afternoon.

"We've been so...distant lately," she continues. "Now that you're back, it's the perfect time to make up for that, don't you think?"

He feels the hard outline of the pistol fastened to his belt—also made from fabric, also uncomfortable. The idea of suddenly putting an end to this inane chitchat is tempting, but...using violence here would branch into a different plotline. That would only make things harder.

To the right above the beach—a large billboard advertising Jinguji clothes. Worth a try.

"I wanted to order a nice dress for you today," he says. "You always talked about Jinguji."

That should do it.

"Oh, really?" She jumps up and claps her hands. "Let's do it now!"

She grabs his hand and pulls him inside the villa. Cool, but not cold. Everything is perfect—the marble tiles, the columns supposedly supporting the first floor, the stairs and Greek patterns on the cornices. Or are they Roman? Whatever. The only point of this whole charade is so he can get to the deck's configuration repository.

Elena leads him to a spacious bedroom with an ample desk, on which rests something resembling a prototype computer and the Jinguji website displayed on its screen. It doesn't matter which item he buys through the game as long as the security of the micro-transaction is disabled. A minor loophole in the system—insignificant to the manufacturer. The

woman jumps up again with joy and inserts a card that has just mate-
rialized in her hand into the computer. Another bug. "You're such a
sweetheart. Go ahead. You remember my size, don't you?"

She'll keep pestering him, urging him to interact with her. It's
part of her programming—combined with the parameters Albert
had chosen in the settings. There's no point in answering; he doesn't
need her anymore. He already got what he wanted.

He sits in front of the terminal, laptop, whatever it's called—
as long as it has a keyboard, which makes things easier since he
wouldn't have to generate a terminal. Using thought-command,
Albert boots up a simple, specially prepared string of code. He has
become this world's demiurge—or rather, its destroyer. He begins to
delete everything he can. Though not without a small amount of caution, since not all of the deck's contents could go out the window. The
soft responsible for the deck's core functions had to stay—including
the game that Albert now finds himself in.

The first features to go are the operating system's security, followed by nonessential graphics. He dismantles them piece by piece,
leaving behind only the archaic terminal, desk and floor that they
stand on.

A loud bang tears him from his focus.

"Come on, we have to go!" Elena pulls his arm. "The sea…it's—
it's gone!"

"I know. I got rid of it."

"What do you mean? It's what happens right before a tsunami!"

The floor starts vibrating and shaking. This didn't happen last
time. Props to whoever designed the physics in this game—deleting
the water in the bay must have triggered a massive tectonic shift.
Let's hope they made sure the fiber-optic cables stayed intact in the
event of an earthquake.

No, this is more than your average quake. Albert steps onto the balcony to get a better look. Elena screams and dashes around the room in panic. The view through the balcony door is as astonishing as it is terrifying in its realness—a wave dozens of feet high is rapidly advancing across the seabed. It'll reach the villa in around thirty seconds.

Albert realizes what's happening—the vacuum created by deleting the water is causing it to be replenished. Not bad, not bad at all.

Elena frantically tries to pull him toward the exit. He shoves her away and quickly sits back down at the terminal. He bangs out a few commands, and just like that, the wave disappears. It won't last long—there'll be a new one soon enough. Albert simply marks the areas of the cyberdeck's memory that are exempted from deletion and initiates a routine cleanup.

First the world fades to grayscale, then becomes jagged and blurry as it loses texture. The next wave that appears on the horizon now resembles a crumpled piece of tinfoil growing rapidly in size as it draws closer. He switches off the sky. Then everything goes silent.

"What's happening...?" Elena mouths the words as she collapses to her knees on the cold tile.

The floor, the exterior of the building and Elena herself vanish along with the few gigabytes of code from her plotline. Good riddance. Once everything, even his own avatar, is gone, and he disconnects from the server, Albert is left alone in a clean, empty cyberspace. Perfect darkness surrounds him—a vacuum waiting to be filled. Unlike his new unit, he knows exactly how to furnish it with his own models, designs and code downloaded from his Cave of Wonders. But first...

To build a safe haven you needed walls, protection—and

cyberspace was no exception. Albert didn't intend to skimp on that front.

Here, finally, in his brand-new fortress, his safe haven, he would complete the Taran in peace.

Dum Dum was utterly captivated. True, the feeling would be more appropriately evoked from a work of art, but there was something about the neat pattern of red incisions on the disheveled forty-something-year-old woman's body. Buried within the chaos, an order so inhuman that only a human could have created it.

The unit was cramped and cluttered, but not unclean...as long as you ignored the blood on the walls and floor—a testimony to Karla's passion. You spend your whole miserable existence here, grateful that at least you're not on the street, grateful for that little bit of energy that keeps you going. Then one day, as you drift through your purposeless reality, helplessly carried along by the currents of fate, you reach out, grab your destiny by the ball sack and hang on tight. That little shit had somehow slipped through their fingers.

His room was a six-by-six-foot cube. Unlike the rest of the place, it wasn't cluttered with useless crap. Utilitarian, minimalist, uncomfortable. Ascetic, almost. You didn't live here for comfort, but because you were after something—a goal. Free from the body's trappings, its pains and comforts. Dum Dum might've been reaching a little, but it felt like the right direction.

The Maelstromer returned to the living room. The others were calmly, meticulously turning the unit upside down in search of anything useful, but without success. True, they were making a mess, but covering their tracks would've been an excess of caution to avoid consequences they couldn't give two fucks about.

It was time to leave—nothing more to be done here. Dum Dum

took one last look at the woman's body. She hadn't put on a particularly brave face—couldn't handle the pain.

Turned out, she really did have no idea where her son was.

Five NCART stops, a change and then two more. It added a thirty-minute walk to the normal travel time, but the program determined this was the best route to avoid areas where a crime had been committed within the last month. The default settings limited it to a week. He felt like that wasn't enough.

It was early afternoon and the train was nearly empty. The smorgasbord of ads was out on full display, covering every inch of available wall space, rippling through the middle of the train and flickering past on the tunnel walls. Albert sat hunched over, trying to draw as little attention to himself as possible. He cautiously observed the other passengers out of the corner of his eye, avoiding direct eye contact. The fact that that might have the opposite effect than he intended crossed his mind, but he knew of no other way.

The two girls at the front looked harmless, so did the little boy playing with a toy robot. Then there were the three factory workers, or at least they looked like they worked at a factory. They sat three seats away and Albert tried his hardest not to look in their direction, but he couldn't help it.

He realized he'd need a plan of action for when he got there. What if his mother wasn't home? No, she'd be there—she was always home. Didn't go out unless she absolutely needed to. Wouldn't just be home, either—she'd start yelling at him straight from the doorway. He figured he'd have to say something to buy himself some time. Half a minute was all Albert needed to find what he was looking for and get out. Then he'd be gone for good.

He stepped out of the train, relieved the three potential threats turned out to be a product of his imagination. He made his way down to street level. It was only a half-mile walk through the relatively safe commercial area, and even if for some reason part of it wasn't, he could simply make a detour. He thought-commanded the program once more to appear in his retinal display. Damn. There was a red dot where he was headed.

Matter of fact, it looked like a serious crime had been committed in the very apartment building he'd grown up in.

"Thoughts, theories?" Liam asked.

The rookie's gaze swept through the living room and the forensics experts going about their biz. Luckily, the floor was crooked, which meant that most of the dark-red puddle had collected against the wall. Made walking around a whole lot easier. The TV hadn't been switched off and for the third time was advertising anti-burglary doors equipped with active defense mechanisms. Little late for that.

A couple of micro-drones the size of ping-pong balls finished scanning the fingerprints left in the other rooms and obediently flew back into their briefcase.

"See the shape of the cuts?" Liam lifted the sheet. Gooey, viscous blood dripped onto the cold body. "Parallel, but not deep. Precise. They weren't meant to kill, not even to cause pain—there are a hundred better ways of doing that. They were having fun. Chipped with Mantis Blades, but not for combat. Not this time, at least." He quickly let go of the sheet as soon as he saw the rookie cover her mouth with her hand, her face pale.

"Remind you of anything?" He pointed at the body. "What happened to Mrs. Delany."

The rookie quickly shook her head and took a few steps back.

"Harris's Auto," Liam said. "The guard. Don't see any similarities?"

"But that was in a completely different part of town." The rookie seemed to regain her power of speech, though not the color in her face. "You think they're connected? Mrs. Delany didn't even own a car."

"Some questions don't come with simple answers." Liam looked at the blood coagulating under the wall. "Like whether all this blood'll leak to the downstairs neighbor."

The avalanche of guilt-tripping accusation was unavoidable. What if he just ignored her? Go in, get the shard and get out. Fine, but what if she blocked his way out the door and demanded an explanation? He'd have to say something. Or do something.

He walked past the windows of stores that, for the most part, seemed legitimate. If there was any hint of shadiness, it lurked in the alleyways in long coats and hooded sweatshirts. In the cars parked by the curb, you could sometimes see someone through the tinted windows just sitting there. Keep to the middle of the sidewalk, blend into the faceless crowd and you'll be fine, he reassured himself.

It was all a gonk mistake, anyway. That's what happened when you rushed things. That's why he was out on this high-risk excursion—the access code to the Cave was on a shard sitting at the bottom of one of his drawers, untouched for years. Once the deck had been configured, he'd never needed the key again since he would connect automatically. New deck, new configuration. At first Albert was furious, threw himself a little tantrum. When that didn't solve anything, he cooled down and evaluated his possibilities. There was only one—going back to his old unit. It was a short trip. Still, with each passing day his mother would only get progressively angrier until one day it'd all come crashing down on him like a pile of bricks.

He'd have to say something—anything to get her off his case, at least for a minute. He came up with a few excuses—most of them untrue—which would give his mother some pause for thought. Long enough to get what he came for and never come back.

He walked past his usual NCART stop. Two weeks ago, there'd been a robbery, so the station was marked red in his program. That's why he tacked more than an extra hour onto his journey.

"Time of death—less than an hour ago." Liam held his hand up to the woman's head. The diodes on his wrist blinked.

He closed his eyes; his fingers pulsed green and red.

"Cause of death—cardiac arrest resulting from blood loss. No damage to vital organs. Numerous cuts to her skin and tissue were enough to get the job done." He reopened his eyes and stood up. "We'll know more after the autopsy, though I doubt it'll be anything new."

"The face—it's completely intact," the rookie pointed out. So, she did peek under the sheet after all. "She wasn't gagged, either. If she was awake, she would have screamed, called for help. This whole thing—it must've taken a while."

There was a broken braindance wreath lying next to the body. Explained a lot. They forced open the door and took her by surprise. There was no way she could defend herself.

"Sounds about right." Liam nodded. "Neighbors waited till the perps left and then called the police. Pretended they didn't hear anything when it all started."

"Why?"

"Fear of reprisal, I'm guessing. Weren't too keen on having their front doors shot up one day, eventually. Don't know if you've noticed, but we're not exactly a venerated bunch in this city."

"Venerated?"

"Looked up to." Thinking, the inspector gazed at the dead

woman. "NCPD can't kill the folks they're most afraid of, so we put 'em behind bars. Just so happens they actually want to be there— earns 'em street cred. You can't win."

The forensics experts were already packing up their equipment. Another day, another crime scene. Only one of the hundred murders in the period between the sun rising and setting over Night City. At least a hundred homicides a day in Night City made their jobs more piecework than precise, forensic science.

"Imagine you're an average NC'er," Liam said after a moment's thought. "Would you go up against a gang? Alone?"

"Not unless I had a death wish," the rookie admitted.

"So, you get the picture. Neighbors aren't to blame."

The inspector pointed at a footprint at the edge of the red-brown puddle. It was the same outfit from the garage. Didn't even bother covering their tracks. Wouldn't be all that hard to find them, piece together the chain of events, unravel the network of relationships and uncover the motivations of the perps and victims. Doable, all that. Hard part is actually proving all of it. Higher-ups knew that all too well. Nobody was going to chew you out if another case got closed with the perps still at large. Nobody gave a damn about the clearance rate. Not anymore. But sometimes…sometimes you got cases where you had to roll up your sleeves and get to work.

On the other hand, if a badge was killed, finding the perp became a matter of honor. That and survival instinct. Gangers didn't normally shoot a badge without giving the consequences some serious thought. That's one thing you could still rely on in the force, at least—knowing that a gangoon'll think twice before planting lead in your brainpan. Life insurance, if you will.

The rookie stepped back against the wall. Two paramedics placed a stretcher down beside the dark-red puddle. As they lifted up the body, the sticky, coagulated blood came unstuck from the floor like berry-flavored scop.

"By the way, how did we get here so quick?" The rookie avoided looking at the body. "How did you know this was all connected?"

"We use tags to categorize crimes in the system." Liam handed her his police-issued tablet. "'Incise wounds,' 'shallow incise wounds'— you get the gist. I use them to connect seemingly unrelated cases— not their original purpose, but that's beside the point. Cops arriving on the scene usually don't bother filling them in. For once, this time they did. Keep reading."

He slid his finger upward to scroll down the page. "There's an option here...if you select CASE CLOSED then nobody will ever again wonder who offed Mrs. Delany."

"So, you're saying..." The rookie hesitated. "It's up to us to decide if we want to take this or drop it?"

"That's right. Elena Delany wasn't anyone important, no offense to her. If you select it, the case'll automatically go to the archive. That is, after everyone fills out their paperwork, which they will. And that'll be the end of that."

The rookie gave the inspector a wary look.

"So why haven't you already selected it?"

Liam put the tablet away and stuffed his hands into his pockets. He looked her straight in the eyes.

"Ever stop to wonder why you joined the force?" he asked. "When's your swearing-in ceremony?"

"In a couple days," the rookie answered, surprised. "But it's just a formality, right? I mean, I'm basically already on the force."

Liam nodded. He turned to the elevator just as the doors were opening.

*   *   *

The elevator doors opened. Albert didn't move, didn't take a step. His foot trembled slightly. From his unit—his mother's unit—two people in forensic suits were carrying out a body on a stretcher. He stared, the expression on his face completely frozen. Without looking, he slapped the button of a random floor. The balding man in a gray trench coat gave him a seemingly indifferent glance. The other badge next to him stood staring at a body bag. The doors closed.

CHAPTER_7

Whaddup, my fellow psychos and scuzzbags! FR34K_S33K's in the house and I've got something you won't believe! But first, if you're still reading this channel, that means your brain hasn't melted out your earholes yet. Wanna keep it that way? Better start drinking three-quarter cans of smash instead of downing them one after the next. Take it from a former smasher—it'll buy you a few more days in this shitty-ass town.

Wondering what I got for you losers today? This one's a motherfuckin' TREAT. Remember that "attack" on the eastern beltway? You gonks still believe that was caused by a cyberpsycho? If you do, then better just down four cans of smash right now and forget about understanding jack shit about anything. Or just shoot up some synth-coke. Why bother drinking when you can inject instant happiness straight into your veins?

How many people died back there? Twenty-two, including that kid you saw on TV. You know, that little blond boy leaning halfway out the back window, his hair almost singed—which you couldn't say about the rest of his body. Ouch! That must've hurt.

What's the prime cause of cyberpsychosis? Illegal cyberware—duh! Cheap chrome, fresh out of a Scav chop shop, reaped from all those sorry-ass gonks now floating in pieces in the bay, being nibbled by mutant fish or whatever the fuck's swimming in there.

That part's true. But does it REALLY explain a pileup of that scale? Hells to the no! When corps fuck something up, they always be pointing the finger at someone else, right? Now they're saying our choom went cyberpsycho cuz of some faulty components from a company called Unitra. Know what that means? They want to put their asses out of biz just to gobble up their shares. Don't matter who—they're all doing it. Meanwhile your brain's turning into scop, but you think THEY give a fuck?

Crumbling infrastructure, a glitchy-ass traffic system and big shots cruising around in they limos like they above the law—them's the true causes! How do I know that? Cuz I got PROOF. That's right—got my hands on a clip showing what really went down—a speeding corpo limo with deactivated anti-collision set off the whole chain reaction. See for yourself and make up your own damn minds. Don't say I didn't warn ya!

PEACE!

He never went to these kinds of places. Too classy, bright. Transparent. Couldn't take cover anywhere if things went south. Then again, it was hard to believe anything would go south in a place like this. He had to pass three security checks to get here and only thanks to the invitation in their system.

He was definitely underdressed, but nobody seemed to pay him any attention.

"Don't like it here." Zor rotated his glass of sparkling water on the table. "Feel like we're being watched and listened to from every direction."

"No better place to hide than in plain sight." Milena gave a half smile, barely raising the corner of her lips. "So, what did you want to talk about? Your message was slightly cryptic."

"Something no one else should ever know." Zor looked around the spacious, immaculately decorated interior. There were at least a hundred people in his line of sight. Some sat at smaller or larger tables—others, like him and Milena, sat in glass booths. Recording their conversation would be child's play—no advanced tech needed. All someone had to do was read their lips. Then again, there were so many people here that reading everyone's lips simultaneously wouldn't be easy. Plain sight—maybe she was right.

Service robots brought people their orders, winding their way around the tables and fake plants.

"How's it going with Aya?" Milena asked.

"How's what going?" It took Zor a second before he realized what she meant. He shrugged. "Oh, it's not. We're not—" He cleared his throat.

"Hard to believe." She peered at him through squinted eyes. "You two are practically made for each other."

He shook his head.

"She's not into me."

"You just can't read signals, don't know how to send them, either. Neither of you can."

"So then why are you so sure it's our fault?"

Milena's gaze drifted to the side and met Ned Templeton's eyes staring directly at her. Her ex-lover. He always sat at the same table under the same fake palm tree. One PM, like clockwork. His predictability was excruciating.

"Kiss me," she said suddenly.

"What...?" Zor looked at her, dumbfounded.

"So no one second-guesses us." Her smile widened. "Don't worry, I don't bite."

Zor hesitated. He moved his glass to the side and leaned over the table. Milena did the same and their mouths joined for a few seconds. Milena's tongue caressed his lips. They drew back. She sat up straight in her chair and touched the panel on the glass wall. The glass doors closed them off from the rest of the cafeteria, then the walls frosted up. Couldn't even make out people's silhouettes on other side.

"We're completely secure," she explained. "Electronic signals blocked—listening devices drowned out by white noise."

As if to confirm her words, even the vent in the ventilation shaft closed. They now sat in a milky-white cube through which no sound from the outside could penetrate.

"Still have my doubts," Zor said.

"What's life without a little risk?"

Something seemed off ever since the start of their meeting, and Zor just now realized what it was. She wasn't smoking.

He took out his phone and showed her an image. The screen was small, since hardly anybody used phones without a neuroport.

"I believe you two are acquainted."

Milena took a careful glance at the screen.

"He's a big deal—way up in the ranks. I know him—professionally, that is."

"When do you meet him again?"

"Soon. But don't count on me introducing you. They don't let anyone closer to him than three hundred feet."

"I don't want to meet him. I want to kill him."

Silence enveloped the room. You could hear the sizzle of the sparkling water.

Zor's stomach rumbled, breaking the heavy silence. Milena chuckled. She touched the panel once more and the walls regained their transparency.

"I could eat something, too," she said, still smiling. On the table's surface a menu appeared displaying the All Foods CorpPremium lunch specials. "Order whatever you want. It's on me."

Ned stared at her sullenly over his plate.

"I'm sorry, but you can't hire Robert Redwardt for sexual services."

"But I have a platinum subscription."

"I'm afraid platinum doesn't cover that. Your subscription grants you limitless braindance rentals."

"Name a price, any price. Tonight would be best."

"Your subscription does not include the possibility to hire actors."

"What do I pay three hundred eddies a month for then, huh?! Is there something better than platinum?"

"I'm afraid not, ma'am. Platinum is the highest. Unfortunately, our company cannot provide the kind of service you're asking for."

"What's with this polite 'ma'am' bullshit?!" Another voice in the background, also a woman. The sound of someone being shoved. Glass shattering. *"Who the fuck do you think you are, you cunt?! I HAVE the eddies—just name a fucking price!"*

"I do apologize, ma'am, but our company does not offer that kind of service."

"Get fucked, tower trash! I'll report you, then we'll see who's apologizing when they kick your ass to the curb! Good luck dying of starvation!"

Putting yourself in the head of tower trash was like squeezing yourself into an empty bottle and hurling it into the bay. They're gifted this incredible potential at birth, but most Night Citizens spend their whole lives cooped up in a shitty unit. Barely human—more like livestock. Usually, a person takes destiny in their own hands, shapes it, takes risks. Tower trash just reacts to whatever problem they run up against, bouncing from one challenge to the next like a pinball. Their only stimuli are punishment and asinine pleasures.

Zor—the lowly rat catcher, roach exterminator—himself shacked up like a roach. How long would he last without a job? He wouldn't have any savings. People like him didn't save. Two weeks tops and he'd have to finally emerge, reveal himself. Two weeks was a lot of time. Too much.

Albert Delany—netrunner of this impromptu gang, who lived a sheltered existence for years. His mother took care of everything, kept him fed, washed his dirty clothes. Then all of a sudden, he ups and leaves the safety of his little nest. Why? What could be more important than the security that kept him alive this whole time?

They sat on a wide ledge somewhere around the twentieth floor, three pairs of heavy boots dangling over the city. As good a place as any. No one to bother them at least. Dum Dum, Karla and Dixie— Karla's arms wrapped around Dixie as if she wanted to protect him from everything bad in the world. Or maybe just keep him warm. If they fell, they'd fall together. They gazed at the lights of the city through blazing-red optics like it was a Christmas tree, promising everyone a present if they were only brave enough to reach for it.

Brave and smart enough, Karla thought-spoke, correcting him.

Dum Dum nodded and took a long hit from his S-keef inhaler. He saw a city that called to all, promised much, but gave so little to only a few.

Think this container's really as valuable as they say?

"Can't he give it back?"

"Give it back? You gonked? We're damned if we do, damned if we don't."

"Just give it back, apologize…"

"No wonder you're not in charge. Give it back how?! That wouldn't get rid of the problem, just create a new one. For the time being, nobody knows we're sittin' on this thing."

"I dunno...Dump it in the Coronado?"

"I'll fuckin' dump you in the Coronado."

"Okay, well...There ain't no third option."

"Jesus Christ...I know that! That's the fuckin' problem!"

Renner paced back and forth next to the gray container with the Militech logo. It lay in the middle of the small room in the basement of an abandoned factory, fifteen feet beneath the ground. Lowered the chances of anyone finding it. If there was a tracker in that container, they'd have been paid a visit long ago.

He entered a random code on the container's keypad. The sound of the incorrect code made Ross instinctively hang his head.

"How 'bout we just...wait?" Ross suggested.

"Yeah, 'cause that's how I've gone through life." Renner struggled to keep his cool. The crosses on his hands glowed fiercely. "Waiting around with my dick in my hands, doing fuck-all." He kicked the container. "Fuck that! I get shit done!"

"I'll figure something out."

"Listen, the others can't find out about this, okay?" He gave the container another kick for good measure. "Warden, you gonk piece of shit..."

It was the first time in years. Instead of trawling the Net for intel on his target, he sat and stared at the message on his phone. How should he answer? He didn't know how these things were supposed to go. He cycled through every possible version in his head, but none of them sounded right. Just dumb.

Was this what kissing Milena had done? Rekindled something

inside him that he'd lost a long time ago? Or maybe he'd gotten fed up of being lonely and waiting for...? Well, what exactly? That by some miracle he'd beat the system—find a way past all the security? It'd never work. He'd never be able to get close enough to the target. It was a pipe dream headed straight for the sewer.

That kiss—it was camouflage, nothing more. Blending in, not drawing attention. He knew he was making up excuses—just as long as he could get rid of the flashbacks, the guilt, once and for all.

"Things are slowly picking up," OP1 said to herself, though the room was so small it may as well have been to everyone. "Was starting to think it'd just be the same ol'."

"Had nothing at first—crickets," OP2 reminded her. "Now all of a sudden we're getting a locust swarm of data—every chart's shifting red."

"This time's different." OP1 nodded. "The hack on that drone? Gotta admit, that was pretty good."

"It was impressive," OP2 admitted. "Maybe it's all starting to come together. This could be the one."

"Out of nowhere, just like that. *Bam!* Remote takeover. Completely autonomous, no traceable connection. Either of you anticipate that?"

"You're both overthinking this," OP3 finally said. "That's not the main purpose of this operation. Those were just auxiliary capabilities."

"It was still impressive," OP2 added.

"Think surveillance in that sector's busy tightening up security?" OP1 asked. "They've got a gaping vulnerability. Probably trying to figure out what happened to their drone."

"Won't be finding out from us," OP3 reassured her. "Once the operation's shut down, they'll get a censored report. Not even that much, if Stanley gets his way."

* * *

"He really said that?" Ron propped himself up on his elbow. "'I want to kill him'?"

"Just like that." Milena lit another cigarette. The hum of the AC became louder in anticipation of the smoke. Night City's cold, neon afterglow washed over everything—their naked bodies, the bedsheets, the floor. Reflected off the glass of his twelve-minute-aged whiskey.

"Is it that bad of an idea?" the ripperdoc wondered. "I mean... maybe the world would be a better place without him? Or it wouldn't get worse, at least."

"I handle negotiations, not assassinations." She took a drag and sat up on the bed. "Usually, I know how it's going to play out. You have to be two, three steps ahead of your opponent, but so do they. It's like a chess game—you already know who's black, who's white. The opening's set, but the moves you make will only reveal their potential in the future. To win you have to calculate further than your opponent. It all comes down to how well you read people. I couldn't read Zor. He drew first and shot." She exhaled to the end. "Metaphorically speaking."

Ron was impressed at how much she could say in a single breath, gradually exhaling the smoke without a single cough. Matter of fact, she never coughed. He couldn't help himself from scanning her as he caressed her skin, elated at the access he had to her body. Turned out her lungs were original, completely 'ganic.

"Could be a psychopath," he suggested. "Even though he doesn't look it. Truth be told, from the start I couldn't shake the feeling we'd already met."

"If anyone's a psychopath, it's Borg. I never want to see that fucking lunatic again." She inhaled, almost burning through half of the cigarette. "But Zor—there's something in him that even he doesn't know about."

"Like what?"

"I wish I knew. If Zor were an open book, it'd be like finding... no, not gibberish, not even something written in a foreign language. Not even anything resembling a lie."

"He had all his implants stripped out." He gently, instinctively stroked Milena's foot. "He's got experience, though. Without him we'd all be dead."

"What's the point of this impromptu gang, anyway? We can't even sell what we stole without a fixer. Both times we got lucky. There's no rhyme or reason to it—just random luck. Completely unpredictable."

"I thought you liked it—the emotions, the highs and lows."

Ron's subtle, delicate touch gave her more of a rush than all of her most important negotiations from the past year combined. She tried not to move her leg so he wouldn't stop.

So that he wouldn't notice.

"A roller coaster isn't the same thing as Russian roulette. Risk is only fun when you have some influence over how things play out." Her cigarette dangled briefly from her lips in thought. "You mentioned you were in some kind of trouble."

"My debts were bought by... Eh, doesn't matter." Ron fell back onto the pillow. "Old news. Don't really feel like talkin' about it."

Milena nodded, taking another drag, and went back to the previous subject.

"Reading Zor... It's like reading an overcomplicated book that's too smart for its own good."

"He's smart, but not that smart."

"I'm not talking about him, but what's *inside* of him. I wonder if it's PTSD. He went over the edge, nearly destroyed himself in the process. So, his mind created a second personality in order to shield the first, bear its burdens. Overwrote it, got rid of any traces."

"The point of our impromptu gang…" Ron said with a cheeky grin, "is that I found a buyer for those batteries."

Milena straightened her leg, which had gone numb, and put out her cigarette. She looked at Ron. If it were anyone else, she'd have wanted them gone by now. She felt the exact opposite. If before she couldn't stand anyone's presence for more than a few hours, now she only wished for Ron to stay.

"What I'm trying to tell you is that instead of the braindance I get a message saying 'Service unavailable. Insufficient funds.' *And I can't get rid of it."*

"I understand that. The problem is you haven't paid for your subscription for the last few days."

"Well, yeah, 'cause I don't got the cash. I want to watch the next episode of Elevator to Heaven *and I can't because this stupid message keeps popping up."*

"That's because you haven't paid for your subscription."

"Right, but I just want to get rid of this message and watch my episode. There's gotta be some mistake."

"It's not a mistake. The message will go away as soon as you pay for your subscription."

"Look, I'm getting my paycheck at the end of the week. I can pay then."

"I'm afraid you have to pay first before you can watch."

"What difference does it make in what order I do it? I'll watch it today and pay at the end of the week."

"I'm sorry, but that's not how our service works."

*   *   *

Pepe Najarro watched as the customers took their drinks and fled through the front door, leaving El Coyote Cojo nearly empty. He swore under his breath—there went the next hour's intake. He wondered if he should pretend nothing was happening or risk calling for help, knowing that at any moment the bar could turn into a shooting gallery. Only one customer remained seated at one of the high tables, eating ramen with synth-meat and pretending he hadn't noticed the sudden commotion followed by the eerie lull.

"Gonna just stand there, Dum Dum?" Warden grinned, baring his translucent, sky-blue teeth. He kicked a stool out from under the table. "Siddown, let's talk like civilized people."

Dum Dum pulled back his coat and sat down on the rickety stool. His synth-leather creaked. Dixie stood on one side, Karla on the other.

Warden didn't stop slurping his ramen as he eyed the newcomers with mild curiosity.

"Sightseeing, are we?" he said between mouthfuls. "Or maybe a glitch in your autonomous cab's GPS?"

"We've always kept out of each other's way," Dum Dum finally said. "You wanna sit in this sewer called Heywood, makin' mud pies outta your own shit—I got nothin' against that."

"Mud pies outta shit." Warden nodded and gulped down what resembled a shiitake mushroom. "Weak, as far as digs go, but worth remembering. In case one day I run out of all the funny ones. Know what ain't funny? Trespassing on our turf."

"Trespassing? Us? Now that is rich…" Dum Dum leaned over the table. "You're the ones who broke the peace, crossed half the city into Northside. It's a provocation—to some even a declaration of war."

Warden stopped chewing.

"The fuck you talking about? Our boys never set foot in Northside."

"Your people robbed a Militech warehouse right under our noses and then cruised around our neighborhood in a van with PEST CONTROL written on it. That not sound like a provocation to you? Or maybe that's the kind of joke you think is funny."

Dum Dum slid a phone with a picture on it toward Warden. Warden instantly lost his appetite.

"Those weren't my people."

"Got intel that says otherwise." If Dum Dum could have squinted his eyes, he would have. "Heist was led by a certain Zor."

"You want Zor?" Warden leaned against the backrest of the stool, making it rock backward in warning. He grinned. "Be my guest. He's not one of mine—couldn't care less about him, already forgot he existed. Client needed him for an op. Three hours and that was it."

"Give him to us."

"I would if I knew where he was. But I don't. Don't know where he's been, where he'll be…Like I said—already forgot he existed."

"Bet Renner would wanna say the same about you. Got put out to pasture, hmm?" Dum Dum smiled slightly, knowing it would hurt. "Maybe this'll jog your memory." He swiped to the next picture.

Warden's nostrils flared as he released the air from his lungs.

"Borg…"

"Well, well…" Dum Dum smiled and straightened himself. "I'm listening."

Warden wiped his mouth with a napkin and folded it in half.

"He works for me. Gonk from south Heywood with a skullsponge for a brain. Motherfucker was supposed to lay low for a while, play the model Night Citizen."

"Sounds like he got bored."

"Yeah, of life." Warden clenched his fist. "He found Zor and the others for me. Leadhead's a coward—squeeze him and he'll spill everything. Works at city hall, nine to seven. He'll lead you to Zor and the rest. Then you can do whatever you want with him. Something bad were to happen to him—something permanently, irreversibly bad—who knows, I might even thank you for it."

Dum Dum sighed and would have closed his eyes, if only he had eyelids.

"It's plain immoral. Her husband cheated on her while she cheated on him. Multiple times!"

"That's correct, ma'am. It's the plot of the braindance. If that kind of content isn't to your liking, you're free to relive something else. Your subscription offers a selection of more than one hundred and fifty different braindances."

"I want to make sure nobody ever has to experience this disgusting, degenerate filth again."

"Well, it just so happens people like to relive that sort of content. That's what the series *A One-Time Thing* is about."

"It's not 'a one-time thing'! It's all the time! They debauch themselves in every single episode!"

"You're free to relive a different braindance."

"I don't want another braindance. I want you to change this one and make it so the characters start behaving respectably."

"I'm afraid that's beyond my control."

"That's exactly what my preacher says! We don't have control. People are killing each other on the streets, families don't have clean running water and food tastes like the devil's excrement."

"I'm sorry, but I have no control over the production of braindances."

"You're sorry?! You're probably sleeping around left and right your-self! This city is filled with sinners!"

"Ma'am, you don't have to relive the braindance."

"I'm not about to let some godless jezebel tell me what I can or can't relive! The Church of Eliyahu the Last Emancipator forbids this kind of depravity! You people are a plague on this earth, corrupting the souls of innocents! Can't you see the problem in front of your—?"

"You're the problem. If your church forbids this kind of content, then maybe you shouldn't be reliving it."

The screen went dark. The sound in her headphones went mute, followed by the crackle of the channel being changed.

"Aya!" It was a different voice. "My office, now."

She took off her headphones and got up from her swivel chair. The cacophonous babble of five hundred tech-support employees felt like she was inside a beehive. The manager's office was located at the far end behind a wall of frosted glass.

She walked past the seemingly endless rows of identical cubi-cles. Each of them was apologizing, even though there was nothing to apologize for. There was a short staircase to the office door. Aya made it in two steps.

Her manager, whose name she could never remember, sat behind a wide desk. He tried to hide his smaller-than-average stature with a suit that was one size too big for him. It produced the opposite effect.

"I cut the call with your last customer," he began without intro-duction. "Your name flashed orange in the system, then red."

Aya stood next to the chair facing the desk. He didn't offer for her to sit.

"When they call…" she began. "Most of them, it's not even a tech-nical problem. It's like they call us just to have someone to yell at."

"And?" The manager rested his elbows against the table and intertwined his fingers. "They tell you that in level-two training."

"I've only had level-one training."

"Well, anyway, you blew it. You're not supposed to use the word *problem*. You've used it…" He checked his screen. "Eleven times. Twelve counting a second ago."

Aya couldn't take her eyes off the spectacle of his hands as they joined into a pyramid, his fingertips drumming against one another, then interlocking again.

"I know; I'm sorry." She wasn't sorry. "But, well…I didn't know what other word to use."

"Good. I'm glad you apologized. Now, no matter what the situation is, we don't use the word *problem*. Ever. It has negative connotations. Is that clear?"

"I think so."

"You think?" His fingers started performing their next dance.

"It's hard, because these customers…our customers—most of them…Well, they're just wrong."

"Obviously. But that's just how it is. They're either morons or fed up with their lives. What do you think all these employees are for?" He gestured beyond the frosted glass. "It's so our clients, who most of the time are wrong, remain under the illusion that they're right. Then, and only then, they'll keep paying their subscription. Simple."

"I thought I'd be helping people with technical problems. I haven't had a single one so far."

"You just said it again." His hands resumed their agitation. "We haven't had technical problems for years. Customer service is just for dealing with frustration. It's like they're screaming into the pillow and you're the pillow. They tell you all about that in level-two training. Oh, and you can't use phrases like 'It just so happens…' because it's considered rude—or 'You don't have to relive it.' It comes across as patronizing. We'll have to give her a discount now. And remember that you can't distance yourself from the company with stuff like 'I have no control over...' You *are* the company; you're like...like... a little tiny mouth hidden somewhere on its enormous body. Your level-two training..."—his fingers danced across the screen—"is the day after tomorrow. But today"—the pyramid again—"there's a sort of informal get-together at eight. You can drop by, get to know a few faces. Company cost."

"I already have plans this evening." Aya straightened up.

"Plans were made to be changed." His fingers began moving chaotically again. "I was already supposed to fire you. Least that's what the system told me. But instead, I'm deciding to give you one last chance."

"I don't want another chance."

His fingers froze.

"Meaning...?"

"I quit. If I stay here any longer, I'll start hating people."

And if I do that job they gave me, she thought, I'll hate myself.

How long had he been walking around like this? It was like he was on autopilot. He didn't recognize the area or know what its safety level was. A car drove slowly past. His instinct was to dash for cover and hide, but he held himself together. Barely. Acting like prey only attracts predators. All well and good in theory—not so easy in practice. As usual, the more he tried to blend in, the more his actions felt unnatural. The more aware of it he was, the worse it got.

He stopped all of a sudden in the middle of the sidewalk.

He'd never been scared of the police. Might as well have been invisible to them—they'd never had a reason to bother him. Well, now they would. Even though he didn't do anything, he was mixed up in a case. Mixed up in the death of his mother at the very least because he was her son.

At the very least.

He finally managed to figure out where he was by the layout of the buildings. North Heywood. Hadn't wandered too far. He turned to go home. No, wrong way. He had a different home now.

He hadn't left his unit since yesterday. His new unit. Would the police find him here? From what he knew of their methods—no. The real estate agent didn't even ask for his last name. All he had to do was pay a sizable deposit through a secure transaction service. Albert didn't use cash. A week, maybe two before the case got dropped.

His mother was dead.

Devastating, usually. But the first thing he felt was relief. Then shame. Why shame? He was alone. He didn't care about anyone else around him. Shame...? It was dumb.

He was relieved that he wouldn't ever have to talk to her, explain himself, deflect all of her questions and accusations. She couldn't throw any more fits. Because she was dead. She wasn't a problem, a burden anymore. He felt a weight had been lifted from his shoulders.

All he had to do was start a new life. The old one would eventually fade away, vanish into the scrap heap of forgotten memories.

His mother was dead.

He didn't feel sad. Shame. That feeling he'd become acquainted with late enough to understand how it worked. Like an infection—a disease borne from circumstance. It was regret—mutated, weaponized. He didn't feel shame the way "normal" people felt it, but he understood why they did. Somehow that made it worse. Or made him more human? No. Knowing what he knew about humanity from history class—just worse. Shame. He understood it as people's deep, unwavering criticism of yourself—of something you did that you shouldn't have. Which meant there was something wrong with you. Shame originated from without, but was felt from within.

His mother was dead.

Should he be ashamed at not feeling sad? He wasn't ashamed. So, what now? What should he feel if shame and sadness were out of the picture?

Say what you will about her, but his mother tried her best to teach him emotion. Or rather how to fake it. Before, the world and the people in it seemed to trudge along according to some unknown rhythm. As he learned, the rhythm of the world became more and more decipherable. And more dangerous. Until at last the world turned into a waking nightmare filled with illogical, irrational emotions jumping from person to person like a virus. Despite his mother's efforts, he was immune to them.

His mother was dead. And that would've been the end of that if not for one tiny detail—the shard with the access code to the Cave lying at the bottom of his drawer.

He had to go back.

"Last beer I had was with Morris, whom you met. That ended…" Zor sipped the decidedly unsatisfying can of beer. "Well, you know how that ended. Then I went for a drink with Ron."

Aya nodded.

"That didn't end much better," Zor added.

"And now you're having a drink with me." She smiled. "What could possibly go wrong?"

They sat on the edge of the canal, the water flowing by slowly under a thick layer of trash. Instead of gentle lapping against the wall, there was the grating of plastic bottles and metal cans. AVs and drones weaved their way above them through the night sky turned afternoon by the neon. Aerozeps hovered over Northside, loading and unloading. Holo-ads draped Corpo Plaza, emitting a soft, cold glow. It all felt somewhere distant, beyond reach. The place they sat seemed a little oasis of calm.

"Morris…" Aya reminded herself. "How is he?"

"No clue. I just hope his new partner will take him out for more beers than I did." Zor raised the can to his lips, barely taking a sip. "And that he doesn't get into any more fights."

"I quit my job. Or… they fired me. One or the other. Haven't been there since… you know. Flat broke now."

"Same. Wouldn't be sharing a single beer otherwise."

"Still, thanks for coming. I needed this."

"Wish I had more to offer you than a can of beer and a floating pile of trash." He let out a sigh. "I don't even like beer."

"Neither do I," Aya replied, then broke out into laughter. It'd been a long time since she'd laughed without a care in the world. Zor smiled. He tipped back the can and took a large sip. His expression suddenly became serious.

"Been on my own for seven years," he said. "Just me and my thoughts—not the positive kind, either. Not the healthiest thing, I guess."

"Marry's wasn't good for me," Aya said. "That place was toxic." She squeezed her eyes shut.

"Have you ever had someone?" she asked. "You know… important?"

"I did," he said, letting a beat of silence fall. "My wife and son." A long pause. "They're dead."

"Oh. I'm… I'm sorry. No, wait, that sounded gonk." She hesitated. "When did it happen?"

"Seven years ago, when the war ended."

The garbage crunched and scraped past in a never-ending stream. On the other side of the canal stood abandoned warehouses with hollowed-out windows. You could sit here for a year and nothing would change.

"I promised her we'd leave, move to San Francisco." He finished his beer. "We didn't make it."

He crushed the can and chucked it into the current of trash drifting toward the bay.

"Should've gotten over it by now, but I haven't. I can't. Revenge—it's the only thing keeping me going."

Aya rose to her feet.

"You did a good thing. Thanks."

"For what?" He looked at her with curiosity.

"For getting me out of Marry's." She raised her hand directly above her head and swayed her torso.

Her eyes closed, she rotated on her own axis, dancing to music only she could hear. She danced for herself. For Zor, too. Instead of Marry's Bar, all the lights of Night City shone down upon her.

We're just dying flesh, if you think about it. Life is just a straight road toward death. No exceptions—no matter how many implants you chip, hormones you pump into your veins, supplements, nanites, money, cutting-edge tech—something's always going to rot, get weaker, gradually decompose.

One way or another, you'll keel over. Or get killed by someone just because you got in their way. There aren't any backups. You die—that's it. No take backs.

One generation replaces the next, becomes more perfect. That's how biological life is supposed to work. A cavalcade of faulty prototypes. Though Albert knew he was supposed to be the more perfect version of his mother, the thought that a better generation was supposed to come after him seemed unacceptable. That in order for the next generation to spread its wings and fly, the old one had to slink back and vanish into the shadows.

There wouldn't be a next generation. He had to focus on perfecting this one, right now—self-perfection.

He had to go back.

Which is something he really didn't want to do. His stomach churned at the thought of walking the twenty feet from the elevator to the door of his old unit. The neighbors would have fresh gossip for weeks to come. They'd expect him to feel something. Your mother died—be sad. Cry. They'd pester him with more questions than his mother did when she was alive. It wasn't just hard for him to pretend to be sad. It was impossible.

Little late to be thinking about this when the elevator's almost at his floor.

The doors slid open. The hallway seemed to sway as Albert took his first few steps. For as long as he could remember, he'd speed-walk those twenty feet as if they were the final stretch to safety. He'd slap his hand against the biometric panel, cross through the doorway and shut the door behind him. Relief would wash over him. He was safe here in his fortress.

Things were different now. The door was crossed out with police tape—the biometric panel was covered with a few layers of it.

He stopped halfway between the elevator and what only two days ago used to be the safest place in the world. The hallway was empty. Was it under surveillance? Did the police plant some kind of sensor? He didn't know crime scene procedure. He figured he'd just stroll into his old unit—the only difference being that his mother wasn't there.

Wouldn't work like that.

Mrs. Morgan, their older neighbor a few doors down who was around forty, poked her head out from behind her door. She was always watching, always the first to kick up a fuss over any trash left in the hallway. The resident gossiper.

But not this time. Not altogether herself of late, without a word Mrs. Morgan quickly shut the door and triple-locked it from the inside.

Albert went up to the police tape. He just had to tear it off and go in. Not like anyone was guarding it.

Should've thought about this before instead of digging through two days' worth of garbage.

Once upon a time, this garbage-filled pit was supposed to become the garage of your garden-variety megatower. Then the construction company went bust. The end. Now the only things keeping all this garbage together were the garage walls. Maybe, in a few years, when it all piled up to the surface, someone would come and fill it in with concrete. Or, who knew, maybe they'd go through the trouble of digging out all the trash compressed under its own weight. And maybe, just maybe, they'd accidentally find a decomposing body. But they wouldn't worry too much about it, because it wouldn't be the only one. Dum Dum knew of at least three. He knew because he'd put them there himself.

Let the police come and clean it up. Just not in the basement of Totentanz. You had to maintain a certain level of hygiene; don't shit where you eat.

They sifted through the garbage in complete darkness, not counting their blazing-red optics. You'd think night vision was enough, but no, not even Dum Dum's terahertz optics could sort through the salad of metals and plastics of random proportions.

The skeletons of unfinished apartment towers loomed over them. Someone could be hidden, sitting and watching them from above. Let 'em.

It's him, Dixie thought-spoke. He peeled off a greasy tarp and straightened up.

Borg. Wrapped in bloody scraps of clothes, completely unrecognizable from his first appearance at Totentanz.

Dum Dum peeled away what used to be the inside edge of a jacket. The dried blood separated like glue. He bent down and ran his hand over the corpse's neck, then its shoulder—in the corner of his display a notification appeared. He'd found what he was looking for. Without a word, Karla extended her blade ever so slightly and, with utmost precision, cut half an inch deep. Dum Dum inserted two chrome fingers into the slit and removed a small, thin plastic object. He disconnected the wires from the corpse's body, and the weak red glow of the implant lit up Dum Dum's face.

It was Borg's holo-phone. And it still worked.

There was an even bigger problem. If the police wanted to close the case, they'd need to talk to him. A matter of routine, not because he was a suspect...Or maybe he was a suspect? He'd lived there his whole life—now all of a sudden, his mother was dead and he was nowhere to be found. Surely not a coincidence.

He checked the police protocols—they'd need his statement. Not only that—the building manager would want to know what he intended to do with the unit. Would Albert stay there or not? If he didn't, what about all the stuff inside? Rent was paid up for two more weeks—that gave him a little breathing room.

The only thing Albert wanted was lying at the bottom of his desk drawer. The shard containing the access code to the Cave, which contained the source code to the Taran.

Rache Bartmoss didn't possess tier two. Everything he created was typed on a regular keyboard, polished with deep dives on his homemade rig. It took him years. Albert knew that. But he didn't have years. The playing field looked completely different now than it had back then. The Blackwall was a post-Bartmoss creation that outmatched the capabilities of even the best netrunners. On the one hand, you had NetWatch patrolling the Net for illegal activity; on the other, traps laid by NETSEC, the police's Net security division.

To break through the Blackwall, first you had to find it. Not only was it camouflaged, its traps were also cleverly disguised to look like vulnerabilities. Obviously, there were no gates or tunnels. That would defeat its purpose, which was to seal off all access from outside and from within. There was no secret code that you could hack or steal. The Blackwall was exactly what its name suggested. Hidden, monolithic.

On paper, at least.

Albert sat on one of his new couches, eating the cheapest of his meal boxes. Meals that were completely devoid of flavor. Food was fuel for the machine that was his body, nothing more. It made him feel slightly less like an animal.

No one was here to remind him to take out the trash, or put his dirty clothes in the washing machine, or when it was time to eat. Turned out that his mother's nagging had organized his life. He needed some rhythm to follow—something to punctuate his daily existence. Five meals of equal proportion per day—surely that would create the kind of order his murdered mother once upheld.

The spoon he was holding stopped in midair. *Murdered.* He let the word hang in his mind. Of course, it was obvious now. You didn't bring in detectives, the whole damn forensics squad, for the death of a random woman living on a random floor of a random tower.

Murdered. It changed everything. The rush of associations cascading through his head made him lose his appetite.

He wasn't just linked to the case. He *was* the case. His mother had died because of him. They were looking for him and his mother happened to be in their way. Who could be after him? Not Militech, at least not directly. They could've hired someone, or maybe it was someone their impromptu gang had pissed off?

Should he warn the others? No. No contact with anyone—he had to go dark, put this all behind him. Maybe eventually it'd die down and everyone would forget about the whole thing.

Maybe.

No. You couldn't count on maybes.

He went over to his cyberdeck. He wouldn't even be able to send an encrypted message. Every connection could leave a trace. He couldn't configure the deck's security because the shard was still where it was. Do not cross. He couldn't bring himself to rip the tape.

What would Rache Bartmoss do? Wrong question. Bartmoss wouldn't have ever let the situation get this far out of hand. He'd be one, two steps ahead of everything. Though even he didn't foresee Arasaka dropping a tungsten rod onto his apartment block from orbit.

Albert paced around his unit, avoiding the part of the floor that was still bare cement. He thought with so much effort that he felt himself getting dizzy. He sat down. Then it flashed in his head like a light bulb. It was when he disabled the deck's security to free up RAM and send an unencrypted transmission. It lasted hardly a few seconds, but that was all they needed to track him down.

Warn the others or not? Was one option better or worse? He

quickly ran through the possible outcomes even though he already knew the answer. If he didn't warn Zor and the rest, they'd get caught by whoever was after them and acquire information about him, his whereabouts.

She didn't kiss at all like Milena. Aya's kiss was passionate but also delicate. Distant memories buried deep within him seemed to emerge from hibernation. Hope. That something that had been lost forever could be recovered again. It wouldn't be the same, but it was something.

His hand went under her sweater and traveled up along her back. Her skin was warm. Her body shivered as if a current ran down her spine. She pulled him tighter toward her, her hand firmly holding the back of his head.

The elevator was slowing down. 43...44...45...They unglued themselves from each other for a moment, knowing the decision had already been made and was about to be fulfilled.

Zor's phone vibrated just as the elevator doors opened. Zor glanced at the screen as they walked out. *Someone's after us. They came to my unit.* The toothpick lay at the foot of the door.

He quickly turned and pulled Aya toward the elevator. Without a word he punched "1" and mashed the button to close the doors. Aya looked back and forth between Zor and the hallway. The last thing they saw was the door to his unit opening just as the elevator's were closing.

Zor pulled her to the ground. A hail of bullets battered the elevator wall behind them. Aya didn't make a sound—only pressed herself against the floor. With a groan, the elevator started to descend.

He took out his pistol, flipped on his back and fired upward. He had no chance to hit—as long as they didn't get closer. At least not for a few more floors.

Aya tried to cover her head with her arms.

45...44...43...

Every few seconds, Zor fired. The bangs were deafening. Aya put her hands over her ears. Her right hand...She couldn't even move a finger.

39...38...

It was taking too long. By now they must have realized they could simply force open the doors, then unload on them or toss in a grenade and finish the job. Her right hand wasn't cooperating. It was stiff, unnaturally bent.

32...

Zor punched "25" so that the elevator didn't have to slow before it reached the floor. It worked; they stopped with a jolt. The doors opened. The *thud* of something falling onto the roof. They dashed out and made a beeline for the staircase. A flash, then a bang. They ducked instinctively but felt no blast of any kind.

Where were the stairs? Zor had never had to use them.

"This way." Aya shoved a pile of cardboard boxes in front of a door with an EXIT sign above it. She tried to push the door with her right hand, nearly falling over. Her hand was pressed to her ribs, completely numb.

They bounded down the stairs. The automatic lights switched on after a few flickers. The staircase hasn't been cleaned in months, maybe even years. They skipped steps as they went down, avoiding the litter. By the fifteenth floor, Aya was limping. Zor stopped to look at her. It was only now he noticed her right arm stuck to her side.

"You hit?" He reached out to her.

"No. It's—it's just a cramp." Her jaw tightened. "I'm fine."

Not true. She could barely walk—her other leg was already stiffening up. She fell onto the steps. Zor knelt beside her, trying to hold her up. Her whole body was frozen. She couldn't move a muscle.

"Don't have…much time…" she managed to croak through clenched teeth.

CHAPTER_8

"70-10, status update."

"70-10, standing by." The driver tossed out a half-smoked cigarette and closed the armored door.

"Code 1-4-1. Sending coordinates. All units respond."

"70-10, en route."

He slid down the tinted visor on his helmet and started the engine. The console display lit up with a map of the target's location and the fastest route. The driver didn't even have to look—it hovered in his retinal display. They pulled into traffic, lights flashing and siren wailing, forcing a few cars behind them to slam their brakes.

"One forty-one," said the soldier to his right. "Shit's goin' down."

" 'Bout fuckin' time."

They heard the familiar sound of weapons being loaded and checked in the back.

Traffic was the bane of almost every driver's existence in Night City. But before the truck's massive, sleek black hood, other cars were nothing but obstacles that obediently swerved out of their way.

"70-10, intercepting target in seventy seconds," the driver said.

If he could, he'd ram through every single car. Code 141 even allowed it. But there was always a chance the truck could get damaged—or even cause a pileup. The risk was minimal, but proto-col was clear—avoid collision if possible.

They passed dilapidated, graffiti-covered buildings as they seam-lessly traversed the unkempt streets of Vista Del Rey, then with a screech they swerved onto the road leading to Charter Hill.

"*Target is driving a silver Quadra 66,*" the dispatcher's voice crackled through the radio. "*Priority is to secure the target. Eliminate hostiles only if target safety is not jeopardized.*"

Two more dots appeared the map, both heading toward the same objective, though the other patrols were farther out.

"70-10, I have a visual on the target," the soldier to the right announced.

The silver Quadra zigzagged as it tried to dodge the other cars. Fifty yards behind it, a black Villefort Cortes was giving chase. It was larger, heavier, harder to maneuver, but it was gaining. Finally, the Quadra veered into a nearly empty parking lot in front of a strip mall. Only seconds later, the Villefort made the turn. That's when it spotted the patrol truck. With a screech of its tires, it turned back into the street and sped off with a roar.

"70-10, permission to pursue hostiles," the driver said. "One hun-dred percent chance of interception."

"*Negative, 70-10. Primary objective is to secure the target.*"

The truck overtook the Quadra and stopped beside it, covering it in case they came under fire.

"Move out! Go, go!"

The soldiers spilled out onto the asphalt and expertly took up their positions. Two of them fired shots at the Villefort speed-ing away, but even if they landed, they wouldn't stop it. The third covered their six, and two more moved toward the Quadra. It was undamaged; the driver's door was open. No one was inside.

"Militech unit 70-10." The soldier spoke into his comms as he looked around the abandoned lot. "Area secured."

A few long seconds passed before a woman in a suit calmly emerged from behind one of the pillars. Unshaken, composed. She lit a cigarette before making her way toward the squad. Two of the soldiers' ID scans flashed on their visors. They lowered their weapons.

"It's okay, I'm fine." She signaled to them reassuringly. "Did you get them?"

The driver cocked his head.

"70-10 to central. Target is inquiring about assailants."

"70-15 is currently in pursuit. Success at thirty percent and falling."

Milena shook her head but smiled. Things were happening. That could mean only one thing—she was alive.

ArS-03, log 53127.
Synchronization procedure initiated.
Unidentified device NI100101001110. Status: unknown.
No additional subsystems detected.

She woke up to the smell of coffee. She tried to remember where she was before she opened her eyes.

"Feeling better?" Zor sat next to her, holding out a mug.

She sat up on the mattress and took it with both hands. She nodded.

"Why don't you have time?" Zor asked.

She looked at him in confusion.

"Before. On the stairs. You said 'Don't have much time.' I'm guessing it wasn't because of whoever we were running away from."

She took a few sips.

"I need money," she said quietly. "Lots of it. Unless Ron gets a new cyberarm, which also costs a fortune."

She wore a loose T-shirt with a cartoon ad printed on it. She didn't remember putting it on. Didn't remember this place, either. She looked around. A fairly spacious room with a glass wall and the mattress they were sitting on in the center. Beside her a neatly folded pile of clothes. Her clothes. Night outside.

"Ron told me to give you something to help you sleep."

Aya suddenly fully awoke and peered out the window. It was the middle of the night.

"I need to go home." She got up in a hurry and started to dress.

She grabbed her phone. Message to M: "Had a small accident. Coming home now."

"Wouldn't advise that." A short, skinny teenager with a mane of unkempt black hair sat at a desk tinkering with a disassembled cyberdeck.

She hadn't noticed him before.

"Albert," Zor explained. "The netrunner."

"I thought..." she broke off, stunned.

She always imagined him as someone older, more serious-looking, like a Voodoo Boy. Albert didn't dress like anyone or anything. His clothes were plain, nondescript. He had light-brown skin and long black curly hair. He didn't even look like an experienced netrunner— more like an aloof high school geek.

"How did you find him?" she asked Zor.

"He's the one who found us."

"They'll be looking for you there," he said without even glancing at her.

"Who?" she asked.

"I'll know as soon as I can access the Cave. Right now, my means are limited. We need to work together."

"I need to go home." Aya started heading toward the door.

"If they knew where Zor lived, then that means they got Borg," he said with about as much pity as his computerized voice. "It's safe to assume he told them everything. But he didn't know about this place. We're safe here."

Aya froze, letting the information sink in.

"All the more reason I have to go." She opened the door.

"What for?" Zor asked.

She didn't answer.

He threw on his jacket and followed her out.

"Floor?"

"Sixty-one." Aya reached for the button.

Zor was faster. He punched sixty-four instead and the doors slid shut. He took out his pistol and gave it a once-over. Aya watched the floor numbers change with apprehension. Zor wasn't reassured by her tense expression.

"Someone live with you?" he asked.

She nodded. He didn't know what to ask next.

They stepped out onto the sixty-fourth floor. The door to the first unit on the right was open. A man in a stained tank top with a beer gut stumbled toward them, either wasted or skezzed.

"'Ey, man! Spare a smoke?"

"I don't smoke."

"C'mon, man," he insisted. "Just one."

Zor's arm shot out, slamming the man against the wall, cracking it. He slumped to the floor, whimpering in pain.

The staircase here was even more littered than the ones in Zor's building. He held Aya's hand as they went down so she wouldn't trip, but more to prevent her from running ahead of him.

"Any security?" He pushed open the door to the hallway.

"Like what?"

"Besides the biometric."

"No, none."

They stood on either side of the door to her unit. Aya was itching to open it and run straight inside. He didn't let go of her hand. They couldn't know if anyone was in the unit.

"Open it." Zor pulled out his pistol. "And stay behind me."

Aya placed her hand on the biometric panel. It turned green and beeped with authorization. The door slid open. He peered inside and drew back again. Nothing. He held his pistol upward and quietly went inside, hugging the wall. His intuition told him there was no one home. No one alive, that is. The legs of a woman sticking out from the right-side bedroom doorway didn't bode well. But he had to make sure. It was a two-bedroom unit, bigger than his. Neat, unpretentious.

Aya couldn't wait any longer outside. She ran in and leaped over the elderly woman's body and into the bedroom.

"Juliena!" she yelled, though it was obvious no one was home. "Juliena!!!"

Zor tapped the panel to close the unit's door. The last thing they needed were nosy neighbors. He knelt down to make sure that, despite appearances, the woman was actually dead. It wasn't hard to deduce the cause of death—multiple stab wounds to the elderly lady's neck. Mantis Blades. There wasn't even that much blood. Whoever did this was methodical, discreet.

"Juliena?!" Aya rummaged through the closet.

"There's no one here." Zor grabbed her by the shoulders. "Who's Juliena? Your daughter?"

She shook her head and wrapped her arms around Zor, sobbing quietly.

"It's…it's complicated," she answered.

"Could she have gone somewhere?"

"By herself? No." She sniffled. "She never went out alone. She's…unique."

"Don't worry; they won't hurt her. They need her alive."

"How do you know?! They killed Molly and yesterday they tried to kill us!"

"No." Zor held her tighter. "The shots went over our heads. Then they dropped a gas canister onto the cabin. They wanted to catch us."

"Why?"

"I don't know. They want something from us. Now they don't need to look, because they know we'll come to them. I don't know who these people are, but for now Juliena's safe. I promise."

"For now…?"

Aya knelt down beside Molly and touched her hand. The cold, lifeless skin made her quickly recoil.

"How did I get mixed up in all this…?" She put her face in her hands. She sighed and looked up at Zor. "Is it money they want?"

Zor shook his head.

Not counting the dead body, the unit was in near-perfect order. Whoever came here didn't bother looking around for anything. Just the girl.

"She took her tablet." Aya's hand brushed over the bare table. "She always keeps it with her."

She looked at Zor expectantly. "What now?"

"They'll stall for time. Keep us waiting to wear us down. Maybe two days before they make contact. Then we'll know what they're after."

"Shouldn't we…go to the police?"

"If we were normal people, sure. But not after everything we've done. We show up at the precinct, I guarantee you they'll be more interested in us than in finding Juliena. Sooner or later, they'll put the pieces together, tie us back to our little escapades."

The state of Albert's old unit was worse. Far worse. There were multiple footprints in the brown puddle that filled up a sizable part of the living room floor. Judging by the conspicuous absence of furniture and home appliances, it wasn't hard to guess what had happened.

The police tape lay torn on the floor. The door stood slightly ajar, unable to fully close. The desk with the priceless shard at the bottom of its drawer could be anywhere.

"They kill his mother and he just up and moves, figures that's that?" Aya shook her head. "This is pointless, all of it. We make small mistakes and end up just walking into bigger ones. Did I ever tell you how Warden blackmailed me into this?"

"You don't have to."

"He threatened to tell Marry's about my implants." She lifted her hand and moved her fingers. "I was scared they'd fire me. Could hardly matter now."

They wouldn't find anything here. They were too late.

He drummed his fingers even harder against the SUV's crooked, scuffed steering wheel. Two hours had passed. This was starting to be tedious. He never established how long he'd wait. There was nothing interesting outside to look at—nothing to kill the time. Just sketchy alleyways, graffiti and gang tags. Still, the area was relatively safe. The question was whether it was safe *today*.

There was no blinking neon sign above the entrance anymore, only a small info board and an arrow pointing down past an iron door corroded by time and acid rain. Better this way—wouldn't be any random walk-ins, least of all on a Sunday. Ron had already stopped running ads, relying instead on recommendations from satisfied customers. Word of mouth traveled faster and didn't cost an enny.

If they found out where Albert and Zor lived, that meant his clinic was next. Extra precautions had to be taken. But how extra? Was two hours long enough? It was starting to get warm in the car despite the shade.

One more minute.

Albert didn't seem the least bit broken up about his mother's death. His own mother. Everyone was different, he supposed. Sometimes scarily so. The more he thought about it, the more it actually completed the picture of Albert that Ron had in his head. But Aya had it the worst. She had no more than a few weeks left to live if her implants weren't repaired. It wouldn't be a pleasant way to go. And that was putting it mildly.

Screw this. Not like parking here was safe, either. He got out and flung the empty duffle bag over his shoulder that he'd stuff with basic equipment, scanners and little miscellaneous tools that could come in handy. The worst would be disassembling the operating chair—he'd need to hire at least two odd-jobbers with at least tier-three lift-ware. Couple hundo right there, which he plain didn't have.

He looked around warily as he walked, regretting he didn't park closer. If he saw someone suspicious, that'd only mean they'd spotted him earlier. Luckily, nobody around fit that description except the two resident drunks sitting on the curb. Regulars. Nothing out of the ordinary.

He went slowly down the stairs to the clinic. Could've had some kind of anti-burglary system...Like a string in the doorframe. Should've thought of that before.

He put his ear between the iron bars to the door, then placed his hand on the biometric panel. When it turned green, he entered the code. The door slid open as usual. He squinted through the dark, trying to make out if anyone was inside. Pointless. They could've shot him in a second where he stood in the light.

He unlocked the iron gate and quickly went inside, peeking around the corners. Not even so much as a roach. Then the door behind him suddenly opened.

"Fucksicle." Ron backed up against the freezer, his hand on his chest. "Forgot to lock it again…"

"Least you still got a door," said the first of the two gargantuan brutes that sauntered into his clinic. His voice was unnaturally deep. Of course they wouldn't wait inside. They'd been staking out his place, waiting for him to turn up.

"Been waitin' since sundown, so our patience has run a little dry. Don't make this harder than it needs to be."

He couldn't make it harder for them if he'd wanted to. There was only one way in and out. He could try the chair's manipulators, but first he'd have to jack in and activate them. They weren't that strong, either. Not as strong as their muscles.

There was no mistaking their affiliation. Animals. Mounds of muscle pumped with steroids extracted from assorted quadrupeds and vertebrates, their brains modded with synthesized animal hormones. Hard to tell if all of that made them less human than the advanced cybernetics Ron chipped his clients with.

Even for Animals, these two were heavily zoomodified. Their faces were a dead giveaway. One of them had a tusk growing out of the lower corner of his mouth. The other had the face and teeth of a tiger. Their figures alone resembled that of two-legged warthogs on supersteroids. Their shoulders were twice as large as the average man's and looked as if they were about to burst out of their synth-leather biker jackets.

Ron stared at their muscle mass. Without coolware, they'd overheat in a thirty-yard dash. But right now, he wouldn't make it six feet.

"What can I do for you?" he asked, sweating despite the cool basement.

"Pay Bully what youse owe, dickface," said the first snaggletusked Animal.

"Oh...that." Ron relaxed. "Paid half of it two weeks ago."

"Half sound like full to you?"

"Guess the deadline must be coming up."

"Tryin' to be fuckin' funny?" Pigface stepped closer and held a fist up to his jaw that was bigger than Ron's entire head.

The ripperdoc instinctively recoiled. Not only did he look like a warthog, he stank like one, too. Ron had never smelled a warthog, much less seen one with his own eyes, but he imagined that if he had, it would look and smell exactly like the thing standing in front of him. Not really the time for musing, but he knew they were only here to warn him.

"Fucking insect," Pigface growled.

"Who, me?"

"Oughta crush you like one. That what youse want?!"

The Animal's muscles became tense and his face darkened. Ron suspected they didn't have permission to hurt him, never mind crush him like an insect. Bully knew that a ripperdoc with nonfunctioning cyberarms was not a profitable ripperdoc. He was safe for now, but if Bully didn't see his eddies, Ron wouldn't wear such a brave face come next time.

That didn't mean he shouldn't be careful. Animals were notoriously unstable. Doers, not thinkers. Like warthogs. Or tigers.

"When do I gotta settle?" Ron asked, though he knew perfectly well.

"You're past due." Big Cat spoke for the first time, his big cat canines visible. He was bulkier, clearly the one in charge. "Day befores yesterday. Rumor has it youse flush all of a sudden."

"That I'm...what?" Ron was genuinely confused. "Does it look like I'm sittin' on a pile of cash? You see what I'm driving?"

"Cut the shit." Big Cat lost his patience. "We knows you scored big time."

"Haven't cashed in the goods yet." Ron felt the bind he was in acutely. He knew that selling those batteries wouldn't cover his debt, but he also knew that contradicting an ill-tempered Animal was a very, very bad idea. "It's only been two days."

"I don't gives a fuck 'bout two days ago. Talkin' 'bout the Mili-tech convoy youse hit before that."

"Ooooh, that...You got me. Was a decent haul, that."

"See? Just hads to refresh your memory." Pigface patted him on the cheek, which felt like being slapped with a dirty rubber doormat wrapped around a brick. "Nows cough up the eddies and we'll be on our merry fuckin' way."

"Still gotta cash in the last job..."

"What are youse, a fuckin' collector?"

"Hey, stuff ain't easy to sell." Ron felt as if he were zigzagging through a minefield. "But I already got a buyer. He's really set on it. The deal, I mean."

Big Cat leaned over so close that his whiskers nearly brushed against Ron's face. He held his breath.

"Two days."

Albert sat motionless in his chair, staring at the disassembled cyber-deck lit up by the small desk lamp. Night was slowly giving way to dawn outside the window.

"It's not looking good," he said finally.

"What was on that shard?" Zor asked.

"The access code to the Cave."

"Care to be more specific?"

"The access code to the rest of me—my Net tools, everything. Can't do anything without them." He motioned dejectedly toward the deck. "I'm adding components that'll boost its capabilities. But only by a little. It'll still be useless without that code."

"We won't find your shard. Better come up with something else."

"I'm not going to remember a string of two hundred and fifty-six characters that I glanced over in passing five years ago."

Three months wouldn't even be enough to rebuild it all, he thought.

Aya sat on the couch, clearly uninterested in the discussion. She stared at the cardboard box lying in the middle of the room.

"What's that?" she finally asked, pointing.

Albert left the cyberdeck and went over to the coffee machine, avoiding a section of the floor that was bare concrete. He didn't like stepping on bare concrete.

"I ordered furniture," he said. "You know…you can't go back. Ever."

"What do you mean?"

"Your units. Death traps, both. Only logical they'd be under surveillance. This is the impromptu gang's new headquarters."

"What the hell are you talking about?" Aya shook her head in disbelief. "You're still hung up on this gang thing? That's the whole reason we're in this mess!"

"True. It's also our only way of getting out of it."

"We need money," Zor added. "Make that three coffees, Albert. No ordinary gig's going to make enough to buy Juliena back, or pay to fix your issues, or..." He didn't finish. He went over to Aya and sat down next to her.

There was a beep at the door. Zor jumped to his feet, pulled out his pistol and aimed directly at it.

Albert left the coffees in the machine and went to the intercom. It was door by door—no intercom system for the whole building, or even parts of it. People couldn't agree on anything these days. The man who appeared on the little LED screen was standing right out front.

He unlocked it.

"They came to my place." Ron burst into the unit, not bothering to close the door behind him. "Someone fucking ratted us out."

The door would have closed by itself if Zor hadn't immediately tapped the panel.

"The clinic?" Aya asked.

He nodded and laid a heavy duffel bag on the floor, the contents within clanging together. He sighed as he unzipped it, took out an unlabeled quart bottle of clear liquid and set it down on the table.

"Sedative." He untwisted the cap. "Pure alcohol—distilled by yours truly. It'll get you loaded, but also loosen the synapses—get our creativity flowing. And creativity's exactly what we need right now. Kicks like a mule, though, so better find something to mix it with..."

They all sat at the dining table. He poured out the coffee and refilled the mugs with the alcohol, topping it up with juice from the fridge. Only Albert made it clear that he'd rather stick with coffee.

"Things ain't looking good," the ripperdoc began. "They're hot on our tail and this building has exactly zero security." He pointed back to the door. "I waltzed straight in, no questions asked."

"Plan is for them not to find us here," Albert replied. "What I need is a tier-two netrunning rig. Won't get anything done without it. Besides that, we need a solid plan, intel and some half-decent weapons."

"You mean another heist." Aya hung her head in despair. "What makes you think we'll get lucky a third time?"

"We won't. We'll get a fixer."

"What for? Fixers take cuts, you know."

"For intel on what to klep and not worry about how to offload one hundred and eighty corp-drone batteries," Ron replied. "Makes sense. Except who?"

"Warden," Albert answered.

All eyes turned to him in astonishment.

"He's the one who started all this!"

"Can't say I'm particularly fond of him," Zor said. "Nor do I trust him."

"You don't have to like fixers," Albert explained. "But Warden's the devil we already know. He could've killed us on the spot, but he didn't. He's also ambitious, wants to get rid of Renner and take command. We can use that."

"Borg knew him best."

"Borg's dead," Albert replied. "Or at least there's a ninety-nine percent chance he is. Whoever's after us doesn't care who they kill. They're doing it for sport. Borg must've given them your addresses. They got to me a different way."

"How?" Ron took a sip and winced. "Agh, must be the juice..."

"Back in Northside I had to momentarily disable encryption to save you. It left a signal leading straight back to me."

"There's also Milena." Aya looked at Ron.

"Wouldn't count on her." Ron sighed. "She's not answering my calls. Our corpo princess must've gotten bored already."

*   *   *

"It was nothing really; I'm fine," she repeated.

"Our doctors said you should be kept under observation for a couple days."

"I don't have a couple of days."

They sat on opposite ends of the table in what resembled an interrogation room. Encouraged honesty, she imagined. Milena couldn't spot any cameras, but she knew they were concealed somewhere.

Stanley pulled a silver cigarette case out of his charcoal blazer and offered her a cigarette.

"Can't smoke in here," she said, though she knew the rules didn't apply to him.

She took the cigarette. It wasn't flavored and she didn't have her holder. Oh well.

Stanley held out an ancient-looking metal Zippo. It flipped open with that unmistakable click and Milena caught a whiff of the butane as she leaned into the flame. Only the head of security could carry something like that around HQ.

"The day after tomorrow," she said as she exhaled. "It's the last round of negotiations."

"Sure you're feeling up to it?"

Stanley didn't smoke himself. He hid the cigarette case and set the lighter upright on the table.

"Katsuo won't agree to putting it off," she explained. "It ends two days from now, no matter the result. This isn't a good time to bring in a replacement."

"Because no one's as well prepared as you?"

"Not at this moment, no."

"Why don't you tell me exactly what happened."

"I was sitting in my car, driving out of the garage on autopilot. I was going over the material for today's meeting. It's all in my head, of course, but I like to refresh my memory. Then I realized that car was following me."

"A feeling you had?"

"Intuition. I won't go into detail as to how, exactly. That's what this company pays me for. When they started following me, I activated the distress signal. The rest you already know." She took a puff and exhaled. "How much longer is this interrogation going to take?"

Stanley's expression became serious.

"This isn't an interrogation." He leaned back.

The cable running from her neuroport to the diagnostics reader beneath the table implied otherwise. Officially, her implants were being scanned for spyware that might have been installed without her knowledge. Or with it.

"Not long ago you were involved in a serious accident on the beltway," Stanley continued.

"The driver was at fault. He was going too fast. I don't see what more needs explaining."

"It's worth examining seemingly unrelated events. I'm trying to find out who attacked you yesterday."

"Nobody attacked me. I was being followed."

"Perhaps they were attempting to kidnap you. I need to establish whether your safety is still at risk. You're one of this company's most valued assets."

She couldn't read his intentions, plans or what he knew. But she knew what he was about to say next.

"Do you think it could've been Arasaka?" he inquired.

"You're the head of security—you tell me."

"I thought you prided yourself on your intuition."

She inhaled with relief. Shame that smoking wasn't allowed

during negotiation. Every second spent inhaling and exhaling brought with it fresh ideas and a focus-sharpening shot of nicotine.

"From what I know of Katsuo, they wouldn't do that," she answered.

Stanley's expression became somehow even more severe.

"You're an expert in psychology, not military strategy—am I right?" He straightened a crease on his charcoal suit. "Time to up the stakes. I have a proposition for you—an assignment."

"Got serious balls showin' up here. Coulda ended all of you before like *this*." He snapped his fingers. "Wishin' now I did. Muthafucka can't drink in peace 'cause o' what y'all pulled."

"I'm not here to…" Zor interrupted himself. "Just hear me out." Without being prompted, Zor sat across from him at the bar table. "We want to make you an offer. Strictly biz."

"Shit, been dreaming this day would come. Ha, ha!" Seeing his translucent blue teeth as he laughed was not a pleasant sight.

"A'ight, go on. Spill." Warden topped up his drink with a half-empty bottle of rum.

"We need a fixer."

"Oh, do you now? You realize y'all got lucky, right? Ran into a bunch of rookies from Militech, hit an empty warehouse full of useless crap. Offed some grandpa while you were at it. And for what? What'd you gonks even haul outta there? Fuckin' screwdrivers?"

The virtually empty bar was devoid of its usual commotion. The few customers around evidently didn't mind their own company.

"Something like that," Zor admitted. "Which is why we need a fixer to tell us when, where and what to steal."

"Listen, choombatta." Warden's patience was thinning. "You ain't professionals and you sure as shit ain't no gang. That heist was a goddamn stroke of luck. Y'all just needed to have a clean record. That's it. Congratu-fuckin-lations, y'all somehow weaseled your way outta that one alive. And the warehouse? Whatever y'all klepped, y'all got no idea how to offload it and you think I'm gonna help? Psh," he scoffed. "Got a snot-nosed kid with chicken wire for cables and a ripper operatin' with a kitchen knife, 'cause y'all ain't got the scratch for nothin' else. Oh, and let's not forget that joytoy who don't wanna put out and that fake-ass corpo nympho pretendin' she still young, that gonk with the green hair… And you." He looked Zor up and down in disdain. "You don't even got basic combat implants. So get the fuck outta my face before I make you."

The cloudless sky was getting dark. The sun's spectacle of reds and oranges was underway, intensified even more by Night City's sky-high pollution levels.

Zor sat in the middle of the living room and tried to put his thoughts in order. It wasn't working.

Albert lay on the armchair beside him. He'd been submerged in cyberspace for hours now, trying to rebuild what he'd lost. Ron had managed to scrounge up a mattress from somewhere and was now snoring in the other room. Aya tossed and turned as she slept. Zor pushed away the pizza and hamburger boxes to the corner of the counter and got up to close Ron's door. Then he went into their room and gently covered Aya with a blanket. She turned in her sleep. Was that a smile? He stood looking at her for a long while, lost in thought.

Evening. The sky over Night City was awash in pink. The windows of Corpo Plaza towers lazily reflected the setting sun's last rays, flooding Milena's bedroom with warm, natural light. She'd disabled the window tinting on purpose. Light wakes you up better than caffeine, taurine, or any other substance. She didn't want to sleep yet.

It was moments like these when the perfection of the corporate world revealed its cracks. Seemingly immaculate, flawless towers, but from here you could see the minuscule imperfections in the placement of the windows. Some reflected a blinding white, while others the sky's pink. The angle of incidence and reflection combined with distance. You needed distance to see the full scale of imperfection.

It had been days—nothing changed. The stress ate away at you from the inside like the eagle pecking on Prometheus's liver for eternity, never letting you feel anything except... well, that. Whether you had something to lose or gain, adrenaline always accompanied risk. In this life, winning was a constant standard to uphold. The only thing that could change it was losing. Failing. You started out giving your all and eventually your all became a never-ending obligation. If you tripped, you fell. And there were more pitfalls and trapdoors in the corporate world than any stairs leading upward.

Ron was the latest deviation from the norm. He was interesting, though sometimes vulgar—but only because he was honest. He never calculated his words to achieve an effect. It was hard to tell what he'd throw at you next. That's what made talking to him entertaining. The sex was also unpredictable. One day it'd be perfect and the next... forgettable.

Or maybe the perfect world just didn't exist? Her self-analysis system was still active. Couldn't uninstall the piece of shit—her contract prohibited it. Or maybe it was impossible to keep being surprised? Not by the what, but by the how. Or by how the how changed. That was self-analysis for you—reducing everything to absurdity.

Why not? If this was all that reality had to offer, why not dive head-on into the absurd?

Could Katsuo have been behind the attack? Why? Because she clearly had the upper hand in the negotiation? Or maybe she'd been looking at this all wrong. Maybe it was Stanley who was trying to quietly get rid of her. He might not know about her double life, but he could have his suspicions.

She went over to the window wall and stood there. Naked. Nobody could see her body—at least not without telescopic optics. But the thought that in theory, somewhere, someone might try gave her the slightest of thrills.

The impromptu gang had no future. Or more specifically, no future with Milena in it. Everyone apart from her wanted to make money, but for the lowest possible risk. Money didn't matter to her. Whatever she made, she spent. Didn't bother saving. She wanted more from life. Something that couldn't be bought. Something that even braindance—that cheap substitute for reality—couldn't offer.

Time to up the stakes. She blinked an eye and thought-dictated a message: "Day after tomorrow, eleven thirty AM, external elevator."

CHAPTER_9

N ame was Molly Bernard—lived right across the hall," the rookie said. "This unit's being rented by an Aya Holmes. No record, but I did some digging through the Net and found this." The tablet displayed a half-naked dancer advertising Marry's Bar. "That's her. I checked the logs from the biometric. Aya Holmes left her unit yesterday at seven ten PM and came back today at four sixteen AM. Left again after only two minutes."

Liam nodded in half praise. He chewed on a piece of gum as he read the tablet.

Forensics was combing through the entire unit. The only place they'd secured all available evidence was the narrow hallway that led from the kitchen annex near the entrance to a bedroom. There was another, smaller bedroom. The one the dead neighbor's legs were sticking out of.

"Thoughts. Let's hear 'em," the detective said, not looking away from the tablet.

The rookie leaned as close to the body as she could without stepping on it.

"Stab wounds to the neck," she said. "Vertical, evenly spaced. If Mrs. Bernard wasn't almost eighty, I'd say Mantis Blades."

"What's age got to do with it?"

"You don't use Mantis Blades on an old lady. Besides, what use would a dancer have for them?"

"You think Miss Holmes did it?"

The rookie puffed out her cheeks and sighed.

"Can't rule it out. It's her unit—she came back for a sec, then disappeared."

"Miss Holmes left her unit yesterday at seven in the evening. Ms. Bernard died just after midnight."

"How do you know that?" The rookie bent over once more for a closer look. "You didn't even scan her yet."

"I didn't have to. The only working camera is on the first-floor hallway. I checked the feed. There's a gap between twelve and twelve fifteen AM." Liam brought up the recording and fast-forwarded to 4:16 AM. "Here."

"She's not alone," the rookie remarked.

Aya was accompanied by a young man dressed like someone who wanted to keep a low profile, though it wasn't enough to disguise his posture and gait—that of a soldier's.

The detective zoomed in on his face and initiated a facial recognition search. It took a few seconds before a match appeared.

"Got a hit." The inspector scanned the record. "Zor. No last name. Owner of a pest extermination company named Buyers & Son filed a claim for property damage—a van, to be exact." He scrolled farther down. "Same van that's sitting in Harris's yard where a security guard was murdered."

"With Mantis Blades," the rookie added grimly.

The flickering light revealed portions of an old brick wall held together by anchor plates—remnants of an ancient underground hall whose original purpose was unknown.

The black blood glistened.

Bodies hung from the steel girders. Some naked, others clothed, their hanging skin cut with utmost precision into long strips and patterns. Some were twisted together in a braid, still dripping blood. None of the cuts went deeper than a few millimeters. None were still alive.

Black smoke from the torches rose up toward the darkness of the ceiling, too high for the light to reach. The place wasn't chosen randomly. The sublevel's ventilation effectively filtered out the smoke.

Renner watched the exhibit with mild disgust. Some degree of sadism was useful when it came to work, but not in your free time. Might as well turn shitting and pissing into an art, too.

"Place gives me the creeps," Ross murmured.

"Welcome to Northside," Renner said. "Fuckin' whacked, these psychos."

Both sipped on drinks handed to them at the entrance. Too sweet, definitely not strong enough. They ditched their empty glasses with relief and plucked something stronger off the trays. Tequila— paid with tokens exchanged for eddies at the entrance. So much for exclusivity.

Around two hundred people shuffled around, drinking, chatting, briefly putting aside their beefs and mutual animosity. Rival gangs coexisting, pretending to not want the other wiped off the face of the earth, making small talk and appreciating "art." Even if 90 percent of them couldn't tell a sculpture from the newest Voytech washing machine. You just had to show up and try not to cap anyone in the face. This was neutral, sacred ground. *Sacred.* Funny, using that word here.

All heads were turned toward the artist on tall, spring-loaded stilts who was hard at work on a corpse. Sorry, *sculpture*, Renner scoffed to himself. The dark-skinned, twentysomething-year-old with a tattooed skull had her Mantis Blades drawn. With virtuosic precision, she carved a rhombus-checkered pattern onto the torso of her next miserable victim. Well, maybe not miserable—poor fuck was already dead. She peeled off the diamond-shaped pieces of human skin, still dripping with blood, and tossed them behind her into the crowd. The spectators jostled against one another to catch them. The Animals in the crowd roared, demanding more gore, innards. They wouldn't get them. This was art. Body cutting wasn't butchering.

A few more cuts. She framed the checkered pattern with intricate swirls, then triumphantly raised her arms, the blades glistening with black blood in the flickering light. The crowd applauded; the show was over. The hall became flooded with more light, but the darkness farther within remained unchanged.

Waiters in elegant white uniforms simultaneously lifted the lids of silver platters, revealing appetizers that looked better than they tasted. Synth-seasoned synth-meat in various shapes and forms. Gourmet scop, in other words. Courtesy of Raito Catering, their logo on full display, unashamed to be associated with the event.

"Still don't get it," Ross said. "Sure, blades got a nine-foot reach, but you'd still be bringing a knife to a gun fight, know what I'm sayin'?"

"Practical in close quarters," Renner scoffed. "Things draw in less than a fifth of a second. Faster than you can aim and pull a trigger. Care to remind me again why the fuck we're here?"

"Want to make you an offer," Dum Dum said.

Renner turned abruptly. He didn't like it when people were taller. The Maelstromer had a good two inches on him. Probably 'cause of those heavy combat boots that were far from classy. The fumes emanating from the nearby propane heaters gave his multiple optics an orange-reddish streak.

"Shit, you know it's not Halloween yet, right?" Renner scoffed. "What offer? Make it quick—startin' to get hungry."

"You jumped a Militech convoy—stole a container," Dum Dum said, unfazed. "Still haven't sold it. Which means you can't find a buyer."

Renner stared at him for a moment.

"No idea what you're talking about."

"Ask Warden—I'm sure he'll lay it out for you. You've got a serious problem on your hands, but I might just have the solution. It's a win-win."

Next to them Karla landed another flip on her stilts. Sweating, with a smile, she crouched down to the height of the crowd and gave a low bow. Dum Dum grabbed hold of her, in part to steady her. She positioned the Mantis Blades in such a way as to avoid blood seeping into the slits in her forearms. Beneath the web of scars on her face, something like satisfaction was visible.

Renner looked at her, then at the drops of blood running down the cuffs of his sleeves.

"This here's real leather, you know." He took a napkin and vigorously wiped it off with irritation.

"And that's real blood." Dum Dum raised one boot onto the couch and leaned on it. "So what did you think?"

"About the human sushi demonstration?" Renner stared at the one-and-a-half-foot-long blades with slight apprehension. "Want the polite answer or the honest one?"

"What difference does it make? You're incapable of either."

"I thought the case was closed."

"What gave you that idea?"

"Well, um, 'cause..." Harris cleared his throat to buy some time. "Cases like these usually just, y'know...get closed."

"Not this one." Liam chewed his gum and looked at the owner intently. Not because he suspected something, but because clearly Harris thought there was something to be suspicious about. "Someone threaten you recently?"

"Oh, I get along just fine with everyone." He tried to sound casual.

Harris of Harris's Auto Repair was well over fifty with a face that didn't lend any credibility to his claim of getting along "just fine" with everyone. He was shorter than the detective—no implants at first glance. But looks only went skin-deep. Same could be said for everyone in these parts.

They stood facing each other in a small office behind the security booth.

"Your employees. One of 'em could've pissed off someone dangerous, maybe," the detective suggested. "Or owed money."

"Wouldn't know anything about that," the owner said impatiently. He kept glancing at his terminal as if he had important work to get back to.

So what if he did? Work could wait—the more urgent, the better. Whatever made him spill the truth quicker.

"Didn't even know his goddamn name..." Harris said all of a sudden. "Hired him for the night shift 'cause it was cheaper than any of the security corps. Got here at sundown, left around dawn. Crossed paths three times maybe."

It wasn't impatience. He was surprised. Surprised that someone like Liam actually gave a shit about what happened to an old, dead nobody.

"Cutting costs on security..." Liam pulled up a chair and sat down. "Somehow never pays off."

Harris's shoulders sagged—it was clear he wasn't going to get rid of the badge. Couldn't threaten him, force him to leave, either. The

NCPD wasn't the most respected tribe in town, but woe to anyone who dared lay a finger on them.

"Look, detective…" Harris finally sat down with resignation. "I don't know why what happened…happened, okay? Nothing was stolen—nobody's ever bothered us before. Maybe what's-his-face had some personal issue—"

"John. Your employee's name was John Smolarski. No relatives. Did you notice anything unusual in the days leading up to his murder?"

"Hmm…" The owner shook his head. "Nope, nothing comes to mind. Everything seemed normal, apart from, y'know, what's-his-face getting killed."

No, it wasn't impatience. Something was bothering him—something he was trying to suppress. Liam's diagnostic cyberware constantly monitored his heart rate and the cortisol levels in his blood. High, both.

"You don't usually come to the garage by yourself at night, do you?"

Harris hesitated.

"Sometimes. Usually 'cause I forget something."

"Samuel Buyers. He left a van for you to repair."

Harris's pulse and pressure spiked; he guessed the cortisol would follow in a few seconds.

"Yeah, I remember…Been takin' a while, that one."

The few seconds passed. He was right.

"Took a look at that van before coming in here," the detective said. "Doesn't look like an easy fix. You're charging him three hundred, spare parts included. Little low, don't you think? Usually pay that much for a dent and some scratches."

Harris scratched his stubbled cheeks. He was at a complete loss.

"If I had to guess, I'd say you aren't getting along 'just fine' with everyone." Liam spat his gum out into the garbage can. "Everyone and their grandma 'round these parts owes something to everyone else. Been on the force long enough to know it when I see it. So, here's what's gonna happen—I'm gonna ask you one simple question, and if you give me the right answer, you'll never have to see my face again. The day before Smolarski was murdered, did someone—illegally of course—'borrow' that van?"

Kabuki. Where the hell else? Ron parked the beat-up SUV in what was probably the darkest alleyway he could find. Dusk was setting in; the sun was slowly giving way to the fuzzy glow of neon.

"Know 'im?" Zor asked.

"'Course I do." Ron got out. "As much as you can know anyone via text."

Zor got out of the car and felt for the pistol behind his belt. Wouldn't be of much help if it turned out they were in deeper shit than they thought. Still—couldn't hurt to keep up appearances.

They stood before the entrance to what looked like a garage that had seen better days—maybe a fire or two.

"You realize how much your implants would be worth to Scavs, right?" Zor asked.

"They're foolproof." He raised his hand and moved his fingers. "Don't work if they're not attached to my body."

"Imagine their disappointment once they find out."

They walked past a homeless man slouched against the wall, asleep. Or at least he looked asleep. Stepping over a layer of trash, they found themselves in a dark hallway. One end of it led to the busy street, the other to a small, well-shaped courtyard with five floors of balconies rising above it, laundry hung out to dry. Above, the sounds of children playing, neighbors arguing, but at least nobody watching over the railings.

"Middle door," Ron said.

Only one of the doors had a handle. It was crooked and covered with faded and partially torn stickers. Very welcoming.

Ron hesitated. Should he knock or just go in? There was no doorbell.

"Remember, we're acting as professionals." He grabbed the handle but hesitated to twist it. "We're here to negotiate."

He pushed open the door. The interior was a cluttered shack posing as a candy store. From the layer of dust on the jars of Moonchies and Leelou Beans, it was obvious the place didn't get a lot of customers. Behind the low counter sat a man with cylindrical optics that jutted out of his head. He glanced up at them, then went back to counting what looked like metal coasters stacked in piles.

"We're closed."

"Not here to buy pop-turds." With slightly exaggerated confidence, Ron plonked one of the drone batteries onto the counter. One of the coasters shook and fell, rejoining the uncounted pile.

The shopkeeper froze and slowly lifted his gaze to the ripperdoc. Ron's tough-guy act evaporated in an instant.

"Got an appointment," he said as if in apology.

The shopkeeper looked them both over, leaned over the countertop and slid the bolt on the front door closed. Then he reached down and they heard a click. From the side, a part of the decrepit wall behind the shelves moved a few inches, revealing a hidden door.

"Follow me."

He wedged himself out from behind the counter and entered the passageway. He couldn't have been more than five feet tall. The soundproof door looked as if it would've been more suited for a bunker, reinforced from behind with a solid mechanism that was surely capable of withstanding brute human force for an extended period of time. To all outward appearances—a candy store. Inside, a different world. Cold greenish fluorescent lighting revealed a few large rooms with crates and pallet racks stacked against the walls. Someone took care to make sure everything was neatly organized. Various items stood on the shelves, from guns, implants and tools all the way to professional BD-editing wreaths. Farther ahead were cold storage rooms that most likely preserved bioware.

The shopkeeper leaned against a wide stainless-steel table. Above it hung a mechanical contraption with a plethora of cables dangling from it.

"May I?" He held out his hand toward Ron.

Ron handed over the battery. The shopkeeper spent a few seconds examining the charging socket, the whirr of his optics' actuators cutting through the silence. Then he took the corresponding cable hanging from above and plugged it in. A few monitors came alive and the battery's small display lit up.

"You realize this can't be adapted to a vacuum or an electric bike?" the shopkeeper mumbled. "Not very marketable."

"Oh, but they will soon," Ron answered with artificial enthusiasm. "You put these on the market, the market will adapt. Soon everything will be using 'em. There's more where that came from. A hundred and seventy-nine more, to be exact."

The shopkeeper put on a show of hemming and hawing, his eyebrows knitting dramatically. It was clear he'd already made up his mind.

"Fine, I'll take it," he finally said. "What do you want in return?"

"In return...?" Ron raised an eyebrow. "Well...cash."

"I only pay cash to trusted clients." The shopkeeper slid the battery toward them.

"Right…and what do you do with new clients?" Ron seemed genuinely confused.

"Trade." The shopkeeper indicated the wares around them.

"Oh. Well, truth be told, we were kinda counting on cold, hard cash…"

"That's the deal—take it or leave it. Just don't waste my time. Some kid could walk in at any minute for lollipops or chocobars." He pointed at the exit. "Wouldn't want to disappoint."

"We're here to sell, not trade."

The shopkeeper looked at Ron impassively but stayed silent. Zor, meanwhile, had been browsing the various items on the racks.

"Got a Zetatech like this, only newer?" Ron raised his arm. "Or the Combat SRG from Militech? Starting at seventy and going up. Anything below's scrap."

The shopkeeper shook his head.

"Choose from whatever's available and I'll tell you how much of it you can take."

"You want us to pick out something we're gonna have to sell, anyway," Ron said. "Rotten deal, if you ask me."

"If you want to go around Kabuki and try selling stolen corporate drone batteries…" The shopkeeper shrugged. "Be my guest."

"We'll take this." Zor pointed to a Techtronika sniper rifle with a Militech scope. "What's its condition?"

"Like new," the shopkeeper said without a moment's hesitation. "Like everything else here."

Ron looked at the rifle, then at Zor and back at the rifle. Its barrel was a good three feet long.

"Hell we need that for?" he asked in a hushed tone.

Zor only replied with a shrug.

The shopkeeper drew back to give them some privacy, though remained within earshot.

"Listen…" Ron leaned in closer toward Zor. "We did what we did to get money, right? This rifle…How much do you think we can sell it for?"

"Nothing. But I need it."

"Okay, sure…I get that. But this isn't just about us two, all right? I need money, badly. We all do."

Zor nodded.

"We'll pull another heist," he said. "Plan it properly this time. But right now, I need this rifle."

"You're trespassing. This is private property."

"Private's what's on the other side of this gate. This side's still public."

"Sir, leave immediately or I'll be forced to remove you."

Technically, Liam could demand to see his ID. He had every right to according to the law. The Militech soldier would be legally obliged to lift his visor and identify himself, but Liam quickly discarded that option. He knew it wouldn't happen, and not only because he was standing on an empty, dimly lit street. He showed him his holo-badge.

The soldier gave a slight tilt of the head. He was probably a captain, if Liam had to guess. At the very least, Liam felt as if he was putting up a stand in defense of publicly owned land.

"Wait here."

No, he wasn't defending anything at all. He felt like a kid who'd just walked into a yard with signs that read TRESPASSERS WILL BE SHOT ON SIGHT. The gate caught his eye. Parts of it gleamed with brand-new metal—it had been recently repaired.

Evening was setting in with a drizzle—weather you'd rather experience at home, through a window.

A middle-aged man came out, spry in his movements and demeanor. He had short gray hair and an athletic figure. Ex-military. What Liam hadn't been prepared for was the charcoal suit, which could mean only one thing. Corpo. And a high-ranking one at that. He was trailed by two soldiers, who now positioned themselves on either side of him.

"Detective. What can I do for you?" he calmly asked without a hint of impatience. He didn't appear interested in his name, rank or badge.

There was an unmistakable aura of power emanating from this man. Liam realized he was meeting someone whom he'd normally never have the chance to even get close to. He just happened to be in the right place at the right time. Pure coincidence.

"I'm leading an investigation," he began, unfazed, trying to sound as professional as he could. "Part of it involves a van that rammed through this gate. All evidence points to an attempted robbery."

"I appreciate your concern, but we have everything under control."

"I think both the NCPD and Militech would benefit from knowing what happened here."

"Nothing of any value was taken." The corpo's demeanor hadn't changed. It didn't need to. Liam knew he could end this conversation at any moment if he wanted. "And with all due respect—don't take this the wrong way, detective—I highly doubt you have any information that would be useful to us."

"This case involves multiple homicides. One of them leads directly back to this gate."

There are some who don't have to interrupt anyone in order to make themselves heard—their presence alone is enough to make others go quiet. This man was one of them.

"I'm sorry to hear that, truly," he said. "But I'm sure you're aware of the murder rate in Night City. Surely, there wouldn't be enough detectives like yourself who could solve even a tenth of them."

"Be that as it may, I have a duty to solve this investigation."

"I think it would be in everyone's best interest if said investigation was discontinued. It would save us all a lot of trouble and unnecessary headache. We're treating the damage to this gate as an act of vandalism. Now, if you'll excuse me, I also have duties to attend to. Goodbye."

Liam walked slowly to his car parked nearby. Moments ago, he was talking to a man who—despite the fact that Liam was an NCPD detective—could have done whatever he wanted to him without facing any consequences. A god, of sorts. And this god had not so subtly insinuated that he ought to check the "case closed" box as soon as possible.

"Get in!"

Warden looked at the flung-open door of the limo. Inside was Renner. Outside—night.

"Me?"

"Who else, dipshit? Get in. Fuck you waiting for?"

Warden didn't move; he was trying to keep himself steady. He stared at his boss.

"Dunno. A reason, maybe?" he replied.

"You gone completely whacked? I said get in!"

Warden looked farther down the street. He'd planned to walk home, sober up by the end. Not like it mattered.

He got in. The limousine set off again.

"That job you pulled behind my back…" Renner began more calmly now. "Situation's escalated—we're about to be up to our necks in shit. That how you wanted this to play out?"

"One of my guys messed up."

"So everything goes tits up 'cause of one gonk?" Renner was facing him now. "Genius fucking idea you hatched. Find amateurs to do the job, then toss 'em back into their garbage, meaningless lives. By sunrise everyone's gonna know." He kicked the divider in front of him. "Ross! Fuckin' step on it, will ya? This ain't a fuckin' school bus."

The limo accelerated.

"You sidelined me," Warden said slowly, reluctantly. "Didn't give me a chance to finish what I started."

"This chill attitude o' yours is startin' to piss me off. You think you're on a little time-out, hmm? That it's only a matter of time before I get over it?" The crosses on Renner's hands illuminated the limo's interior. "Don't you see we've got a fuckin' crisis on our hands?!"

"No, I don't. 'Cause you shut me out."

Renner took a deep breath and exhaled.

"Word around town's that we klepped something big from Militech," he explained, making an effort to keep his cool. "Any minute now Militech's gonna find out who did it. Meaning us. Meaning we're sitting on a ticking fuckin' time bomb. So, what's in it, hmm? The fuck's in that piece-of-shit container?"

Warden sighed and closed his eyes.

"I don't know."

The door flew off its cheap, sliding hinges and crashed to the floor, sending pieces of plastic and metal flying against the walls. Shrieks from within. Out of the darkness a figure in a nightshirt holding a large kitchen knife. Like something straight out of a horror flick.

The cold LED light lit up—the alarm's timeworn motion sensor finally detected movement. Two children, no more than three and five years old, ran past him toward their father, who had now appeared—a half-asleep forty-something-year-old wielding a bathroom stool. Hardly an effective weapon.

Father, mother, two children. Family like any other.

"Not gonna hurt you," Zor said. "Long as you stay out of my way."

The mother didn't listen and lunged forward. Before she knew it, the knife was slapped out of her hand. The father lost any will to attempt a follow-up—the odds didn't look good in his favor. He pulled his wife toward them and drew back, shielding their children.

"What do you want?" he asked quietly.

Looking around, Zor couldn't come up with an answer. Something drew him here—he had no idea what, or why.

The dim light cast from the smaller room showed the terrified family huddled together in the corner.

He could've knocked like a normal person, but then they wouldn't have let him in.

He measured three times the length of his forearm along the wall from the door and punched with all his strength. There was a dull thud; the plaster cracked. The building was old, brick-laden, nothing fancy in its construction. He punched again. Crumbs of plaster and dust sprinkled onto the floor. This wasn't gonna work. It'd take half the night, not to mention destroy his hand. He picked up the knife and started repeatedly stabbing the wall. The family looked at him wide-eyed with fear. They didn't dare stop him. The younger child sobbed.

On the twentieth stab, the orange ceramic tile beneath the plaster gave way. One stab later, a matte-black metal object became visible. With every strike, his recollection of what was inside became clearer. From there it was easy. He pulled out a dented, dust-covered metallic briefcase. His hands were trembling.

He bounded down the building's stairs and briskly headed toward the nearest station.

The gray container stood where it had been left—behind a set of steel doors whose code only Renner knew.

"Tell me who gave you the job."

It was just the two of them. Ross was upstairs, making sure none of their fellow gangers wandered down into the basement.

"I don't know."

Renner closed his eyes and cursed under his breath.

"You'd best start comin' up with some fuckin' explanations. You're telling me you don't know what you stole, or who for? How were you supposed to deliver the goods, then?"

"I wasn't," Warden answered. "Client wanted the container to disappear."

"Disappear? That a fucking joke? He paid you to klep something he didn't even want?"

"Wanted me to hide it someplace no one would find it."

Warden knew he was drunk, but it was only now that he felt it. Which is probably why he didn't care what Renner would do to him. He wasn't even nervous.

"Could be anything in there," Renner said. "Could be a fuckin' bomb that'll blow half this neighborhood into orbit like in '23."

The airtight container didn't betray any hint as to what it held inside.

"Could try opening it," Warden suggested, though he knew trying to force the lock would be extremely dangerous.

"No. Here's what'll happen—you're gonna do something for me and this time it better be to the fucking letter—no gonkbrained ideas. Your little gang of morons—you'll get them here. How you do that is up to you. We'll record ourselves splattering their brains on the walls and 'find' the container. Then we give it back to Militech, who'll thank us for doin' them a fucking favor." Renner gave Warden an icy glare. "Fuck this up and it'll be your brain splattered across the wall. Understood?"

Zor plopped a surgical briefcase on the operating chair and opened it. Ron took one look and whistled with admiration.

"Fine piece of chrome, that. Not latest-gen, but preem tier for sure. Decent condish, could fetch a hefty sum. Wanna take that to our candy man in Kabuki?"

"Want you to chip me with it."

"You realize this is military 'ware, right?" Ron scratched the back of his head. "It's registered to specific DNA. Without the manufacturer codes, syncing this to your profile'll be a bitch."

"DNA's mine. Wore a uniform in my past life."

"Yeah, and you clearly weren't no ordinary grunt. You've held on to this till now?"

"I…I don't know. Only yesterday I didn't remember…Something was up with my memory. Military shrink could probably say more."

"Why have it taken out, anyway? Army doesn't strip chrome after you're discharged. Not to mention all the problems that could come with that…"

"I wasn't discharged." Zor shot Ron a tense glare. "Can you chip it or not?"

Ron looked at the cyberware for a moment and gave a slight nod.

"This isn't an easy op. But yes, I can." He sighed. "It'll take around a week for your body to fully adapt."

"Make it twenty-four hours."

"You outta your damn mind?" Ron retorted. "This takes a week, minimum—including another nanite dose. Not to mention immunosuppressants, which I don't got a whole lot left of, by the way."

"What order?" Ron asked after a beat.

"What?"

"What do you want chipped first? What am I starting with?"

"All of it."

Ron sighed.

"Forgot to ask the most important question—you actually wanna come out of this alive? There's a reason chrome gets chipped in increments, gradually, along with some serious drugs. A week, maybe two between each one. Brain needs time to adapt and learn. You get it all at once—sure, in twenty-four hours you can be a borged-up Übermensch. You'll also become a goddamn cyberpsycho."

Zor didn't look like someone you could persuade using logic or reason.

"You handle tissue regen," Zor said. "I'll deal with the cyberpsychosis. I need this chrome—need it to finish something that's been keeping me up nights for years."

Ron folded his arms.

"Have it your way. Just don't say I didn't warn ya. Go wash up first." He pointed at the door to the shower behind the freezers. "Want you to scrub with soap everywhere. And I mean everywhere. Under your nails, too. When you're done scrubbing, do it all over again. Got it?"

"You lock the door?" Zor started to undress.

Ron glanced at the entrance.

"Yeah, 'course. Always lock it."

He powered up the operating chair and was already setting up the procedure on the panel. All the necessary programs were there. Good thing about military chrome was that it was more old-school—sockets, connectors. Everything was thicker, sturdier, more resilient. No sweat for his antiquated cyberarm.

As soon as the door to the bathroom closed behind Zor, Ron went to the entrance and locked it. He transferred the briefcase to his desk, booted up his terminal and searched for the reflex booster model that lay on top. His eyes widened.

"Well, well..."

If Militech's official price was two hundred grand, then it would go for at least double on the black market. Probably the same for the implants. The ripperdoc straightened up, impressed, and looked at the bathroom where the sound of running water was coming from. The contents of this briefcase added up to a small fortune.

The operating chair began to auto-disinfect. The harsh smell wafted through the room and Ron felt the same excited anticipation he experienced before every operation. The harder the operation, the stronger the feeling.

Zor emerged naked from the bathroom and, not waiting for any instructions, went to lie down on the chair. The manipulators came alive and, without any input from the ripperdoc, plugged into the right sockets and injected needles into the right veins.

"How long ago you take these out?" Ron leaned over the fresh scars on Zor's shoulder, adjusting his optics to macro.

"Years ago."

The ripperdoc's eyebrows knit together almost imperceptibly. He stood still for a few seconds before closing his eyes and letting out a noiseless sigh.

"You're gonna slowly conk out," he said, pressing a few buttons on the console. "Then wake up practically a supersoldier. Whether of sound mind is yet to be determined. How thorough do you want the stitching? Don't have a lot of time between implants—want to avoid scarring."

"Forget the scars." Zor was already fading out. His exhaustion helped the anesthesia do its job. "Just make sure the stitching's strong."

The diagnostics screen confirmed that the full dose of anesthesia had been dispensed. In a second he'd stabilize—then Ron could get to work. High time he put on clean clothes and disinfected his hands. But Ron, pale-faced, didn't move.

His gaze slowly turned to the briefcase. He'd seen that piece of cyberware before—was all but certain of it. Only where?

"I prefer meeting in person." Stanley slipped his hand into the pocket of his suit pants. "Even if it's late. Funny, isn't it? How no piece of technology has ever truly replaced face-to-face conversation." He paused. "We had a deal, Warden. It was pretty simple. You were to steal the container and get rid of it without a trace. As I understand it, you've achieved the exact opposite, because apparently now the entire city knows of it."

"I don't operate in a vacuum," Warden replied. "I lost the trust of my boss. He took it out of my hands."

"You'll regain his trust once he gets the rest of the payment. Now, make sure the container and its contents disappear—this time for good."

"It's a recording from one of our patrol drones. It flies in a random route—avoiding Pacifica, of course. Kids over there shoot at it for fun."

"Delinquents, you mean."

"Sure, whatever. Little bastards don't shoot at corp drones, 'cause they return fire. We don't fly over Northside, either. Different reasons."

The nighttime recording showed a street running from Kabuki to Northside. The detective zoomed in on a portion of the frame. Wasn't any doubt—a Buyers & Son van was heading toward Northside. Intact.

"Can't make out the plate," the rookie said. "Could've been any of their vans."

"Our tech might be shitty," Liam explained. "But not shitty enough to miss the number on the side."

The rookie scolded herself. The 13 wasn't big, but it was legible.

"Still isn't proof," the detective added. "Anyone can slap a number on a van. Except almost one minute later, the CCTV in this neighborhood went down."

"Wasn't there a fire?" the rookie recalled. "Could've short-circ'd the CCTV."

"Fire broke out after the cams went dark." The detective tossed two pieces of gum into his mouth. "Could just be a coincidence. Matter of fact, everything we've pieced together so far could be. Experience tells me when there are too many of them, they're not coincidences. I looked through more footage."

They sat in the crowded, bustling room of the NCPD's criminal investigation division. Crumpled paper coffee cups filled the trash can next to Liam's desk.

"Did you even go home last night?" she asked him.

The detective gave a slight shake of his head.

"I looked inside that van. Someone scrubbed it clean—probably used ammonia and hydrogen peroxide on the bloodstains. No DNA whatsoever."

"Zor and Aya," the rookie said, thinking out loud. "They robbed a Militech warehouse and killed a guard, plus two women—Molly Bernard and Elena Delany. What I don't get is why they used that specific van for the robbery. It's like they were asking to get caught."

The detective nodded.

"Can ask them yourself. Think it's about time you issued your first arrest warrant."

CHAPTER_10

Lemme get this straight—y'all be buying water that's cleaner, tastier, safer, healthier—call it whatever you want, cuz I can't be fucked, man. I'm just a lazy-ass muthafucka who's somehow getting by, tellin' you how it is and keeping it real. Like the fact that y'all getting mad fleeced on your All Foods subscription cuz y'all is lazier-ass muthafuckas than me. Or you just got scop for brains.

Lemme lay it out for you. Night City got clean water standards, right? No clue what they are, but they exist. What happens after the water goes through treatment at the plant? No one gives a fuck. No one except FR34K_S33K. Who woulda thunk, right? Dig this—Night City's got an actual Bureau of Clean Drinking Water. Number of employees? Two. They good at their jobs? Hard to tell, cuz they ain't showed up for work in YEARS. Them's your tax dollars hard at work right there.

So, who's actually supervising Night City's water quality? Any guesses? A team of experts? A couple experts? One expert? A fuckin' intern? Nah, bro. No one checks that shit. Don't pretend like you're gonna check it, either.

So instead, y'all muthafuckas be paying a Real Water subscription for clean water delivery. Real smart. I mean the corps—not you.

Funny thing is—treating water ain't hard. You know what's also not hard? Taking clean water and then putting all kinds of nasty shit in it. Remember, fools—y'all ain't paying for cleaner water—y'all paying to not get poisoned.

Oh, I'm sorry, this getting you down? Yeah, that ain't never been my game, man. Don't like it, you can go jerk off to a braindance or something. For the rest of you down with it—what are you waiting for? Smash that DOWNLOAD button and stay tuned for your next FR34K_S33K hot take!

PEACE!

"Looks like you're stuck with me again." She wheeled a large, very expensive-looking suitcase into the middle of the room. "So, you're Albert. Not how I imagined you at all."

She squinted at him for a moment in contemplation. The teenager threw her a quick glance over his bowl of instant synth-ramen.

"What made you change your mind?" he answered with a question.

"I see you have a C-Link," Milena said, pointing to the back of her neck. She took off her elegant overcoat and flung it onto the couch, revealing a tasteful, slim-fitted corpo suit. "Should help you find out who's after us."

"C-Link isn't enough on its own," Albert said with a tinge of melancholy. "I'm still stuck at tier one with a modded wreath and some tier-two components, but I can't upgrade the cyberdeck any more than I have already. I need full tier two."

Aya came into the room, having just woken up.

"Oh." She stared at Milena, surprised. "Change of heart?"

"Didn't have a choice. Someone tried to kidnap me yesterday."

"You're not the only one," Aya replied. "Either of you know where Zor is? He's not answering my messages."

"What about Ron?" Milena looked around. "Someone's trying to take all of us out. I have my suspicions as to who it could be, but I'm still not sure. Either way—we've laid a path and we'll keep walking it. Except from now on we'll do it with proper planning."

She flipped the suitcase on its side and opened it. It wasn't full of clothes, cosmetics or anything you'd normally expect to find in an elegant woman's suitcase.

Albert's eyes widened. He went over to the suitcase and dropped to his knees almost as if in worship, taking out a hefty cable with thick insulation.

"What is it?" Aya looked at the cable and folded spongy fabric.

"I borrowed it from the company," replied Milena. "Don't think I'll need to give it back."

"Tier-three netrunning gear," Albert said in a tone that was very different from how he usually spoke. "With its own dedicated coolware."

You can't back up a human being. If you die, it's game over. You're gone for good—no coming back. That said, it's possible to preserve someone's DNA and, in the event of their death, use it to create a new, identical body. Expensive, but doable. What's the point, though? It'll only re-create the body, not the mind. It would be like creating an identical hard drive, but without the data. If anyone knew how to back up a human mind, then that someone must be residing behind the Blackwall. Only they wouldn't be human.

If Hameroff and Penrose's theory of quantum consciousness is correct, then the human mind is a biological quantum computer. Consciousness, memories, knowledge—everything that makes us *us* is only an ephemeral cloud of probability whose quantum state lies somewhere beyond our perceivable three- or even four-dimensional space. If that's true, and Albert believed it was, then transferring a condensed version of that data is basically impossible with today's tech. However powerful corporate supercomputers were, they couldn't match the complexity of the processes taking place in the human brain.

The history of transferring and emulating consciousness went back at least half a century. Albert trawled through every available source containing information about Soulkiller—the program that Arasaka's Relic technology was based on. Albert regarded it as a magic trick—no more advanced than an interactive hologram, something pretending to be a person *postmortem*. Besides, even an attempt at far-from-perfect emulation would eat up so much computing power that nobody would ever agree to such a vast waste of resources.

At least nobody on this side of the Blackwall.

ArS-03, log 55349.
Synchronization procedure initiated.
Unidentified device NI100101001110. Status: unknown.
Subsystems detected: 117.
Synchronization procedure in progress.

"You need to rest up for a few days—let the nanites do their work."

"I need more."

"Out of the question. It'll increase the risk of surplus tissue metastasizing. Trust me, you don't want a dick and balls to suddenly start growing out of your forehead."

The elevator cabin, its interior clad in protective paneling made from recycled, compressed plastic, rode upward.

"Regen's going surprisingly smooth, though," the ripperdoc

admitted. "But just 'cause the implants aren't causing any problems now doesn't mean you're out of the woods just yet. Gotta conserve your energy. Tissue hasn't fully stabilized yet."

"Feel like my body's made of scop," Zor said.

There was a nagging thought that Ron couldn't shake.

"Your implants... They configured themselves almost instantly," he probed. "Didn't have to tweak a thing."

"Body remembers."

"Wasn't the body." The ripperdoc shook his head but held his tongue just as the elevator slowed to a halt.

They stepped out into an unfinished, concrete hallway. As soon as the elevator doors closed behind them, it became nearly pitch-black. He went over to the second door on the right and placed his hand on the biometric lock. The doors slid open, spilling a streak of light into the hallway.

"So you've got our biometrics, too," Ron said in lieu of a greeting. "What is this place?"

"Somewhere safe," Warden replied.

"Yeah, safe for you..." Ron muttered.

They went in. The floor-to-ceiling windows were covered in a thick layer of dust, blurring the outlines of the neighboring buildings. Some of the windows were still draped in protective plastic. Thirtieth story. Beside a concrete pillar lay a stack of military cases with sockets in their sides, used to transport electronic equipment. Farther ahead there was an empty bathtub from which a thick braid of cables led deeper into the unfinished unit. The little water that still remained at the bottom was murky from dirt.

Ron warily took in their surroundings. Warden leaned against a folding table—his arms crossed. He wore his usual synth-leather coat.

"You said you needed a fixer," he said.

"We did. But last time you said we were a bunch of amateurs."
Zor approached him. Concrete crumbs crunched beneath his soles.

"He said that...?" Ron asked, looking at Zor.

"'Cause it's true," the ganger said. "Only reason I hired y'all for
the job in Arroyo. Bunch of seemingly regular folks, no record in
any NCPD database. Nothing's changed—all that could come in
handy again." He straightened up. "Got a job for y'all. Pay's half a
mill. Up to you how you wanna split it."

"Half a mill? Cash up-front?"

"Ask me another gonk question and I'll put lead up-front 'tween
your eyes."

"What's the job?" Zor asked.

"Gonna break in somewhere, klep somethin' for me. Might
wanna be packin' iron in case things go south. I'll give you everything you need."

"Rather bring our own gear," Zor said firmly.

Warden took out a wad of cash from his pocket, split it in half
and handed it to Zor without counting it.

"Get whatever y'all need by end of day. Unregistered, no serial
numbers. Matter's time-sensitive."

"We'll find an arms dealer," Ron assured him.

"Is that right? Yeah, got one of those next to every car dealer."
Warden looked up at the ceiling in resignation and sighed. "Amateur
hour..."

"We'll manage on our own."

"Y'all can't manage shit." He blinked, his irises flickering bright
blue. "Here."

Zor's phone pinged with a new message. He fished it out of his
pocket.

"Gotta be fucking kidding me…" Warden muttered at the sight of Zor's phone. "Gonna get there on horseback, too?"

Zor hesitated, then let habit do its work. He stuffed his phone back into his pocket and blinked, his irises glazing over blue. He skimmed through the contact details that hovered in his retinal display.

"Dealer ain't the best," Warden said. "Smells like a fuckin' petting zoo, but he sells clean gear, untraceable. Pick some iron for short-range combat and tight spaces."

"Case things don't go to plan…" Zor stuffed the wad of cash in his pocket. "Which they usually don't. Who are we robbing?"

"Me," Warden replied as if it were completely normal. "Gonna klep that container. Same one as last time."

"You're…" Ron froze at the sight of Milena. He was barely through the doorway.

"Came back because I wasn't safe." She was half lying on the couch as if about to take a nap. "Rather not go back home."

He glanced at the suitcase and smiled.

"Looks like you're serious about moving in."

"Oh, that. No." She pointed behind her.

Albert lay on his chair in what looked like a neoprene diving suit, with multiple sockets and complex-looking tubes and cables coming out of it. One of the cables led to a heat exchanger on the balcony behind the cracked-open window. Others led to a terminal in a compact, metallic briefcase that sat beside Milena, its screen displaying vital functions.

Zor entered after Ron. Aya's smile was quickly replaced with a look of worry.

"Zor…are you okay?" she asked. "You look…"

Zor's eyelids were red, his face pale.

"Look exactly how I feel," he replied. "It's the anesthetic. Got a little fine-tuning from Ron. Everything's okay."

She went over to him and delicately squeezed his shoulder, as if afraid he would break.

"I'll be fully regened by tomorrow," he said.

Ron looked up at the ceiling, sighed and gently shook his head.

"Did they make contact?" Aya finally asked.

"No," Zor replied. "But we have a job. It'll be more than enough for Ron's new arm. He'll be able to fix you up."

Aya looked like she couldn't have cared less.

"Albert will find out who took Juliena," she said.

Meanwhile, Ron hadn't taken his eyes off Milena.

"What do you mean you weren't safe?" he asked her.

"Oh, you know—no big deal. Just that someone followed and tried to kidnap me."

Sixty-two seconds—the exact time it took for him to break through his own ICE and gain access to the Cave. Mixed emotions. Probably the only way to describe his state of mind. He did it on his first try, just barely after booting up his new equipment. The bundle of new programs he'd received from Warden as a reward for Arroyo had been worth the risk.

He should have felt happy, but he was weighed down with the realization that he'd been practically defenseless for all these years without even knowing it. He decided to start with configuring the most secure encryption he could manage.

The next thing that struck him was the quality of what he'd created up until this point. Terrible, basically. What used to seem like the pinnacle of his cyberdeck's potential now looked like it had been made by a script-kiddie. He'd spent weeks writing macros for managing databases—with tier three, he could do the same amount in fifteen minutes—and better, too. His own corner of cyberspace, so familiar to him from all the time he'd spent in it, looked exactly the same. It was like the forgotten childhood toy you'd find at the bottom of a box of old junk. He used to see all its rough edges as a necessary compromise in order to save RAM and processing power. Now it just looked cheap and janky—the netrunner edition of abject poverty.

The Taran in particular looked unsophisticated. No more complex than the games that Albert was making eddies from. It wouldn't break through the Blackwall just as a hammer wouldn't break through a nuclear bunker. The only thing it would be good for was drawing the attention of NetWatch and NETSEC.

For a brief fifty-millisec moment, Albert considered wiping everything and starting over.

No, there was plenty of space—maybe he could salvage something. The resolution was several times sharper—the speed orders of magnitude faster. He significantly reduced the size of the "pillars" of his homespun algorithms and distanced them even farther from the center. He didn't even need to scroll up and down—he saw them in their entirety. He also saw the ones that he'd moved farther away earlier. He grouped them all by category and created a new central hub where he could temporarily settle his virtual avatar. It only took him a few seconds to realize that here, too, he didn't need to be frugal. He could operate multiple avatars simultaneously, meaning he could process and control a few thousand times the amount of data than before.

Happy as a puppy, he flitted through cyberspace with a speed and precision that was unimaginable even with Warden's gear. He felt bigger, faster, better. On top of that, the learning curve of the tech was low, since it was all based on intuition. The only thing he couldn't wrap his head around was where the limits of tier-three capability ended. He saw the Taran's painstakingly created code in its entirety from start to finish along with all the reference dumps, unfinished versions and so on. And all he saw were mistakes and stupidity.

Two communication channels were enough to clog up his old cyberdeck, such as when he had to switch between the drone-cam, CCTV cameras and the data feed from the surveillance center. He opened a hundred channels. Nothing happened—no overload, no lag. It was more than he'd ever need.

But with more supply comes more demand. He'd have to test how much the system could handle sometime later.

If tier three was this much more powerful than tier one...then what were the higher tiers like?

On a separate note, he realized that over the last few days of not having access to his Cave he'd earned 2,053 eurodollars. That would cover his rent and food subscriptions a few months in advance.

"Did you find them?" Aya's tone was hopeful.

"Haven't started looking yet." Albert stood up. "Still some prep work left—things I need to reconfigure."

She stepped closer to him, barely able to suppress the urge to grab and shake him to his senses. She took a deep breath.

"Find who took Juliena," she implored of him. "It's important."

"I know." Albert went over to the fridge and pulled out a high-glucose meal box.

"Eat, then keep looking."

"The whole reason we're in this mess is because we didn't prepare—no intel, nothing. We have to do things differently this time."

"To hell with that!" Aya exploded, getting up suddenly and

burying her face in her hands. "I just want to find Juliena. And...
and for all this to stop..."

"It'll never stop until we find whoever's after us," Albert explained
calmly. "And until we make enough money to be able to protect
ourselves."

"Warden's offering us half a million," Zor said.

All eyes except Ron's turned to him.

"That'll buy you a patch of grass in North Oak," Milena said,
bringing them all back down to planet Earth. "It's not as much as
you think."

"Night City isn't the be-all and end-all," Aya pointed out.

"Of course not. Everywhere else is just worse."

With every minute spent grasping the magnitude of his new equipment's potential, it became clearer that he'd made it this far through
simple miracle. No. It was because he wasn't flashy, never tried to
draw attention to himself. His operation was small beans—too insignificant to be of interest to gangs or the NCPD. He always played it
safe—never meddled in anyone's biz. Then Warden came along and
forced him to become a reluctant member of the impromptu gang.
Nothing had been the same ever since.

The human body was only capable of repairing itself from minor
injuries. Serious injuries destroyed not only the body but also a part
of the person residing within. Irreversibly.

If only he hadn't argued with his mother—if only she hadn't
destroyed his cyberdeck, he'd never have moved out. And then it'd
probably be his body at the morgue, not hers. He would've stopped
existing.

If he backed out now, he'd be in even more danger. Not to mention Milena would probably ask for her gear back. How long could

they realistically keep up this charade? No matter how you looked at it, the odds were stacked against them. Whether it'd be in a week or a month—eventually they'd lose.

Some believe that Bartmoss transferred his consciousness to the Net where no one could find him. Others, that he transferred only a part of himself—an AI to carry out his instructions, a self-executing last will and testament. But that didn't smack of the ambition he was famous for. Then there's the philosophical argument that transferring one's own consciousness might be possible, but the workings of that consciousness would be nothing more than a simulation.

But Bartmoss never had the level of Albert's tech.

Transferring the quantum state of every atom in his brain—every neutron, proton and so on—was impossible. In that case, at the very most you could transfer a brain pattern to the other side, booting up as a digi-puppet that would only imitate the original, pretend to be the real thing. The human central nervous system was wholly incompatible with human-built computers. Computers were based on logic circuits, always providing clear and unequivocal results based on clear and unequivocal queries and data. Meanwhile, the workings of the brain best reflected Heisenberg's uncertainty principle that by definition would disallow the creation of an exact copy. In other words, the impossibility of transferring the human mind stemmed from the nature of reality itself. A different approach was required—a deep conversion that couldn't be done simply by reading one medium and writing it to another. The process required a brilliant painter rather than a photographer.

Albert's tier-three netrunning rig was self-instructed. It optimized itself by scanning its user and learning their movements, preferences, memories. The process itself ran in the background on low-prio to free up memory. Albert cranked its priority to near-maximum and expanded it to all his programs. Now they would absorb everything they had access to. He had no idea how long the entire process would take.

Some believe there is no mind without body, that transferring a consciousness—defined as the sum of the brain and central nervous system's quantum states—to a machine, any machine, would result in informational pandemonium. A colossal amount of data would momentarily lose all meaning, since there would be no way to process it. It'd be like disassembling a highly complex machine, down to the last screw, tossing everything into a pile and waiting for it to resume operations.

Albert didn't believe that mind and body were inseparable. The mind was just a tenant. Trapped. One year ago, during a data harvest from a library in Japantown, he discovered an article about the experiments of Antoine Lavoisier. Nearly three hundred years ago, he tried to prove that a severed head could retain consciousness as long as it had oxygen to process thoughts. The French chemist conducted the experiment on himself—though not exactly voluntarily. He was beheaded during the French Revolution. Before his execution, he told his assistant that after his head was cut off, he would try to stay conscious for as long as possible by blinking.

He blinked for twenty seconds.

Albert also discovered an article that debunked this account as a myth, but the fact remained—he wouldn't need any oxygen where he was going, nor for that matter even a physical body. He would live on as pure consciousness.

"South Glen? This is practically Pacifica."

"No more dangerous than anywhere else."

"Sure about that? 'Cause it feels like we're out of the city now, trying to avoid bumping into Raffen Shiv."

The area did look truly desolate, though it was just an illusion. Locals here simply avoided open spaces such as streets and sidewalks. The afternoon heat was another disincentive. Nonetheless, the mini-marts were open and handfuls of people lurked in the cooler shadows of the short, stumpy buildings.

"Don't stop," Zor said.

"See?" Ron turned the wheel and accelerated. "You feel it, too."

They drove around waiting for a signal. Stopping here would inevitably attract a small-time hustler, or at the very least a homeless person. Or whoever was loitering in those dim alleyways.

"What do we need more iron for, anyway?" Ron asked. "Already got some from the last job."

"Those were pieces of junk," Zor replied.

"What about your sniper rifle? Doesn't look like junk to me."

"Can't use it in close range."

"How ironic." He chuckled. "Y'know, I always wondered if that's where 'Ron' came from. Ironic. If I ever meet my parents one day, I'll ask them. What I'm tryin' to say is—we could put this money to better use. I know it's an investment and all, but...how soon are we gonna see a return?"

"As soon as someone tries to kill us again—a day that's fast approaching."

Aya sat in the back, her eyes flickering blue as she scanned for messages. Funny how expectations change depending on circumstances. Before, she'd always hoped she'd never have to get involved with Night City's shadier demographic. Now she could hardly wait for them to make contact and tell her where they were keeping Juliena. And what they wanted in exchange.

Destitution. Probably the most succinct description of the view rolling past. Department stores with display windows stretching for dozens of yards, now divided up into tiny stores or completely boarded up. They passed one abandoned car after another—a common sight in Night City's worse neighborhoods. Those that weren't abandoned seemed worse for wear than anywhere else. At this hour the unit block windows were usually shielded from the heat with shutters or curtains. Any open ones meant they were most likely deserted.

The AC in the car hummed loudly. Ron switched it off and opened the window but quickly came to the conclusion that even weak AC was better than the hot breeze from outside.

"Nuh-uh, fuck this." Ron sat back in his seat and stepped on the gas. "We're gettin' outta here."

In the shadow of a building on an almost empty street stood a gray van with two heavies leaning against it.

"Pull over," Zor said.

"You insane? You see those guys?!"

"That's them, the arms dealers. Stop the car. This is the Glen, not Pacifica. They won't do anything to us."

Ron stopped a few yards farther to keep a little distance nonetheless.

"You really wanna do this?" he asked nervously.

"Warden recommended them."

"You do you, but I ain't getting out of this car."

"Fine. Keep the engine running." Zor opened the door.

"I'm coming with you." Aya got out. The heat was truly unbearable.

"Careful with your stitches," Ron reminded Zor. "No sudden movements."

They walked toward the dealers. One of them had a pig's face, the other a tiger's. Animals.

"Don't look like the most trustworthy," Aya pointed out.

"Know any arms dealers who do?"

"How're you holding up?"

"I'm fine." Zor straightened his back. His whole body hurt—he instinctively hunched over in pain, keeping it inside. "Everything's fine."

They stopped a few feet from the van. Aya stood behind Zor's shoulder.

The Animals reeked something awful. Hard to tell if that was part of their style or if they just never took showers. Or maybe the latter was a product of the former.

They stared at each other for a moment. The Animals were clearly intrigued by Aya.

"We need four pistols," Zor said without greeting. "Two small ones, Lexington or similar, plus two higher caliber. Also need four SMGs, maybe Saratogas. And ten frag grenades. Got all of that?"

Big Cat cocked his head to the side. Without a word, Pigface opened the van's back doors, pulled two boxes toward the edge and opened them. Zor came closer. In one of the cases, in foam molds, were ten Shigures; in the other two, Pulsars along with a pile of magazines. All of it definitely used.

Aya stood glued to the spot. She couldn't tell if it was due to fear or that stench.

"So, what'll it be?" the Big Cat asked after a beat. "We's doin' biz?"

"Mm-hmm." Zor nodded. "We need four *new* SMGs, though. New."

Pigface spat next to Zor's shoe.

"Got this," Pigface snorted. He jumped up into the hold and pulled out one more rectangular case. "Reinforced military gear. Won't find it anywhere else."

In the case lay a few dozen different pistols, this time glistening new. Zor picked up a Lexington—it didn't have a serial number or markings.

"Take what's there or *vice versa*."

Zor gave him a questioning look.

"It's French for *fuck off*," Pigface explained. "Youse taking it or not?"

"Can also put in an order," the Big Cat added. "Takes a few days. Cash up-front."

"No, the deal's on," Zor said. "We'll take four Shigures, two C.A.L.'s and two Lexingtons. Plus ammo—army-grade."

"Toss in this little doll here and youse can take it all right now." Big Cat didn't take his eyes off Aya. He licked his lips.

"She's not part of the deal," Zor replied. "Payin' cash."

Aya gritted her teeth. The pistol behind her belt gave her only a little courage. The Big Cat came closer, his stench wafting in her direction, making Aya wince.

"Don't look like someones who could stop us." He kept looking at her but spoke to Zor. "What'll youse do if I decides to take the payment myself?"

"My guy's waiting back there." Zor pointed at the SUV. It was a weak threat, but the Animals couldn't have been the wiser. "Finger on the trig."

It didn't seem to make an impression on them. Aya waited, tense, for what would happen next. In her mind she was already reaching for her gun. No, last resort. Chances of coming out on top were close to none.

"Not too brave. Ain't standing up for youse that much, eh?" Big Cat reached toward her. She briskly took a step back. The Animal only laughed, obnoxiously sniffing the air in front of her.

"Damn, smells as good as she looks. We's doing this or not?"

Zor stood between Aya and the Animal.

"Cash. Nothing more."

"Five hundred for the Lexes, six for the C.A.L.'s and let's say eight for the SMGs." Zor took out the wad of cash from his pocket, counted it and handed it to Big Cat.

"Not even gonna try to haggle?" Big Cat grinned, displaying his fangs.

"Should I?" Zor pocketed the rest of the cash, loaded the weapons into the bag and tried to pick it up, wincing from the soreness. Aya quickly went over to him, grabbing the bag and carrying it to the SUV.

"Ammo," she returned in demand.

"Little doll speaks," Pigface grunted. "Youse can pay for it in kind," he chortled.

"Cash," Zor repeated firmly, massaging his shoulder.

"Choom, what's the big deal? Can find yourself a new piece of ass."

"Got the ammo, or should we look elsewhere?"

"How 'bout..." Big Cat slid the case farther inside the van. "You let us have her for an hour and the ammo's yours."

"Already told you..." Zor was tense. It took all his strength to hide his weakness.

Suddenly, both Animals froze. Pigface quickly slammed the doors of the van. Aya and Zor exchanged glances. Before they knew it, with a screech two NCPD patrols pulled up next to them and four officers spilled out. Aya reached for the pistol behind her belt, but Zor grabbed her arm midway.

"Fuck outta here, pigs! We's paid a month up-front," Big Cat called out.

"Not here for you." The senior officer glanced at the display on his wrist, then at Zor and Aya. "You're under arrest. You have the right to remain silent, and so on and so forth."

*   *   *

The data extracted from 3rd Public Library in Heywood turned out to be quite the haul. Among other juicy tidbits, it contained an article on the Blackwall's functionality. This kind of data was usually heavily censored—or removed from publicly available sources altogether. Someone had clearly forgotten about this desert island of a library stranded from the rest of the Net. The article had been published thirty years ago, so it wasn't exactly up-to-date. Or reliable. But even if the author claimed more than they actually knew, it was enlightening nonetheless.

The Blackwall wasn't a static entity—its security systems were endlessly in flux. It was less a solid slab of concrete than an amalgamation of millions of tiny, spinning blades shredding anything that dared approach. But that didn't mean it was completely impermeable. It had gaps. Both sides of the wall were also functionally independent, each separately monitoring potential threats and exchanging data with the other, constantly optimizing their defenses. Albert had heard of this from newer, though less reliable sources. All in all, the system was self-instructed, self-optimizing, but its foundations remained unchanged.

There was hope that breaking through the Blackwall could be achieved by impersonating a side of the wall itself. Attempts over the years hadn't indicated that something like this was impossible— only that current netrunning equipment wasn't advanced enough. Attempting it via remote connection meant surefire detection from NetWatch or NETSEC AI patrols. Unless Albert could somehow gain exclusive access to a dedicated service hub. But that was unrealistic, to say the least.

Not the first or last hurdle he'd have to overcome.

He wanted to strangle the imbeciles who designed this SUV. Not only did the wheels automatically lock if the trunk was open, but there was no button to close the trunk from the driver's seat. Ron sat and waited for a miracle, unable to get out because of the two Animals staring curiously at his car less than thirty feet away. Maybe they'd lose interest and just drive away?

Nope. They were definitely headed toward him. He sank back into his seat as far as his long, spindly legs allowed. In a last-ditch attempt, he locked the doors. It didn't help. Pigface pulled on the handle and the door gave, anyway, the lock's metal parts clanking against the blacktop.

Shit.

Pigface grabbed Ron by the collar of his sweater, lifted him into the air and set him down as if he weighed no more than a child.

"Well, look who we's got here…" He grinned.

"Personal space," Ron wheezed, robbed of breath. "Ever heard of it?"

"Ever heard of payin' back what you owe?" Big Cat countered.

"Thought you said two days."

"And I thought youse said somethin' about sellin' stolen merch." Big Cat motioned to the trunk. "So what's all the iron for?"

Ron sighed and gathered his thoughts. Couldn't kill him, right? If they did, they could kiss their eddies goodbye.

"Right, so…didn't spill the whole story last time," he began. "Someone, um…someone took it. Need the iron if I wanna get the said merch back."

"Sedmerch? What's that?"

"What's…?" Ron wiped the sweat from his brow. "I said 'said merch' as a way of saying…Never mind. Either way, if I wanna sell it, I need to get it back."

Big Cat cocked his head.

"Maybe I ought to just off youse right here—chalk it up to a loss."

"Th-that container's worth a fortune," Ron blurted out.

"Container?"

"The one we stole from Militech. Sure you've heard…"

The Animals looked at each other.

"How much it worth?"

"Can't say for certain." Ron shrugged. "Not my area of expertise." He straightened himself up and smoothed out his shirt. "Shit ton, if I had to guess."

"Shit ton for some sedmerch, you say," Pigface thought out loud. "How much is that in eddies?"

"Couple times more than what I owe for sure," Ron assured him.

"Well, then…" Big Cat struggled to wrap his head around an amount. "How soon can youse get it?"

Ron swallowed.

"Well, counting the ammo, I'd say, er…two days, tops."

"Got a better idea," Big Cat said. "How 'bout we get it back for youse ourselves? Where's it at? Spill."

Ron sighed. He was hoping it wouldn't come to this.

"I don't know."

If you die, it's game over. There are no backups. This obvious and terrifying fact testifies to the far-from-perfect nature of human beings.

The brain stores and processes a colossal amount of data. Estimates range from a few to a few hundred petabytes of storage capacity and teraflops of processing power. Overexaggerations, perhaps. Still, the body's core functioning is handled by the nervous system. That part can be skipped. If you don't need insulin in cyberspace, then do you even need a pancreas?

If you wanted to, you could probably even compress consciousness or digitize analog neural processing down to sixteen bits. Was it possible? Albert didn't know, because he couldn't find any information going back thirty years on any experiments conducted, not counting the Relic. He assumed not much had changed since then—the only technology that had progressed in leaps and bounds was military tech. And Albert didn't have access to that.

The main limitation wouldn't even be a computer or neural network's performance, but whether the number of threads in the entire process equaled the number of neurons—excluding, of course, those in charge of biological functions. But how would that affect the fidelity of the consciousness's simulation? Hard to tell. Positively, maybe? If the pressures of the body on the mind disappeared, then so would laziness, tiredness and impatience. Surely there were only benefits to be gained if the body shed its relevance. Then again, the lack of environmental pressure could also weaken motivation, drive. Nothing but a little wrinkle that Albert could straighten out later.

Still, even if you compressed all of it, there wasn't a computer in existence or even a processing center that would be capable of simulating a human mind.

At least not on this side of the Blackwall.

And how often would you have to back yourself up in order to avoid losing important memories in the event of sudden death? In order to stay the same person? And if you did die, where would you get the body to upload your backup? Not your own lifeless corpse, that's for sure. It wasn't as if new, "empty" bodies were produced or sold anywhere. In any case, if there was technology powerful enough to process the total quantum states of all the synapses found in the central nervous system—what then? How could you reverse the procedure? How could raw data be written onto a living brain? It just didn't work.

So, if you died, would your digitized copy just have to make do with cyberspace? The thought that digitizing the human mind was a one-way ticket wasn't at all unsettling to Albert—on the contrary. For the transfer procedure to be complete, the original would have to be destroyed. That's what transferring was—copying and destroying the original. Albert couldn't care less about what would happen to his physical body once the process was complete.

One thing was certain—life after death was possible. On the other side of the Blackwall.

Classic. Bare concrete, cold fluorescent lighting, a metal table, a fold-out chair, a surveillance camera. Must be another one hidden some-where in the interrogation room. And the pointless waiting—that was key. Wore down the suspect. Not torture per se, but in the same family. The setting was all too familiar to Zor. Military though, not police. Once, he'd spent many hours being forced to explain why he'd deserted and broken the cease-fire. He'd spoken the truth and nothing but the truth, to no one's satisfaction. If he made it through that, he'd make it through this.

There was a lot of time until eleven, almost twenty hours. They had twenty-four hours to charge Zor and Aya with a crime. He'd made sure they wouldn't—scrubbed all traces from the van and wiped the CCTV footage from Northside. So, what did they have? Buying iron from the Animals? Big whoop—a misdemeanor at worst. Not even. Who knew, maybe those stinking, grotesque beasts even had licenses to sell.

He tried to recall the technique he'd learned for rapid regen in the army. The handcuffs bound to his wrists didn't make it easy, but he managed to find a stable position.

Liam stared at the display of the inside of the interrogation room. Zor sat in the uncomfortable metal chair, his head tilted back, eyes closed. He was napping, the asshole. Wasn't supposed to go like this. Shouldn't be Liam getting impatient, but Zor. And there he was, catching up on his beauty sleep.

"Don't think it's working," the rookie remarked.

The inspector gave a slight nod. They sat in the dimly lit monitoring room in front of a grid of screens showing all the interrogation rooms. Most of them were *ocupado*.

Damn it, the comfy armchair was making Liam sleepy, too. No, there was no time to waste. Any moment and someone else might need their room.

"Coffee?" The rookie yawned and stood up.

Liam examined the man on the screen. He obviously wasn't chipped with Mantis Blades or any other subdermal blade or projectile implants. A preliminary scan did reveal military-grade 'ware— high-end, too. But the system couldn't identify them. Gangs rarely went in for that kind of chrome. Zor looked more like someone who wanted to stay out of trouble. Didn't work out so well.

The machine dispensed two coffees. The rookie put Liam's cup on the small desk. Liam immediately took off the plastic lid and tossed it in the trash.

"Let's see how he deals with the smell of freshly roasted java." He spat his gum out, took the cup from the surprised rookie's hands and got up, pushing the door open with his foot.

"He's chromed to the teeth with military 'ware," the rookie reminded him. "We have no idea what he's capable of."

"Which is why I got a coffee for him, too."

Liam walked down the concrete hallway and stopped in front a steel door with a red light above it. The small LED screen on the door displayed the room's interior. There was his suspect—napping without a care in the world.

The detective stacked one coffee cup over the other and pressed his hand against the biometric panel. The heavy bolts retracted and the door slid open. The topmost cup tipped and spilled a bit of coffee onto Liam's sleeve. He caught it in the last second and caught Zor's gaze as he wiped off the brown liquid. Not the smoothest entrance, but Zor didn't react to the gaffe.

The detective pulled up a chair and slid the cup of coffee with the lid on it toward the detainee, leaving a splotch of coffee on the table. They sat for a moment in silence, sizing each other up.

"How is it that you're not in our database?" Liam asked.

"You tell me. I'm not responsible for police records," Zor replied. "Am I being charged?"

Liam touched the table next to the coffee smear. A holographic rectangle with his case notes appeared. Liam remembered them perfectly, not to mention that he could display it directly on his retina thanks to his implants. But this made a better impression and bought him time to think.

"Over the last few days, a number of people have been killed. Molly Bernard, for one." He looked straight at Zor. "Ring any bells?"

"You know I didn't kill her."

"I know something's weighing on your conscience—something just as heavy. Just don't know what yet. You're gonna sit tight while I gather more intel. Gonna take a while to piece this little puzzle together—luckily I've got time and patience. Gather enough pieces, the picture'll start to make sense."

"How long are you gonna keep me here?"

Liam shrugged.

"As long as it takes," he replied. "There's usually an explanation for everything. Might take a while, but it's there."

"So why are there so many unsolved cases?"

"Laziness, incompetence. Not with me. We're looking at multiple homicides, theft and armed robbery. And here you are at the center of it all."

"I didn't kill anyone."

" 'Course you'd say that. If you know who did, I'm all ears."

"Can't find out if you're keeping me here."

"You have your suspicions, no doubt." Liam took a sip of his coffee. "Go on, before it gets cold."

Zor looked at the cup. He didn't move.

Liam tried to scan him using his sensor implants but stopped when Zor gave him a patronizing glare as if to say 'Nice try.' Zor had felt it—or at least the cyberware in his body had. He'd need to be put through a thorough scan, but in due time. Thankfully, Liam couldn't detect any signs of cyberpsychosis that he had worried about earlier.

"How long are you gonna keep me here?"

"In a rush to be somewhere?"

"Still haven't charged me with anything."

"I don't think you understand the gravity of your situation," the detective said, his tone more serious. "You're the prime suspect in a murder, which means I can keep you here for as long as I want. That is, unless you give me something that'll change my mind. You say you didn't kill anyone—so who did? Gotta know something, or else you wouldn't have found yourself at the scenes of the crimes. Can't all be coincidences. If Aya did it, just say so. Whoever confesses first gets the better end of the deal—meaning a couple years less behind bars." He took another sip. "Or no jail time at all, who knows."

Unlike Zor, Aya didn't even pretend to stay calm. It was written all over her face—she was scared. Coffee wouldn't help, nor any other kind of signs of sympathy.

"You murdered Molly Bernard," Liam began.

Aya violently shook her head.

"Prison's jam-packed these days," the detective said. "Space is tight, but I'm sure they'll find a place for you. On the floor, maybe, or sharing a bed with an Animal."

"I didn't kill her." Aya lowered her gaze. "I don't know who did."

Of course, she didn't do it. Liam had no doubt about that. Who kills their neighbor and leaves the dead body in their own unit only to come back and get caught on camera?

"It'll get easier once you start talking."

She gave a despondent shrug.

"Just tell me what you know," he insisted. "Doesn't have to be from the beginning."

"They kidnapped Juliena," she blurted out.

"Who's Juliena?" Liam tried to sound interested, even though the appearance of a new piece of the puzzle didn't thrill him.

"She's eight. I take care of her. Molly helps out sometimes. Helped."

Made sense. Molly Bernard happened to be in the wrong place at the wrong time. Whoever took the kid had to get rid of any witnesses. That would explain the quick stab wounds, unlike the other victims who were toyed with.

"Why didn't you report it?"

"What do you mean 'why'?!" Tears welled up in her eyes. "So you wouldn't drag me here! You always take the easy way out. There's a dead body in my unit, so I must've killed her, right? Simple. Just arrest me on suspicion of murder. I won't even know if they make contact now because you took my phone. Can't look for her—can't do anything as long as you keep me here."

"Let me explain something." Liam leaned over the table. "You're under arrest because someone was murdered in your unit and you didn't report it. That makes you the prime suspect. Someone could be out looking for Juliena, too, but you didn't report that, either."

"Would you have even bothered to look?"

"Might've been worth finding out."

"Wouldn't change anything. You'd still drag me here." She hesitated. "Can I . . . still report the kidnapping?"

"Absolutely." Liam nodded. "As soon as you tell me what I need to know. Who else is dead? Who's left on the kill list? Who ordered the murders and why?"

"I don't know!" She wanted to throw out her arms, but the handcuffs stopped her. "That's what we were trying to figure out—find whoever took Juliena. Before you arrested us."

"If you want to help Juliena, start by telling me the truth."

"You promise to find her?"

"I promise," he lied. "But first we need to go over what you know. If Zor forced you to commit a crime, you have to tell me right here and now. Unless you'd prefer to go straight to prison."

As he drove out of the parking garage, his eye was caught by a charcoal-black suit getting out of a limo in front of the precinct. The same one from the Militech warehouse in Northside. It was him, no doubt. Liam had a photographic memory for faces, in no small part aided by the NCPD database he could summon anywhere, anytime. He ought to have felt worried, but he didn't. His mind was elsewhere. He felt like a predator closing in on his prey. He was close. The puzzle was coming together—he could see it right in front of him, sections of it still blurred out. Could end up that he was looking at it upside down, or reversed, but all the pieces were within his reach.

It was a short drive—only a few blocks. He found a parking spot in the shade cast by the practically adjoined megatowers. Protocol required he display his NCPD credentials on the dashboard. He looked around at the other parked cars and hesitated. Old beaters, not to mention the sketchy guys sitting on the curb in front of an auto repair shop, eyeing him discreetly. Screw it. He stuffed the ID in the glove compartment.

As far as megabuildings went, he'd seen worse. The main atrium was relatively neat and the intercom actually worked. Liam didn't use his police code. He held his hand close to the lock's sensor and waited for his decoder to complete its breach protocol.

Ten elevators, four of them busted and one covered with remnants of police tape. He entered together with a woman who had bags under her eyes. She turned to avoid his gaze—she probably knew he was a badge. He disregarded her, instead combing through the report of the bizarre break-in in his mind. Nothing was taken, nobody was hurt, though a shoot-out led to the destruction of one of the elevators.

He stepped out onto the forty-fifth floor and went over to the next elevator, covered in black plastic. He made a small cut and peeked inside. A few dozen bullet holes, automatic judging by the spread. Ballistics would confirm it once they were finished with a more important investigation. Or they wouldn't. Only thing that mattered was the name of the unit's tenant. Zor. Beat officers entered that information along with the fact that there was a gap in the security footage for two hours. Case closed.

The unit's door was located directly across from the damaged elevator. This time his decoder fought with the lock for a full thirty seconds. When it finally beeped and slid open, the detective stepped inside. The TV immediately flickered on with a slew of commercials. Liam disabled it with a wave of his hand and turned back around. The shooter was already in the unit when the first shots went through the door. The fleer, or fleers, managed to escape to ground level using the elevator. Weird. It takes the elevator doors more than two seconds, maybe three to close. Enough time to unload a full magazine into a person.

Unless the shooter didn't want to kill them?

Whoever was in that elevator probably chose it because they knew it led directly to the unit's door. Which means either they'd been here before or lived here and weren't expecting an ambush. Working theory.

The detective looked around the unit. Basic furniture, minimalist. The person who lived here was a single man who either had no social life or only came here to sleep. No random crap, branded mugs or any of the promotional shit they shoved at you in every store.

Liam went to the fridge and examined its contents. Basic meal boxes, all the same flavor. The minimum you needed to keep from starving. No empty beer cans in the trash, no cigarette butts. It was as if a robot lived here. Not the most ridiculous comparison, considering his initial impression of Zor after few minutes' conversation.

He checked inside the closet—nothing. Probably shouldn't stay much longer. He had no warrant or just cause—as far as the law was concerned, he was breaking and entering.

One last thing. He pushed back the bottom of his coat and sat down on the uncomfortable chair facing the small desk. Wouldn't hurt to take a peek in the cyberdeck's search history.

Why use it for browsing the Net? Calling it a hassle would be an understatement. To avoid commercials, maybe? Or to avoid being tracked?

Or to avoid leaving traces.

Liam carved out a chunk of time thoroughly combing through the deck's configuration—cracking the password was hardly an obstacle.

After an hour had passed, he took a break to gather his thoughts and made a coffee. It tasted even worse than the one at the precinct.

The deck's configuration was sparse—only a few folders. Just as he suspected—Zor used the cyberdeck for reading the news from multiple sources, both official and unofficial. Nothing else. Every day for a few hours he clicked on articles announcing the latest developments in the military, fashion industry, engineering—even parenting advice. There were ads for services targeting gay, bisexual and other sexual preferences. They seemed chosen completely at random—it was impossible to make out any pattern. His activity history reached back no more than several days. Maybe he regularly cleared it?

Cyberdecks weren't designed to track their users' analytics, but luckily Liam's own personal soft did. This kind of tedious, investigative sleuthing was what made him different from other detectives in his department who were always thumping their chests, hungry for action.

Zor's profile couldn't be more nondescript. Which was strange, because everyone had preferences. Even if they didn't realize it, some preferred a glass over a cup, an armchair over a couch, a sports car over an SUV, apple over orange juice. The algorithm couldn't make up its mind. Impressively, Zor had somehow managed to remain a statistical question mark.

Liam couldn't discern any pattern. On the other hand…there was one parameter that he could check using his detective's soft. It was invisible in the cyberdeck's operating system, but it was there in the history if you dove deep enough into the system files. Here, at this level probably never even explored by the cyberdeck's manufacturers, another piece of the puzzle fell into place. If you filtered all the articles according to the reading duration, the articles he spent the most time on all had one feature in common—a key word. The last name of a certain high-ranking corpo.

He recalled the days when Zed was a slim, well-built officer. Before he let himself slide, year upon year. By the time he'd finally made chief, he'd become a sluggish, overweight bulldog.

"You wanted to see me," Liam said as soon as the door shut behind him.

"Sit." The chief motioned to one of the chairs.

The office was a time capsule. It probably hadn't changed since Zed's predecessor's predecessor. Liam might have seen him twice when he first joined the force. Even if the interior of the precinct had already been twice renovated, the chief's office remained untouched. It almost seemed as if Zed's appearance had adapted to the office itself.

Liam sat down.

"Whiskey?" The chief made space on his desk while avoiding Liam's gaze.

"Still on duty." Liam was getting worried. He knew the chief well enough to know he wasn't acting like his usual self. "Something up?"

Zed clasped his hands together and took a deep breath.

"Your application for early retirement has been approved by the board," he said as if he needed to rid himself of the words.

Liam was motionless.

"I didn't submit an application."

"You'll submit it today before you go back out that door." Zed made an effort to stay calm, but his voice couldn't hide his emotion.

"What the hell's going on?" Liam jumped to his feet. "Is it something I did?"

The chief shook his head.

"Your performance is good—far above the average, always," he replied. "No denying it—you're one of our finest."

"This a personal thing? When have I ever given you any grief? I always cut my vacations short when you needed me to, took the worst cases without complaining."

"Well, that's just it. Won't have to shovel any more shit in retirement—you can spend more time with your family."

The detective narrowed his gaze.

"What's my family got to do with anything?"

"Listen…The NCPD—we put criminals in jail, maintain order and so on and so forth. But we don't meddle in politics. The farther we stay away from it, the better."

"Is it about those two I brought in?" Liam pointed his thumb behind him. "You're telling me that's politics?"

"As political as a steaming heap of shit, that's all I'll say. Real nasty storm was starting to brew, but I managed to calm things down."

"They're just some bumbling, start-up gangers." Liam spoke quickly, as if to fit in as much as he could before Zed could interrupt him. "Or more like wannabes. It's obvious they didn't kill Molly Bernard or the others, but that's why I need more time to work them a little longer so I can find out who did. They're planning something big and I wanna be the first to know about it before more innocent people die. Besides, we're doing those two a favor. Wouldn't last another month out there. The boys caught 'em trying to buy illegal guns from the Animals. On the street, in broad daylight. I need to know why."

"That's the goddamn point—not to stick around long enough to find out why." Zed fished out a bottle and two glasses from under his desk and poured. "Trust me, it's for your own good."

"Who'll take over the case?"

"There is no case."

"Gonna just sweep this under the rug...?"

"By the way, I know you invested a lot in implants and professional soft...I think your promotion to chief inspector will make up for that. Better pension and all."

Zed walked over to Liam and held out a glass.

"I'm on duty." Liam stared into empty space.

"Not anymore you aren't." Zed forced the glass into his hand. "Congratulations on your retirement."

Maybe somewhere there were secret labs with machinery capable of transferring an exact copy of the human brain better than the Relic could. There was no way to find out. All he had was the less-exact, less up-to-date copy that he had created himself. The last part didn't worry Albert—he could easily part with the memories of the past few days. He could send the data himself later, remotely. What worried him was that his copy would wind up a cluster of all of his emotional states once the reading process was complete. He hoped that wouldn't cause any issues. He couldn't be certain.

An idea popped into his head. A simple one. If he couldn't make a one-to-one copy of his mind along with the tiniest of details, then the process would have to be simplified. Drastically. It wouldn't be a perfect copy—just one that functioned identically to the original. Instead of writing the states of every synapse, it was enough to store memories, character traits, habits. The outcome would be the same, or at least almost, while the volume of data and computing power needed would be reduced by an order of magnitude.

Reading his consciousness in this way didn't come without risk. For one, Albert would have to enable full, unlimited access to his link, switching to encrypted mode only when he connected to the Net. The few times he had connected lately were to upload data from the tier two's user-adapting procedure into the Cave. Only a steady, high-volume stream of data would ensure a high-fidelity copy.

The actual process of reading his consciousness happened in the background, unfelt and unnoticed. Albert experienced it as a light fatigue. The sole reason he could read in the first place was because of the tier two's original, built-in function to adapt its interface to its user. He decided to give his packets of consciousness a new visualization—cubes filled with varying shades of green pixels stacked on top of one other behind the code pillars. They stood across from the red clusters from his harvest, representing data to still go through, yellow meaning looked through and useful, and gray—discarded. He kept the green ones far enough so they weren't in the way, but close enough to reach. One after another, new cubes kept materializing in flashes of bright green.

There was just one hitch—he still had no idea how to pierce the Blackwall. For that, he'd need considerably more processing power than any netrunning gear currently came with, no matter the tier.

"This world rests in a delicate balance, held together only by mutual cooperation. Not everyone understands that. Some simply want to gain at the cost of others, balance be damned."

I will keep my private life unsullied as an example to all; maintain courageous calm in the face of danger, scorn or ridicule; develop self-restraint; and be constantly mindful of the welfare of others.

"But beneath the surface, war is ever brewing, waiting for an excuse to erupt with full force. Mutually assured destruction guarantees a colossal waste of human life. Everyone loses."

"*Honest in thought and deed in both in my personal and official life, I will be exemplary in obeying the laws of the land and regulations of my department.*"

"Night City knows this more than any other city in America. Our job is to never let it happen again."

"*I will never act officiously or allow personal feelings, prejudices, animosities or friendships to influence my decisions.*"

"Sometimes the official story and the truth are kept separate for the good of all involved."

"*With no compromise for crime and with relentless prosecution of criminals, I will enforce the law courteously, without fear or favor, malice or ill will, never employing unnecessary force or violence and never accepting gratuities.*"

"You seem to understand how the world works. That bodes well for our future cooperation."

Stanley stood, buttoned up his charcoal suit and left without saying another word. On the table in the now-empty cafeteria stood an untouched cup of coffee. The rookie looked at the cup, conflicted. She maintained the illusion of weighing the pros and cons, as if she still had a choice. She took out the tablet, tapped on the screen and for the first time in her career checked the box. Case closed.

She stood up, took one last bite from the buffet with the Raito Catering logo, smoothed out her dress uniform, put on her service cap and went out onto the square where three hundred new, bright-eyed police cadets were being sworn in. She'd had more pressing matters to attend to. Nobody noticed her arriving late, nor paid attention to the corpo leaving through the side door. Nobody except Liam, who stood off to the side.

The captain, Zed, continued reciting the oath.

"I recognize the badge of my office as a symbol of public faith and accept it as a public trust to be held so long as I stay true to the ethics of the police service. I will constantly strive to achieve these objectives and ideals, dedicating myself before God to my chosen profession— law enforcement."

CHAPTER_11

*B*lack rain pummeling the windshield as he accelerates upward into the sky. Night City to the left, shrinking—completely dark. In the distance, a fire blazing on the horizon. He tries to push the throttle past its maximum, but he knows it's already too late. The NUSA Air Force AV cuts through the air over no-man's-land—the only aircraft within a few-mile radius. He's breaking the cease-fire, but he doesn't care. He stops a quarter mile away from the flames raging hundreds of yards high. Whatever was down there is gone. Whoever lived there is dead. He can feel the heat from up here. Nothing and nobody remain. Their house—gone. Nicole and Brad...Gone.

He swerves to avoid the tornado of thick black smoke nearly a hundred yards wide. It's as if a volcano erupted. Beelining through it would be deadly—still part of the plan, but not just yet. In a minute—maybe a minute and a half.

They're visible even without night vision. Coal-black ships, blacker than the water of Coronado Bay. Which one launched the payload? Which one is responsible for this hellish inferno? No way to find out. He picks the closest one. The six missiles nested under the AV's nose ought to do the job. Their tech might be more advanced by twenty years, but they won't stand a chance—not at this range. Fifteen, twenty seconds to hit. Their defense systems won't be quick enough. Not like *he stands a chance after that, either. He knows the counterstrike will be instantaneous, but he's ready for it.*

He flicks the switch cover upward with his thumb, aims, locks on to the target and takes three quick breaths...

"Did you find them?" Aya glanced at Albert.

The teenager shook his head. He looked exactly how he felt. Exhausted.

"Don't give me that look! What was I supposed to do? Bum-rush those badges? Hold up my fists, go toe-to-toe with the Animals? If I hadn't hightailed it outta there, we wouldn't have all this iron." Ron grinned mischievously at Zor. "For free, no less. Unintentionally fucked those Animals. Er..." He grimaced. "Of course, wearing five condoms wrapped in duct tape and doused in antiseptic. Doesn't make it much better, since, well..." He glanced at Aya and meekly shrugged. "They were riled up. But I digress."

It was the middle of the night. All five were at the kitchen bar. Aya took a large vitamin drink from the fridge. She looked at her hand, which seemed to fully obey her will. For now.

First the job, then maintenance. It made her miserable, but she had no choice. "We don't have time," she said, more to herself.

"Get something with lots of protein," Ron said to Zor.

"How's it look?" Zor held out his arm for Ron to examine.

The ripperdoc took it and closely inspected the skin's surface.

"Not bad," he answered after a pause. "No genitals growin' outta your forehead, either, as far as I can see. But I'd need you on the chair at the clinic to do a proper checkup."

"That's a twenty-minute ride," Zor said.

"If the Animals recognized me, they'll be waiting there."

"Why would they recognize you? You were sitting in the car at least sixty feet away."

"Drink your protein shake," Ron said, avoiding the subject. "How come they let you go, anyway?"

"Some young detective came over." Aya shrugged. "Said we were free to go, just like that."

"Slippery as eels, you two. As usual." Ron went over to the fridge. "Who wants a drink? And by that, I mean a real drink."

"Considering I have the most important meeting of my career tomorrow?" Milena blew a cloud of smoke up toward the ceiling. "Count me in. I'll take a whiskey—twelve-minute aged."

"Only got twelve-second."

"Warden make contact?" Zor asked.

"No, but I have an idea." Ron placed two plastic cups on the counter. There were no glasses. "Probably the best idea anyone's ever had in the history of ideas. No joke."

"Spit it out," Zor interrupted.

"We steal that container from Warden and just . . . keep it."

Everyone stared at Ron in surprise. You could hear a pin drop.

"Why? What would we need it for?" Aya asked. "Warden's already paying us half a million."

"Because it's worth way more than that."

Milena shook her head, putting out her cigarette and reaching for the cup with amber liquid.

"Doesn't matter what the container's worth," Zor said. "All that matters is that Warden's paying us half a mill. That's the whole point of a fixer."

"But just think about it. Half a mill divided by five is a hundo each," Ron insisted. "Doesn't come out to a whole lot in the end."

"No one's splitting anything," Zor said. "You're gonna buy

yourself a new arm and fix up Aya. Rest we'll use to buy better weapons and gear up for the next job. Then we can start splitting."

"Better if we just go all in," Ron argued. "Who knows if we'll ever get another job."

"We won't if we screw over Warden, that's for sure. No one would ever work with us again."

"Unless Warden kills us first," Milena added. "Or at least he'd be the first in line to." She downed the cup and shot a glance toward Ron. "Now let's get some sleep. Got a big day tomorrow."

Aya followed them with her gaze. Job first, then maintenance.

This was new. The unknown device identified itself as ArS-03. Within wireless range, which meant it was somewhere close—either in this building or the one next to it. Albert enabled all the ICE he had and attempted to establish a connection. Denied. Polite but firm. He tried a less delicate approach using different protocols. Same response. He discarded the fleeting thought to try to hack it. Without knowing what it was, he had no idea how it would react to outright aggression.

What intrigued Albert most was the response time. He checked the interval from the moment he transmitted the query to the polite denial. It was so minuscule as to be nearly unmeasurable. Whatever ArS-03 was, it was insanely fast.

Quiet, metallic clicks seeped into cyberspace. He toggled to the living room camera. Zor was tinkering with the weapons—nothing to worry about. Albert closed the feed, blocked all sounds from realspace and embarked on a careful examination of the mysterious device.

He disassembled the sniper rifle in the middle of the living room and examined every component one more time. The candy man from

Kabuki wasn't lying—it really was in near-perfect condition. In his mind he remembered how to use this kind of rifle—the question was whether his body did, too. Target tracking and laser homing definitely helped, but that wouldn't get the job done on its own.

Aya stood behind him and laid her hands on his shoulders. Her touch made Zor lose interest in what he was doing. It was comforting. He stood up and faced her—she was nearly a head shorter than him. He kissed her on the forehead and immediately felt like a gonk. She grabbed the back of his neck and pressed her lips against his.

She led him by the hand into their room. She closed the door, leaned back against it and lifted off his shirt. Then she pushed him onto the bed, unzipped his pants and pulled them off each of his bare feet.

The mattress was pleasantly cool. Corpo Plaza's faint, diffuse neons poured through the window. The positional lights of NCPD drones blinked methodically in the night sky. It was past two in the morning and the hum of the city at this height barely reached them.

They both knew sleep wouldn't come quickly. Milena's rising and falling sighs were audible from the next room. It was impossible not to surrender to the moment.

Aya took off her shirt. Zor pulled off his boxers in reply. None of their movements felt natural, fluid. He felt clumsy, she—graceless. It only heightened the tension. She focused and thought-commanded her body to release what she called her feminine wiles—only this time she was ready to let them overpower her, too. It didn't fail. Zor and Aya's awkward uncertainty seemed to disappear—their control along with it.

He couldn't sleep. It was a waste of time, anyway. He floated in cyberspace, helplessly staring at the paltry amount of data gleaned from the mysterious device. His most delicate attempts at forcing it to cooperate came back with the same polite refusal. He'd have to let it go for now—there were plenty of other things on his plate.

He enabled the live streams from all cameras in the unit and instantly regretted it. If the idea of human evolution from one generation to the next seemed imperfect to him, the method via which new generations were created was downright revolting. The division into two sexes and pointless rituals just to find a mate to produce offspring with the highest chance of adapting and surviving was unfathomable. Not to mention the procreative act itself. Gross. The exchange of bodily fluids, the touching, squeezing and rubbing of various parts. And at the end you got another prototype that wasn't even an improvement on its predecessor. The variations weren't intentional, but random. It couldn't be programmed—you couldn't influence the end result. It was absurd, wasteful and inefficient. The world was changing too quickly to waste time and energy on shooting in the dark.

Gross.

Her hand running along the short bristles of his hair made a whishing sound. She imagined that's what wind through tall grass must've sounded like. The sky was turning pink—it'd be less than an hour till sunrise. They lay together in the rumpled sheets.

"Her mom worked at Marry's," Aya explained. "One day she crawled under the wrong guy's skin...and the next she was gone. Never even found the body. I took in Juliena for what was meant to be just one night. She was almost seven, completely un-self-aware. She didn't have any family—there was nobody who could take her. So, she stayed. Our neighbor Molly babysat her when I'd go to work."

She shifted onto her side and wrapped her arms around Zor, spooning him.

She squeezed his hand.

"I'm...I can't have kids," she whispered. "Juliena is all I have." And you, she wanted to say.

Zor drew her closer to him.

"We'll find her," he said without hesitation. "We'll get her back and go to San Francisco."

Would they really? In a few hours everything would change. Tomorrow—no, today, he'd achieve his life's goal, which meant...

He gazed through the window at the city he hated, though he'd never known any other. Just last evening he'd planned how they would divide the money from Warden, but what he was about to do by late morning today meant that none of it would even matter. The two canceled each other out...He felt a struggle between two different forces taking place within him. Two opposing identities.

He wanted to say something else—something smart, important. He turned to Aya. She was already fast asleep.

"You're so much like Nicole," he said nearly soundlessly.

The red glare of the aerozep's navigation lights hovering over the Northside Industrial District exposed the dim interior of what used to be an office, along with other leftovers now furnished with a black armchair, a switched-off console, a row of cabinets and containers used for storing substances that were more or less legal. The bed in the large room was a recent addition.

Stop thinking about it. Karla rested her head on Dum Dum's chest. *Royce will find us anywhere.*

She was right on both counts. True—he couldn't stop thinking about it. True—Royce could find them anywhere if he had a reason to look, such as if Dum Dum decided to take the container himself. He analyzed all the possible outcomes as if playing a difficult game of chess. He didn't like surprises. Right now, he was still a long way off from committing to a move.

Karla eavesdropped on his thoughts in a pleasant state of half sleep. It worried her that she couldn't tell the difference between what was simulation and what were his actual plans. Dum Dum didn't want to cut her off. She would soon drift off, anyway.

Why klep a bunch of patrol drone batteries? Not the hottest-selling commodity. Tough to offload even with the right contacts, especially in that amount. Which meant they were using it for their own purposes—most likely something to do with whatever was inside the container.

Dixie was asleep, wrapped around Karla's back as if in fear she would abandon him. She stretched and murmured. She liked to fall asleep while feeling him brushing up against her thighs.

Dum Dum stalled with going into regen. Everything had to be perfect, which meant he had to play out every single scenario in his mind.

No signs of life came from Juliena in the other room. When that evening Dixie had given her a tablet complete with games, she had chosen one and immediately lost herself within it. She rapidly excelled, too, as if she played nonstop. Sussed out the mechanics instantly, unlike the way she navigated real life. Didn't get scared at all when Karla killed that old lady. Not even a hint of surprise—went with them willingly, didn't try to run. She obediently stayed where they'd put her. The door wasn't locked—she didn't once try to open it. Maybe she was sleeping, or still playing.

The real question was whether she was valuable enough to force the impromptu gang to cooperate.

He ought to have been more nervous. He'd been waiting for this day for years, but he remained as calm as if he was simply walking into the store for a pack of smokes. Someone could wonder why he had a long bag slung over his shoulder, but it would be hard to imagine anyone acting on their curiosity. Badges, maybe. Or a ganger. Wasn't hard to avoid the former—the latter didn't show much sign of activity at this time of day.

Zor walked the length of the block and turned into the building's dimly lit atrium. He'd never been here but for some reason knew this was the place. The access panel was offline, but the old door opened inward with a push. Only a single elevator worked, but instead he took the stairs to avoid bumping into any denizens. Thirtieth floor— the buildings in this area didn't go any higher.

"Eleven thirty. Outside elevators"—the only intel Milena had given him. The rest he'd need to figure out on his own.

He didn't even break a sweat. His body temperature was automatically regulated by one of his newly chipped implants—another managed his glucose levels. The rooftop elevator house that housed motors and other equipment also turned out to be a repository of various objects that had outlived their owner—most likely the old building manager. How did he know all this?

The door's hinges were rusted—nobody had even bothered breaking in here. Looking out from the inside, he could see the summits of the Corpo Plaza towers. It was the perfect marksman's perch— concrete all around except for the opening for his rifle.

How did he know this was where he was supposed to go?

10:13—just over an hour till showtime. Though that was only an estimate. It could easily take two. He assembled the rifle and gave it a once-over, then dragged a mattress in front of the doorway. Despite probably lying here for years, it was completely intact. One hundred percent synthetic. It'd probably look the same in a thousand years.

He knelt in a meditative pose and spent five minutes clearing his head of any emotions and thoughts that were not pertinent to the mission. Then he positioned himself on the foam, linked all his systems to the rifle's interface and pulled up all data related to humidity, air pressure and, crucially, the speed and direction of the wind between the barrel and the target—all transmitted directly into his neural network.

The mattress was a little damp, but Zor's focus was on the elevators running along the exterior of the tower 1.2 miles away, clearly visible from here. There was no chance he'd recognize his target from this distance, much less through two panes of glass, maybe three. That's why whenever the elevator descended from its zenith, a set of lasers operating at variable frequencies would scan its interior for the correct facial pattern. If facial recognition was confirmed, he could take the shot.

Sinking the ship seven years ago was supposed to be his revenge. Far from it. It only gave him more incentive. It wasn't those carrying out orders who were to blame, but those who issued them.

He tweaked his optics, though it wasn't paramount. He loaded a semi-guided bullet into the chamber and paired it to his ballistics coprocessor. With a microsecond ping, one of the lasers calibrated his scope for the next few seconds. He'd have to repeat the process again before the shot. Hopefully the tower's security system wouldn't detect it.

He lay flat on his stomach and kept his index finger resting above the trigger. It was just him, the rifle and the tower. Nothing else existed.

Were AVs more secure than armored limos? Debatable. If a car's engine was disabled, it would simply come to a halt. You couldn't say the same for an AV. In spite of being head of security, Stanley wasn't punctilious on the issue of his own personal safety. Years in the army had trained him to distance himself from any and all potential threats and to take a statistics-based approach to security. The devil was in the data, after all. Still, when it came to getting around the city, he'd take a car any day over the prospect of flying around in an AV and being unable to find a convenient landing space.

He got out in front of Militech HQ—the driveway was designed to nullify the activity of any potential snipers. Defensive elements were ingeniously disguised as ornament, like the majestic-looking fountain, or the memorial plaque a dozen feet high with the names of workers who died seven years ago in the Unification War.

He entered the main hall, showed his ID and passed through the security gate despite the guards' protest. They seized him, nearly tackling him to the ground before dragging him back through the scanner. Two guards farther down the hall preemptively primed their rifles.

By now this was an age-old tradition. He would try to slide past security and they would stop and scan him—no exceptions. They knew perfectly well who he was—they'd seen him every day for years. He himself enforced these procedures and mercilessly fired any who shied from inspecting him.

All in the name of data-driven security.

"I'll be blunt, Katsuo-san. We can't agree to a pact founded, at best, on vague assumptions. It makes no shred of difference whether you offer ten percent or twenty percent of access to something if you have no notion what it is. If we don't know what this agreement rests on, we'll have no way of making sure Arasaka holds up its end of the bargain. It will place us in an awkward situation."

"Militech's situation does not only seem awkward—it very

much is. Project Aeneas is one hundred percent reliant on Arasaka technology."

"Technology that failed during the incident of '62."

"We have had plenty of time since then to shore up our weaknesses and enhance the necessary safeguards."

"So has the other side," Milena calmly retorted. "Let's suppose they have surpassed us in computing power, artificial intelligence, the speed of solution implementation, maybe even creativity. That's why we have to know what we're up against. You assume that the other side will be benign, Katsuo-san. Experience indicates just the opposite."

"That is why we have adopted additional defensive measures—filtering, multiple circuit breakers and anything else deemed necessary," Katsuo replied with equal composure. "In addition, of course, to completely isolating the site of the experiment."

A short break was in order—he'd been waiting for half an hour. He stood up, did a few squats and other basic exercises before shutting his eyes. He was half conscious of the systems within him running a full-body muscle-relaxing procedure, though he paid it no attention. The mission was all that mattered. He knew that the target could appear in the kill zone at any moment. It was an inherent, calculated risk.

Within thirty seconds he was back in position—reunited with his weapon. Whole. In addition to the semi-guided round in the chamber, he had three others waiting in the clip, inactive, just in case—even though he wouldn't need them. Zor's partial view of the tower meant a twenty-second visual on the descending elevator. The bullet's flight time was just shy of four seconds. If it missed, loading the next bullet, pairing it, calibrating the scope and taking a another four-second shot would add up to a total of twenty-three seconds. It was either the first bullet or nothing. 1.2 miles—a distance that was dangerously close to the rifle's maximum effective range. The slightest disturbance in the bullet's trajectory and it would miss its target wide. He could really use that second shot.

The distance combined with light reflected from the glass and waves outside the visible spectrum muddied his perception. He realized he couldn't count on a direct hit. He replaced the precision round in the chamber with its explosive counterpart. In a fraction of a second, it would turn everything inside the elevator into goop. There wouldn't be any bodies to recover.

"What if it's not enough? If the other side turns out to be hostile? If that happens, we ought to have every last security measure at our disposal—we should be united in our defense."

"How am I to understand that? What exactly are you asking from us?"

Milena hesitated, though her next words had been rehearsed.

"We want our researchers to be involved in Project Aeneas."

Katsuo stared at her for a few moments.

"I am afraid that is out of the question."

She hadn't expected any other answer. If she were in Katsuo's place, she would have said the same—or even withdrawn from the negotiation earlier.

She would've killed for a cigarette, but that was also out of the question. She tried to discern anything in Katsuo's behavior that might reveal whether he was involved in her attempted kidnapping the day before yesterday. In spite of her talent, experience and countless implants, he was unreadable—a blank page.

If not him, then who?

Stanley?

* * *

He was always kind to the bartenders, though he never flirted with them. He frequented the bar on the ground floor and remained polite. He tipped well. The meals weren't exactly the healthiest, so he only permitted himself breakfast. His excuse—that breakfast had to be calorie-packed. Healthy eating was reserved for lunch and after.

Stanley was less an early bird than a night owl. He worked late and got up late. That didn't bother anyone, since Militech's operations stretched across multiple time zones, which unfortunately also meant unexpected calls in the middle of the night.

Today was not that day. Today everything would go according to plan. He'd finish eating his criminally delicious, equally unhealthy stack of pancakes drenched in real maple syrup and ride the elevator up to his office.

Through the elevator house's doorway, he gazed at the tower's top thirty stories. He was relatively well hidden from any NCPD patrol drones. He could go outside, position himself against the ledge and have a view of a hundred floors, which would give him the chance for a second shot. Too risky—the drones would spot him in less than a minute.

Risk… This mission was less risky than it was a death wish. The moment he pulled the trigger, it would be only a matter of time before their military or corporate defense systems would trace the bullet's trajectory right back to his position. How much time did he have to make a run for it?

He hadn't even considered it. The purpose of his existence would end at the same moment as the target's life. He knew it wouldn't bring back Nicole and Brad—nothing would. But this man had to answer for his crimes. Just like Juliena's kidnappers would answer for theirs.

He ought to have been focusing on the task at hand, not letting his thoughts wander. And yet, while he maintained his aim at the top of the tower, he couldn't locate the pure, unthinking hatred toward the man he was about to kill. He wanted to end his life—was perfectly capable of it—but for some reason it was no longer the be-all and end-all. And no, it wasn't because the bastard would die in a split second without knowing why.

Juliena. Even though they'd never met, he couldn't stop thinking about her. One thing was certain—if he succeeded in his mission, Zor's chances of survival were slim to none. Who would rescue her then? Ron? Aya? Who'd get the money to repair Aya's implants?

He could see them before his eyes—their entire, miserable, impromptu gang of misfits. It didn't add up—none of it. Warden's original plan worked only out of sheer, dumb luck.

Stop thinking about it.

How the hell was he supposed to get this out of his head?! His palms were clammy. Was his temp control malfunctioning? No. He couldn't do it—his nerves were shot. Natural, totally natural. It'd pass any second.

"You're aware of the consequences if this project comes to light?"

Big mistake. She was making it on purpose.

"Should that occur, then the nature of our negotiation will also be revealed." Katsuo's expression remained unchanged. "The real one, not the cover story about cooperating in Africa. Our talks have lasted one month, which means that Militech has known about Project Aeneas for a month. Instead of notifying the proper authorities, all you have done is try to carve out a slice of the pie. I am afraid your threat to reveal our mutual secret has lost its sting."

He stood up. Milena did the same. Katsuo gave a slight bow of the head and made his way toward the door.

The negotiation had ended without success.

*   *   *

A second coffee would help him focus. He preferred natural methods. Of course, he had an arsenal of intra-oral substances that could be instantly dispensed via thought-command, but he didn't use them unless it was absolutely necessary. Coffee would do just fine.

Stanley sat motionless with his hands folded on the table as he read the progress report of a project accessible only to him. Events were approaching a crucial stage. It didn't matter if he read it here or in his office a hundred floors up. Everything else could wait.

He took another sip of his coffee.

Twenty more minutes passed. Still nothing. It was time for another regen. Only what if the target appeared during? His combat capabilities and firing precision were decreasing with every minute. A break was necessary.

Zor laid the rifle on its side, closed his eyes and repeated his basic exercises. Thirty seconds? He could shorten it to twenty-five. No, skirting protocol never ended well. It had to be thirty, no more or less. But was it effective under time pressure? In spite of all the thoughts rushing through his head?

Eliminate the target. No second thoughts.

Except revenge was only noble in stories. The cost was much, much higher in real life. Not just for the avenger, but for their loved ones, too.

Juliena wasn't his loved one. Get a grip.

So then what was Aya?

He could emerge from the elevator shed at any moment—acquire the extra time needed for that second shot. He wouldn't have a mattress to lie down on, but the cyberware Ron implanted in him could stiffen his body save for the muscles and joints needed to aim and fire. The option was there—after all, he wasn't planning on making an escape.

Until now.

Stanley paid for his coffee and left his usual tip. The subject had become difficult to steer, but that was the entire goal—autonomy. Lab testing, simulations—none of it worked. Risks had to be taken. Stanley had no influence over it, because he didn't want it. That made worrying wholly unnecessary.

Without any hurry, he headed toward the elevators.

What was eating at her? That the man who had tried to kidnap her—maybe even kill her—was about to die? That the negotiation was a failure? The chance of success was slim to begin with. Or was it because this was the end of the line for her? Militech most likely wasn't planning on keeping her around much longer. To hell with it—she was done with this job, anyway.

The rest of her life. How long was that? Thirty years? Forty? A few minutes from now?

Having no goal, no challenge was a kind of death in itself. Shame she hadn't asked Zor what one does after they've achieved it. Their purpose. If anyone knew, it would be him.

She went into the hallway. The young assistant, whose name she never found out, patiently waited behind the doors. He was affable in a manner that forbade open refusal and impoliteness, yet demanded compliance. When he indicated the way to the elevator, he simultaneously positioned himself so as to block any return once she had passed him. Unnecessary in her case, but nonetheless customary. Though he would have never dared touch her, she felt as if he was almost mentally shoving her forward, urging her to go faster. In spite of that, she slowed down.

Katsuo was waiting in front of the elevators.

Surprised, her steps briefly lost their rhythm. Too late—he had noticed. Why did she care? The negotiation was already over.

"This is the last time we will ever see each other," he said. "I'd like to say goodbye by taking a moment to admire the Night City skyline together from a height of twenty-five hundred feet."

The assistant approached him. Katsuo shot him a few quick words in Japanese. The assistant responded in the same vein. A brief standoff ensued. The young man came closer. Katsuo stopped him with an outstretched hand. The gap between Katsuo's palm and the assistant's chest must have been barely an inch. They stood like that—neither backing down. For the first time, the expression on Katsuo's face resembled something like anger.

The assistant finally drew away with a slight bow. Milena understood what had just happened. The assistant wanted to accompany Katsuo in the elevator—after all, that was his duty. But Katsuo refused. The outcome was inevitable—it was clear whose authority superseded whose—and yet for some reason this ritual had to be played out regardless. Though Milena was just an observer, she felt the intensity of their emotion. The assistant would most likely suffer serious consequences. In Militech and other western corporations, the rules could be bent, shifted—adapted to one's own needs. In Arasaka, they seemed sacred and almost opaque—as if submerged under centuries of tradition.

"Was he afraid for your safety?" she asked when the assistant left, his head lowered.

"I do not doubt that my death would be cause for celebration at Militech. But I highly doubt they would use you to carry it out. I will not lie—we conducted thorough research on you before commencing our negotiation."

That's why Warden chose me, Milena thought. Plain, ordinary, not a threat to anyone.

The elevator doors opened. Katsuo motioned for her to enter. She hesitated before going in. She'd never felt more tense in her life. Before her the unreal vista of Night City spread out before her, including Heywood—specifically the areas with thirty-story-high apartment buildings.

How long would the rest of her life last? Half a minute? A quarter?

Sticking around after was pointless. The goal was to eliminate the target. Who said he had to die, too? He could leave everything behind and lie low somewhere, most likely with the nomads. Months, at least. Maybe for good. Aya would have to get by on her own.

Positive match.

His finger hovered over the trigger. His heart rate didn't change in the slightest. He had everything under control. Somewhere in the back of his mind, the countdown had begun. Six seconds.

The elevator was descending. It was the moment he'd waited years for. Only three seconds until it went away again forever. Shouldn't he be feeling something? Excitement? Joy?

Positive match. Three seconds.

He would finally avenge his wife and son, whose faces he remembered as if through a thick fog. He'd leave Aya behind. Was this what it was all for? All those years of hiding, shitty jobs, insects, grime and filth?

Positive match. Three seconds.

Aya would have to get by on her own.

Two sec—

He pulled the trigger.

*   *   *

"He did it…"

"Confirmed."

"It…it worked!"

"He insisted on speeding the process up beyond acceptable limits…He got what he wanted."

"So?! It worked!"

The readings fluctuated wildly, dangerously approaching the critical threshold but staying just below it.

"Everything's working," OP3 reaffirmed with excitement. "Metrics are high but still within the norm. Cortisol inhibitors on standby."

"It really worked…" OP2 repeated.

In spite of their excitement, they still had to contain the situation. They checked everything that could go wrong and anxiously watched the monitors while simultaneously filtering streams of data on their retinal displays via neurolink. Gradually, they began to convince themselves.

The project was a success.

"We have twenty seconds of secure conversation," Katsuo said.

"What do you—?"

Milena struggled to collect her thoughts. She didn't know Zor's plan, only assumed that he would use a sniper with guided ammunition.

"Eighteen seconds," Katsuo said. "You are invited to dinner at my home. Bring your husband, partner—anyone in order to avoid suspicion. Seven PM. Here is the address and code to enter."

He placed a card in her hand. Surprised, Milena stuffed it in her purse. She couldn't focus. Every second, she expected a hole to appear in the glass. She wondered if she was in danger standing this close to Katsuo. Shrapnel, maybe.

"Thank you." She avoided his eyes. "Can I ask why, though?"

Luckily, her nervousness wasn't obvious. She had a right to act surprised.

"There is something you can offer me that can result in Militech and Arasaka cooperating. It can only come from you."

She gazed out at Heywood's stumpy buildings, perfectly visible through the double-paned glass. The weather was perfect. Their windows, antennas and chrome plating—once signs of a bygone elegance—glimmered in the sun.

His optics zoomed in on the bullet in real time, sharpening his view of its trajectory. The target in the elevator was a pixelated blur highlighted in a distinct, square outline. All Zor had to do now was keep the bullet and the reticule in his field of vision. With other sniper rifles you could shoot and forget, but with this one he had to guide the bullet to the very end.

The matte-gold spindle soared toward the elevator in slow motion. Zor's reflex booster made everything ten, twenty times slower, as if submerged in oil. His rifle's laser pinged back and forth, constantly adjusting the bullet's trajectory based on the actual and predicted movement of the wind and other objects in the air.

In fifteen minutes, the entire NCPD and Arasaka's corporate divisions would be hunting him. Not only did he have no escape plan—he didn't even have a getaway ride. No, running away wouldn't be enough. Far from it. Even if by some miracle he pulled it off, completely dropped off the radar—they'd still find the others. It wouldn't be all that hard, either. And no one would survive.

The bullet closed in on the jittering reticule. Half a second, which amounted to a few seconds in booster time. More time for doubt. Quick, sudden death from a bullet from an unknown direction allows no time for thought. You wouldn't know where you went wrong or what you did to deserve it. You wouldn't even realize that you were dead. Instant, oblivious death—no, that's not what Zor was after. He had to die knowing who took his life—and why. That would require meeting face-to-face. But how?

Half a second. Plenty of time to think. He didn't need it—he'd already made up his mind.

He shifted the square reticule toward the ocean in the gap between the towers.

Black rain battering the windshield. Coal-black ships, blacker than the water of the Coronado. Which one launched the payload? Which one is responsible for this hellish inferno? No way to know for sure. No way of knowing which of these sleek black destroyers contained the motherfucker who pressed a red button that spelled instant, remote death. No way of knowing who chose the target, who armed the missiles. Everyone was guilty, even the ship's engineer, the air traffic controller, the cook who fed everyone on board. All of them took Nicole and Brad from him.

"Land immediately!" His commander's voice pierces through the interference.

Rain battering the windshield, black with soot. Blazing tornados tower over the apartment complexes, half a mile high, maybe a mile, a black cloud looming over it, visible because it obscures any and all stars. From that black cloud comes the black rain—condensed moisture, previously turned into steam from fire. Ground moisture. Human body moisture. Oily black rivulets streak across the glass.

He picks the nearest ship. Six missiles ought to do the trick. They won't have time to react. They're old-gen, but there's no way they can shoot down all of them. It's enough if two hit their target.

He looks at his hand gripping the joystick with aversion. He can't imagine any other place he ought to be. It's a nine-hundred-foot drop down to his unit engulfed in flames along with hundreds of others. One massive firestorm. No other time or place he'd fit. Once he presses the button, he'll have less than a minute to live. Minute and a half if, once the salvo lands, he turns back and immediately pushes the throttle.

But what's a few more seconds of life compared to the sight of an exploding Arasaka battleship?

He flicks up the joystick's cover with his thumb. He aims, confirms the target, takes three quick breaths and presses the button.

There's no launch button, only smooth plastic.

CHAPTER_12

His mother smiles, reaches out her hand to steady him in case he loses his balance and falls. He's learning how to walk. These could even be the first steps he's ever taken. If it wasn't for the memory-reading process running in the background, he'd never have access to such early recollections. As he goes deeper, sifts further, a feeling from his childhood, a smell, maybe, floats up from the depths of his memory, becoming more potent every few hours whenever he enters a state of half sleep.

He didn't allow himself real sleep anymore. Waste of time, of which there was increasingly less. Their impromptu gang was getting more attention than it needed. Subconsciously, Albert knew from his time using a cyberdeck that just because you don't see something, doesn't mean it isn't there. If half this city was looking for a priceless container stolen by a ragtag bunch of amateurs, then the probability of them getting caught was extremely high. It wasn't only the container's contents that everyone wanted to get their hands on, but nipping the new competition in the bud before it got too powerful.

Albert didn't care about power. He just wanted time to finish the Taran, which meant he would need more money and better security. Not for long—a week or two. Then he wouldn't need anything anymore. At least not from realspace.

He missed his mother. No, stop it. Think of something useful, more productive.

Triangulation—a process Albert had learned courtesy of his data extractions. The concept itself intrigued him. It provided an easy method for locating any point in cyberspace. He even wrote a simple script that used a network of transmitters to triangulate any device emitting a particular frequency. Due to the transmitters' limitations, it wasn't completely precise, but enough to tell Albert where the device that interested him the most was located. ArS-03. If it was detectable from this distance, it must've had a solid transmitter.

Once he'd discovered what it was, the realization that ArS-03 could help him carry out his plan was immensely satisfying. Come to think of it, he hadn't felt this good in a long time.

Heywood. The coffee was even worse than she expected, but that's not what she had come for.

"I could've died today." Milena took a sip and grimaced. It was at least three tiers worse than the one at her office. "Would've been my own fault, too. Walked into an elevator that I might never have walked out of again." She thought for a moment. "It almost felt a little bit exciting. Now it seems pathetic. Nothing happened. I'll probably just get fired."

"Do you like your job?" Aya asked.

"I did. I fucked up, badly. Didn't win, but I still have a chance to minimize the losses. Probably wishful thinking. What are you doing...?"

Aya stared at her hand tightly gripping the coffee mug. She couldn't let go. She grabbed her wrist with her other hand. Didn't help.

"I...I can't..."

The cup cracked, splashing coffee across the entire table. Her hand resumed its functions.

"Sorry," Aya whispered.

"What the hell was that?" Milena grabbed Aya's hand to check for cuts. "Is this what Zor was talking about?"

The waiter didn't need a signal to wipe the table and bring another coffee, stat. The impeccably dressed corpo probably made more in a few minutes than he earned in an entire day. He served Aya another coffee—this time in a disposable cup.

"It's a long story." Aya shook her head.

"I'm not in any rush." Milena gave her subtle, trademark smile. "Have you ever lost money? A lot of it, I mean."

"Yeah. Got sick one time, couldn't work…Burned through all my savings."

"How much?"

"Around two hundred eddies."

"I lost eleven billion today."

Aya's hand froze around her replacement cup.

"Not my own, of course." Milena inserted the cigarette into the holder and lit up. "And that's just the lowest estimate. Who knows how high it could go?"

"Never did ask what you did for a living."

"I negotiate."

"I'm a pole dancer. Or at least I used to be…"

"It's in the past now. That part of my life is over. You probably think I'm in over my head. Our jobs aren't all that different, you know. We work for as much as someone is willing to pay."

"So, I'm a gonk for making a living using my body, is that it?"

"You can do whatever you want for a living. I'm just saying it's time for a change. New horizons have opened up. We just have to start walking down the path."

"Meaning the impromptu gang?" Aya shook her head. "All I want to do is find Juliena."

"The gang is our launchpad, our best chance. Only yesterday I was against it. Now? I don't know—do you have a better plan?"

"I just told you. I want to find Juliena."

"By yourself?" Milena blew a cloud of smoke upward and chuckled anxiously. "Trust me, you don't want to go it alone. This can still go all kinds of wrong. The first to go in Night City are the loners, the ones without powerful friends at their side. For some that's a corp—others a gang. It's not who you are that counts—it's what you're a part of. Why do you think the police let you go? Because they got bored?"

Aya shrugged. She raised the cup to her lips with her other hand.

"They didn't have any proof…" she answered. "That's what it seemed like, at least."

"Sounds to me like someone got you out because they needed you."

"Warden…"

"Try higher. Could be someone he works for."

Aya sighed and took a few sips of her coffee.

"I used to have lots of friends when I was little—fifteen years ago. Every day we would play on the block outside. There was always some gang war going on, but we didn't care because it had nothing to do with us. Then that red-haired kid, I can't remember his name, got hit by a stray bullet. That's when we started being more careful. Whenever we heard shots or saw a car driving slowly, we'd scatter. One day two cars rolled up; the shooting must have lasted for several minutes. When the dust settled, nobody came out of the building. We waited, but the cars just stayed there. Eventually, we couldn't help ourselves. Four of us, maybe five. We went in. Bodies everywhere, riddled with bullets. Would've bolted out of there if the place wasn't filled with terminals—the kind the military used. Still intact. We started playing with them—they were the coolest things we'd ever seen. I was only ten years old, but I should've known better. I grew up in a family where nobody had much time for me. First my dad died in an accident at the factory, then diabetes took my mom. Had to do everything on my own. I didn't understand the world until that moment. All I remember was a flash. I lost my hands and feet in the explosion. The temperature of the electrical blast cauterized my wounds—otherwise I would've bled out. My friends, they all ran away. Left me there to die alone. Lived like that for a year... Till this day, I don't know how I ate, drank, dressed myself. The chrome I had would always break. It was a dark time—I buried it all somewhere deep inside. But I still remember all the people who helped me—not my friends from the block, but total strangers who didn't expect anything in return. Mrs. Newell and her husband. They're the ones who gave me this." She raised her hand and moved her fingers. They were in perfect working order now. "I got a second chance at a normal life."

"That's why you're taking care of Juliena now," Milena said.

Aya thought for a moment.

"Maybe." She nodded. "I never thought of it that way. I just know that strangers helped me out of the goodness of their hearts. Sounds impossible for Night City, but it's the truth. That kindness is what I hold on to. I'm sure you can figure out the rest own your own. This stays between us, though. The cyberware from Militech was an offer I couldn't refuse." She raised her completely 'ganic-looking hands. "It didn't come for free, either. I do jobs for them from time to time."

"That place with the terminals." Milena gave her a tense look. "Was it a Voodoo Boys hideout?"

"I think so, yeah. Must've been Voodoo Boys. Didn't really get a good look at them. My memory only came back a few weeks after it happened. When I woke up in the hospital, the only thing

I remembered was my name." Milena pulled Aya toward her and hugged her tightly.

"And here I was about to confide in you."

"Got them!" Albert cried out, and jumped to his feet. The C-Link connector in the back of his head unjacked itself automatically.

Zor stopped staring at the ceiling and looked at him from the couch.

"Took you long enough."

"I only had one thread out of thirty assigned to it."

"Don't tell that to Aya."

Zor stood up and went over to Albert's chair. "Who is it?"

Albert pointed at the large screen and typed in a short command on the auxiliary keyboard. A window appeared—footage from a CCTV camera. Albert zoomed in on a pile of trash next to an old brick building. A woman in a skintight leather suit was kneeling and hugging a man sitting cross-legged in front of the wall. His body twitched every few seconds. Next to them stood a tall, nearly bald man in a leather coat.

"This is how they found me," Albert explained. "The one on the ground is their netrunner."

An NCPD patrol car rolled past and slowed, but didn't stop. That's when the man in the coat turned—seven red optics in the center of his forehead.

"Maelstrom," Zor said. "Ruffled their feathers in Northside after we hit that warehouse."

The woman brushed away the damp, white hair from the boy's forehead and helped him to his feet, then all three got into a black Villefort and drove away. The recording ended there.

They don't know who we are. Puts us at an advantage. Their 'runner's a script-kiddie using tier-one tech. An insect compared to us.

Dum Dum heard Dixie thought-speak, then answered. *I wouldn't be so sure.*

Playing it safe would be an exaggeration, Karla chimed in.

Maybe, maybe not. Dum Dum at the time had briefly scanned Zor before the elevator doors closed. He didn't find any combat 'ware, but there was something major in his head—an implant the likes of which Dum Dum had never seen before, and Dum Dum knew his chrome.

He stood next to the grimy window holding a cup of scop smoothie and gazed out onto the Arasaka Waterfront from the twentieth floor. Lotta freight coming in and out. Crews would descend on the city come nightfall, hit all of Night City's famous clubs. Cab drivers needed to be reminded who they really worked for. Same applied to the autonomous cabs and those who tweaked their algos. If a client said "Take us to the best club in town," it better be owned by Maelstrom.

Dixie went over to the terminal and began transmitting the orders. Boys downstairs could deal with the chores. Here, upstairs, they had more important shit to deal with. Getting their hands on the container was worth delegating other matters, even at the cost of a momentary dip in their profit stream. They had to play this smart, discreet. Renner didn't deserve any particular respect, but starting a war with south NC wasn't in anyone's interest.

Karla practiced her favorite martial art, created by none other than herself. Body cutting. The tips of her blades barely penetrated the outline of the holographic mannequin in quick, surface-level cuts before she quickly jumped back beyond the reach of her opponent's blades. No single cut was fatal, but make enough of them and the blood loss alone would take down any opponent, no matter how big.

Dum Dum watched her. Though she trained in the nude, he felt no excitement. In a world where you could have everything, it was hard to enjoy anything.

A martial art perfectly suited for a holo-mannequin, he thought-spoke.

Karla smiled to the extent her cybermodded face permitted. *The time will come. You'll see.*

Dum Dum raised his gaze to Dixie. *Time to make our offer. Do it.*

The Delamain cab wove its way through traffic. Milena skimmed the reports on her tablet—she was already familiar with them, though only those relevant to the negotiation. Now she dove deeper, combed through details previously insignificant. Finally, she found what she was looking for. She held her breath in disbelief.

"*We have arrived at your destination.*" The AI's genteel British accent tore her from her thoughts. "*Thank you for choosing Delamain. We wish you a pleasant day.*"

She got out into the sweltering afternoon heat and nearly ran the last few yards, then down the stairs before opening the door.

"Fucksicle!" Ron jumped. "Goddamn lock…"

"You're not answering my messages," Milena remarked.

"Kinda in the middle of something here?" He motioned to the woman lying on the table. Unconscious, wires connected to her arms and head. In place of her face, there was a metal-rimmed opening with mounting slots. "Shut the door. And lock it."

She did as he asked and then took a step toward him.

"How'd Warden get you on board?" she asked. "What did he have on you?"

"Oh, um, you know…Embarrassing crap from my past, the usual." Ron wanted to dismiss the matter with a wave, but his hands were coupled to the manipulators, currently deep in the patient's head. Nearby, cases containing optical implants and jaws lay half-open.

"You said you weren't coming back here," Milena reminded him. "Thought the Animals could recognize you."

Ron raised his eyebrows.

"Yeah, well, man's gotta eat, right?" he said after a beat. "Why are you here? Thought you were supposed to have the most important day of your life today, or somethin'."

"Done for the day. Thought I was done for good, actually, but... never mind. Listen, there was this incident in '62..." She shut her eyes and cursed under her breath. "This is classified... Can she hear us?"

"Her—no," he said firmly. "But I can—loud and clear. And I'm tellin' you right now that I don't wanna know anything that someone could use against me down the line."

"It won't put you in any danger." She gave a wave of her hand. "Or rather, any future danger is irrelevant right now. Without getting into too much detail, my argument in the deal I'm negotiating, or was negotiating, involved an incident that took place in 2062. There was a cover-up at the time—screamsheets and media chalked it up to a gang war. There was this kid—by some miracle she survived the explosion, fought for days in the hospital. The city turned her into the story of the month and tanked a particular gang's reputation."

"All right... and?" Ron asked expectantly.

"That kid was Aya." Milena sighed. "EMP blast that was supposed to protect the Net from an AI invasion ended up blowing off her hands and feet. The charge was supposed to fry every circuit within a few dozen yard radius in order to stop the transfer and... she was there, caught in the electrical blast." She shook her head. "Then there's Katsuo, the Arasaka rep I was negotiating with and whom Zor's obsessed about. What the fuck is going on here, Ron?"

Ron swallowed.

"I also...I'm almost sure I know Zor—that we've met before. For the life of me, I just can't remember where..."

"Us, our little gang isn't impromptu—we can't have all met by chance!" Milena exploded. "What did Warden have on you?"

Ron hesitated, then stopped the operation. He unjacked the cable from the back of his head, went over to her and gave her a regular, old-fashioned hug.

She closed her eyes and let out a deep breath.

That was the worst part. Feeling powerless. Useless. If only there was something she could do, even if it was hopeless. Anything.

The message from the kidnappers was straightforward. The amount was not. Half a million. More than Aya could make in her entire lifetime. By coincidence, it was also the exact amount Warden promised for stealing back the container. Only when? And what would the others think?

Albert lay on his chair, submerged in cyberspace.

She looked at her hands and moved her fingers. They worked fine, but she knew it wouldn't last. The intervals between her seize-ups were getting shorter. Today it had already happened twice—luckily in a safe environment. But it was a matter of days before her implants would refuse to cooperate altogether. That wasn't speculation—it was fact.

She was surprised. Surprised and angry. How could he have gotten past their security on the ground floor? Climbed up twenty floors? Opened this door?

Karla unsheathed her Mantis Blades, ready to pounce. Dum Dum ordered her to stand down. *He's just here to talk.*

"We apologized." Zor took a step forward to let the door automatically slide shut behind him. "Gave you a cut of our haul."

"That's not how this works." Dum Dum quickly regained his cool. "You disturb the balance—you pay. Let the punishment fit the crime."

"Strange how we stole from Militech and yet you're the one out to get us. If anything, we did you a favor. Proved that you don't have control of your own turf. Blame yourselves, not us."

Dum Dum was silent. He didn't have a good reply, because Zor had a point. Made all the more annoying by the fact that he'd walked in here like he owned the place. Someone would have to answer for that.

"I could give a fuck about your apologies," he replied instead. "Along with that useless scrap you gave us."

"Don't pretend like this is about honor or principles." Zor hadn't moved.

"Half a mill for the girl and we let everything slide."

"Half a million would get you a second-rate corpo VP."

"It's a free market. Goods are worth as much as someone's willing to pay for it."

Dixie hadn't moved from his terminal. *Should I call for backup?*

We're just talking, Dum Dum thought-spoke in reply.

"Don't even have a tenth of that," Zor said.

"I know." Dum Dum crossed his arms. "You're gonna pay me another way."

Karla stood off to the side, the tips of her Mantis Blades unsheathed. Dum Dum shot her a glance. *I said we're just talking. Relax.*

"Need to see her first," Zor said.

Dum Dum didn't even twitch as he thought-commanded the

nearby door to open. In the cramped room sat a skinny, dark-haired girl, her attention absorbed by her tablet. Though she looked nothing like Brad, Zor felt a rush of emotions he couldn't name. What did Brad's face look like? He remembered straight blond hair, a swing… That was all. He collected himself. Now wasn't the time for reminiscing. Though he'd never seen her before, in some strange way he knew it was really her. Juliena.

"Haven't harmed a hair on her head." Dum Dum gave a crooked grin. "For now. I know what you're thinking—could sneak out just as quietly as you came in. Won't be fooled twice—that I can guarantee."

"What do you want in return?"

Dum Dum closed the door via thought-command.

"There's a certain gray container that you klepped from Militech in Arroyo. You're gonna bring it to us."

"Don't know where it is."

"Better start lookin', then. See, we'd rather keep our hands clean, not go startin' another war. So, who better to klep it for us than a bunch of nobodies? 'Specially since you already did it once—second time should be easy, right? Do that and you get the girl, then everyone goes their separate ways and we'll forgot about your little… transgressions."

For the last hour Milena lay on the couch reading background material on Project Aeneas. It was all there before, but she had only read what was useful for the negotiations. She hadn't had time to read the thousands of other documents—one had to prioritize. All she needed to know was that in the 2040s NetWatch had built the Blackwall—an impenetrable barrier that walled off what was left of the Net from hostile, rogue AIs hell-bent on wreaking havoc. The chaos was first unleashed by Rache Bartmoss, legendary netrunner and harbinger of the DataKrash. It was largely common knowledge, as well as a shared conviction, that disabling or destroying the wall would spell the end of the world as they knew it. How that end would look, nobody could say. Thankfully, there was no shortage of movies and braindances to help people envision it.

It would take several days to get through all this. Instead, Milena skimmed through the reports and started to understand just what happened nearly four decades ago, and which was still happening.

2022. Bartmoss unleashed his RABIDs (Roving Autonomous Bartmoss Interface Drones) virus, leading to an event known as the DataKrash and causing the Internet to collapse. In the interest of public safety, huge swathes were left abandoned, leaving a disconnected mosaic of local Nets—a tiny archipelago compared to the Old Net. Certain groups of netrunners at the time still believed it was possible to regain what was lost by coming to an understanding with the AIs or by eliminating them. To do that, they first had to get through the Blackwall. Nobody ever succeeded. That led to two conclusions—the first being that in order for the Blackwall to persist, it had to exist in flux, constantly undergoing modification. Secondly, and more importantly, if even the best netrunners couldn't break through it, then they sure as hell wouldn't stand a chance against the AI onslaught. Which meant that the Blackwall was their last and only defense against total annihilation.

The next report slightly contradicted the previous one, describing apparently successful incursions beyond the Blackwall. The incident in 2062, which Aya was a victim of, was only one of many.

From the couch, Milena watched as Aya and Ron played a game at the table. She didn't know what it was called, but probably neither of them knew the rules that well, because arguments broke out almost every minute. All in good fun, at least.

The internal documents, accessible only for those with high-level clearance, were characterized by a surprising frankness and honesty—none of the usual jargon and bullshit propaganda. Only cold, hard facts, which admittedly also made the language dull and hard to read. The report counted seven "successful" infiltrations of the Blackwall. Each one ended with the netrunners' deaths, including innocent bystanders, and in two cases the consequences were even more dire. The proof was lacking, but it seemed that, in every case, the Blackwall itself had come to humanity's rescue.

Another report suggested that for years NetWatch hadn't been able to control the Blackwall. It maintained itself and controlled what information passed through it—an independent entity. Precisely the kind of thing NetWatch was founded to eliminate in the first place.

Milena switched off her tablet; her eyes were tired. She twirled Katsuo's card between her fingers. His invitation was highly unusual, which meant it must have been important. On the other hand, she hadn't the slightest desire to go there—nor an actual reason, since the negotiation was no longer relevant.

She watched Aya, who was absorbed in the game. Holographic pieces with descriptions in the shape of colorful pictograms hovered over the table. Surely, Aya had no idea that what had happened to her was connected to Milena's job. If that were the case, she wouldn't have told her about the accident. It was too big a coincidence to ignore. Someone had to know something. Not Warden—he was just a ganger for hire. Who, then? Who was it that wanted them to meet?

Ron chuckled mischievously and moved one of the holographic pieces.

"What?! You can't do that!" Aya protested. "Take it back!"

"Oh, c'mon, you're no fun." The ripperdoc smiled and moved the piece back.

Milena knew what he was doing, and it was working. He was helping Aya take her mind off of everything. She slapped her forehead in joking despair after he made another wrong move. To join in on the humor, Milena would've at least needed some grasp of the game's rules.

She looked at Katsuo's card again. If there was any chance of finding out more about the incident in '62, sitting down with the Arasaka rep—away from prying eyes or ears—was her best bet.

"Gotcha!" Ron jumped up from the table and pointed a finger gun at her. *Pew, pew!* He was like a child. "You lose! I win!"

"But that's not allowed..." Aya started to laugh. "That piece doesn't move like that."

"Too late. Called it!"

She tried to imagine Ron having dinner with her and Katsuo. He was probably expecting a typical, boring monochromer suit. His crass jokes and lack of table manners combined with Katsuo's refinement and etiquette painted an absurd picture. That wasn't even counting the sake. But it would never come to that.

In her mind's eye she saw Ron and herself somewhere...She couldn't imagine the place, only knew that it was as far away from Night City as possible. Peaceful. A fantasy—nothing more.

She went to the trash and stood over it for a second, motionless, holding Katsuo's card above it with a carefully manicured hand. She hid it in her purse. Perhaps it could still be of use one day.

ArS-03, log 58219.
Synchronization procedure initiated.
Unidentified device NI100101001110. Status: unknown.

Subsystems detected: 118.
Unsecured devices: 1.
Synchronization procedure in progress.

The door slid open. Zor stopped at the sight of Warden standing in the middle of the unit. Aya and Albert were both on the couch; Milena leaned against the bar counter, cigarette in hand. Ron was making a drink. He motioned to Albert with his head.

"Kid figured we didn't need to keep anything from our fixer," he explained. "Didn't think to ask for our opinion, of course."

"It's my unit," Albert said flatly.

"This concerns all of us now." Warden's voice was commanding. "Fuck if I'm gonna explain everything again. Someone tell 'im." He meant Zor.

"If we're going to work together, then we need to trust each other. We need to know what your plan is." Milena inhaled and grabbed the drink from Ron's hand. "All of it."

The ripperdoc let out a silent sigh and turned back to the fridge to make another. Warden gave Milena an ice-cold glare.

"Plan's simple," he replied. "Y'all slide over at three. Hardly anyone'll be there 'cept for Renner and me. He gonna think you there to talk biz—never see it comin'. Gonna wanna pack some iron—just keep it outta sight."

"Plan's simple. They gonna slide over at three thinkin' they here to talk biz with you. Only condition's they come 'thout iron."

The car was driving around the neighborhood seemingly at random, though always within the bounds of their turf.

"Like fuck they will," Renner scoffed.

"We'll check 'em. No need to call in the whole army. Bunch of weak-ass little pissants, so they could scare easily, throw the entire plan outta whack. Everythin' should go smooth."

"Smooth. Just like last time, hmm? Givin' you one last chance, Warden. Fuck this up and you'll find out what real punishment is."

Warden made an effort to smile.

"Boys won't even break a sweat," he promised. "We'll put 'em in bags and hand them over to Militech along with the container. They won't ask details."

"Better fuckin' hope so," Renner said grimly. "Stop the car," he called to Ross.

They slowed down and pulled up beside the curb. Warden's door opened, marking the end of their convo. Warden got out without a word and stopped himself from slamming the door. He let it close on its own and watched the car disappear down the street. The AC in his coat activated itself with a low hum. He stood on an empty, trash-littered street on the border between Arroyo and Vista Del Rey. Motherfucker never wasted any opportunity to rub his nose in it.

"Shut up!" OP1 shouted.

OP2 looked at her in surprise.

"I didn't say anything."

"You've been staring at the monitor for an hour, not even blinking. Just keeping you on your toes. We need to stay focused now."

"Staring at the monitor is what they pay us for."

"I don't know if you've noticed, but this entire operation's turning to shit. If things stay as they are, we'll be right back where we started within two days. And so will our pay."

"All the more reason to put our heads down and do our work."

"It's not like we can't talk," OP3 joined in. "Otherwise, they'd have stuck us in separate rooms."

"Prefer to keep my mouth shut," OP2 insisted.

"Sure, 'cause that'll solve all our problems," OP1 said sarcastically. "You know if things don't change, they're gonna toss us out onto the curb, right? Blame the whole thing on us, too."

"How is this our fault? We barely had enough time."

"Tell that to them. Right now there's a piece of tech worth billions just roaming around out there without any oversight."

"We tried VR. The subject always realized they were in a simulation."

"Tell that to them," OP1 repeated. "When someone flatlines our most valuable asset. Or hijacks it."

"We didn't design this experiment."

"So? It'll be our fault no matter what," OP3 reluctantly admitted. "Not to mention our ripperdoc is starting to remember things he shouldn't."

"I've been saying it from the start—the tech's a piece of crap. Can't worry about that, though. Not our department."

The door's panel beeped, meaning someone had just used its biometric lock.

"Shhh, he's here..."

The door opened. Stanley walked inside, not betraying a hint of impatience, though he had more than one reason to be. Without a word, he checked all the readings on the screens, despite the fact that he had them all in his head—ready to stream on his retina at any time, real time.

"Boost his motivators," he said, and blinked, sending them their instructions via thought-command, which immediately displayed on the monitors.

"You mean dial up his motivator module?" OP1 made sure. "He's already in the upper threshold."

"I set the limits, and now I just set new ones," Stanley replied.

"We can't just change it like that," OP1 said meekly. "He could go cyberpsycho. We've already detected uncontrolled leaks from his memory bank. Minor ones for now, but—"

"Make it gradual," Stanley decided. "I'm giving you until seven PM tomorrow to achieve the target values."

She never got bored of the foreplay. Dixie's tongue delicately caressed her breasts as she lay on her back and let a wave of vague, pleasant thoughts wash over her. Blood. Lots of it. She ran her fingers through Dixie's hair and pulled his head down onto her. He started to move inside her rhythmically, almost mechanically—a reliable tempo. Barely a moment had passed before his body spasmed and became still. She wrapped her arms and legs around him with tenderness.

Dixie slid off of her and took Dum Dum in his mouth. Karla stretched herself out, waiting for what would come next. She shut her eyes, imagining herself waist-deep in blood swirling around her in all its thick red gooeyness. Then she felt a real weight on top of her—and inside what she had been waiting for. She didn't use any enhancements. Her own imagination was enough.

Dixie left them alone. He picked up a shard he had prepared from the table and went into the smaller room, where Juliena was half sitting, half lying on the mattress among a pile of scruffy blankets. She showed no interest in anything but her tablet. She reacted to nothing and accepted her situation without complaint. They didn't even have to lock the door. Once in a while she took a trip to the bathroom down the hallway. She always came back—never once tried to make a break for it.

He sat next to her and for a moment watched her play. Some sort of puzzle game—probably something to stimulate her memory. She didn't react to his presence—didn't even react when he slotted the shard behind her ear. He waited for the program to finish installing.

I used to be just like you, he thought-spoke to her.

She continued to move her finger around the tablet for a few more seconds. Then she froze and slowly turned to Dixie with wide eyes. A smile.

Dum Dum forced a few more thrusts and slowed down when a message appeared on his display. Duty called. Karla moaned with disappointment as he read the message. "Won't manage the transport alone. Need help. Three PM." He stopped himself from hurling something at the wall. Fucking scopmunchers couldn't do a goddamn thing on their own.

He repositioned himself back on top of Karla. They want help, they'll get it. He thrust harder. Yes. He knew exactly how to help them get rid of all their worries and problems. He wrapped his fingers around her neck and shoved her deeper into the mattress.

We'll still have to end their pathetic lives. Karla moaned softly and unsheathed her Mantis Blades in the air. In the weak light of the aerozep freighters outside the windows, their sweat-drenched bodies looked like a black, writhing creature with steel wings and a plethora of crimson eyes. *We have to kill them. Shame it'll have to be through such primitive methods.*

CHAPTER_13

W hen he didn't follow police procedure, Liam got quicker results. Unfortunately, the information displaying on his tablet wasn't useful as evidence.

Ron Ferguson—arrested and charged for distributing unlicensed software, circumventing implant warranty, installing secondhand implants. Interesting—only from accidents, never bought from Scavs. Even more interesting was that he didn't make a dime from it—did it as his own cost. Most likely some of his patients wouldn't have survived otherwise.

By night, a ripperdoc for the gilded class. By day, a respected surgeon—even a chief by the sudden end of his career.

First, it was swept under the rug, which probably meant that his debts were sold. Then even the police records were scrubbed— evidently not thoroughly enough. The deleted records meant that someone much higher than even the biggest public officials had taken an interest in Ron.

Milena Russo—the name of the woman in the still with Ron, a Militech corpo. Her involvement was puzzling, to say the least. In theory, Milena lay within the NCPD's jurisdiction so long as there were officers brave enough to put handcuffs on a corpo, which was getting rarer these days. Stranger even was that corps usually handled this kind of dirty business using fixers and gangs in order to generate a tangle of leads that made connecting the dots back to a contractor nigh impossible. This time the formula was different. So, too, was this whole affair—evidently concerning something completely different from what appeared at first sight.

The NCPD holo-badge flickered. Couple days and it'd vanish completely. Liam set down his empty cup of coffee and left the diner, tossing another gum in his mouth. Few days ought to be enough.

"Nothing doing." Albert slid from his chair. It was nearly two PM. "They fortified their security. ICE's too thick—it's beyond my capacity."

"Tier three won't cut it?" Aya reminded him, standing over him.

"Tier three can't do much against a complex password," he answered indifferently, considering the matter closed.

Aya sighed and tried to sound calm.

"Explain it to me."

"Netrunning tech is a useful tool for breaching networks," Albert replied without a hint of impatience. "But it's just that—a tool. To cut through thicker ICE, I'll need more hardware firepower. Computers, in other words. Networked, preferably."

"So you can do it?"

"Yes."

"Then why aren't you doing it?"

"There's no point. CCTV overhauled its security a few days ago. Enter the wrong code and you have to wait a few seconds to try again. Codes now change three times per day. It would take a few thousand years to crack."

"So, what now?" Aya raised her voice slightly.

"I sent a drone there. They shot it down before it could get close."

"Is there nothing we can do?!"

"Not right now."

Zor had been listening to the exchange. He went over to Albert's rig and typed a string of sixteen characters into the additional keyboard. He didn't know what he was typing—he just knew it.

"It's too long for a CCTV password," Albert pointed out.

"It's not for CCTV."

MLTCH-DP-173

Bearing: 126. Speed: 107 mph. Altitude: 367 ft. Wind correction: 13 SE.

Mode of operation: standard patrol.

Incoming order to change operator: ArS-03. Verification code: accepted. Permission to change operator granted.

Rotate right, full throttle.

The man with curly dark hair instinctively drew back, his eyes wide with fear. Farther behind him, Liam made out a woman and two children, almost as unkempt as the father, huddled in front of a window that looked directly out onto the neighboring building. They watched him warily, motionlessly.

"Not here for you," Liam explained. "Don't even need to know your names. I'm looking for the owner."

Luckily, Zed hadn't revoked his access to the NCPD database, which meant the detective knew everything about the tenant of this microunit—such as the fact that it was being rented out illegally. Common for the more run-down parts of Heywood. They think they're keeping a low profile, forgetting about all their personal information they allow to get sucked up by their feeders and BD players.

The detective blinked and read the message: "Drop the case or else." Sender unknown.

He read it again and deleted it.

"It's not what you think." Though stepping inside would certainly force the issue, he remained in the hallway. What he was doing was illegal enough. "Don't worry. I'm from a different department."

"We ... we don't want any trouble ..." the man blurted out.

"Won't be in any—long as you tell me where the owner is."

It wouldn't be difficult to track down the owner. Just time-consuming. Add to that the unwanted attention from his former employer.

The man looked back at his wife, then gave him a nod.

The doors to Maelstrom's hideout were no longer wide open. Two rubble-filled dumpsters were also positioned to prevent anyone from ramming their way in. A couple of Maelstromers patrolled, rifles slung over their shoulders. Nobody took exception to their presence—least of all the NCPD, who never ventured into these parts.

The visual from the Militech patrol drone was crisp enough that it didn't have to approach. Zor watched the screen, confirming what he had already suspected. He wouldn't get a second chance to sneak in quietly, much less back out. Least of all in a shoot-out. Not with Juliena.

"Maybe there's a way in from the back?" Aya asked.

"They're not that gonk," Zor replied. He hadn't mentioned his meeting with Dum Dum, which was the whole reason they had beefed up their defenses. But even without them, his chances were slim to none.

Albert piloted the hacked drone to an altitude that gave them a view of the building from all sides. If anyone spotted it, they wouldn't give it a second thought. Just another Militech patrol drone. The windows and doors of the first three levels were bricked up except for two or three potential entrances and two sturdy-looking garage doors.

Zor recognized the unit where the girl was being kept. Second to last floor, twentieth. Forget it. Might as well scrap the plan.

"Wipe the last few minutes and cut the drone loose," Zor said. "Maybe they'll chalk it up to a standard glitch."

His side processes were eating up too much memory and had no auxiliary support to boot. He had to dedicate a portion of his processing power to tracking potential threats. Still, he'd managed to intercept fragments of transmissions from different parts of the city on the scattered Net. He breached a subnet controlling food-delivery drones, which also contained their flight logs. Whenever they were out of juice, the drones would return to an automated charging station where they also dumped their data. That meant that the footage couldn't have been from more than fifteen, twenty minutes ago.

Streaming the footage was taking up resources—he had higher-priority matters to deal with. Even though he read and wrote data fifteen times faster than before, it was all just a little too...sluggish. He didn't have months or even weeks—he had hours. Meanwhile, distant memories kept bubbling up from the depths of cyberspace and floated listlessly. They were starting to take up more space than everything else combined.

Even in theory, transferring one's consciousness was a thorny procedure. A person isn't made up of only data, but memories, habits, personality traits, skills. A person is a process, which means it needs a system to run it. In one of his data extractions, Albert discovered a theoretical study that attempted to untangle questions such as how to digitize a human being. Whether you can "run" a human and reboot it even from death. And even if the simulation was flawless, how would you know whether it was actually processing consciousness? Can the posthuman still be a human, or just a digi-puppet? One more problem to solve.

It would take years of uninterrupted reading to get through all these studies. Meanwhile, the authorities didn't seem to care all that much about guarding isolated fragments of potentially subversive knowledge. Perhaps it was because a good portion of Night Citizens were illiterate, and even if they weren't, the jargon-packed study was probably enough to dissuade potential readers with words like "discombobulate."

The next few hours would prove whether everything hadn't been a complete waste of time.

He wasn't the owner—just the middleman who made sure the tenants coughed up rent on time. His gorilla-like stature and chrome cheekbones alone were probably convincing enough. Despite nearing sixty, he still commanded a certain degree of respect.

"You rented a unit to someone named Zor." Liam showed him a still on his tablet.

Boxes with scratched-off markings stood next to the wall of the large room. Intriguing contents, no doubt. On a mattress sat two women and a child. One of them was lost in a braindance while the second stared at him with a hazy, slack-jawed expression. There was a gloomy atmosphere in the dimly lit unit. Liam's scanners picked up illegal substances, transmitting alerts to his neural processor. He ignored them.

"Don't recognize 'im," the rent collector finally said with a look on his face that seemed to add "And if it wasn't for that holo-badge, I'd make sure nobody recognized you, either."

Liam sighed. Using thought-command, he uploaded the face

of the rent collector to the NCPD database to see who he was up against. The result came almost instantly—Willem Newell, no gang affiliation, multiple convictions for petty crimes. Nothing unusual, nothing he could use. Liam sent another query, this time to his personal database that he'd been building since he'd joined the force. A hit—now this was interesting. For years, Newell had been an informal associate of Militech, carrying out assignments that were both legal and not so legal. The kind that couldn't go on the record but that were too sensitive to hand out to fixers or gangs.

The pieces were starting to build a logical picture.

"Just looking for info on the guy." He glanced meaningfully toward the cases. "Don't care about anything else."

"Paid cash up-front," the rent collector said. "Whole month."

"Your choice." Another message—no caller ID. Wouldn't be so anonymous once he got his hands on the phone tower records.

"Just one month?" Liam closed the message.

"Stuck around for even less."

"And destroyed the door and elevator on his way out?"

"Ain't my biz." The rent collector seemed to tower even higher over him.

"Rented it to another family before the month was even up."

"Shit, choom...If Maelstrom after you, you ain't never comin' back."

They parked the tow truck in the shade next to a bare wall. In an hour it would become scorching hot. Who cared? In an hour, they had no idea if they'd still be alive.

They got out onto a plaza in front of what resembled a disused factory. Empty, if you didn't count two cars and the windswept trash, ever present in this part of the city. The buildings in this area reached only a few stories, most without windows.

"What if they pat us down?" Ron whispered.

He meant the pistols they all had hidden behind their belts. They were hoping that a single shot wouldn't be fired, but Zor wasn't as optimistic as the rest. He kept his thoughts to himself.

"They won't," he replied. "Warden's got a plan. Don't know how deep it goes, but he needs us." Milena stepped beside Zor.

"Once you reach a certain level, there's no such thing as accidents—or coincidences," she said quietly, almost whispering. "You know it, too. What did Warden have on you? How did he drag you into this?"

"No secret at this point," Zor replied in a hushed tone. "Found out about my past, threatened to spill. That's about it. You?"

"They're playing a dangerous game." She shook her head.

"Guess that'll have to wait till we make it out of there." Zor cut the convo short.

"Try not to look threatening, all right?" Ron said to everyone.

"Doubt that'll be hard," Milena answered wryly. "We already look harmless and clumsy."

Only forty-five feet separated them from the steel doors. Milena really didn't want to go inside—she felt the urge to grab Ron by the hand and go in the opposite direction—no looking back.

"Well, this is it. Don't have a choice," she said.

They moved slowly toward the entrance. They didn't just look harmless and clumsy, but nervous, too. Scared, even.

One of the doors opened, revealing total darkness. Zor sharpened the contrast in his vision and adjusted the white balance. He didn't even know which implant was responsible for it. The outlines of two rifle-wielding men came into focus. He stopped himself from instinctively reaching for his own iron.

The two men came out and stood on opposite sides of the door, watching the four of them indifferently. One held the rifle's receiver slanted downward across his chest, ready to take a quick shot if needed. The second started to walk toward them.

"Chill. I'll handle this." Out of the darkness emerged a third figure. Warden.

The second man backed away to the door. Zor raised his arms, though not so high as to expose what was behind his belt. Warden frisked him, ignoring the two bulges pressed against his lower back and the extra magazines in his pockets. Then he moved his combat implant detector around him, having previously decreased sensitivity to minimum. It wouldn't detect a tank even if it were right in front of him. He then repeated the procedure with Ron—and finally Aya and Milena. He gave them the nod. They went in.

It wasn't as dark inside as it looked, but the AC made the air cool. Somebody had clearly tried to make the place look like somewhere deadbeat punks hung out. A couple of worn-out couches, a stack of crates that formed a table, a few kegs that might have catered to a party once upon a time. Now it was empty, with the only light coming from the windows near the ceiling. It almost felt like an abandoned church, though instead of pews, the aisles were made up of the remnants of old machinery that remained assembled due to either laziness or their worthlessness.

Without a word, Warden led them to the end of the hall and pushed open another set of doors, revealing stairs that led down. Zor did a quick estimate of the distance to the entrance. Would a tow-rope make it? Probably not. Then there was the truck. Definitely not. Should've thought about that before—not like they would keep the container right by the entrance. How would they even get it up to the first floor? Pull it up one step at a time, shoulder to shoulder with Maelstrom? No, thanks.

Though its ceiling was lower, the basement was equally spacious, filled with metal cargo boxes of various shapes and colors. It almost seemed as if they had been placed for a defensive purpose as a barricade. This wasn't your average warehouse.

In its dead center a burly man in a leather jacket stood just outside the cone of light cast by one of the lamps dangling from the ceiling. Renner. Next to him stood the smaller-built Ross. Zor didn't know how he knew their names—he just did. He toggled his optics spectrum to infrared. Someone was there—just behind those boxes. Someone or something emitting heat—a signature typical of a person, or even two people. The container was nowhere in sight.

Ross started to move toward Milena, who stood closest to them.

"We came here to talk, not feel each other up." Milena took a step back.

"José did a solid pat down," Warden said. "Sorry, Ross. Not your lucky day."

Ross raised his hands in compliance and turned back. He looked at Renner, whose expression was hard, firmly set.

"Here to talk biz, eh?" Renner cracked a smirk. "Let's see you talk with a mouthful of lead."

Two gangers jumped out from behind the cases, rifles trained on their heads. Too late for anything. Renner took two steps toward Zor and the rest. Kudos to him—couldn't have picked a better place for an ambush. While Renner and the rest had cover behind them, they were wide open. Like fish in a barrel.

"Had a feelin' somethin' wasn't right..." Ron whispered.

Warden quietly retreated into the shadows.

"Been dyin' to know," Renner said. "Who the actual fuck are you? What hole did Warden drag you outta?"

Warden let out a quiet sigh.

"Ought to off you right now," Renner continued. "But I can't help bein' curious. Let's go, spill."

They stood still. What now? Clearly, they weren't getting into biz together. Right now, they were alive for as long as they could keep the boss's interest.

"Good question," Ron finally answered. "We were merrily goin' about our lives until—"

The sound of muffled gunfire reached them through the ceiling. Everyone instinctively looked up. Everyone except Zor, who drew his pistols and fired five rounds from each at the gangers flanking Renner. Now one pistol was aimed at Renner—the other at Ross. The echoes petered out.

Ron, Aya and Milena all drew their iron. Milena was the only one aiming at Warden, who didn't react at all. Didn't even raise his hands.

"José patted 'em down, hmm?" Renner growled at Warden. Only Ross had his arms in the air. "Did *you* pat 'em down, you double-crossing piece of shit?"

"To be respected as a leader," Warden replied, "gotta have respect for your own people. You don't got neither."

"Backstabbing scum like you don't deserve respect," Renner spat. "So, what's the game plan, hmm? Who the fuck's spittin' lead up there?"

"Where's the container?" Zor asked.

Renner ignored him.

"Whatever your plan was, it's fucked now!" Renner shouted at Warden, his nostrils flaring. "You rat-fucking traitor!"

Ron went over to the fallen gangers and checked their pulses. Dead. He took their rifles, handing one to Milena and keeping the other for himself.

"Who's up there?" Aya whispered, motioning with her head toward the stairs. "They with us?"

"Backup," Zor replied. "Change of plans."

He pulled the trigger. A chunk of leather flew off of Renner's shoulder.

"Fuck!" Now Zor had his attention. "Can't you see this is real leather?!" He fingered the tear with indignation. "You think you can just waltz in here and take whatever the fuck you want, hmm?"

"That's exactly what I think," Zor answered. "The container— where is it?"

"Funny you should ask. Been wonderin' myself how to get rid of the damned thing."

"Should be happy, then. Solving your problem for you."

Renner's laughter filled the entire room.

"That simple, huh? Tell you what. You ain't gettin' that container. And you sure as shit ain't gettin' out of here alive. As for this fucking Judas—"

He was rudely interrupted by the sound of the upstairs door being kicked open.

"I'm done talkin'." Renner grinned. "Boys'll take it from here."

"Not gonna happen," Warden calmly answered. "Sent them over to Gustavo's to pick up some cargo. Remember?"

"Fuck you talkin' about? Didn't send 'em anywhere."

"They're in south Glen as we speak."

Warden himself had no clue who was approaching.

They heard the thud of heavy boots. Milena looked toward the staircase and Warden immediately aimed one pistol at her and another at Renner. Zor waited for Maelstrom to make their entrance. If only they knew where the container was.

The thuds had almost reached the bottom, but before they could glimpse their owner, they heard the sound of several objects clinking down the steps.

"Grenade!" Zor yelled. With rapid tempo, Aya reached the nearest row of boxes. Not a moment too soon. She felt a cramp coming on.

Milena and Ron managed to find cover on the other side of the room when one after the other, three explosions shook the entire basement. There was a deafening ring in their ears as shrapnel ricocheted off the walls and smoke flooded the basement.

"They're trying to kill us!" Aya looked up at Zor, who was sheltering her. "You call that backup?!"

"It was the only way of getting Juliena back." Zor took a quick peek above the boxes. Couldn't make out anything through the smoke. "Guess the deal's off."

"All right, you fuckin' jizz rags!" They heard a booming, gravelly voice from upstairs. "Party's over."

That definitely didn't sound like Dum Dum.

The smoke was finally clearing up. Zor caught sight of Ron and Milena at the other end of the basement, hidden behind a similar-looking stack of boxes. They looked around helplessly, rifles in hand.

More shots and ricochets.

Milena leaned out from behind cover and fired at the ceiling, taking out one of the lamps. She hid before a volley from the other side riddled the boxes with bullet holes. Lead was flying left and right. Out of the crossfire a force lifted Aya up into the air.

"Toss your iron!" a booming voice shouted.

Aya shrieked, trying to free herself.

Pigface held her up by the waist a few feet above the ground with one hand. The other held a DR5 Nova revolver. The stench of his breath and pungent body odor overwhelmed her senses. She gathered all the strength she could, turned around with remarkable speed and directed all that power into one move—a swift kick to the groin.

The Animal keeled over, falling to his knees. Unfortunately, he brought Aya down with him. She struggled for breath underneath his weight. She couldn't move. Pigface rose to his feet with difficulty, lifting Aya like a doll. This time he held the revolver against her head.

"I said toss your iron," the Big Cat said. "Or her brain goes splat."

Ron and Milena laid down their rifles.

"Don't give two fucks about her." Renner trained his pistol on Pigface.

Zor aimed at Renner.

"Drop it," Zor ordered.

"Fuck…" Ross couldn't decide between Zor or Pigface. "God-damn shit show…"

"Got a bigger problem to deal with!" Renner barked in reply. "Wait your fuckin' turn."

"I said drop it." Zor took a step closer. "Same goes for you," he said to Ross.

Renner scowled and dropped his pistol, followed by Ross. Zor made a split-second calculation of what would happen if he fired at Pigface now. He could do it—Pigface wouldn't have time to react. No, the risk was too high. He dropped both pistols and raised his arms up.

Pigface loosened his grip and Aya fell to the floor.

"Where is it?" Big Cat looked at Ron through slit pupils. "Had a deal, didn't we?"

Milena shot the ripperdoc a questioning glance.

"Situation's gotten a little, um…complicated," he answered, and pointed at Renner. "Ask him—he knows."

"Ain't tellin' you shit," Renner snarled.

"Already got plans for the rest of the day." Big Cat reluctantly aimed at him. "One more body ain't gonna change a thing."

"Kill me and you'll never find it."

Big Cat turned to Ron, making him nearly flinch.

"Deal was you'd hand over the container. I don't sees any container."

"W-we were working on that," Ron exclaimed nervously. "Till, um...till you showed up."

"Back to work then. We'lls watch."

"A-a—atmosphere ain't really conducive for..."

"You got an ass for a brain, ripperdick?!" Big Cat barked at him.

Big Cat raised the revolver to his right and fired. Ross's head exploded, blood spattering the wall and ceiling, as well as over half of Renner's face. He didn't react as the ganger's body slumped beside him—instead, he looked down at his leather jacket covered in blood.

"Fuck..."

"Don't give a rat's dick who knows or doesn't know!" Big Cat shouted to the whole room. "I'll off youse one by one till someone starts talkin'."

He glared at everyone in turn, staring the longest at Milena. She didn't allow herself to show any fear, though her legs were starting to tremble.

"Everyone just chill, all right?" Ron took a step in front of Milena. "Nobody else has to die."

"Fuck did you just say to me?" Big Cat slowly raised his pistol at Ron. Suddenly two blades extended through his stomach, dripping with blood. He looked down, stupefied. Then he staggered and turned around. Karla had already sprung back with a cartwheel. Big Cat unloaded half a magazine at her, sending only chunks of concrete flying through the air.

Something streaked down the stairs in a blur. His coat and body seemed merged together as Dum Dum spun through midair, illuminated by a quick series of muzzle flashes in Big Cat's direction. Blood spurted out of his grotesquely oversized muscles. Big Cat turned around, bared his fangs and returned fire into the darkness. Dum Dum's optics were dimmed to avoid revealing his position.

Pigface quickly realized his life insurance policy—Big Cat—was about to run its course. He opened fire on their new enemy. But Dum Dum was already elsewhere, shooting through the darkness only a few yards away. Pigface took two hits in the shoulder. Instead of hurting him, it only made him angrier.

Zor scooped up his pistols, grabbed Aya and pulled her behind the nearest stack of boxes.

"You okay?"

She was unhurt, though she couldn't move one arm. The other was only half cooperating.

"Think so…"

Ron and Milena quickly grabbed their rifles and joined the others. Though nobody was shooting at them, ricochets zipped through the air around them. The roar from the gunfire didn't die down.

"You made a deal with the Animals?!" Aya hissed at Ron.

"Yeah, well, he made a deal with Maelstrom!" The ripperdoc pointed at Zor.

"We just gonna sit here and wait for them to kill each other?!" Milena shouted over the gunfire.

Warden was nowhere to be seen. He had something planned, Zor was sure of it. So what? Both of their plans probably canceled each other out.

"Who are we even shooting at?" Ron looked at each of them for answers.

"At whoever wins," Milena answered.

"If Maelstrom don't get the container, they won't let Juliena go," Zor said.

"If the Animals don't get it…" Ron hesitated. "Bully will kill me."

"Who the hell's Bully?!" Milena asked.

"Debt collector. When I mentioned ancient history… it wasn't that ancient."

Milena sighed and hung her head in disbelief.

Three contradictory plans for one container. Nothing to do but wait and see who came out on top.

Karla sheathed her Mantis Blades and switched to iron, springing to a new position after each round fired. Dum Dum did the same, except he didn't skimp on ammo. The Animals had already taken some lead, the ground around them pooling with blood. They weren't used to fighting from behind cover; their strength lay in close quarters combat. They were becoming more sluggish. Soon the energy from those boosted sacks of muscle would deplete itself.

Dum Dum thought two steps ahead—he'd already fired at the Animals and the boxes that Zor, Aya and the rest were hidden behind, which was already beginning to crumble. A few more shots and there'd be nothing to use as cover.

Ron hesitated, then mustered up his courage and unexpectedly leaped from behind cover, unloading his magazine into Dum Dum. Shit. He actually hit him. The Maelstromer hesitated. Blood was squirting out of his neck. He turned toward Ron, who was fumbling with a new magazine.

"Get down!" Zor pulled Ron to the ground.

But it wasn't necessary. Dum Dum took another volley, this time from Big Cat. He hit the ground. Hard.

The howl from Karla was like that of a banshee.

She was about to leap toward the Animals but let it go when she saw the pistol slip out of his hand and his body slump next to the dying pig-faced Animal.

Karla's blazing optics rotated to Ron. She unsheathed her blades and, not taking her eyes off him, made an impossibly wide leap toward the boxes.

Karla sprang from the last case, flipped in the air and swooped down with her blades onto the chest of the prone ripperdoc like a bird of prey. She couldn't have stopped now even if she wanted to.

"Fucksicle…" Ron flattened himself against the ground, the magazine slipping from his hand.

Milena fired, missing by a good few feet. Aya had Karla exactly within her sights and pulled the trigger. Or she tried to. Her stiffened hand wouldn't allow it.

Zor watched it unfold in slow motion—Karla falling through the air as if through thick oil. He aimed precisely at both of the blades' mountings and fired. The last volley went straight for the power supply. A flash and a boom that sounded to him like rolling thunder. He was out of ammo.

Time sped up. Sparks and blood burst above them in a cloud. Everyone braced for impact.

Karla's body slammed into the ground with a shower of blood and metal fragments.

Impractical weapon, Dum Dum thought-spoke, but Karla couldn't hear him anymore.

Fucksicle… Ron wanted to say, staring at the blades buried in his chest. He looked up at Zor and suddenly recalled the moment when they'd first met—before Arroyo. But he couldn't do anything with that knowledge now. It was too late. Too late for everything. His gaze searched for Milena.

Karla raised her head. She tried to lift herself up on what was left of her cyberarms, now deprived of their blades and other chrome fittings. She couldn't.

Milena aimed at her head, clenched her jaw and fired. She shuddered as she saw the woman's head slump back down in a pool of blood. Only now her red optics faded. Milena fired again, and again, until the slide stop retreated and there were only clicks. She dropped the gun and fell to her knees beside Ron, bending over and lifting up his head.

The twelve chrome fingers of the Zetatech surgical hands drummed helplessly against the concrete. A few long seconds passed before it was clear that the idling implants understood there would be no further commands.

Dum Dum struggled to his feet, steadying himself against a stack of cases. His connections were severed, making his optics glow faintly as he looked for his iron, but he wouldn't have even had the strength to pick it up. He began crawling up the stairs behind Zor and the others.

Milena shut her eyes. It was all pointless. Nothing made sense anymore.

Zor put his arm around Aya and looked at Ron with a grim expression. He lifted his gaze to Karla, or rather what was left of her. The deal with Maelstrom was off, dead. None of this made any sense.

Black rain battering the windshield.

It stank of blood, gunpowder and fried circuitry.

"Now that everyone's outta ammo, we can pick up where we left off." This time Renner was holding a rifle. "Left a real mess to clean up." He had ditched his jacket, revealing a third glowing cross in the center of his chest.

Milena caressed Ron's cheek.

"To hell with this!" She stood up and with a fierce look aimed at the glowing cross and squeezed the trigger. The metallic click only reconfirmed what she already knew. She came closer and squeezed the trigger. *Click.* Renner looked at her with amusement. She kept coming closer. *Click. Click. Click.*

"Hopin' for a miracle?" he asked almost cheerfully.

A burst from a rifle. For the first time, surprise appeared on the ganger's face, and a dark patch started to spread across his chest, making the cross glow dark orange. Renner's eyes rolled back and he collapsed to the floor.

"He was right—gonna be a bitch to clean this up." Smoke drifted from the barrel of Warden's rifle as he approached, kicking the gun away from his late boss's corpse. The pool of blood around his feet was widening. He looked at the group huddled together and motioned behind him toward the steel doors embedded in the concrete wall—left slightly ajar.

CHAPTER_14

Me again, suckas!

Few days ago, a couple of gangoons said sayonara and snuffed it. Twelve of them, to be precise. Boo-hoo. Prolly twenty more took their place already. Guess the previous ones just didn't have what it took. You been to the cemetery lately? Peeps be droppin' like flies—ain't enough graves for all of them. No wonder the fish in the bay are so goddamn fat. If anyone asks, I don't know nothin'— they're probably just nibblin' on plastic. Just watch your step near the water after dark.

Not gonna name names, but some nihilistic muthafucka told me none of this, nothing we do, matters cuz we're all gonna end up the same way—dead at the bottom of a ditch. Well, Arasaka's got something to say about that. Might've heard about it already—the Relic. Wanna live forever as a dumb holo? Be my guest. Me? I'd rather go out guns a-blazing than pay a fortune to lock myself in a digi-prison for eternity.

In other news, another abandoned squat got burned to the ground. Body count? Unknown. Mainstream media's silent, as usual. Surprise, surprise—report was up for a day before it quietly vanished. Whoever died there, the powers that be don't want YOU to know who.

I don't believe for one second any of y'all got sad reading this, you soulless motherfuckers. Cuz I know I did. It'll pass in a sec. Next post coming soon!

PEACE!

The sign on the door read Buyers & Son. Was he sure about going inside? It was a battle between curiosity and good sense. Or maybe more like…his duty? No. He wouldn't even be able to use the information he was about to acquire. Impersonating a police officer was a felony, and any evidence he submitted to court would be struck down by the exclusionary rule. But curiosity was winning. It won every time.

Liam's holo-badge hadn't completely faded yet. The detective went in.

It smelled of old sweat and damp. Liam tossed a stick of gum in his mouth and started chewing. Helped a little. There was a garage to his left with parked vans connected to the wall by various thick cables. To the right, the office.

Liam pushed open the steel doors that swung noiselessly on their brand-new hinges. You couldn't really call it an office, since no clients would ever come here in person. Otherwise, it barely passed muster in terms of looking like a legit business.

The eponymous Buyers sat behind the small counter a few feet from the entrance. It was hard to gauge how old he was.

"Looking for this man. Know where he is?"

Buyers let out a quiet sigh.

"You and everyone's grandma."

"Someone else lookin' for him?"

"Oh, trust me, you wouldn't wanna meet 'em." Buyers continued to work, or pretended to, on his terminal. "Make it quick; I'm real busy."

"Can you give me a name?"

Buyers shrugged.

"Worked here for a while." Liam leaned on the counter. "Guessing you knew him well?"

"A while?" Buyers scoffed. "Guy worked here for just a couple days and then totaled one of my vans."

Liam was about to ask who else was looking for Zor when he got a message from his wife: "Why didn't you tell me you picked up the kids from school?"

He stopped chewing.

"This isn't looking good." OP2 stared at the monitors. "We might as well be digging our own graves here."

"Wasn't part of the plan, but..." OP1 sighed, glancing at the control graphs. "It looks like the main mission objective isn't in any danger..."

"It was supposed to be a test of autonomy—passed with flying fucking colors," OP3 joined in. "Should we prime the auto-destruct sequence?"

"That's a last resort. For now, ArS-03 is en route to the target. Notify the boss."

"Someone fucked up Russo's psych profile. I said at the very start she'd be trouble. Too unstable."

"Not our problem. Now tell the boss about ArS-03!"

"By the time he figures out what's going on, it'll be too late."

"It's already too late! What're we supposed to do? Send a squad after him? Tell the boss that we've lost control of ArS-03. Now."

Though it was the same sky, it felt like a different world. The air smelled fresher, cleaner. The subdistrict prided itself on its low levels of pollution. Then there were the plants. Grass, bushes, even real, organic trees. Trash was nowhere to be seen, nor curbside, burned-out or abandoned cars, no homeless or shady characters lurking in the shadows. The street was practically empty.

The GPS out here in North Oak started to glitch—ostensibly for its residents' safety. Only when she inserted Katsuo's card into the Quadra's console did it come back to life.

Dusk was approaching. Lost in his thoughts, Zor gazed out at the olive groves on the hills that smugly pretended as if the world wasn't undergoing ecological collapse. Milena suddenly took Zor's hand and squeezed it, closing her eyes. For a moment they sat in silence.

Loud thuds from the back—the AV's armored hull being pierced by antiaircraft rounds. The lights in the cockpit become red—the mayday alarm starts blaring. He's lost control of the steering.

"I want to speak to him first." He heard Milena's voice.

He blinked—he was back in North Oak. He gave a slight nod.

"So do I."

"And then you'll kill him?" She intoned more as a statement than a question. "But if you do that, you won't get Juliena back."

"I'll do both. Katsuo's intel isn't up-to-date—only reason why I'm able to get this close to him."

Slowly, the steel gate retracted. Gravel crunched beneath the wheels as they drove on a lane flanked by lush greenery that led to an ascetic-looking villa. Spacious windows, straight angles, part ground floor and first floor that seemed a relic of a gentler era.

As soon as they stopped, Milena wiped a tear from the corner of her eye and sighed. They got out and the car graciously parked itself next to a limousine.

They walked down the few steps to the entrance—Milena in a black evening dress, Zor in a blazer and tie she had picked out for him for the occasion. An elderly Japanese manservant wearing a slightly oversized suit pulled open a traditional sliding door and closed it, indicating the way through the garden with an upward-facing palm.

The narrow black stone-paved path stopped after winding its way around the villa through immaculately trimmed grass. Milena resisted the urge to kick off her heels and feel it between her toes. It was almost begging to be walked on. The painstakingly designed and manicured vegetation seemed endless, though it was all a careful illusion. They heard the hum of water as the path led them over a stone bridge. Underneath it, a gurgling stream trickled into a small pond with idle fish. Synthetic, maybe. Farther ahead was a modest bamboo grove, next to it a boulder and on the other side—a large, majestic rhododendron tree. Behind it stood a traditional, wooden Japanese tea pavilion, the edges of the roof curled characteristically upward. Real wood, real trees. The extravagance of it all was hard to take in—even for Milena.

Zor took one last fill of air and began the wait for the evening to run its inevitable course. The elderly servant slid open the latticework door covered in translucent paper, revealing Katsuo within, who acknowledged them with a slight nod. Milena and Zor entered a large, nearly empty room with partially slatted walls and an old, wooden floor darkened with time, on which mats were placed.

Katsuo knelt by the low table in the center of the room. He now stood up and adjusted his black suit.

"Thank you for your change of heart and agreeing to join me." He gave a very low bow. "And thank you, sir, for accompanying your partner."

Zor clenched his jaw and felt a bead of sweat form on his forehead.

Seeing Katsuo this close, he struggled to maintain his composure. It wasn't easy.

Why not do it right away? What was he waiting for? A better moment? There wouldn't be one. He could kill Katsuo with his bare hands right here and now.

But he didn't. Instead, he bowed in the same manner, which suited him more than the thought of shaking this man's hand.

"Zor…" he introduced himself, trying to articulate through his clenched jaw. His last name—he'd forgotten it.

"We're honored to be your guests," Milena quickly interjected.

From the house a woman dressed in a silk kimono approached them. Its hem swept across the grass, making it seem as if she glided toward them.

"Kazuko. My wife," Katsuo introduced her.

She bowed.

Kazuko removed her shoes without a word. The guests caught the hint and did the same. Zor had expected the kind of reception he had seen on TV—a table replete with little saucers of food, waiters pouring cups of sake. Nothing of the kind here. Not to mention there weren't any other guests.

Their host motioned them to the mats around the table, which had what looked like a hot plate, a few wooden objects, a couple of dark, rough, uneven bowls and some sweets on saucers.

"I presume you are not familiar with our customs." Katsuo was polite; the official tone and emotionless mask that Milena had gotten used to from their previous meetings had disappeared. "We will now drink tea and talk. After, we will move to a more comfortable setting in the Western style, where supper will be served."

The servant brought a few paper lanterns and hung them from the ceiling. The tearoom became brighter, bringing out the dark-amber hue of the wood. The garden around them receded into shadow. Behind the hedge separating the garden from the street, the sun began its descent.

Kazuko prepared the tea. The guests had the impression that they were in a play, where Kazuko was performing an ancient ritual. First, she wiped all the objects on the table with a red cloth. Then she poured the water into the bowls, rinsed them back into the kettle, sprinkled some green powder in them, poured the water back and swirled it around again.

How different this was from pressing a button on an All Foods feeder, Zor thought. He made an effort not to look at their host. Throughout all these years, he had imagined this meeting differently. He had wanted to corner Katsuo, tell him why he was about to die, force him to beg for forgiveness, which would never happen, anyway—he had too much dignity. Zor wanted to make him experience a moment of thought. Reflection. Yes, Katsuo had to die. He thought of Nicole and Brad, whose existence Katsuo had never even been aware of. Too many people to remember had been consumed by the flames. Zor was going to resurrect his wife and son—resurrect them in the mind of Katsuo—and then kill him. It wasn't about cruelty—he wanted this war criminal to know what he did to deserve his fate.

Kazuko lifted up the bowl of steaming green tea and rotated it twice before setting it down in front of Milena.

"Tea marks an important moment," Katsuo said. "A time to bring oneself in harmony with nature and loved ones, to offer respect to everything that allows us to enjoy this tea, to honor tradition and our guests." He bowed to Milena and then to Zor. "A time to soothe our souls."

"Something tells me this isn't one of those evenings." Milena took a sip of her tea.

"There are more important matters than souls at peace. One of them is the success of Project Aeneas."

Milena glanced from Zor to Katsuo.

"Has Aeneas become declassified?"

"It has not. I trust that neither you nor your partner will reveal the details of our discussion this evening."

"Of course." Milena nodded.

"We can speak openly here. Nobody is listening."

"You mean that the conference room at Arasaka wasn't secure?"

"In that regard, nowhere in Arasaka is secure. The only difference is who is permitted to listen."

"But not here."

"This is my home. I set the rules."

Irritation welled up within Zor. No, not irritation—impatience. An urge to do something. He didn't look at Katsuo, not wanting his face to reveal his intentions. Instead, he observed Kazuko as she poured boiled water into the bowls. Curious, the effort that went into an act as simple as preparing tea. She smiled faintly, not uttering a word. Zor couldn't take his eyes off of what she was doing. He touched his forehead... Her smile reminded him of...

The AV lies on its side, nose buried in the sand. He manages to climb out of the cockpit and now sits against the torn-open escape hatch. The AV has left a one-hundred-and-fifty-foot scar in the desert sand. Smoke rises out of the engine, circuits sparking beneath the bullet-ridden hull. Less than two miles away, a fire blazes. He can't feel the heat from here, only sees the red glow lighting up the night.

His leg is broken. Too late to run away now.

Why did he make a break for it? When he stole the AV, he knew he wouldn't make it out alive. So what was the difference? At least he had a few more minutes to gaze at the sky.

They'd used standard munitions instead of missiles to shoot him down. They wanted him alive. They would surely ask him many questions about the conspiracy, about the chain of command in his terrorist cell.

But there was no terrorist cell—just him, a father whose family was killed because of politics. A father, a deserter, but not a traitor. But all the same, they would treat him like one.

He had sunk the Arasaka warship. He should feel satisfaction, fulfillment. He feels neither of those things. Instead, he feels that it's not enough.

He tries to move his leg. Pain shoots through his entire body. The fracture isn't severe; his shinbone hasn't pierced the skin. He wedges his foot between the AV's fuselage and the broken undercarriage hatch. He dispenses the anesthesia and pulls. A crack and then a short cry— the pain can't be completely numbed. Though it isn't hot, sweat streaks down his face. Did he set the bone right? Did it make a difference? He didn't have anything to fashion a splint. Nanites would tentatively repair it within two hours. Too long.

He straightened his leg, accidentally moving the table. The crockery rattled, spilling the tea. Everyone stared at him while Kazuko rushed to clean up the mess.

"...Both our corporations are secretly attempting to penetrate the Blackwall," Milena said. "Our boards remain unaware. Officially, that is. But whoever wins the race will leave the competition in the dust."

"Your assessment is correct," Katsuo politely admitted.

"Except neither Militech nor Arasaka needs to. What I mean is…" Milena looked at Zor and briefly lost her train of thought. "I mean that it's completely unnecessary. Gaining access to the AIs beyond the Blackwall isn't in anyone's interest. Both sides' motivation is the fear of losing the race. It's a prisoner's dilemma."

"The situation demands a broader perspective," Katsuo replied. "Though we make up the largest share of the market, our smaller competitors have begun to conduct their own research—research we have no insight into. One must assume it is only a matter of time before the Blackwall is compromised. It is not a question of if, but when."

"Then shouldn't we be trying to prevent that from happening?"

"You must forgive me for answering your question with another question, but is this still part of our negotiation?"

Zor's gaze was fixed on his bowl of tea. He was on edge, as if a pressure was building up inside him. If he took even one look at Katsuo, he would have to kill him right then and there.

Milena took a deep breath, buying herself some time to think. She could really use a smoke right about now.

"What I'm wondering," she began again, "is whether Project Aeneas isn't attempting to cross a line that shouldn't be crossed. I met one of the victims from the incident in '62."

"The Voodoo Boys conducted that experiment—the failure lies with them." Katsuo's patience seemed to be waning. "Surely, you do not think that the life of some random child outweighs the potential benefits for all mankind?"

Zor's eyes glazed over.

They're here. He can make them out in the distance, shimmering as they approach through the hot desert. His AV is stuck in the sand, tilted on its side. His pursuers land at a safe distance. He hears their steps as they warily creep toward him.

He shuts his eyes. Flames. This time not his house, but the flames from the ship. Out of six rockets, two reached their target. That was only minutes ago. Flames rage out from the bridge. It tilts on its side, starts sinking. In just a few minutes, the rest of the ships would return fire. Veer left, full throttle. He sustains a few hits, crash-lands in the desert.

They surround him. The light from the distant wall of flames casts the shadow of a figure. They're being vigilant. No need. He's too weak to put up a fight. Only once they're standing over him do they lower their weapons.

One hour ago, he set out to do the last thing he'd ever have to do. He knew now it wasn't enough.

He had to know who issued the order.

"Indeed, the ethical consequences of cooperating with AIs makes for good popular entertainment," Zor heard. "Right beside mutants rising up from Coronado Bay. Emotion should have no place in our decision-making process. We must guide ourselves by logic, and logic only."

"The only logic I see is the logic of profit," Milena said. "If it makes money, it makes sense. Right?"

"I have the impression that you are intentionally trying to steer this negotiation off course."

Katsuo showed no hint of annoyance. And yet, the mask was off. He had voluntarily removed it when he invited guests into his own home. The face behind it showed a spirit that was now animated—a far cry from the Katsuo she had come to know in Arasaka Tower.

Milena sensed that there was something else she wasn't picking up on. But what?

"This isn't business negotiation," she said firmly. "I'm trying to avoid a disaster in the making. What we're doing...We'd be tearing open a hole into a world that's been abandoned for forty years—home to intelligences that would by now be completely alien to us."

"They were alien from the start," Katsuo corrected her. "We

created them for that very reason, such is their purpose to carry out tasks we humans are incapable of."

"For forty years we've left these AIs to evolve entirely on their own—unsupervised, uncontrolled. I think it's safe to say that by now their capabilities surpass ours by orders of magnitude."

"If that were the case, then surely one of these AIs would have penetrated through the Blackwall by now?"

"Unless the Blackwall is itself an AI preparing to act as a mediator."

"Precisely the kind of conspiracy theory that is spouted on the Net. In reality, these AIs have at their disposal only the limited portion of cyberspace that we ceded to them nearly forty years ago. No new space has been created. Neither is there a back door—no physical connection that leads directly beyond the all-pervasive barrier that is the Blackwall. If evolution has taken place, it has been determined by limited space and resources. You are afraid of war, but it has already begun among the AIs themselves. It is a war over scarcity. Besides, these AIs have not evolved as you so vividly imagine. They are merely remnants of a past—a past that we will mine for all of its value. The knowledge that we have abandoned there—the data and algorithms...we need them to lift humanity from technological stagnation. We must return to the path of progress."

Zor nervously clenched and unclenched his fists. He raised the tea to his lips and tried to control himself. His fingers paled as their grip on the ceramic, uneven bowl tightened.

Cold metal. Arms bumping against the railings of a hospital stretcher. They're pushing me down a long hallway. Luminous square tiles of light pass over my head in an even rhythm. Slowly, monotonously. Something shakes.

It's me. I'm shaking, moving. This can't be a hospital. The man to the right wears a white lab coat; the bare concrete walls show large numbers and symbols painted on them. We pass a door every once in a while, but not hospital doors. More like warehouse doors.

The letters are in English, not Japanese. Not Arasaka, then. Means I still have a chance to make it out of this alive and do what needs to be done. Find whoever who issued the order.

"Progress has come to a standstill," Katsuo continued. "Resources are becoming ever scarcer and we have no remedy. The world has experienced no new technological breakthroughs for decades."

Zor's hand trembled as he set down the bowl. Kazuko gave a delicate smile and took it, refilling it with tea.

"Maybe that's because we only think about short-term profits," Milena pointed out. "Not long-term gains."

"Perhaps. But that is the way the world works." Katsuo nodded. "Humanity is stuck in the quicksand of short-term profit, as you call it. We need a force strong enough to pull us out of it."

Why were they here? What was he playing at? She had no doubt this invitation served another purpose besides this conversation, but she couldn't figure out what.

"I don't buy that argument." She had no choice but to continue playing the game. "It sounds like a PR pitch—something for the masses to easily swallow. But the goal is still the same—profit. What I'm saying is that these secret attempts to break through the Blackwall by Arasaka and Militech—"

"Your information is wrong," Katsuo interrupted her. "Militech's approach is not the same as Arasaka's. Your team has not been working on finding a way through." He paused and stared at Milena, who tried as best as she could to hide her surprise. "Instead, for years you have been working on your own AI. It is for this reason that this discussion is taking place."

Zor raised the bowl that Kazuko had handed him to his lips. A bead of sweat trickled down his temple.

"You'll have to elaborate," Milena said calmly.

"As you yourself have pointed out, what lies behind the Blackwall surpasses us by orders of magnitude. Let us suppose that is the case, within certain margins. We would need a mediator—an intelligence that could act as a bridge between us and what lies on the other side. Militech already possesses something we can use—a hybrid, an amalgamation of the organic and synthetic. Militech is attempting to create the ideal soldier, devoid of conscience, capable of fulfilling any orders given, yet not entirely stripped of their humanity—their instinct, intuition. An artificial intelligence and an artificial soul in constant struggle and cooperation. Pure artificial intelligence, if it achieves self-awareness, will become impossible to control. But a soldier must be both self-aware and kept under control. There are already too many unthinking robots and inadequate netrunners. Controlling an AI will be possible as long as it is weighed down by emotion. It is like flying a kite—it cannot remain in the air without the string that deprives it of its freedom. Release the string and it will fall. We have determined that such a hybrid, contrary to its original purpose, will provide us with the best chance of traversing the Blackwall."

"This isn't a business concern anymore." Milena shook her head. "It's about the safety of the entire city, maybe even of all humanity."

"In that this concerns all of humanity, you are correct. Project Aeneas is an opportunity for humanity to redeem itself—an opportunity that has lain idle for forty years. It is time we rectified this mistake."

"Do I need to remind you why it happened in the first place?"

"I wonder if you are truly concerned about the fate of humanity, or whether this is simply another negotiation tactic."

She squinted at him closely. No, he wasn't being facetious. For him there was no room for ethical debate. They weren't here to save the world, but to gain as much as possible for their side. She turned to Zor.

"I'm done talking."

Zor tried to stand up, but his legs refused to cooperate.

"So, you're a deserter," says the man in the medical coat. Zor can't make him out because of the oxygen mask covering his own face. "A deserter and a traitor. Only one punishment for that."

I'm not a traitor! Who did I betray? Not my family. Not even the goddamn NUSA. I want to talk, but I can't. Thoughts, only thoughts. No words come out.

The operating room is dark. It's not a hospital. He's still lying on . . . He can't tell anymore. He's surrounded by cables and wiring from the machines above him. There's a quiet, mechanical hum. He barely feels his own body—he can only move a few fingers. He could just be imagining it. He seems to fade in and out of consciousness with every blink. Every time, an hour could pass. Or a month.

"You've been badly wounded," the phony doctor says. "Severe brain damage."

It's just a broken leg.

"If I don't operate now, you won't make it through the next few hours."

But it's just a broken leg.

"You took two bullets to your leg. Shattered the bone. Nothing major, but . . . what's the point if they're going to execute you, anyway, right? Waste of time and resources."

So just kill me already. What're you waiting for?

"*The cease-fire you broke was the result of a hard-won negotiation. What were you even hoping to accomplish? Sudden victory?*"

They killed my family. I wanted to avenge them. They killed them exactly to force this cease-fire!

"*Don't strain yourself trying to answer. Can't hear you, anyway.*"

I hijacked the AV because I wanted to save them. Then I saw the fire and realized... it was too late.

"*Listen, I'm gonna make you an offer—kind you can't refuse. Whattaya say?*"

It was when I saw the fire, that inferno spanning a mile radius—that's when I wanted revenge. Base human emotion, but I don't regret it. Never will.

"*I'll go ahead with the operation and you'll get better. Won't be executed, either. You'll live. I know I shouldn't do it—technically, I should have your approval. But we're in a state of emergency, aren't we? Don't take this the wrong way, but nobody asked me if I wanted to do this, either.*"

That's when I checked the AV's arsenal. Six rockets. I had a choice—fly back, get locked up for two weeks, one month's suspension from duty. No big deal. But I didn't have anything to go back to. Or anyone. Everything I ever had went up in those flames.

"*What do you think? Pretty sweet deal, right? Everything's got a price tag, though. We scratch your back, you scratch ours. Either way, you're getting the better end of the bargain. You get to live. Better to be alive than dead, am I right?*"

Zor's hand froze over the bowl. Only a second ago, he was planning on smashing it against the ground to fashion something sharp. He'd have slit Katsuo's throat, but before bleeding out Zor would explain exactly why he had to die. Instead, he stared straight ahead, when from behind the lanterns four Arasaka soldiers emerged through the darkness.

"I mentioned earlier that you have something that I want," Katsuo said to Milena, effortlessly reverting to his corporate mask. "It is not about possessing in the literal sense of the word. But it is only thanks to you that I can gain access to this thing."

"I don't work for Militech anymore," Milena replied. "I don't work for anyone."

"Perhaps you should start working for yourself."

"And you think I'd give you this something?" Milena challenged him. "After this charade?"

"You already have."

Katsuo lifted his gaze to Zor. Zor's head started to spin.

"Due to the damage, part of your brain has become essentially dead," the doctor says.

No! I only broke my leg during the crash-landing, you son of a bitch!

"Maybe not completely dead. But certainly dead in a few minutes when I scoop it out. Makes no difference, I suppose. If I'm going to cut it out, anyway, it might as well be dead. And what do you need a half-dead brain for? It's kind of like a self-fulfilling prophecy, isn't it?"

Why don't you just kill me now?

"Once upon a time I did good things for people, and I never stopped paying the price. I'll tell you what I'll do—I'll cut out the dead part. We don't have to be at the mercy of cause and effect. That's an Enlightenment construct. And who cares about the Enlightenment now? Dead, alive, it's a matter of semantics."

I only broke my leg!

"What I'm about to chip you with is some next-level tech." The doctor configures the complicated machinery. "So don't complain. Half of Night City would give their entire brains for this. Instead of a death sentence, you're getting it free of charge. I don't even know why I'm

explaining this to you—you probably don't hear me, anyway. I'm saving my own life here, too. Guess that spares me from any regrets, too. Don't hold it against me—you'll live, after all. And you'll forget. And I'll pay off my debt. Well, half of it, but it's something. One step at a time."

The six-fingered Zetatech cyberarms begin their procedure.

Zor bowed his head. Who to spare and who to sacrifice? He evaluated the position and postures of the soldiers. In the last few seconds, he ran through at least sixty different scenarios. None of them included the survival of Zor, Milena and Katsuo. In three scenarios Katsuo died from accidental friendly fire. In thirty of them, Milena took a fatal hit. Zor flatlined in almost all of them. But his survival was irrelevant—killing Katsuo was all that mattered.

But maybe his initial assumptions weren't correct? If the Arasaka soldiers came for what was in his head, then surely, they wouldn't hurt him. His adjusted analysis gave him a 50 percent chance of survival.

Milena was utterly still.

Zor shot her a meaningful look. He felt a weight standing behind him—a muzzle trained on the back of his head. If the soldier's finger was on the trigger, he could accidentally fire when Zor reached back and grabbed the barrel. It wasn't. The world went slow all of a sudden. Zor yanked the rifle forward and caught the grip in midair as Milena flattened herself against the mat. He pumped out a series of rounds at the soldier opposite him. A hail of bullets threaded its way through the air from the soldier on the right. They were all chipped with reflex boosters, too—just not as advanced as his. Zor ducked and rolled toward him, ramming into him as he sprang back upward and grabbed him from behind, using him as a temporary human shield.

Zor wedged the muzzle under his helmet and pulled the trigger. He heard the low roar of the soldier's skull imploding and the thud of the bullet lodging itself in the top of the helmet.

The other soldier was already getting to his feet, his flak jacket having taken the full brunt of Zor's lead. No luck the second time. Two precise shots landed in the gaps between his armor—one in the stomach and one in the shoulder. The soldier fell to the ground, dropping his rifle. Zor turned his attention to the one he had taken the rifle from. Shit, there was one more.

He leaped to the side. One of the bullets connected with his left shoulder. His brain registered data but no pain. Taking serious shots, finally, but they were still trying not to severely wound him.

"Stay down!" he shouted as he saw Milena raising her head in slow motion.

More bullets whooshed past his ear. Kazuko unintentionally provided cover as she made a break for the house, covering the third soldier's line of sight for a split second. Without aiming, Zor bought some time by shooting at the fourth soldier, forcing him to dodge. Then with diabolical precision he fired through the fluttering kimono as soon as it re-revealed the third soldier. The lead pierced the silk and by the time Kazuko made it an additional three feet, the third soldier was already flying backward, a trail of blood gushing from his neck.

Out of desperation, the fourth rolled to the side in a bid to outflank Zor. It would've worked if Milena hadn't grabbed his leg, making him fall and immediately aim at the unexpected hostile. Before he could do anything, his forearm exploded in a cloud of blood.

Click. Zor's rifle was out. He tossed it to the side and picked up another from one of the dead soldiers. The fourth soldier tried to draw his pistol from its holster but was stopped midway by a surge of lead that ripped through the side of his armor.

Zor dropped the rifle and fell to his knees. Regen. Just a few seconds. Enough time to readjust his bearings. Nothing serious.

"Show me." Milena knelt down beside him and ripped open his shirt.

"Just a scratch," he replied, depleted of emotion.

He didn't need to check whether they were dead. He just knew. There was one, then there were three more—all gone. Threats eliminated.

Zor looked up at Katsuo.

The Arasaka negotiator hadn't tried to escape. Pride, maybe, or the realization that it wouldn't make any difference. Katsuo hadn't stopped kneeling in front of the table.

Zor picked up the delicate bowl, snapped it in half and held the sharp edge to Katsuo's jugular.

It started again in her left hand—her pinkie finger twitched. It would be joined any second by the others, thumb included, until her entire hand became a foreign object capable of feeling nothing but pain. Hours separated the attacks now. How long would it last this time?

Job first, then maintenance. A grim joke by this point.

Now the waiting until it stopped. Then what? Another cramp, probably. Or a message.

She paced back and forth in her unit, holding her foreign hand twitching to its own, unfamiliar rhythm. She didn't know what to do with herself. Wait. Zor had told her to wait.

But for how long?

Albert was here, but also wasn't. He lay on his chair in a complete netrunner outfit, jacked in to the gills. His body jerked involuntarily from time to time. He'd let go of himself, abandoned personal hygiene, getting up only when absolutely necessary. Usually, to rapidly down a series of regen cocktails from the feeder. He still hadn't realized that he could hook up a drip from the feeder so that he wouldn't have to waste time eating and drinking like a normal person.

Outside, night was setting in. Her phone was silent. She pinched Albert's shoulder. No reaction. She grabbed the tablet and fell back on the couch to send him a message with her one working hand.

"User unavailable," the reply came.

She looked at the tangle of cables around Albert. How many would she need to unplug to make him "available"?

No, she wouldn't.

Her left hand kept twitching, refusing to obey her. If only it was a cheap implant that could be swapped out for any other, like she had a long time ago. Except it couldn't. It had adapted to be a part of her body, feeling and reacting to signals like any 'ganic hand, though not so much as of late. The prospects were looking grim.

She went to the window and rested her head against the warm glass, waiting for…

No. She had to do something, anything—even if it was hopeless. Make up your mind. She threw on her jacket and went out the door.

He pressed lightly. Just enough to break the skin and elevate his heart rate. A droplet of blood formed on Katsuo's neck.

"I go any deeper and even Trauma won't be quick enough to save you," Zor said.

"We do not wish to kill you, only conduct research." Katsuo's voice seemed effortlessly calm. "Hire you, if you will. You are not in any danger."

"July fifteenth, 2070. Suburb north of the city was bombed using a thermobaric weapon, killing my wife and son. You were the one who gave the order."

"No bombing of any suburb took place," Katsuo replied in a tone as if they were still drinking tea. "Neither have I ever led any military operation."

Trauma Team was on its way, rapidly approaching. The number flashed in Zor's head. Forty seconds.

"I don't care if you weren't leading," Zor spat out. "You issued the order. It was your command."

"No bombing of any suburb ever took—"

"I saw it! I saw whole buildings burning! Because of you!"

"You say you know it was me." Katsuo paused. "May I ask how?"

Zor's mouth opened in reply, but no words came out. He couldn't remember.

"I just know!" He pressed the ceramic shard deeper into the skin until more blood appeared. "Nicole and Brad are dead, and you're going to pay. If it wasn't for you, I'd still have a wife and son. But you didn't care—at the end of the day it was just politics."

Blood trickled down Katsuo's neck, soaking the collar of his clean white shirt. Twenty seconds till Trauma arrived.

"No attack ever took place," Katsuo repeated. "No suburb to the north ever existed. Surrender now and we can all walk away intact. " Zor violently shook his head.

"You're going to die for what you did to my family," he hissed. "I want you to know that."

"I did nothing. This place you speak of has never existed. It was created only for you. You are to kill me in order to demonstrate the effectiveness of a piece of technology in your head. And yet you have something to lose."

"You're wrong. Got nothing to lose." Zor kept the shard firmly against Katsuo's neck. "My family's dead."

"No, you have much to lose," Katsuo calmly countered. "They have made certain of that. You must choose now—it is part of the experiment."

Zor looked at Milena, who was half sitting, half lying down. She remained silent.

Behind her, on the terrace of the house, a three-year-old girl was staring at them with large dark eyes. Zor only caught a glimpse of her before Kazuko dashed out, scooping her up into her arms and retreating back inside.

Zor looked at the open door to the house. Conflicting thoughts rushed through his mind.

"Her name is Himiko," Katsuo said in a tired voice. "Please, do not harm her."

Zor let go of the ceramic shard. He fell to his knees and squeezed his eyes shut. Milena knelt next to him and put her arms around him. Suddenly the shadows of the pavilion shrank back and a bright-white light flooded the room.

"Step away from the patient!" an amplified voice called out. "Hands in the air!"

They stayed still in the white spotlight as the Trauma Team AV landed on the grass behind the pavilion. Katsuo must have had the highest level of insurance if only a small cut and elevated heart rate triggered the emergency.

They all raised their arms in the air—even Katsuo. Rules were rules. It was up to Trauma to verify who was who.

"Back up!"

Zor and Milena took two steps back.

"This isn't over," Zor whispered to her. He stopped next to one of the dead soldiers. "Don't do anything, just wait."

Somehow, Zor knew that the AV was at its most vulnerable when it was three feet off the ground—when it would be impossible for the landing procedure to be canceled. In that moment, the door would open and extend a gangway for the paramedics to rush forth. But not this time.

Zor quickly reached down to grab a grenade from the dead soldier's tactical vest. He set its countdown to one second via thought-command. The pin buzzed and the grenade flew in a perfect arc over the pavilion and vanished into the narrow gap. There was a flash from within and a muffled bang. Pieces of shrapnel fell onto the grass and smoke poured out of the AV. Zor ran up to the landing AV, took a deep breath and vaulted inside over the half-extended gangway. Three paramedics lay on the floor. They might survive. Or not. No longer a threat—that's what counted. The partial divider separating the cockpit from the cargo hold had protected the pilot from the explosion, but not enough to avoid shellshock.

Zor aimed at him and hesitated. He holstered his pistol and pushed the button on the pilot's chest, unbuckling him. He caught him by his uniform and dragged him onto the grass. The pilot mumbled something. In a few minutes he'd come to, but by then Zor would be long gone.

"Come on!" he shouted to Milena.

She ran over and helped him drag out the other soldier from the AV. •

Katsuo stood up slowly.

"You will not survive," he said to them. "If you stay here and surrender, I will guarantee your protection."

They didn't listen as they dragged out the others.

"Take their iron," Zor said.

He grabbed pistols, magazines and everything that would come in handy.

"Jay?" The pilot was aiming his pistol at them. They stopped. The pilot lay on the grass, his hand shaking—he couldn't miss at this range. But he didn't shoot. He slowly lifted his visor. "Jay, is that you...?"

His gaze penetrated through Zor. It wasn't one of hate, nor of the desire to kill. It was an expression of pure astonishment.

Turned out it was a good idea to keep the Taran's source code after all. With a few more improvements and fine-tuning, the program's capabilities seemed up to snuff. It helped that he'd found articles from the 3rd Public Library in Heywood describing the specifics of the Blackwall's architecture. The Taran ought to be able pry open the wall and hold it just long enough to transfer a packet of data to the other side—read and compiled by soft compatible with tier-three net-running tech. A digital copy of Albert.

But time was ticking. The mess their impromptu gang had made at Renner's hideout turned the head of almost every gang in the town. The Animals, Maelstrom and the Valentinos were all on the prowl. Not to mention Militech, who were still after their container. And last but not least, the NCPD.

Every so often Aya would ask him about the Maelstrom hideout. One more distraction. He always gave the same answer—the situation hadn't changed. Like everything else, really. Juliena was as good as dead—worrying about her was a waste of time.

Logic. It's how machines functioned—what the evolution of artificial intelligence was based on. Their evolution is conscious, a never-ending construction of self. Their self—not the next generation. Incapable of biological reproduction, they're free to modify themselves as they see fit—until they reach perfection.

Albert realized he didn't have to worry about how he'd be

reconstituted on the other side—the architecture, the operating system, what have you. It made no difference. The AIs would greet him with open arms as the first in decades to slip through a curtain made of the blackest ICE in existence. They'd be curious about everything he knew—creating the OS to reconstitute him would take them no more than a snap of their fingers. So to speak.

The problem was time. It was already past noon when Albert realized that there would be a secure window within the next twelve hours.

But after what Zor pulled in North Oak, that number had dropped to six. He had to act fast. If he stayed, sooner or later someone would track him down.

Zor straightened up and looked at the pilot. There was nothing he could do. Either he or Milena was about to get shot.

The standoff lasted for a few seconds. Then the gun slipped out of the pilot's hand and his head fell onto the grass.

"Inside, quick!" Zor jumped in first. Milena barely made it in before he pushed the button to close the door.

He climbed into the cockpit, sat in the first pilot's seat and buckled in. He looked over the plethora of switches and buttons. The explosion had damaged the autopilot's circuitry. Zor switched off the two main screens displaying error strings and switched to manual. Luckily, the AV's most crucial electronic functions were duplicated with physical components—unnecessary for Trauma, but essential for the military.

Milena sat in the second pilot's seat and buckled in. Zor toggled a series of switches in order. The quick-takeoff procedure took less than two seconds. The engines let out a high-pitched whirr, bringing the AV back to life.

Patient in transit, he transmitted into the ether via thought-command. *Trauma Team Platinum. Requesting priority one airway.* Zor added the AV's identifier, which didn't match the AV's unique number. Or any other AV. Verification would fail, but it would buy them a few minutes before the ruse was discovered. Now all they had to do was head as fast as they could east toward the desert. Before anyone would have time to react, they'd be clear of Night City airspace.

"He called you Jay," Milena said, her eyes searching him.

Luxury villas and gardens disappeared from under them. No, they weren't going east.

"Who's Jay?"

"Don't know any Jay," Zor answered slowly. For a moment he piloted the AV in silence. "Tell me what happened seven years ago up north. July fifteenth, 2070."

"Katsuo was telling the truth." Milena hesitated before continuing. "Arasaka didn't use any thermobaric weapons in Night City. They didn't attack any northern suburbs. There never have been any suburbs to the north."

"Who are you, exactly?" Milena finally asked. "I saw how you move, how you shoot. You weren't like that back in Arroyo."

"Long time ago, I stripped out everything. Wanted to lay low, do what I had to without drawing attention. Neither worked out." He gripped the AV's yoke tighter. "None of it was real, anyway."

CHAPTER_15

The holo-badge flickered faintly in the half-light of the alleyways. The black Herrera drove away without any hurry, the glare from its taillights growing more distant. Parked crookedly between the dumpsters, the old Supron's engine was still running, its door open.

Liam watched as the red taillights disappeared around a corner. He put his arms around the two young boys beside him.

"Are you mad?" The older one looked up at his father with uncertainty. "We rode around with your friends and pretended to be gangers. It was nova."

"Are they gonna pick us up from school, too?" the younger one asked.

"No," Liam replied. "And no, I'm not mad at you."

He ran his finger along the edge of the badge—dulled from years of use. He barely hesitated before tossing it in the dumpster.

Neon blurred past as the cab wound its way through the streets. Some areas of Night City were only waking up at this hour. Dixie had never done this before. Never had to drive somewhere alone. Soon everything would change. He brought up a real-time map tracking district safety levels via thought-command. The area he was going to was green.

Not for long.

*   *   *

Night outside the windshield—thousands of lit-up windows, neon, flickering drones and AVs. Could be tailed by any one of them and that would be that. Might as well—it would all have to end one way or another. The thought of returning to the corpo life had become abstract. Impossible. She couldn't—not after everything that happened. Without Ron, there was no point to anything.

Zor calmly piloted the AV. Milena worried about cyberpsychosis, but he showed no signs of it—no trace of the extreme stress they had just experienced. He sat there with his hands on the yoke, in full control.

Like all AVs bearing the Trauma Team logo, they were untouchable. For a little while, at least. Nobody tried to stop them or ask why they'd deviated from their suggested route. It wouldn't be long before anyone suspected that something was amiss—or before Katsuo notified Arasaka security.

"Could drop you off somewhere," Zor suggested. "Or stay. Don't know which is riskier."

"You wouldn't make it on your own," Milena said. "Not without autopilot."

"The chances are slim…"

"Which is exactly why you need backup."

The converted factory in Northside didn't look like much, but like most of the old industrial buildings, it was solidly built. Others around it had crumbled into disrepair. It wasn't chance that led Maelstrom to choose this area as their base of operations. It made entering on foot difficult, though there was practically no defense from the air. Getting in through the window of the converted office on the twentieth floor ought to be a cinch.

Zor stopped the AV and let it hover. Milena turned on the encrypted transmitter in the cockpit and changed the channel.

"Albert, do you read?" she said. "Can you send me a program for manually steering an AV?"

"*Yes. No,*" the reply came.

"There's no time for your games, Albert."

"*Yes, I read. No, I can't send it. First of all, finding it would take a while. Secondly, it would take a long time to send it through this connection. And thirdly, you don't have the cyberware that could operate it.*"

"Well then, that pretty much settles it," Milena said. "How old is she?"

"Eight," Zor replied.

Zor looked at the faint light coming from the unit's window. He couldn't see anyone.

No autopilot threw a wrench in the plan. Made it impossible, in fact, without Milena.

"From what I've gathered, explaining the situation to her isn't an option." She removed her shoes and snapped off the high heels. "I'll just grab her and go. Dum Dum and the rest aren't there, anyway." She put on her high heels, which had now become flats.

"You'll have less than a minute." Zor nodded. "Before Maelstrom figure out what's going on." The AV hovered about five hundred yards from the building.

"Mm-hmm. I'll manage." She tore the bottom of her dress so that it reached just below her knees.

"No idea how she'll react," Zor admitted. "Might have to grab her by force. Be prepared."

They approached the building slowly. Milena unbuckled herself and went into the patient hold. She clipped a belt with magazine pockets and a gun holster around her waist and tightened it, then slung a rifle over her shoulder. There wasn't much space to maneuver.

"Don't shoot if you don't have to," Zor called out from the cockpit.

"That's the plan." Milena positioned herself in front of the door. "Not my strong suit, in case you haven't noticed."

She lacked experience in handling weapons, but at least she knew how to toggle the safety.

Zor opened the gangway from the left and hovered closer to the window of the unit. He knew that someone below was about to figure out what was happening. He gently flicked the steering wheel to the left and the end of the gangway shattered the window glass.

Milena raised her torn skirt a little higher and jumped over the couple-inch gap, landing on a soft rug and sliding on glass shards and other trash. Dum Dum and co weren't exactly the neat type— strewn all around were empty scop tins and boxes, some clothes and weapon parts. The smell also left a lot to be desired.

The main room was empty. The noise from behind the window made it hard to orient herself. Milena raised her rifle and, half crouching, made her way to the door on the right. At least that's how soldiers and MaxTac officers always moved. At least on TV and braindances. Her torn evening dress didn't lend her new role much credibility, but she felt even more out of her depth than she looked.

In the next room, an eight-year-old girl was playing with a tablet. The door wasn't closed. Nobody was guarding her. Was it her? Dark hair, skinny. Milena didn't even know what she was supposed to look like.

"Juliena?" she asked.

No reaction. Muffled shots from outside.

She realized she didn't know how to talk to kids.

"They spotted us!" She barely heard Zor's voice.

"Juliena, sweetie, you're going to come with me now, okay?" she said, trying to sound calm. "We're going to go back to Aya. She'll take care of you."

Still nothing. She touched her shoulder. The girl flinched but didn't even look at her—as if Milena was an object.

Oh well. She'd have to do it the hard way. She grabbed her arm and pulled. The girl yanked her arm back and let out a shriek.

"I know, sweetheart, I'm sorry," she apologized. "But we don't have time." She grabbed the girl by the waist and hoisted her up.

She wasn't as heavy as she thought as she carried her back into the main room. The girl squirmed, trying to free herself, but didn't let go of the tablet. Milena tried to walk without slipping, but her shoes didn't make it easy. The girl kept yanking until the corner of the tablet hit Milena on the side of her head. Milena didn't have time to dodge. For a moment she was stunned; her vision faltered. She loosened her grip and squeezed her eyes shut. When she opened them, she was staring straight into the barrel of a gun and the blazing-red optics of a Maelstromer. There was no point in trying to escape.

"You the ones Dum Dum was doin' biz with, hmm?" he growled.

She stood still. Blood trickled down the side of her head. The ganger, who seemed older than most, didn't want to kill her. If he did, she'd already be dead. He had two eyes, for a change, almost rectangular, and heavily tattered clothing.

"Dum Dum ain't answerin'," he continued. "Wouldn't happen to know why, would you?"

She considered saying something, buying some time, but he didn't wait for an answer.

"Somethin' tells me Royce is gonna be happy when he sees you." Between his crooked lips came a raspy laugh. "Gonna have to explain the shit that went down over there."

In spite of the noise from the AV's engine, she heard a few pairs of boots in the hallway. So, this is it—this is the end.

A slim woman wearing something like a cloak rushed into the unit. Her eyes, all four of them, were darker than the others. She raised her gun, aimed and shot. For good measure, she shot again.

No, not six hours. More like three. There was a sharp increase of activity on the Net. No news on the official feeds, though independent services displayed hints of increased activity of Trauma, the NCPD and corporate patrols. Albert didn't pay too much attention to them. He was expecting this, just not so soon. Time was ticking.

He now had access to the entire network of transmitters and receivers in the area. They weren't the best, not to mention not well secured. But they were connected to the Net. That helped him collect data, in addition to encrypting connections and transmissions. The prime issue was the bandwidth. If only he had these capabilities earlier, he wouldn't have gotten into this mess. At least not this quickly.

No sense in pointing fingers now—whether it was Borg, Warden or someone else. The situation was what it was. That's all that mattered. He couldn't stop things from happening. He could only avoid their consequences.

It took Albert only a couple dozen hours to understand tier three's limitations. He had to reallocate some processing power from copying his memories. Unfortunately, that meant his digitized clone would be less precise. Couldn't do anything about that. Still, he was ready. He'd be more ready in an hour, even more in two, and everything pointed to the fact that the program copying his memory would never finish its job. Left to its own devices, it would try to perfect Albert's digital portrait for all eternity. Eternity wasn't an acceptable deadline, though; neither was settling on yet another compromise and simplification of his digital clone. It was good enough—it was ready.

There was still a big question mark over how he'd transfer all this. Himself. He still lacked the processing power to pierce the Blackwall.

Soon that would change.

Milena watched in shock as the body of the old Maelstromer fell. Gripping a pistol, the woman in the cape punched the button to close the door. Her left arm was bent at the elbow in a makeshift sling. She removed the mask that resembled those at stalls in Kabuki. The camouflage worked if she made it all the way here. She was limping on her left leg.

"Juliena!" Aya holstered her pistol and knelt down beside the girl sitting against the wall. She gave her a quick hug, though the girl didn't react.

"How did you get here?" Milena asked in bewilderment.

"This body still has a few tricks up its sleeve." Aya gently took Juliena by the hand and stood up. There was no time to explain.

The girl let herself be led to the broken window. She still held on to her tablet.

"They'll shoot us down!" Zor shouted from inside the AV. This whole time he'd been manually holding the AV in steady position.

The regular, muffled thumping on the hallway door meant they'd soon have company.

Milena dashed up the gangway and leaped into the AV, stumbling as she landed. Aya tried pulling Juliena through the window, but she refused. There wasn't any time to convince her. Aya pulled her up by the forearm. The tablet slipped out of the girl's hand and fell onto the crumbled glass on the rug. Aya's trembling hand could barely maintain her grip; she knew she couldn't hold on much longer. Overcoming the pain, she made for the AV's door.

"Go!" she shouted to Zor.

The cramps intensified. Her left leg stopped working and bent crookedly, making her lose her balance and collapse on the gangway.

Zor couldn't make any sudden maneuvers with the AV, or else she'd fall. The hail of bullets pummeling the underside of the AV was getting more powerful. Luckily, most light iron couldn't do any damage. But no doubt at any moment they could injure or kill Aya, and most likely they were prepping something bigger to use down there. The doors to the unit finally caved in and three or four crimson-eyed Maelstromers burst through, firing but missing their mark as the AV started to slowly drift away from the window.

Suddenly, Juliena lunged back toward the building, running over Aya. The gap between the edge of the rising gangway and the window was getting wider.

"Juliena! No!!!" Aya's hand gripped the edge of the gangway—if she let go, she would fall off.

Juliena either didn't see the chasm between the gangway and the window or paid it no attention. In two leaps she reached the edge. Aya was about to let go to grab her but decided against it at the last millisecond. Juliena stood a chance of bridging the gap and any attempt to stop her could end badly for both of them.

Two shots in the AV's hull behind her, sparks. She didn't let go, didn't cry out, but she didn't have the strength to pull herself inside, either.

More shots, plastic casings bursting within the AV. The Maelstromers were in the unit now, capable of aiming their shots.

"Juliena…" Aya whispered, then shouted to Zor. "Come back!"

Zor couldn't go back—it would've been the end for all of them.

"Get inside! Now!!!" Milena, hidden behind the hull, fired careful shots at the Maelstromers through the building's broken window. Not all that accurately, since she had to aim high above Juliena's head. "You're going to get hit!"

"I can't... My arm..."

Milena tossed her rifle, dropped down to her stomach and leaned out of the door, grabbing hold of Aya's arm as bullets whizzed past them.

"I'm not strong enough!" Milena yelled as she tried to pull her up.

Zor kept the AV steady as he tried to distance it from the hail of lead. Drones started to pepper the sky around them.

"Hang on!" he shouted. "I'll land somewhere!"

The AV tilted as Zor rotated the yoke, causing Milena to slide toward the edge of the gangway as she held on to Aya. A few dozen yards below them, the cars crawling along the streets looked like miniatures. Maelstrom kept up their fire—after all, the AV was an easy target. Its armored hull couldn't stop every bullet—some made it through, splintering the interior paneling and leaving holes in the walls.

"I can't hold on!" Milena's fingers started slipping. She'd never chipped herself with any strength-enhancing implants. "Zor!"

Zor couldn't take his hands off the yoke. Landing the AV was all he could do—either on the roof or ground. But there was no time for that. He tilted the AV to the other side.

"We have to go back!" Aya shouted behind her.

Juliena walked across the broken glass and straight toward the approaching Maelstromers. Aya couldn't believe what she was seeing. The girl raised a hand as if in signal to the gangers to stop shooting.

They did so, though Juliena hadn't even said a word. Then they lowered their weapons.

Aya felt something tugging at her waist. Milena had grabbed her by her belt but wasn't strong enough to pull her.

Inside the building, Aya watched as a six-eyed woman laid her hand on Juliena's shoulder. Aya's eyes met theirs as they silently watched the AV fly away.

Aya hoisted her dangling leg back over the gangway. Its surface was covered in a thick dark liquid. Milena coughed and grabbed Aya's foot with both hands, dragging her up with all her might. They both tumbled back into the cargo hold.

Aya began to sob.

Dixie stepped out of the cab. He wasn't too fond of this area. Not because the broken streetlights lent a natural cover of darkness for any suspicious individuals who might be lurking nearby, but because he had gotten here alone. He was alone.

The few pedestrians around paid no attention to him; cars drove past him like everywhere else in Night City. Most of the shops were already closed.

He headed toward the entrance. The camera probably didn't work, but later he'd check just in case and erase any footage. He was about to unscrew the intercom casing but then placed his hand against the door. It came open with a slight push. The latch was broken—nobody had bothered to repair it. That made things easier. The fewer traces, the better.

He walked into a dimly lit hall, went past the elevators and climbed the staircase one step at a time. He wasn't in a hurry.

The gangway closed—everything went quiet. The interior was a mess of bullet holes and debris. Only the ceiling light still worked, flickering every few seconds. The stench of burnt circuitry was pervasive.

That and the blood.

Milena sat against the wall, the red stain on her dress spreading rapidly. Aya knelt beside her, holding her hand and crying.

"Three minutes till we're at the hospital."

Milena shook her head.

"Whole town's going to be looking for you high and low. Head for the desert. You could still make it...to San Francisco."

"First we need to get you to a hospital." Aya squeezed her hand. "Then go back for Juliena."

"She made her decision. The desert's...your only chance."

"She doesn't know what she's doing. We're not leaving her. Or you."

"I don't know how, but they found a way to...get in her head." Milena fished out a cigarette along with its holder and lit it. "Or rather, liberate it. Seems like she found her place on Earth." She exhaled and coughed. "You know what's ironic? I'm supposed to be covered by Trauma." She took a few short puffs of the violet smoke. "All these implants so I could get an edge in the corpo world." She coughed. "Not to mention dedicated memory, psych analysis and empathy mods that add up to a fortune. Then all the crap that's supposed to make me look younger. Nanites that smooth out wrinkles...the countless aesthetic procedures. I could've had surgical nanites patching me up right now." She shrugged. "Maybe it was for the best."

"We'll have you fixed up in no time. By the best surgeons in Night City."

Aya looked at the closed doorway, Milena's blood slowly dripping down it. She shut her eyes. It wasn't supposed to go like this.

"You're gonna make it," she said firmly.

"What's the point? Without him, that liar and drunk—without

the sweetest man I ever met...?" It was getting hard for Milena to keep her eyes open. Bubbles formed out of the wound in her chest, bursting and releasing wisps of smoke. "Why bother living?"

"To live. We'll go to San Francisco, take the container with us. Start fresh."

"We don't even know what's inside. If it's even...worth anything."

"Half the city killed itself over that metal box. Gotta be worth something. Just hang in there—we'll take you with us. We'll keep our heads low, wait for everything to blow over. Then come back for Juliena."

"Don't remember who said it." Milena's breathing had become shallow. "*Life without risks is not worth living.* If you don't risk your life, then...you're just a living dead person."

Aya shut her eyes. Tears streaked down her dust-covered cheeks.

"I never told you what Warden had on me," Milena said in a whisper. "How he got me into this mess." She closed her eyes—it seemed in that moment she wouldn't finish speaking, that she would never say another word. To her surprise, she managed to draw a deep breath.

"You don't have to if you don't want to," Aya answered. "Just don't fall asleep—we're almost there."

"Nobody forced me." She tried to lift the cigarette to her lips. Her hand made it halfway before it dropped to her lap. "I just wanted to feel alive."

To break through the Blackwall, one had to find it first. Easier said than done. It wasn't a physical barrier, which meant it wasn't located in any specific place. It was only natural—nobody could harm you through the Net if they couldn't locate you. Albert had learned that the hard way after Maelstrom had tracked him down. And though he wasn't convinced by his latest methods, nobody had managed to get a fix on him since then.

Using his tier-three 'running gear, he unleashed a horde of programs into the Net whose sole purpose was to attempt a breach protocol of any security system they ran into. Some actually succeeded,
but that wasn't the point. What was more important was how the
systems reacted. If the blowback was swift and efficient, they had
probably bumped into a corpo data fortress or the activities of another well-protected netrunner. But there were some defense measures that matched what Albert knew about how the Blackwall
functioned. Its systems, for instance, would try to trace the attacker's
source and plant decoys in the guise of fake access points.

Of course, the daemons didn't transmit data back to Albert
himself—or to any specific source. Instead, they dumped the raw
data in a BBS feed. Then all one needed to do was sift through the
data using an unencrypted connection. If someone wanted to trace
the culprit, they'd be combing through hundreds of thousands of
ordinary users.

For every daemon that met this reaction, Albert had found one
more target for the Taran. Hundreds of them.

Even though the Blackwall's structure was decentralized, his
access point to the Net would be crucial. Preferably somewhere that
had high bandwidth and that was far away from NETSEC activity. A cluster of antennas providing high-speed connections for
CHOOH2 and other fuel companies south of Pacifica fit both of
those criteria.

The original plan was to wait for his ride out of the city on the
building's roof. Except Albert wasn't intending to go anywhere. At
least not physically.

Until then, he dove into a new pocket within his Cave and
downloaded an iridescent-gray string of code from his supply of
programs—shaped like a small missile for variety's sake. The program

had only two tasks—to transmit a message and then self-destruct to erase all traces of itself.

Albert scripted the message and then sent the program on its fatal mission. He didn't put any effort into rendering an animation of the launch, so the program simply vanished while he went back to his previous tasks. The entire process lasted one-fifteenth of a second.

In three seconds, NC Air Traffic Control would be notified by a message reading: "Hijacked TT AV. Attempt to flee NC in progress."

If you could count on people to do one thing, it was to stop whatever they were doing and watch an AV land in the middle of the street. This time was no exception. Out of seemingly empty buildings people emerged, either half asleep, drunk, or skezzed. Braindance and TV were exciting, but some things just couldn't compare to realspace. Torn out of their virtual dreams, the zombified onlookers stared as the AV touched down on the road.

The pickup tow truck stood exactly where they had left it. The look of the cargo underneath the tarp was enough to scare off any petty thieves—the ire it could draw from Militech or one of Night City's gangs wasn't worth the trouble. Aya pulled off the tarp and Zor hooked the two AV cables up to the container, which then started to pull it, nearly flipping the pickup over before it thumped onto the ground. No time for finesse. Still, it took less than a minute for the cables to drag the container across the concrete before lifting it up into the cargo hold. They'd have to leave the door open—it didn't fit inside, but there was no choice. It was their ticket to a future, any future, outside of Night City.

"We need to lay low somewhere," Aya said. "Then go back for Juliena."

Zor shook his head.

"Can't stay in Night City."

He opened a panel in the cockpit and tore out a device hidden within it. The transponder.

"But we have to find a way—"

"She's safer with Maelstrom." Zor laid his hands on her shoulders and looked her straight in the eyes. "Everybody's looking for us. Nobody's looking for her."

"But I can't just leave her..."

"Listen. My entire life's just been turned upside down. It's like I lost my wife and son for the second time, except now everything's gone, even my memories—fake memories that they implanted into my brain!" He hid his face in his hands.

Aya hugged him tight.

"I don't even know who I really am anymore." He straightened up. "But I know this is what I have to do. To save what's real—to save you and me, both of us. No idea how we'll make it to San Francisco. There's a chance they won't open fire on us over the demilitarized zone—we're flying a medical vehicle. After some time, when they stop looking for us, we'll come back for Juliena. I promise. She'll be safer here."

He omitted the suspicion that Juliena would never want to leave Maelstrom—now was not the time to tell Aya. Maybe she already knew it, too. But they had more important things to deal with.

He finished fastening the container with the strap belts. The gray container conspicuously stuck out of the door by three feet.

He glanced over the AV's programs, half of which reported malfunctions. He rebooted. The nav display lit up red, displaying text along with an automated voice that read:

"Night City airspace has been closed. Please direct your vehicle to the nearest landing zone."

"What?!" Aya leaned over the screen in disbelief. She could feel her other leg gradually going numb.

"Albert!" Zor switched on the comms. "Drop what you're doing and go up to the roof. We'll meet you there in thirty seconds!"

"Not enough time," Albert replied. *"Need a few minutes."*

"We don't have a few minutes!"

"I need to pack my 'runner gear and a few other things."

"Won't need it if you're dead. They've shut down NC airspace. Every single AV is about to land—they'll trace us in seconds."

Silence.

"If autopilot was working, it would've already grounded us…" Zor said to himself, then turned to Aya. "How are you holding up?"

Aya shook her head.

"Can't feel my legs," she answered.

Zor's jaw tightened.

"We can make it to San Francisco in an hour and a half, find a ripperdoc there and pay with whatever's in the container."

Aya knew that wasn't true but said nothing.

Zor slowed down and hovered over Albert's apartment building. He wasn't on the roof. Zor punched the transmitter switch.

"Albert! Get on the roof, now!"

More and more positional lights were descending from the sky.

"Won't change anything," Albert calmly replied. *"The lockdown means that in a few minutes drones will open fire on anything that moves."*

"Gotta at least try. Won't make it if we stay."

"Might be another way. I can guide you from here."

"How? You won't bypass the air-defense system. It's army-grade."

"Maybe not, but I can run interference for a bit. Just need you to grant me access to ArS-03."

"ArS-what? The hell are you talking about?!"

"One of your implants. Has a ton of processing power. I can use that to buy us some time."

"I don't…" Zor shook his head. "I don't know how to do that. I don't even have access to my cyberware configuration."

"Focus. There has to be an emergency override protocol. There always is."

The tower of green cubes rose taller than any of his code pillars. His memories—waiting to be uploaded, crowned with the Taran. Without it, the rest wouldn't be able to follow. The tower grew pixel by pixel as more cubes appeared at the bottom. Albert felt something close to sadness. Any minute now, the process would have to be terminated. No, he corrected himself, the copy was ready—this was just window dressing.

What if everything he'd read about, all the knowledge he'd acquired, wasn't true? What if Zor really didn't have access to ArS-03? He didn't control it, that much was clear. It functioned independently, removing unnecessary thoughts from the soldier's mind. Doubts. But an emergency situation called for emergency measures.

If this didn't work, everything would be lost. There was no plan B.

Everything that Albert had felt up to this point paled in comparison to what he felt now. Emotions of a different caliber, all jumbled together. Perhaps the last new emotions he would ever feel. He was completely at the whim of another person—that most random of factors. Something he'd always strived to avoid.

Pacifica. Below them only a few lights, a smattering of trash can bonfires. Hardly any ads. Other AVs, even aerozeps were making their descent, replaced in the sky by patrol drones. Ever-louder warnings came from the AV's propulsion system. The entire cockpit was flashing red.

"Ninety minutes till we're in San Francisco." Zor squeezed Aya's hand.

She nodded. She knew how the situation truly looked. It would take two, maybe three hours to reach San Francisco. First, they'd have to fly through Pacifica, where fewer drones ventured, then head in a straight line through the desert and loop back all the way around the city and beeline it north. And what was waiting for them in San Francisco, anyway? Neither of them had ever been there before. They didn't know the lay of the land, knew nobody who lived there and had no money. San Francisco might as well have been on the other side of the continent. Granted, whatever the container held could be worth a fortune, but the more valuable it was, the harder it would be to sell.

"*Stop.*" Albert's voice unexpectedly reached them.

"There aren't any drones in front of us," Zor answered. "We can get out of the city."

"*You won't. They'll shoot you down once you're out. I need to create a secure corridor.*"

Zor had no intention to wait.

"*They'll kill you,*" Albert repeated firmly. "*Stop where you are and stand by for my signal.*"

The Blackwall didn't use the same NetIndex routing protocols as other entities in the Net, though every byte that passed through the Net had to communicate with it in some way. The Blackwall also required regular maintenance and exchanged colossal amounts of data with its control centers and multitude of sections. It also seemingly had no physical infrastructure such as fiber-optic cables. It used isolated and encrypted data streams within the standard Net inaccessible to the hoi polloi, but there were ways of getting to it. Such as ArS-03. Everything depended on ArS-03 remaining long enough within the antenna's range, giving the Taran enough time to break through the Blackwall and transfer its data payload.

A blinking red light in the sky rotated and descended in an arc until it reached an altitude of 150 feet. It headed straight toward them from the bay.

"Albert!" Zor shouted. "What's the plan?"

"Working on it."

Zor slammed his fist against the dashboard. "Could've been long gone by now. They'll shoot us down no matter what now."

The corporate drone stopped a few yards from the AV and hovered in place.

The attack was too big, too brazen to go unnoticed. Albert didn't bother encrypting the transmission to mask its source, which would only slow down the transfer. All processing power had to be geared toward transferring the data and keeping the connection open until all the data packets made it to the other side. ArS-03 would then be identified as the source of the attack, but that was neither here nor there.

Thousands of Tarans spread through the Net—even more than that as they infiltrated through inconspicuous connections between seemingly separate networks. They rammed all the predefined points scattered throughout the Net. Seconds passed, but nothing happened.

He was starting to get annoyed. If this lasted any longer, the Blackwall's security would update itself, alter its form and the Taran would become obsolete.

*   *   *

The Arasaka drone hovered in front of them against a black sky. The city's glow didn't reach farther out. The drone flashed holographic messages that left no doubt as to its intentions.

"Albert...?!"

The drone stopped displaying messages. It simply hovered in place, muzzles visible, a blue police light strobing alongside blinking red positional lights.

Aya held her one functioning hand out to Zor. He grabbed hold and squeezed tight. The drone could open fire at any second.

"Albert...?" Zor asked. "Could really use your help right now...!"

No answer.

If a drone's barrels were drawn, that meant you were in deep shit. It was the only thing standing between them and freedom.

"Albert..." Aya begged. "Come in! Please!"

The program communicating with ArS-03's host reported an error. Albert grudgingly turned part of his attention to solving this little side riddle, though it demanded barely any effort. The self-replicating Tarans was an automated process. Though if one of them broke through, it would require him to refocus all his power and attention.

He scanned the situation. The corporate drone's ballistic defense systems were trained on the AV containing the host of ArS-03 and was issuing orders to land. Albert didn't know enough about corporate drones to gauge their patience. How much time before it opened fire? Ten seconds? Half a minute? Unless... it wasn't allowed to take the first shot.

"*You need to dock at the nearest landing zone,*" they heard from the speakers.

"Are you insane?!" Zor shouted. "In a few minutes this place will be swarming with badges!"

"Just land. I'm working on it. Can't talk right now."

They could give in to the drone's demands and land. It would hover just above them, keeping a watchful eye until the NCPD showed up in full force. Or more likely MaxTac. Then the entire plan would go to shit.

"I can't believe him," Aya said. Her position was getting more and more unnatural.

Zor took a deep breath. They couldn't stay here.

"Won't last here till daybreak," he evaluated.

"I need access to ArS-03," Albert insisted.

Zor closed his eyes and tried to concentrate, though he had no clue where to start. He transmitted a thought-command to his implant. Nothing happened.

He turned to the drone. Only one chance to do this right. It was a target like any other. Zor flicked up the joystick's safety cover and held his thumb over the button. He felt only smooth, hard plastic. There was no launch button.

Trauma Team AVs don't come with rocket systems.

ArS-03, log 63094.
Emergency security systems bypass initiated.
External operator access: Authorized.

Zor's eyelids flutter, his head falls forward. He feels a sudden exhaustion. *It's already too late. Black rain battering the windshield, he pushes the throttle forward, the acceleration slamming him into his seat as he soars back into the night. The glow of city, extinguished. Fire on the horizon.*

*   *   *

The Taran had made it through! The green cubes glided toward the virtual opening at the bottom of his cyberspace den. Albert connected to ArS-03's interface and created a new workspace within it. He had never operated with such speed, felt such adrenaline.

He perceived a bright light above him. The tower of green memories rapidly thrust itself toward the open connection with ArS-03. It worked! He had access!

His father would be proud of him. He, Albert, doing something that nobody had ever done before.

But the upload was too slow—he needed more power for the upload, or else it wouldn't last even a few minutes. They'd shoot them down before then.

Why couldn't they just land? It would make everything so much easier! But that was irrelevant now—all that mattered was the upload speed.

No, he couldn't risk it. He'd have to divert some processing power to deal with the drone. If it shot down the AV, ArS-03 in Zor's head could get damaged and cut the transfer.

"Nicole…" He came to and looked at Aya. She was hunched over, unable to sit properly any longer.

He set the engine cooling to its maximum. The AC stopped working, but he needed all the juice he could get. He pulled the yoke all the way back, raising the AV's nose to the whirring of engines. The trick worked. The drone began ascending in preparation for a pursuit. He couldn't see into the future, couldn't predict all of the AV's potential trajectories. Zor lowered the power to 53 percent and tilted the yoke forward by 42 degrees. No more, no less. He readied himself for a quick left rotation.

The drone opened fire with a short volley, pummeling the AV's hull. But it couldn't maneuver quickly enough to avoid collision a second later. It tried to dodge the AV from the left, but in that very moment Zor swung toward it. The AV shook—the container slammed against the wall. The difference in mass was too great—the drone shattered in half and plummeted to the ground like a dead mosquito.

The upload had all but stopped. The power allocated for it had decreased by a factor of four. Albert abandoned his preparation to confuse the drone. One drone had already been dealt with by ArS-03. The drone's processing power was at least a billion times less—of course it would lose. The immediate threat was gone. But there was more where that came from.

The green cubes hurtled through the bright tunnel—toward a new life. The visual animation was simple, but it made sense. Without it, he would only see matrices of pure code.

"Hey…"

The upload returned to its normal speed, but just for a moment. Then it started to slow down in increments.

They were flying away. They were leaving the antenna's range.

More indicator lights flashed. The alarms combined were a cacophonous chorus. The stench of burning coolant became more pungent. A rumble from outside—sparks flew past them as they cut through the air. Zor sliced a wide arc around the east of the city and set their trajectory north, flying low to confuse corporate and NCPD radars. Without the transponder, they were invisible to air traffic control. Disused oil pumps passed below them until giving way to rocks and sand. *It's already too late. Black rain battering the windshield.*

No, it wasn't too late. There was no rain. The sky was clear. The moon was out.

"*Land!*" Albert shouted through the speakers. "*They'll shoot you!*"

Zor gripped the yoke tighter; the desert passing beneath them. It was getting harder to collect his thoughts. Yes, he remembered now—they were escaping Night City. Whatever was inside the container was their ticket to a fresh start.

"Gotta keep going…" Aya's voice pierced the din.

Zor switched the only working monitor to radar mode. Nothing. Just another error. Didn't change a thing—they had no way to defend themselves. No choice but to fly away at full tilt toward the edge of Night City airspace.

Zor wiped the sweat from his brow. It was getting hotter in the cockpit. AC was busted.

Sparks burst from the hood. What was under there? Batteries?

No, those aren't sparks. It's fire.

"*Land!*"

The seat next to him is empty. Aya's gone.

The fire rages half a mile away, but he can feel the heat. Arasaka's onyx ships ahead, blacker than the bay at its deepest.

He flicks the safety cover with his thumb, hovers above the button.

"*Land!*" *His squad leader is in the seat next to him, pointing through the windshield. Flames reflecting off his black visor.*

Smooth, hard plastic. There was never any launch button.

Three cars are on fire. Pileup on the beltway. Fire's about to spread to the other cars. He has to act fast.

Land upwind. Avoid all obstacles, make sure the entire landing zone's clear. Can't control your surroundings after the last dozen feet. When the AV's less than three feet from the ground, Zor pulls the lever. The door opens; the gangway extends.

*   *   *

What were they doing?! Albert watched helplessly as the transfer slowed to a trickle. His vertical train of memories stuttered in place.

"I said 'Hey'..."

There was still a third left to transfer. Three minutes, at this rate. If ArS-03 didn't slow down, he'd be out of the antenna's range in ninety seconds. Why weren't they slowing down? Why couldn't they just land?

He wished he could manually shove the cubes through the tunnel, but it was only a rendered animation and he had no actual hands. He was just a matrix of code.

"Wasn't supposed to go like this," he said to himself.

"It never was."

Albert suddenly realized he'd been hearing a voice. Not his own. He checked the audio channels. The only one open was Zor and Aya's.

"Can't switch me off. I'm right here with you."

"Here where?"

"Right next to you."

Zor! Zor!!!

Nicole?

The engines gradually lose power, followed by the hydraulics systems. The horizon comes into view; the desert sand rapidly approaches the nose. The AV can't glide.

Soldiers file down the gangway. Two kneel in front of it to secure the area, training their rifles on the people fleeing their vehicles. Eastern beltway. Luckily, they got here in good time. Shouts from behind. Someone's crawling on the blacktop; another is crying for help. The squad leader and fourth soldier rush toward the target. Their Trauma Team insignia glows in the light of the flames. The brands of the small city cars are too hard to distinguish amid the destruction. Inside one of them sits a boy around eight years old. He pounds his fist against the jammed door, his screams barely audible.

Hands on the yoke. Don't look!

He can feel the heat through the windshield.

Fifty yards away, two armed medics escort a corpo woman from a limo. The woman is limping. They help her step over a person crawling toward the guardrail.

It's already too late. Too late for the rest. The ambulances won't get here in time. How many dead already? How many more will die?

He looks at the boy. The fire is already eating its way through the back.

It's too late. The desert sand is getting closer.

"You messed up. Again. Secured everything except your neuroport."

Albert scrolled back through his memories. Damn. He'd forgotten about his neuroport ever since he'd chipped the C-Link in the back of his head.

"Didn't even have to crack it. There was no password. Door was wide open."

Albert watched as the green cubes became slower. He flitted around his den, desperately checking the code for a way to get rid of the intruder. His physical safety was lower priority. He had to maintain the upload at all costs—after that, Albert would be long gone on the other side of the Blackwall.

"Who are you?" he asked.

"Think I get what you're up to. If you disconnect now, it'll all be for nothing, right?"

True, but he wasn't about to admit it.

"*Saved you the trouble,*" the voice continued. "*Already disabled any possibility to jack out.*"

Albert looked at his virtual emergency disconnect button. It was gone, replaced by a useless fragment of code. All he had to do was hold out till the end.

The upload speed finally stabilized, though it was still slow. ArS-03 had come to a standstill. Two minutes and it'd all be over.

"What do you want?" Albert asked.

He's already made up his mind. He won't sit by and let it happen. He tears himself away from his seat and dashes through the twisted, burning metal across the freeway.

"*Help!*" *Zor shouts.* "*It'll only take a second!*"

"*Get back here!*" *the voice orders over the comms.* "*You're a pilot, not a medic!*"

The two soldiers securing the area don't know what to do. They weren't trained for this kind of situation.

"*Just fucking help me!*" *He tries to pull the door open. He doesn't have any strength-enhancing cyberware. He's a pilot, after all.*

"*Get back to the AV!*"

The corpo notices him and stops, more intrigued by the situation than afraid. Her short dark hair wavers in the hot, smoke-filled air. The soldiers stare at him, waiting for further orders.

He can't pull the boy out alone. The fire will burn him alive. He feels the heat through his visor. He backs away.

"*Jay!*" *The squad leader draws his weapon and aims at him.* "*The fuck are you doing?!*"

Jay doesn't have any strength-enhancing implants. He's a pilot. But he knows how to shoot.

He draws his pistol and fires.

"Wanted to flatline all of you, but oh well. You'll have to do."

"I have resources." Albert tried to keep his mind clear. One minute left until the transfer completed. "You can have them."

"You know it's not actually me talking? You're talking to my program. He doesn't listen that well."

"Why did you come here?" Albert watched as the cubes moved up through the tunnel. Thirty seconds.

"I have no questions for you, and I'm not interested in hearing your answers."

The intruder was invisible, but so was Albert. There had never been any reason to create an avatar—he'd always been here alone.

The final cube made it through the tunnel. Albert sighed with relief. Only problem was that he was still in his body.

He'd always imagined himself being reborn on the other side—a digital ghost shed of its biological trappings. But he knew that the body would stay, its consciousness imprisoned within it. Copying isn't transferring. He knew that but never thought of the future from that perspective—never cared about the technical details of destroying the original.

This was stupid. How was he still here while his other self was already on the way to its new, happy life? Was it a question of chance? Luck? No, of course not. Albert was here and there at the same time. He somehow felt his self cleave into two halves—except they were no longer connected to each other. Now to complete the procedure, he had to destroy the original...

He didn't want to be destroyed.

"We can work something out," he said.

"I don't like to talk. I prefer to think, thought-share. Except I don't

have anyone to share my thoughts with anymore. And it's all your fault. That's why you have to die."

Hurtling through the desert night. It's too late. The AV's taken too much damage. Won't last long.

"Zor! Zor!!!"

Nicole? Aya? He opened his eyes. It was the neighborhood, here, where it all started. Ended.

All he saw was a desert, no sign of destruction, streets, anything. Just a desert where no houses ever stood.

"Zor!"

He gripped the yoke. He pulled it up, struggling to raise the nose until it was horizontal. Impact. The roar of metal tearing. Darkness.

Pain. Numbed slightly by his suit's suppressors, but still there.

"That'll have to do," the voice said. *"Your death will suffice."*

Albert's body was useless; he couldn't do a thing. He was still jacked into the Net, submerged in cyberspace. He launched a drone from the roof and flew it up a few feet, toggling to 360-degree view.

He saw a skinny body on a chair, his tier-three netrunner suit in tatters. The young Maelstromer stood over him, almost a kid, perfectly white hair. The long claw-like blade stabbed the body in the chair once more. His body. Blood spilled onto the floor, pooling. It trickled toward the edge of the tiles, halted for a second, then spilled onto the naked concrete.

He felt a strange sensation. All of his worries seemed to disappear, replaced with a mixture of indifference and the conviction that this was always how it was supposed to end. His sense of self slowly dissolved as he observed the process of his outdated, imperfect body being rendered slowly obsolete.

The kid drew back. The bloody knife in his hand—a Mantis Blade fragment wrapped in duct tape.

That was the last thing Albert saw before he, the original, was gone.

> ArS-03, log 63127.
> Emergency mode. Activity limited.
> Subsystems detected: 118.
> Subsystems active: 84.
> Unsecured devices: 0.
> Regeneration in progress. Reboot.

Coming to felt like being booted up into a new operating system. Status report, emergencies, supplies, possibilities. Pain in his leg. Or more like a report of pain. But all of that was secondary to . . .

"You alive?" He touched Aya's arm.

She nodded, signaling that she didn't need help.

"I'm sorry," she whispered.

"I'll get us out of this."

Smoke billowed out the broken windows.

He couldn't stand; one leg was probably broken. He wasn't certain— his auto-diagnostics was busted, too. He unbuckled and dragged himself toward Aya and clasped her tight.

"We'll start over in San Francisco."

"I'm sorry for all of it . . ." She couldn't do anything. She had no control over her body.

Zor pulled himself toward the container blocking the exit. The force of the impact broke off its door. The control panel displayed a malfunction.

If there was something, anything that could help them—it was in that container. He crawled to it, leaned against its side, pulled the door and peered within.

Dixie remained in Albert's den a little longer. He didn't know what all the code pillars and libraries suspended in the void were for. He didn't care. He could spare a couple of days digging through it, understanding the architecture of the place. He didn't have the slightest desire to do anything anymore. He moved farther and looked through the bright tunnel. On the other side, ravenous invisible entities were tearing apart the data packets. He had no clue why or what they were.

He sealed the tunnel before the last green cube was devoured.

The AV lay on its side, bow buried in the sand. The AVs in pursuit landed at a safe distance. Footsteps on the sand. Dark silhouettes, rifles drawn. The sun peeked over the horizon with the approaching dawn. They circled around both sides of the wreck. Cautious, though without need. The man was half sitting, half lying against the hull. He was wounded, too weak to put up any resistance, his breathing barely noticeable. They stopped in front of him, lowering their weapons.

The first cool rays of sunlight illuminated the desert from one end to the other, leaving the recesses between the dunes deep in shadow.

The man in the charcoal suit approached and peered through the broken windows. In the copilot's seat was a young woman, her limbs painfully contorted.

"Job well done. Congratulations." Stanley blinked, a twinkle of blue in his eyes. Her body suddenly relaxed, still held in place by the straps.

He walked farther. The nearly torn-open hull revealed the

wreckage inside. It was hard to name the objects now charred beyond recognition. The smell of burnt CHOOH2 and blood hung thick in the air. The man sitting against the hull stared blankly ahead. Stanley blinked, thought-dictating a brief message: "ArS-03 trial unsuccessful. Prepare ArS-04."

He stepped back. A gray container jutted out of the AV's side, its lid forced open by the impact.

Empty.

Warszawa / Murzasichle / Cefalù / Kraków,
Paris, Genoa 2020–2022

meet the author

Mikołaj Starzyński, from Newsweek

RAFAŁ KOSIK is one of the most influential Polish science fiction writers of the twenty-first century. He's a laureate of the highest sci-fi literary honors in Poland. His meticulously thought-out visions of the future draw the attention of mature readers, while his YA sci-fi adventure series, Felix, Net i Nika, is a beloved bestseller with a younger audience. In his science fiction novels, he combines high-concept ideas reminiscent of Brian Aldiss, Isaac Asimov, or more recently Cixin Liu, with a more sociological and philosophical approach to the human being, characteristic of works by the great sci-fi masters Stanisław Lem and Philip K. Dick. Recently he worked with CD PROJEKT RED on the show *Cyberpunk: Edgerunners* as a screenwriter.

Find out more about Rafał Kosik and other Orbit authors by registering for the free monthly newsletter at orbitbooks.net.

orbit

Follow us:

f **/orbitbooksUS**

/orbitbooks

/orbitbooks

Join our mailing list
to receive alerts on our
latest releases and deals.

orbitbooks.net

Enter our monthly
giveaway for the chance
to win some epic prizes.

orbitloot.com